The Melancholy Howl

"The brisk narrative is bolstered by stellar dialogue … A smart and indelible crime tale with skillfully interwoven storylines."

— Kirkus Reviews

"Packed with beautiful descriptions of Colorado's wilderness, razor-sharp dialogue and savvy insights on the state's burgeoning marijuana business, Stevens delivers a commanding mystery and compelling portrait of intriguing characters grappling with timely issues. When Allison Coil comes across a man tied to a tree, she becomes entangled with dangerous smugglers and also finds that a friend of hers is missing. Very few authors do dialogue as deftly as Stevens does, and paired with poignant prose, interwoven plots, and smart twists, Stevens has given us yet another gem of a novel that's impossible to put down."

— Christine Carbo, author of the *Glacier Mystery Series* including *A Sharp Solitude*

"The Allison Coil series hooks from the very beginning and only gets better with each new book. This one is no exception. *The Melancholy Howl* transports readers to the true Colorado: where behind every majestic mountain, inside every wild wilderness, and beside the so-called solid politician is a shadow hiding something dark and dangerous. The refreshingly stripped-down prose makes the novel move like a raft through class IV rapids. A thrilling, surprising ride alongside great characters. And a ride well worth taking."

— Erik Storey, author of the Clyde Barr thriller series including *Nothing Short of Dying* and *A Promise to Kill*

"I don't know what I enjoy most about Mark Stevens' Allison Coil mysteries: his spot-on descriptions of the Rocky Mountains in all their cruel grandeur or his pitch-perfect dialogue. *The Melancholy Howl* is a wonderful addition to a captivating series and to the subgenre of outdoor mysteries."

— Paul Doiron, author of *Stay Hidden* (The Mike Bowditch Mystery Series)

"In *The Melancholy Howl*, heroine Allison Coil sheds light on the dark side of Colorado's marijuana industry, while author Mark Stevens delivers plenty of outdoor action and smokin' hot suspense."

— Margaret Mizushima, author of *Burning Ridge* and the Timber Creek K-9 Mystery series

"Stevens masterfully weaves his story back and forth, building narrative tension every step of the way—until you have to know how it all ends. His best book yet."

— Stephen Singular, New York Times best-selling author

Lake of Fire

"Thrilling, irresistible."
— Kirkus Reviews

"Lake of Fire swirls into an environmental inferno that reads all too true—Mark Stevens writes like wildfire."
— Craig Johnson, author of the Walt Longmire novels, basis for the hit series Longmire

"Mark Stevens is one heckuva storyteller, and Lake of Fire is a riveting page-turner of the highest order."
— Scott Graham, National Outdoor Book Award-winning author of *Mountain Rampage*

"Mark Stevens just gets better and better ... An absolutely must-read thriller!"
— Chris Goff, author of *Dark Waters* and the bestselling Bird-watcher's Mystery series

"You'll revel in Mark Stevens painted descriptions and sharp dialogue. And most of all, you'll root for the smartest, coolest heroine this side of the Mississippi: Allison Coil. Try not to tear the pages as you turn them furiously."
— James W. Ziskin, author of Stone Cold Dead and the Ellie Stone Mystery series

Trapline
Colorado Book Award winner

"A chilling tale."
— The Denver Post

"Allison's third adventure ... combines a loving portrait of a beautiful area with an ugly, all-too-believable conspiracy that could have been ripped from today's headlines."
— Kirkus Reviews

"Readers will enjoy the fast-paced action."
— Mystery Scene Magazine

"A well-executed and suspenseful narrative ... The book is a thrilling read."
— The Aspen Times

Buried by the Roan

"Buried by the Roan is flat-out terrific. Everything you expect from a first-rate mystery is here: Savvy sleuth Allison Coil, hunting guide on-top-of-her-game, gorgeous Colorado mountain setting, gripping story where the pages practically turn themselves, and eloquent writing to boot."
— Margaret Coel, New York Times bestselling author of the Wind River Mystery series

"Mystery fans can delight in Mark Stevens."
— Fort Collins Coloradoan

"Stevens, a former journalist, has an eye for well-paced narrative, vivid characters and telling details."
— High Country News

"A suspenseful tale featuring an easy-to-like protagonist and a landscape Stevens clearly knows well, and treasures."
— Grand Junction Sentinel

Antler Dust

"I stand ready to devour the next one."
— The Summit Daily News

"The Colorado crime scene has gained a strong new voice, as well as a new character to watch in Allison Coil."
— The Rocky Mountain News

"With its unique setting and diverse cast, Antler Dust makes a fast-paced, intriguing addition to the list of new thrillers."
— The Denver Post

"Prose and plot sing in perfect harmony."
— The Aspen Times

The Melancholy Howl

An Allison Coil Mystery

MARK STEVENS

First Edition
First Printing, 2018
Book interior design by Jody Chapel
Cover design by Jody Chapel
Cover photo by Mark Stevens & stock photography
Edited by Karen Haverkamp

Library of Congress Cataloging-in-Publication: 2018904383
ISBN: 9780990722472
Printed in the United States of America

Third Line Press
2509 Xanthia St.
Denver, CO 80238

The Allison Coil Mystery Series

Antler Dust
Buried by the Roan
Trapline
Lake of Fire

"The illegality of cannabis is outrageous, an impediment to full utilization of a drug which helps produce the serenity and insight, sensitivity and fellowship so desperately needed in this increasingly mad and dangerous world."

— Carl Sagan

"Legalize it."

— Peter Tosh

Part One

One

What is the scent of desperation?

Of near death?

Allison Coil gave the breeze a sniff.

Maybe she should improve her ability to identify certain smells, but how? With red wine, on the rare occasion she wasn't sipping tequila, she only picked up notes of red wine, overtones of red wine and earthiness of red wine.

So, what were the vultures waiting for?

Allison's eyes traced a line from the axis of gliding scavengers downward to an imaginary point a couple hundred yards uphill, beyond the first bank of trees.

Something was dying.

She hopped off Sunny Boy. "It's not like we don't have time." She tied her horse to a long-dead snag. "No complaining, okay?"

Twenty paces off, she tried to gauge whether her olfactory system worked any better outside of the Horse Zone. Still, she caught a whiff of sweaty equine. But that could be because she'd been riding for three days, checking on the luckless bow hunters in her two camps. Only a hot shower or three would shed eau-de-horse.

Maybe she still smelled horse because Sunny Boy was giving her the stink eye.

"Okay, I'll hurry," she said. "How about a little patience around here?"

Sunny Boy knew they were headed home. When it came to

echolocation, he could give the whales a lesson. All the comforts of his barn waited mere hours down the trail, in Sweetwater.

Allison groaned as she forced herself up the slope, her quadriceps balking at the switch in function from horse grippers to main motors.

A field of snags dotted the berm and then gave way to a thick growth of spruce. Allison's boots turned dry grass and pine cones to mulch. The Rat Mountain Fire had wiped out a huge chunk of the northern section of the wilderness one summer ago. To compound matters, the drought had dug in its heels and meant to stay. Every branch, plant and weed drooped. The dead things drooped. The dirt drooped.

Whatever mammal was waiting to die, it was no chipmunk. Vultures didn't put on a party for a snack. Their feasting possibilities included dead or dying elk (but she hadn't seen any all summer), deer (ditto), bear (unlikely), coyote (possible) and mountain lion (better odds in Vegas).

Any of the beasts in question, depending on their distance from death, could prove dangerous. She toted zero weapons, per usual, with the exception of a decent knife on her hip and another in Sunny Boy's saddlebags.

Allison found a dead branch from an old spruce and whacked it in half against the trunk of a neighbor. The splintering knock bounced around the forest like a gunshot.

Makeshift club in her grip, feeling not one smidgen more secure, she walked with her focus cranked up, her gaze riveted ahead. The forest grew tighter. The dark birds flashed overhead. The grade eased and then went all the way flat. A flicker swooped across her view, flash of red in the wings—*flap-glide, flap-glide*. A pine squirrel chittered gibberish. Allison tightened her grasp of the ersatz weapon and wondered which of the so-called muscles on her nonthreatening, five-two frame were going to Popeye up and save the fucking day, should the need arise.

But there was one mammal Allison had overlooked—the species that smoked tobacco.

The cigarette butt wasn't such an unusual sight, but it suddenly jacked her alarm for what might be ahead.

The stub was fresh. Its tan filter had not yet faded under the high-elevation sun. The smoker had a high tolerance for harsh. Only a thin rim, a sliver of white, remained. The trash went in her back pocket.

Allison peered ahead with refreshed zeal. Nearing the edge of the tree line, and almost surprising herself, she caught a low whiff of rot. If *she* smelled something, it could pull in vultures from Utah.

Or Uganda.

The ridge dropped off to a broad, flat plain. Straight north stood Turret Peak.

In the wide sweep of landscape, a towering spruce stood guard like a forgotten sentry. The tree was separated from the forest by thirty yards of scrub and sage.

At the base of the spruce, Allison spotted the reason for the birds.

Two reasons.

At the outer edge of the spruce, a deer carcass lay inert on the ground. A thick cloud of flies partied above it, a buzzing black smudge on a high-definition photograph.

And at the base of the tree, a man.

Allison's arms flashed with prickling goosebumps. Her throat went full Sahara.

The man stood, but he was bent at the waist like he'd been punched. His arms flopped halfway between full crucifix and at-ease, each wrist restrained by rope connected to a branch above.

Sweat soaked his tattered T-shirt. Hair sprouted wildly. A full, orangey beard dangled well below his neck.

He strained against his limits like a snarling dog. He panted like he'd been fighting. He turned as if he had read the question in her worried look. He gave her a side view of his waist, to show where a third rope attached.

He grunted.

Then shouted: "Get me out of here!"

Two

Friday Afternoon
Duncan

The fire at King's Crown Mobile Home Park turned one trailer home into a pile of smoking rubble. Blisters and scorch marks marred the neighboring units. Their exteriors were splotched caramel and black, like an over-roasted campfire marshmallow.

The call to the Rifle Fire Protection District had come in at 11:25 a.m. and now, nearing 5 p.m., Duncan Bloom put the finishing touches on his story, coming together on the wafer-thin tablet perched on his lap. He typed away in the roomier shotgun seat of his rust-and-green Camry.

The Rifle police had made quick work of arresting the married couple that used to live in the obliterated unit. How they had escaped injury required the kind of belief system reserved for holy sites. Duncan didn't need all his years as a reporter, including nearly half a decade based in Glenwood Springs, to know that the pair were not the churchgoing type.

The lack of piety showed up in the pictures posted online by the Garfield County Sheriff's Office. They had wasted no time putting the mug shots up on Twitter and underscoring their status as husband and wife.

Jimmy Enriquez, 18.

Marsha Sykes, 47.

Jimmy had narrow, thin shoulders and a sapling neck. His buzz cut made him look younger than his years, but he fought the high school freshman effect with three loops of barbed wire tattooed on his neck and earlobes distended by stark white gauges the size of half-dollars.

Marsha led with a bulbous neck worthy of a bullfrog. Her chin disappeared into the puffy sac of floppy flesh. Her brown hair shot up in random, greasy spikes. Her mug-shot gaze set a new standard for stoners worldwide. Her eyes drooped and her mouth hung agape like a fat, wrecked fish.

The records showed that the odd couple had pulled a marriage license in Grand Junction eight weeks earlier. Marsha had worked janitorial jobs. She hailed from Walsenburg and left behind a steady trail of criminal mischief in Montrose, Grand Junction and blip-size De Beque.

Jimmy had dropped out of Coal Ridge High School before finishing his junior year.

Duncan had his editor on speed dial.

Chris Coogan, as if his hand hovered over the phone, picked right up.

"Pictures come through?"

"Yes," said Coogan. "Perhaps words to go with them?"

"Coming up."

"*Drudge Report* and *HuffPo* have already got it, a perverse double whammy for viral explosiveness."

"Already?"

"Warp speed." Coogan waged an ongoing campaign to highlight the nation's whacked-out standards for what constituted national news. "Everyone is wondering, who got the hots first? I mean, she's straight out of a freak show."

"She was on her second husband the day he was born." Duncan had done the math. Marsha's first marriage lasted six months.

"Neighbors?"

Duncan pictured Coogan's pinched, beaver-like face. He laughed once a month, whether he needed to or not.

"Talked to a few," said Duncan. "I got a few choice words about hash oil and the stupidity involved. Quotes of fury."

Through the windshield, Duncan watched as one of the collateral victims, a feisty truck driver named Cleo Bilhorn, chewed on the ear of a patient television reporter named Stan Greer, who had pulled up when Duncan had started writing. Bilhorn stood with one foot up on the shiny chrome step rail of a new Ford pickup.

"How about a jailhouse interview with the odd couple?"

"I can try," said Duncan. The chances of getting it were slim, but it was always better to sound agreeable. Besides, he didn't really mind. Putting in a request was a pretty basic thing to do.

"And what's up with the hash oil buzz?" said Coogan. "Even before they tightened the law, you'd think with legalization there would be no need to go to the trouble."

"Are you assigning me a story on the endless styles of drug-induced buzzes? It will take time and I can't guarantee a professional receipt every time I need to claim an expense."

"Hilarious," said Coogan. "I wonder if hash oil fires are a bigger problem in counties without retail weed."

"I could go down to the Green Joint or the Green Dragon and find someone who thought about making hash oil but then de-

7

cided it wasn't worth the risk."

"I still like the jailhouse. Get these two lovebirds to say how they feel about torching the neighbors' homes."

Coogan wasn't prone to good-byes. Not even a heartwarming "see you later."

In Duncan Bloom's time at the *Glenwood Springs Post-Independent*, following his layoff from *The Denver Post* during the Great Newspaper Meltdown, Duncan had grown comfortable with his role as a bigger fish working for a much smaller fish wrap. He liked the lack of competition and the wide-open Western Slope. His role in uncovering a private prison conspiracy and helping expose the violent plans of religious extremists helped raise his stature. The arrest of the religious shitballs landed him a few moments of marginal fame on network news shows. Being interviewed by Gayle King did not suck. Getting calls and emails from former Denver journalist buddies and the likes of Kerry London, the national news reporter superstar, allowed you to walk around in a cloud of self-importance.

For a few minutes. Ribbon-cuttings and school board meetings had a way of balancing things out.

Stan Greer packed up his gear, but Bilhorn didn't stop talking. Greer reached out to shake a hand in the universal gesture of "gotta go." She ignored it.

Duncan pulled out his phone, scrolled through his contacts, punched the number. Greer dug his phone out of his back pocket.

"Looks like you could use an exit strategy," said Duncan.

Stan Greer turned, slow motion. "How did I miss your snazzy rig?"

"Among all these other limos here in Beverly Hills?" said Duncan. "Seriously."

Greer held the phone up for Bilhorn. "My newsroom," he told

her. "Gotta go."

Cleo Bilhorn folded her arms across her chest.

"Meet you by the entrance to King's Crown," said Duncan. "Up on Twenty-Fourth Street."

Greer, a one-man band, arrived in his Jeep Cherokee, a rolling billboard for 9 News. Being a mountain reporter, blue jeans were the norm. So were simple shirts with button-down collars.

"Shouldn't there be a less combustible means of making concentrates?"

"You should give lessons," said Duncan.

"It's all about the purity, especially if they were going after shatter."

"Who needs to dab when the stuff they make now is so strong?" Duncan enjoyed the occasional hit. A puff of the right pot and finding a fun way to disrobe Trudy made a regular party special. But acetylene torches and titanium nails made concentrates look complicated to produce. How much trouble was it worth?

"It's a mystery," said Greer. "Did you see those mug shots?"

"Yeah. The whole world, too. I do feel for the neighbors, living next to those two."

"It's gotta suck. You would think that legalization had taken out the incentive for the DIY crowd."

Greer had shot and produced a series about the thriving black market for all legal and illegal drugs, including one harrowing sequence in which he demonstrated how to cook concentrates.

Black market entrepreneurs knew one basic rule of business. All they had to do was undercut going retail prices to keep customers. And legalization made it easier to move around with the basic supplies, since anyone could grow up to six plants. What army of state bureaucrats checked all those homes?

"I can't believe you went undercover without getting recognized," said Duncan. "I know you didn't pull into those towns in your work truck."

"You're right about using the news truck. We didn't. But don't forget—nobody is watching the news anymore unless you're a politician or you were born before 1980. My mother recognizes me in person, but that's it. You're the one with celebrity status."

"Got my three minutes," said Duncan.

"Warhol said it was fifteen."

"Three minutes is the new fifteen," said Duncan. "I should quit now and avoid the slow fade."

Could he keep doing this for five years? Ten? Twenty? Other than the loving companionship of Trudy and encounters with Allison Coil, who had retreated further into herself over the past year, the forecast had one theme: Do what you did yesterday. Do it again tomorrow. And prepare to do it again the day after that. And watch your bank account suffer. Duncan had carried debt with him, including hefty student loans, from his days at *The Denver Post*, when he had his sights set on *The New York Times* or the *Chicago Tribune*. Then, the trajectory of his career promised to cover what he owed. Now what he earned didn't put a dent in what he owed. It barely met the needs of the minimum monthly payments.

"You tried to reach our vixen cougar and her high school sweetheart?"

"I'm going to try," said Duncan.

"Good luck," said Greer. "Find out if they were after shatter, budder or wax."

"What's the difference?"

"Potency, taste and serious credibility. You know how to cook up pure shatter, you know your shit. It's like see-through amber. The hit will alter your reality at warp speed."

"You tried it."

"Gotta know what you're talking about."

"Worth blowing up your place and the neighbor's too?"

"That can be your first question when you get to Jimmy and Marsha."

The Camry fired up after its usual bout of petulance and an embarrassing exhale of blue-gray miasma.

He jumped on the interstate and headed east along the Colorado River to Glenwood Springs. Despite one layer of woe—financial—it wasn't hard for Duncan to list the good stuff in his life, starting with the many comforts and intriguing ways of Trudy Heath.

Would he be reporting forever? It was all he knew. More than that, he still loved the work.

He had friends in Denver who had jumped from the journalism ranks to swank PR firms. Or lobbying. Or entrepreneurship. One launched a brewpub that drew throngs. Duncan had always thought it would be journalism or die, but the paradigm crumbled. He had surfed the rockslide down to a stable situation, but salaries in Glenwood Springs did zip for his debt. And in all this time, he hadn't revealed his true financial health to Trudy. Living rent-free under her roof helped, but the hour or so commute to Sweetwater meant more trips to the gas station and more wear and tear on his cranky car.

He was slipping further behind.

He needed a winning lottery ticket. He wondered more and more about making a transition to the hottest business in the state. The switch could alter his life in every single way he could imagine.

It meant he would be getting into the business of weed, oils, dabs, kush, budder. And shatter.

If it ever came to that, it might be a good idea to bone up on the terminology.

Three

Friday Afternoon
Allison

The man grunted. He coughed. He spat. His arms fought against the odd double tether. He didn't have enough slack in either rope for one hand to reach the other. Given his size and apparent strength, getting him into this position must have required a two-on-one. Or one mighty struggle.

"What the hell?"

She'd come within ten yards.

He took in a breath, studied her. "Get me out." He strained against the ropes, neck bulging and crimson. "Fuckin' get me out of out here."

"What gives?"

She ran another inventory on the weapon supply, to make sure she hadn't overlooked a .44 Magnum in a back pocket.

The dead deer spewed a rancid stench. Rotting meat wouldn't take long in this heat. Two vultures settled on the carcass, ignoring the flies. Four others lit on the ground. Allison flashed her arms like wings. The birds chatter-growled and hopped away.

Sweaty grime covered the man's cheekbones above a floppy beard, not quite worthy of ZZ Top. He had sunken cheeks and furry eyebrows. His forehead was coated in a sweaty sheen. Shoulder-length brown hair fell in tangles.

"You gotta give me something," she said.

Two bold vultures hopped back on the slit belly of the deer, beaks tearing at the flesh.

The wasted meat pissed her off as much as the tied-up man.

"Ain't none of your business." He tried for a touch of composure. It didn't work. "Just cut me loose, go on your way."

As a matter of pure fact, it was not her business. Her business was the straightforward income generator of supplying hunters with camping spots, tents, horses, food, warmth, comfort, and guidance on the good spots where they would have a better chance of filling their freezer with a winter's worth of elk or venison. And one thing she knew was that keeping the Flat Tops Wilderness free of crazy stuff and treed-up wild men would keep customer satisfaction high, given that most customers preferred to deal with dangers only from weather, ornery wildlife or drunk companions.

Plus, as a former city girl turned self-confessed outdoors enthusiast, her half dozen years in and around the wilderness had produced a keen dislike for anyone who thought they could exploit the Flat Tops for its resources or deep cover.

"Give me a scrap," said Allison. "A morsel."

The man issued a doglike grunt, shook his head.

Door one, do nothing and leave. Then, get help. Or point in this direction.

Door two, release him and somehow coax him back to civilization to find somebody who could explain what the fuck was going on.

Door three, release him and let him go wherever he wanted. Hope for the best—that he wouldn't hurt her.

She put him at six two. Maybe an eighth of a ton. With her

puny size and recently fueled system, she liked her odds in a foot race back to Sunny Boy.

The man glared as if indignation alone could change her mind. For their first couple years together, Colin had thought the same thing. He knew better now.

A dark scrape blotched the side of the man's right shin. The same ankle looked puffy and purplish black. Laces on the tan running shoe around it were untied, unlike the one on the left.

"You hurt?"

He shrugged.

"Sprain?"

"Fucking bullshit." He tried again with the flexing and straining routine.

The injured ankle was double the size of its healthy brother.

"Who killed the deer?"

The man shook his head.

A fourth option dropped into view.

She'd be back by midnight, or maybe sooner, depending how long it took to bring Parks and Wildlife up the road to Sweetwater. And Duncan Bloom would have a reporter's front-row seat for the dawn arrival and arrest of the inscrutable stranger, a man found tied to a tree and left, perhaps, to die.

"Who killed the deer?" She stepped around the carcass. The vultures hopped off again, didn't go far. She didn't have time to study it closely, but the killing wound might be underneath, on the side she'd fallen. "How many days have you been out here?"

"Get me out." He struggled to sound matter-of-fact.

"Who did this?"

"I'll go my way, you go yours. I swear."

With objections shouted in her direction, strong at first and in heavy rotation, but then not so loud and not so frequent, Allison put her back to the crazy scene. She pondered her choices and picked her way back through the woods.

Sunny Boy balked at the bivouac and his delayed appointment with a fresh batch of hay. She knew he had an aversion to the smell of rot and no doubt he would pick up the rank deer corpse soon, if he had not already. He picked his way up through the rocks and sage and scrub. She felt his petulance in her thighs. She walked Sunny Boy back to the man and climbed down.

She stepped with care and stopped a few paces beyond the reach of a flailing arm.

"What are you doing?"

"Leaving you a little nourishment."

"What if you just cut these ropes?"

"Do you want some water or not?"

"You can't leave me here."

She held up the bottle. "Yes or no?"

He nodded.

She held a bottle of water to the man's lips. He stunk like no man should. He sucked down what didn't splatter on his T-shirt. She fed him five Fig Newtons and two long hunks of Colin's homemade elk jerky. She slid a water bottle in each pocket of his baggy shorts.

"One last chance." She climbed up on Sunny Boy. "Start talking."

"Cut me down. You never saw me."

He stared right through her.

Allison circled the tree on horseback, searching the ground for boot prints, trash or any odd bits to fill in the story. A cold campfire pit sat outside the tree's canopy on the opposite side from

15

the dead deer.

Southeast from the man and the tree, thirty yards from the deer carcass, a foot-shape impression stared up at her from a sandy patch of earth. The print pointed straight east, toward Sweetwater, in the same direction she would be heading. She hopped off Sunny Boy and led him on foot. It took a minute to find three more matching prints. One print gave up the detail of an intricate tread. The owner of the prints either played basketball or worked as a clown in the circus. Her boot looked like a child's by comparison.

Two hours of daylight remained. Already, the second half of the ride to Sweetwater would be dark.

She walked Sunny Boy back to the tree, still scanning the ground and trying to ignore that sinking feeling of trouble.

"Who was the other guy? What the hell happened?"

His mouth still didn't work.

"Start with your name." She hated the thought of leaving him but had no reason to trust him if she cut him down. "Tell me now, or tell all of them later."

"Them?" His eyes widened.

"All the people who care about the death of that deer. And all the people who will want to know the name of Big Foot, if he was the guy who left you here. Was he the smoker, too?"

The man cocked his head, puzzled.

"Was there one other? Two? Three?"

She climbed down again, snatched a ground blanket from her saddlebags.

The vultures scampered to the sky. Holding her breath and pulling with every ounce of scrawny muscle she could muster, she flipped the dead deer onto the blanket. A bullet hole sat dead center on the lungs. She knew better than to dig the slug out. She gathered all four legs and folded the blanket over like a partial shroud.

Allison punched holes in the corners of the blanket with her knife. She ran a rope through the openings and around the legs to cinch the blanket tight. The vultures might peck their way through, but she had to try and protect what evidence remained. The wildlife officers wouldn't approve of her hacking at the carcass or hauling it anywhere.

Back on Sunny Boy, she gave the scene one more check.

"Don't." He yanked hard against the ropes.

"Last chance," she said.

"I'd tell you," he said. "But I don't remember much."

She turned Sunny Boy and gave him a last look over her shoulder. "You'd have to do better than that."

"I mean, after the plane crash."

Four

Friday Afternoon
Trudy

"I don't know what it is." Trudy Heath stood on a small rock, fighting every childish urge to give up. "I can't seem to get it."

"There's always a break-in period."

Producer Chuck Cline was compact, bald under his well-worn New York Mets cap, and full of opinions on lighting and angles.

"This will come as naturally as anything else you do. At some point. You have to not overthink. We are a small crew with simple video gear, but guess what? We don't exist. We aren't here.

17

The camera is a portal to your growing legions of fans who want a bit more of your essence, however they can get it. Think of the customers, friends, and loyal supporters. When they watch this on their televisions or laptops it will be you and them, one to one."

"I practiced," said Trudy. "Lots."

"It's not the same because the camera is so goddamn soulless. You have to reach right through there and pretend like you're chatting with a customer."

The idea sounded good—well, reasonable—when the producer from NatGeo called. Nat *freaking* Geo. The idea was a series of shows that would spotlight all the wild bounty in the forests, all the overlooked food. The idea of the show was to provide a series of how-to lessons for the amateur forager, from mushrooms to mallow, from dandelion to dock. The show was pitched as an outdoors Martha Stewart of the Colorado forests.

Except she'd have a co-host, the gentle soul now waiting between her muffed takes.

He sat cross-legged in the sun, a burgundy moleskin notebook on his bare knees. One hand held the notebook open, the other tapped a pen against his bearded chin. He could be working up ideas for a poem or sketching the horizon. At times, he tipped his head back, closed his eyes and let the sun blast his face.

Sam Shelton.

The Sam Shelton.

Ex-rock star.

He stood, stretched like a cartoon bear with a guttural yawn, half howl, and headed their way. He wore tan cowboy boots and blue jeans held in place by a bright red-and-white macramé belt. The remaining rock star affectations were a thin gold necklace that dangled loosely over his purple T-shirt and a pinprick gold stud in each ear.

"You gotta get to a point where you think *fuck it*." Originally from County Cork, Ireland, fuck was *fowk*. "You gotta get to a point where you say, this is my goddamn show and I'm going to own it."

"That's it," said Cline. "Dig down for that easy confidence—we know it's there."

"In your *mind*, you know." Sam Shelton tapped his temple with a finger, raised his eyebrows. "In your mind, give a fist pump. Own the mother."

"You had stage fright, right?" said Cline.

"Of course I had fucking stage fright—all the time," said Shelton. "Glug of whiskey and pump up my bandmates and, yeah, maybe a wee bit of nerves at first, but we'd settle down and find that groove. Or at least go looking for it. I mean, some nights, nothing. Other nights, bang, it's right there and you ride it all night, if you know what I mean. When it happens right, you disappear. You don't exist. You climb inside the music and go."

Known around the world for his kiln-dry vocals, Shelton required all manner of quirky stage movements as he dug for notes and feeling. Sam Shelton released an album every three or four years. He blended gritty rhythm and blues with punchy, horn-heavy, white-boy soul. He snatched gems from the previous decade and hit the recycle button. He recorded a duet with Mick Jagger and, in the video, Shelton played the wise old head with the cool gaze to Jagger's prancing and hyper gyrations.

NatGeo dreamed up the co-host combination. He would demonstrate his newfound home gardening techniques. She would focus on foraging in the wild.

The show would not mention or involve Sam Shelton's previous celebrity. It would play off it but—*not* play off of it.

Sam Shelton, tomato man.

Three years earlier, he had chucked his rock star status for country boy and holed up in western Colorado to become another farmer dude.

Each half-hour show would end with one of them demonstrating a recipe, either in his kitchen or, for Trudy, over a campfire deep in the wilderness.

"Let's give it another whirl," said Cline.

Trudy took a deep breath, closed her eyes. One reason she thought she could even consider standing in front of a television camera was Allison's friend Devo, who had been the star of a short-lived reality show, *Longitude/Latitude*, filmed in the Flat Tops Wilderness until authorities evicted them for camping much longer than regulations allowed. The earnest, pint-size Devo and his tribe of devolutionists made TV work look easy. In fact, they made it seem like second nature, which was ironic given all the modern audio and video gear that tracked them day and night in their attempt to live more like the wilderness-savvy men and women of the nineteenth century and less like a bunch of corporate office softies.

Maybe Devo and his flock had stage-fright jitters at first, too.

Maybe she needed to push through, find a routine.

"Consider the humble dandelion," said Trudy. There were no dandelions this late in the season, but they were shooting a sample show that would never see the light of day. "By the way, it doesn't think it's humble. It's queen of its world."

How do you see through a camera when it's sitting right there on a tripod, staring back?

"In the city, you may think of the dandelion as a blight, since it destroys the look of all those lawns—"

She hung her head.

The *look*. She should have said *appearance*.

"It's okay, believe me," said Cline. "We will get it."

"Shake it off," said Shelton.

20

Cline's television credentials included shows about underwater dredging for gold in the Bering Sea and commercial fishing off the Aleutian Islands.

"Consider the humble dandelion," said Trudy. Maybe if she didn't look right at the camera. "I'm sure you have. In the city, you may not be fond of its appearance and how it dots your lawn with its bright yellow flowers in spring. But these weeds are mineral-packed beauties. Their deep underground taproot sends out rootlets that soak up minerals from the soil, all on behalf of the aboveground stalk."

Her thoughts sailed off a cliff, full speed.

And into nothing.

"That's okay," said Cline. "We got a few sentences, you know, that's okay."

"Another breath." The coaching this time from Sam Haze, who handled audio and lugged most of the gear. "Back up a bit and pick up the flow."

"I don't know," said Trudy. "I'm sorry."

"It's okay," said Cline.

"Par for the course," said Haze.

One future idea involved a month long forage from New Castle to Buford. They would set a course a half mile east of the road as it cut north-south through the Flat Tops Wilderness. She would eat what she found in the way of edible weeds and flowers. She would demonstrate cooking techniques and healing properties, etcetera. The project sounded fabulous, if she could get this part down.

Trudy stood. "Give me a second."

She wore hemp shorts and a simple, white cotton top with blue-green embroidery across the shoulders. A wide-brimmed straw hat shielded the piercing August sun. Sweat coated her lower back. She had a long relationship with television—as consumer. It had been her window to the world back in the epilepsy days, when her husband kept her trapped. Despite living on the edge of the wilderness, she liked to keep up with the news and she'd seen so many of these quasi-reality shows that she knew the formula by heart.

But *still*.

"You'll get into a rhythm," said Cline.

"Yep," said Shelton. "I mean, I decided the cameras were my best friends. Inanimate cold bastards but still, my best friends."

Legend had it Sam Shelton used to drink a bottle of brandy all by himself, rock star-style, in first-class cabins when he flew—and still perform the same night. Trudy had spent a few hours online, digging into Shelton's career, before jumping into this project. His public persona wasn't too bad, by rock star standards. Now his eyes were as white and alive as a newborn's. He'd lost a medium paunch and developed muscles. Age added charm and a well-weathered countenance.

The switch from stage to dirt had come out of the blue. He had flown to the United States, bought a farm outside of Meeker, started growing tomatoes, let his beard grow, wrote poetry and vanished into the hard-working ranks.

His self-designed rock star protection program couldn't bury that giveaway Irish brogue and, soon, word got around. The Meeker locals assumed the tomato infatuation was a brief fling, a respite between world tours, but they were wrong.

Shelton agreed to an interview with *The Denver Post*, but the reporter started off the story saying his fans would be disappointed. Under the terms for the interview, the reporter could ask only two questions about his music career. The remainder of the interview would be one topic.

Tomatoes.

Duncan, much to Trudy's surprise, loved the idea of the Sam

Shelton–NatGeo project. Perhaps he wanted to get close to Shelton, too. Allison, as always, expressed support. But Allison's thumbs-up included a caution that nothing good ever came out of seeking publicity.

The NatGeo offer, when it arrived, seemed like a natural extension of everything she had accomplished. They claimed they had been looking for a "spirit guide" of sorts to team with Shelton and though she loathed the moniker, she caved under the gentle, unfaltering pressure applied by Duncan. He approved of the money but urged her to get an agent if they went into full production. And he asked her to consider the downside of not taking the chance.

Besides, she felt as if she had jumped outside her comfort zones so many times over the past few years that she deserved a medallion or giant *R* on her chest for *Riskwoman*:

Helped expose her ex-husband's big-game poaching conspiracy.

Survived and fought her way back from brain surgery.

Launched a successful business.

Then another.

Dumped an overly earnest boyfriend who was more concerned about profitability of the business than its people.

And helped Allison and Duncan, as much as she could, on two "situations." The second of those two now meant that every trip through the Hanging Lake Tunnels involved an exercise in mind over memory.

So what was up with shooting a simple video?

Trudy drifted away from the camera and crew. She breathed with purpose. She stopped where the incline opened up. In the distance, mountains poked their summits above the tree line. She performed the first few vertical moves of sun salutation, balanced on a rock not much wider than her side-by-side hiking boots.

High overhead, a straight-line white contrail looked as if someone had stuck a white straw on a blue ceiling. She could make out the gap between the tail of the silver jet and its tracks in the sky. The boulder where she perched shifted as she craned her neck to follow the jet's unrelenting course and as she hopped off, stumbling, the rock shifted, rolled halfway over and stopped again, its underbelly exposed. Red ants scurried from the dark cavity.

"Sorry," she said.

Cline munched on an almond butter and banana sandwich straight from her kitchen.

"Join me?" he said.

"Let's do this first," said Trudy.

The take flowed. She found a sweet spot at the crossroads of relaxation and concentration. "The oldest written records in Japan reference dandelions as food." The camera as friend. She pictured Allison, who might smirk. She pictured Duncan, who might stroke his chin in mock sincerity. "And in Japan scientists have patented an extract of dandelion to fight cancer. The roots are roasted and boiled at low temperatures to produce a syrup, and roasted dandelion root coffee is popular in Japan and many other countries."

She saw herself mixing dandelion seeds with vanilla, dates and water to make a nutritious morning milk. "The pollen is the sexual dust of the plant world and is considered a potent source of fertility around the world," she said. "The whole plant is edible—every bit of it."

She followed Cline's ideas for retakes. Her mind dug for tid-

24

bits they hadn't discussed—how to make a wild sauerkraut with the roots, the powerful effect of the "weed" both as an aperient and a sedative. She improved on the spot. "Among the Hindus of India, dandelion tea is used to cool the body and provide internal balance. The style of medicine is called Ayurvedic medicine, which includes herbal remedies, mineral supplements, opium and the application of oil through massages."

She could do this.

Behind Cline and behind the camera, Sam Shelton whacked his moleskin notebook against a bare palm.

Clap, clap, clap.

"By George, you got it," he said. "What the *fowk*!"

Five

Saturday Morning
Allison

The story required a couple run-throughs. How he'd looked, how he'd behaved, what he'd said, what he hadn't said, the dead deer, the whole eerie tableau.

Duncan listened carefully, asked the right questions to flesh out details.

"And he wouldn't tell you anything about the plane crash?"

"Nothing. He thought I'd get sympathetic at that point."

"Which might make sense, right?"

Allison had survived a commercial airplane crash on takeoff at LaGuardia Airport. She was one of the flukes, injured but alive.

"Correct," said Allison. "And I wasn't going to trade stories, you know? He was, like, pissed off the whole time he was describing what little he decided to tell me, which wasn't much. He didn't know where they'd crashed, but it sounded more like a hard landing. They wrecked the prop and had to hike out."

"Jesus," said Duncan. "Nobody killed?"

"According to him."

"You told him you'd cut him down if he gave you more?"

"Believe me, I gave him plenty of chances to explain."

"So cops are coming here? I'm supposed to head to Glenwood for a work thing, but *hell*."

"By the time they get up here and make the round trip to the tree where he's tied up, it will take the better part of the day." Allison knew she wasn't factoring in time for the cops to poke around at the scene. Parks and Wildlife officers were coming, too, for the out-of-season deer. She had made calls from her A-frame last night, slept fitfully and then walked across the meadow to look for either Duncan or Trudy. She had worried the whole ride down and all night if she had done the right thing and how this would end. Even a couple of well-built deputies might have trouble corralling Mr. Tree and convincing him to climb on a horse. She couldn't picture him cooperating—with anyone.

"Trudy got off okay this morning?"

Trudy had left before dawn to head to Meeker and Sam Shelton's spread. The transformation of Trudy from trapped wife of a brutal wild man to the local authority on organic food and purveyor of fresh herbs would never cease to amaze her. And now, a soon-to-be national television star.

"A bit apprehensive, but yeah," said Duncan. "She'll figure it out. She always does."

"Why don't you cancel your appointment in Glenwood and

ride along when we go back up?" said Allison. "Heck of a scene up there."

Duncan said, "I'll pass. Some businessman wants to meet up, not sure if it's a tip or what, but I'll be back when they come down."

Together, they raided the refrigerator. Duncan scrambled eggs and stirred in goat cheese, scallions, chopped cherry tomatoes and pickled jalapenos. Allison handled the toast.

She studied a pile of weeds that sat limp next to the sink. "No garnish for me," she said.

"Experiments in tea," said Duncan. "Trudy's next big venture. She froze a whole field's worth of dandelions last May. And she's working on a dandelion pesto with cashews, lemon juice, garlic and parsley."

Trudy's phases always sounded iffy at first, but every interest transformed into another smart business. A line of teas made perfect sense. She already produced three varieties of pesto that were a statewide hit among the organic crowd.

They shoveled in the eggs with homemade sunflower bread, drank coffee and cleaned up. They worked together in an easy rhythm. Life in Sweetwater with Trudy had mellowed Duncan Bloom. He had started out projecting a big-city image of always being in high demand and behind schedule. He once seemed to relish angering local officials and creating a ruckus with his questions. Trudy's style had cooled his thrusters. And now Allison couldn't think of a better guy than Duncan Bloom to support her friend's dreams, even if at times it seemed that he had four things cooking at once. It didn't matter. He treated Trudy well and had saved her life, which earned him enough brownie points to last this lifetime and the next few.

"I've got a point-and-shoot," said Duncan. "It's a cinch to use. Could you take a few shots before they take him off the rope?"

"Wouldn't feel right," she said. "But there's still time to change your mind and come with."

"Last time I rode a horse I didn't walk straight for a week."

"Cops will shoot plenty of photos," she said. "You must have sources who can hustle them up."

"It all depends on their mood."

"If Man-in-the-Tree still isn't talking, they might be plenty motivated to put out a photograph, see who knows anything about a plane going down. If they think he's telling the truth."

"You don't?"

"I think after I bring the cops and wildlife officers up there, my job is done."

Six

Saturday Noon
Duncan

Two minutes after the meeting started, Duncan already regretted the trip to Glenwood Springs.

He knew he should be working the phones about Allison's bizarre discovery. Or he should be trying to get an interview with the hash oil chefs, Jimmy and Marsha. This meeting with Clay Rudduck smacked of weird.

"Thank me?" said Duncan.

"For your care. Your *touch*."

"It was a building dedication," said Duncan. "Anyone could have written that story."

Clay Rudduck had been singled out by the mayor as one of six local businessmen who played a role in financing a new low-income housing complex.

"You did a good job," said Rudduck. "I also wanted to compliment you on the story you wrote about the fight in Basalt, the story about the heavy smell coming from the marijuana operation. The grow."

The grow in Basalt supplied the raw materials for an "apothecary" in Aspen, further up the valley. "Do you live up there?" said Duncan.

"No," said Rudduck. "But I liked how you measured the distance from how far away you said you could smell the darn thing. That one quote from the neighbor, what was it?"

"That they might as well be living next to a foul dump in the hot summer," said Duncan.

"That's it." Rudduck laughed. "Great quote."

Their oversized, comfy chairs faced a massive fireplace in the elegant lobby of the Hotel Colorado. In this August heat, however, the fireplace sat cold and dark. The room was such a throwback to the early days of Glenwood Springs that Duncan wouldn't have blinked if Teddy Roosevelt came strolling down the staircase.

Clay Rudduck wore a dark green, short-sleeve work shirt with extra pockets for hiking or fishing. He wore beat-up blue jeans and rough cowboy boots. At the mayor's groundbreaking, he'd gone mountain casual, too. His eyebrows needed a chainsaw. He had a wide face and deep-set eyes with a heavy stare. He was losing hair. He fought the balding with a comb-over that struggled for respect. Long ears coupled with that distant gaze gave him a wise old look, but Duncan put him at late thirties. He filled his comfy chair, but he was by no means overweight.

Next to Rudduck sat Helen Barnstone. Duncan guessed she

was a few years younger than Rudduck. Fit, trim, medium height. She wore powder-blue shorts and brand-new yellow Nikes. A rim of white ankle socks poked above the shoes, setting off her tan legs. Duncan looked for a flaw. Even the kneecaps were clean, youthful. The calves were sculpted and smooth. A purple-and-white checked top covered a smallish frame. Short dark hair suggested sleek and easy. She didn't twiddle with her phone, which sat on the armrest. At introduction, she said she was a devoted reader of the newspaper and knew the Duncan Bloom byline well. Her relationship to Rudduck, business or otherwise, wasn't clear.

"You're opposed to legalization in general or only that particular situation?"

Rudduck managed a weak smile.

"I appreciate you and your newspaper recognizing that there are issues," said Rudduck. "That's all. The history of journalism and its reliance on hard-drinking reporters, along with the media's left leanings, makes it easy to think that you all think marijuana should be as available as a can of Coke."

Nobody ever emailed a reporter to express appreciation, let alone called a meeting. Duncan still didn't quite get the point of this gathering.

"When it comes to reporter leanings, you're going off an old movie." Duncan knew several ultraconservative reporters at *The Denver Post*. "And no matter our leanings, facts are facts and smells are smells and I wouldn't want to live anywhere close to that grow in Basalt. I didn't know you were active in Pitkin County anyway. Or perhaps I haven't been paying attention."

"It's the whole valley," said Rudduck. "I would hate to see that kind of grow plunked around here."

"Silt fought them off. What about retail?"

"The city council seems to have represented the people here

in Glenwood and everything seems to be fine the way it is, don't you think? A few retail shops are up and running and civilization has not imploded. Stoners toke, drinkers drink, all is good."

"So any new grows, you'd be opposed?"

"Garfield County has already decided that issue. No different than saying we don't want Coors or Budweiser building a giant brewery. It wouldn't be a good fit."

"And you want to encourage me, to put it in its gentlest terms, to keep up the negative coverage of those operations?"

"Only to thank you for your coverage to date," said Rudduck.

"Which, forgive my cynicism, makes me think that you have a stake in the status quo."

Barnstone crossed her legs, looked at Rudduck. The gaze appeared to be more pupil than partner. Still, Duncan wasn't entirely sure.

"Do you decide how things get covered?"

"The totem pole in a small-newspaper town is as tall as my desk, but It's easy to find reporters because they are always on the bottom."

"But, still," said Rudduck.

"Now my question. Do you have a stake in retail marijuana?"

During the ensuing pause, Duncan could have debriefed Teddy Roosevelt about plans for building the Panama Canal. "I have many investments."

"I'll take that as a yes."

"And so?"

"And so why did you want this meeting?"

"This may be a touch awkward, maybe a bit unusual—I don't know." Rudduck looked at Barnstone. She nodded as if she knew what was coming. "So if you ever have a question regarding the future of Glenwood Springs or the county situation as a whole, I wanted to let you know that I am available. As a resource."

Rudduck didn't have a clue how reporters worked. Sources developed, one baby step of trust following the next. They didn't hold up their hand and say "use me."

Barnstone leaned forward. "We both admire your coverage and of course we know how deep you dig, given your work on the tunnels and all that awfulness last year."

The *tunnels*. That's how it was known. A sweeping story of anti-government defiance reduced to shorthand—the conspiracy's target.

"I always appreciate having sources," said Duncan. "I turn down very few. Check that—I turn down nobody. But what is your interest in retail marijuana?"

Rudduck's expression remained an inscrutable hunk of granite. Perhaps he had expected a "sure thing" from Duncan, a handshake, and be done with it. Barnstone gave a pop-up smile, lips closed. In the long moment it took Rudduck to form an answer, Duncan realized that he might be missing a golden opportunity.

"It's a matter of public record," said Rudduck. "The state is clear about what you must disclose and, you know, the whole vetting process."

"And?"

"And why would I try to spare you the joy of homework?"

"So the retail shop is already well supplied by a grow operation, though we aren't saying which one, and the status quo is your strong preference. But the commissioners seem pretty set against any county involvement in grows, and Glenwood Springs, of course, has enough trouble managing retail. Doesn't seem to me like you had to go out of your way today for this little chat, though I can tell you that reporters so rarely hear a thank-you that I don't want to leave the wrong impression. But where's the threat?"

Rudduck managed a smile fainter than a faded pastel. "You need to think like a businessman with investments."

"There's one commissioner seat open and he's a Republican," said Duncan. "Enough said."

"If you say so." Rudduck shrugged, turned to Barnstone. "Guess there is no need to worry."

"Can I ask you something?" Duncan cleared his throat to buy time.

"Sure," said Rudduck.

This time, Duncan set the pace. Deliberate. *Asking* would be harmless. "Are you still looking for investors?"

Duncan's phone chimed. It was a number he didn't know. He answered without Rudduck's permission. The call would show Duncan was busy. *Needed.* Let Rudduck mull the questionable question.

"Hello?"

Silence—but not dead silence.

"Don't leave downtown without going to the office."

"Who is this?"

An odd, slow voice. And female.

Duncan stood up. "Who is this?"

Two girls played a choreographed slapping-clapping game as their parents studied the bill at the registration desk. Another group headed for the hot springs across the street, towels draped over all four shoulders, two moms with two boys.

"You there?" said the voice.

"What's at the office?"

"You'll see."

The connection went dead.

"What the hell?" said Rudduck.

Duncan looked around again, looked at the phone again. "Not

sure."

Rudduck said, "Before you leave I want to say I was unaware that journalists could ask to invest in a business that is a source of controversy. And that they are covering."

"It would have to be done carefully," said Duncan.

A lie. It wasn't even a close call. Journalistic ethics were unequivocal. Receiving financial gain from a business you covered? A big fat no-no. But his bank account danced in hope, so close to relief.

"If there was an opening," said Rudduck. "Theoretically speaking. What about all that paperwork with the state? Your name on the corporate papers, etcetera?"

Duncan found his mouth had run dry. "And my question was theoretical as well."

"Really?" said Rudduck. "I could see the eagerness in your face."

The debt dogged him. He felt at times like he was tugging a bulldozer by a rope with his teeth through mud, walking backwards. The mere thought of being able to drop the rope and let his incisors rest provided a swift surge of happiness. Plus, no more fibbing around Trudy. He wanted the thing with Trudy to work out. Long term.

"Theoretically, would it be possible to work out a side deal?"

"So how much would you have available?"

"Theoretically, right?"

"If you insist."

"Call it eighty-one thousand."

He had $81K from his grandmother's will, but it was roughly one-third his debt, piled up from student loans and years of credit card debt plus a whole hell of a lot of interest. He needed the $81,000 to find a way to fuck like rabbits and multiply.

"It's not much, is it?" said Duncan. He had heard horror stories about electric bills for grow operations—the lights and ven-

34

tilation alone.

Rudduck offered a sour smile. "It's not nothing."

"So maybe a handshake arrangement and you turn my money into something more substantial."

"And the terms?"

"Whatever the other investors receive."

"We would shake hands but also write an agreement, of course," said Rudduck.

"If you want."

If there was an invisible signal, Duncan missed it. Barnstone stood at the same moment as Rudduck, and the two stepped away for a chat, their backs to him with no body language to read.

Barnstone spoke first when they returned. "We have new situations we are pursuing," she said. "We will let you know."

Duncan crossed the bridge with a lift in his step, a sensation like he'd walked through a magic mirror.

Maybe there was a way to make all the debt go *poof*.

Cars filled the hot springs parking lot below. The interstate hummed with traffic. Three blue rafts floated in the late-season water of the Colorado River. The eastbound Amtrak inched into the station on the south bank of the river, where a gaggle of passengers waited to board. Glenwood Springs, at times, looked like the outdoorsy Colorado equivalent of Times Square.

Duncan walked quickly. Trudy had long since cured him of extravagant use of gasoline. He adored her whole lifestyle, wanted to find that same calm. Anyway, walking would be faster. The parallel bridge was backed up with traffic. The vitamin D didn't hurt, not that he was in short supply. With Trudy busy filming the pilot with the crew from NatGeo, Duncan's original plan was to head down toward Redstone and use the afternoon for a hike on the lower flanks of Mount Sopris. That plan was scrapped in favor of returning to Sweetwater to wait for the return of the pissed-off man that Allison found lashed to a tree. Duncan had already called the FAA—but no reports of missing planes in Colorado. What the hell?

"Your hash oil flamethrowers bonded out."

Chris Coogan mother-henned the newspaper as if society might collapse if he wasn't there to edit every breaking story.

"I'll find them," said Duncan. "First thing Monday." Coogan did not need to know that a public defender had rejected his request for a jailhouse interview.

"So why are you here?" Coogan's question arrived fully annotated. No scholar was needed to write the subtext—*my extra hours and dedication are par for the course, what's your reason?* "When you said you heard reports of a plane going down in the Flat Tops, I assumed you'd stay up there."

"Heading back in about two minutes. Have you ever heard of a guy being tied to a tree but he won't say why?"

"That's the kind of quirky stuff that will go national. Twice in one week. Glenwood Springs, Crazy Town USA." Coogan gave a sideways head nod to the new feature writer. "By the way, we've been making a few calls."

Marina Fuentes wore a wireless headset and took notes on a tiny wireless tablet cradled on her blue jean lap. She glanced up, shook her head and scrunched up her cute nose. At least she was getting nowhere. What was there to get until the cops came back with Allison?

"I don't need help." Duncan smiled. He didn't want Fuentes to think he was jerk. Or possessive of his stories, but this one was his, all the way. So was the hash oil blaze. "Okay?"

"She's just making the routine calls," said Coogan. "Don't worry. Did you know a box was delivered with your name on it?"

A cardboard container sat atop a pile of newspapers on the corner of Coogan's desk. Block letters covered the top: FOR DUNCAN. It was wrapped every which way with duct tape.

"When did it show up?"

"It was leaning against the front door. Don't you have friends on the bomb squad?"

Coogan laughed. Duncan didn't.

Maybe Coogan was chickenshit. Maybe he decided right then to stand up from behind his desk and pretend to need something off his bookcase. Coogan's reaction ratcheted up his own sense of alarm. Fuentes, proving her own mettle or sheer innocence, drew close. She smelled like jasmine.

For its size, big enough for a pair of combat boots, it didn't weight much. Duncan jabbed the pocketknife through sticky layers between lid and box where the tape had no purchase. After three sides of slashing, the lid flipped up like a coffin top.

The box exhaled an edgy, earthy aroma.

Inside, well-yellowed newspaper crunched as Duncan dug down. Coogan came back to his side, chickenshit moment over.

Below the newspaper, giant bear teeth in a jumble snaked together on a funky piece of leather.

Duncan knew it.

The fact that its owner had been separated from his trademark accessory gave Duncan a jolt.

"What the hell?" said Marina.

"One of a kind," said Duncan.

"And?" said Coogan. "Know whose it is?"

"It belongs to the man who made it," said Duncan. "Devo."

Seven

The vultures, from a distance, had treated her makeshift shroud as a temporary annoyance. They had jabbed their way through the blanket and feasted again.

The birds served as a partial indicator of her trustworthiness. From sixty yards out, Allison willed the man to step around from the other side of the tree and reveal himself.

"Fuck." She said it under her breath, looked around at the other three. "Did I say that out loud?"

At the tree, Allison climbed down first.

Nobody said a thing because nothing needed to be said.

The deer carcass proved she wasn't crazy. So did the left-behind rope, sliced ends mocking her.

Alone, she circumnavigated the tree. She felt them watching. She studied every patch of bare, sandy earth, as if looking for the outlines of a trapdoor. Halfway around, she spotted two sets of faint impressions. Again, the clown. And perhaps the other set were the tree man's running shoes. If so, he'd be favoring his right leg on the long haul. Eight more impressions—six sneaker, two boot, three left, five right—lined up so well they could have been confined by railroad tracks. Unless it rained, they would be a cinch to track.

"I assume he didn't have a knife." Boyish Deputy Sheriff Giles Reed appeared, at least, forgiving. He flicked up his dark sunglasses to study the frayed ends of the rope.

"His captor came back," said Allison. "Two sets of tracks that head straight back into the Flat Tops."

Deputy Reed crouched between ends of the rope. He wore a blue baseball cap that sported the Garfield County Sheriff's Department logo. His babyish skin meant he had to shave his face maybe twice a week. He kept his dark hair short. His knees didn't make a sound when he stood up. Ah, youth.

"I should have let him come with me."

"Not if he was as uncooperative and ornery as you described."

The stench of dead deer kept their mouths tight, their words choice. Vic Allen, the Parks and Wildlife officer, came prepared with a big red kerchief for covering his nose and mouth. He looked bank robber scary, but all the way up he'd been the conversation driver and she knew his heart—kind with a wary streak as cynical as any urban cop or city prosecutor. He had jumped at the chance to ride Hercules, Allison's stalwart mule.

"Found this," said Allen. He held up a plastic baggie. Weighing down one corner, mucky from its previous home inside the carcass, sat a bullet. "It's not archery season, not black powder season, not rifle season, not anything season."

Deputy Reed bagged the rope in an oversized pouch, taking care not to manhandle the thing too much in case a flake of DNA from the captor or captive could be gleaned. Cop-to-cop chatter between Deputy Reed and his cohort, the more jaded and quiet Deputy Darren Walls, confirmed there had been a crime involving kidnapping or unlawful restraint, but they both knew they would need the victim, and his complaints, to build a case.

Following Deputy Reed's direction, they imagined a grid created by the general footprint of the tree's canopy and began a thorough walk-through. She crissed. He crossed. She found a spot where the dirt cratered like the caldera of a mini volcano. The guy relieved himself, apparently, only once. She didn't spot another, but he hadn't had much slack in his restraints. He had enough slack on one arm to unzip, but not enough to untie knots on the opposite hand.

The number of piss spots and lack of human scat put possible parameters on the length of his outdoor incarceration.

Evidence bagged and photographs taken, Allison led the way cross-country on horseback to a rocky outcropping that offered an unbroken view of the broad valley. Four stubby fingers of forest reached into the open bowl. They paused to take in the view. They were two miles from the vulture tree, five hundred feet up. Allison scanned every available square inch through binoculars. She wanted to spot the backs of the two men running or the tail of a jet poking out of a tree. Despite her own need for further validation, her buddies from the land of officialdom did not appear doubtful.

"Stop glassing and eat." Allen and the others sat cross-legged on the grassy slope. They had brought chain store submarine sandwiches, chips and bottled water.

"In a minute," said Allison. She had chopped the view into a grid—one hundred squares, ten by ten. Within each view, binoculars propped on her knees, she zip-scanned top to bottom, left to right. She gave each square its due.

Nothing.

The hum started low—an electric clipper buzzing in the next room. Ten seconds later, nobody in her group could have heard her if she had shouted with every spare ounce of lung power, though mere yards separated all four riders and all five horses.

The sound flattened them.

A prop plane chewed through the sky, a ridiculous chunk of metal with wings. Nothing in the all-too-brief history of manned, powered flight could move any slower and remain aloft. Tires on the struts bore faint treads. A wide, fat wing sat atop the fuselage like a brooding brow. Rust pimpled out of the underbelly of the powder-blue skin. The blue bug crabbed so low Allison caught a whiff of oil as it spewed exhaust, and she gagged before burying her mouth in the crook of her shirtsleeved elbow.

The plane hugged the contours of the landscape as if a topo map had been programmed into its brain, but Allison didn't figure this floating junker for sophisticated avionics. It reeked old school. Bush.

The plane rattled down the slope and gave them all a view of its high wing, from above.

"What the hell?" Vic Allen put a hand on his hat to hold it down in the mild wake.

Allison pulled the binoculars from Sunny Boy's saddlebag. The plane reverted to an unobtrusive noise level, banked to the left and set a bearing for Allison's least favorite tree in the Flat Tops.

At least, she thought, now she had one.

The plane reached the tree, tipped its wing and set a course to the northwest. A brief mechanical gargle caromed off the empty bowl of wilderness. The crotchety oversized blue bug did not belong. She watched it cruise but willed it to crash, about the last thing in the world she wanted to witness. Would it be possible for the same person to watch one plane crash from the inside and another from the outside? She didn't want to find out, but she didn't want to lose the plane. She watched it until the blip vanished, but already her mind spun back to the double set of prints she'd found by the tree. The plane had locked like a laser on the exact same course those prints were headed.

"Anybody else want to go with me?"

Allen eyed her horse like he might have missed a hidden jet pack. "Don't think you'll catch up."

"They might not land 'til Utah," said Reed.

"Or Idaho," said Allen.

"Or over the next ridge," said Allison. "You all can make it down okay? Cut south from here, you'll hit the trail and it's a four-lane highway back to Sweetwater."

Eight

Saturday Afternoon
Trudy

The necklace-in-a-box discovery had punched Trudy in the gut. Quirky, savvy, tough, determined, a bit reckless and very smart, Devo and his funky campaigns had always found a supporter in Trudy. He adored Allison, and it wasn't just because she once saved his life in a snowstorm. He had been critical help in two "situations," one with the murder of a man over property rights and one with a purposely set wildfire that took the life of a prominent environmentalist. Trudy had watched every one of his YouTube Channel clips on wilderness survival and, when he went to cable network, every episode of his quasi-reality show.

Lately, Colorado's most famous devolutionist and his erstwhile band of followers had faded from the limelight. Trudy had heard from friends in Meeker that Devo had reassembled the group, taken in a few new recruits and was making another push back in time. He wanted to toughen up the collective DNA and start a new society. This time he was doing it on private land with less publicity and no threat of government interference.

"You told the police?"

"My cop friend DiMarco took the box. He said he'd have the techs wipe it down. And they were going to pull security camera footage from all along Grand Avenue, see if they could spot whoever dropped off the box."

"We should go up there—to Meeker," she said.

"Coogan already wants an update." Duncan found a way to turn every side trip into a byline. It wasn't a bad thing. "Are you as worried as me?"

They sat on their front porch, watching the whole lot of wonderful nothing going on in the flat light of dusk. Duncan sipped IPA from a bottle. She drank a cooler with cucumber, chickweed, mint and apple.

"Why send it to me?"

Despite the beer and the setting, Duncan seemed anxious, edgy.

"Because you'd recognize it."

"So?"

"So how many people is that?"

"All the ones who saw his show," said Trudy. "So, millions I suppose. But there were a whole bunch of stories last summer when he got kicked off the Flat Tops. And you wrote the ones about his flock having to disperse."

"I guess."

"Are you okay?"

"With going over there?"

"With everything?"

Trudy put a hand on his leg. "You seem distracted."

"Sorry," he said. "Decompressing."

"You're worried?"

"Aren't you?"

"Maybe he sent it, knowing you'd come."

"Devo without his necklace is like Daniel Boone without his

coonskin cap. And maybe here comes the other thing I've been waiting on."

Duncan pointed his beer bottle up the road.

Jesse Morales, one of Allison's most trusted and steadfast hands around her outfitting business, rode up bareback on a dappled gray horse.

"That's Bella." Duncan made a lighthearted point of showing off his familiarity with Allison's livestock, even though he didn't trust horses.

If she had a hundred cats, Trudy would know every name and each one's quirky ways. Horses baffled her. She didn't mind riding them, but had no clue how to read them. Felines amused. Equines, she thought, endured.

Jesse, as always, arrived in inscrutable fashion. He could have won the lottery. He might have an arrow in his back.

Jesse slowed Bella to a walk to cross the meadow that separated Trudy's house and Allison's A-frame. A worn, curving path connected their front steps.

"They're at the barn unloading," said Jesse. He'd grown a pair of fuzzy sideburns, but kept the rest of his brown face smooth. Despite working around a barn and horses most days, he always looked clean. He kept his dark hair long, usually in a ponytail that jutted down from a black cowboy hat.

"And?" said Duncan.

"It's the cops," said Jesse. "The two cops and the dude from wildlife. And a dead deer that reeks to high heaven."

"Not the guy? The guy they went to retrieve?"

Jesse pulled Bella up close and climbed down.

"Guess he was gone," said Jesse.

"Allison said he was tied up," said Duncan.

Jesse shrugged. "Somebody came back. The deer was still there and all of that. Ropes and stuff."

"And Allison?" said Trudy.

"Cops said she stayed up there to scout."

Allison heading off by herself was no cause for alarm to Jesse, but Trudy had to force herself to not think about all the wacky ways that events could spin out of control. The elements were risky enough.

"Cops talking?" said Duncan.

Jesse looked around, straight-faced. "You wouldn't want me to do your job, would you?"

"How long have they been back?"

The barn stood a quarter mile uphill, at the end of the Sweetwater road.

"They should be coming down any minute," said Jesse. "But don't worry. I asked them to stop. The one sheriff's deputy said he knew your name. They all did. They got a few stories out of Allison on the way up, and one of the deputy's wives has gone vegan and started keeping bees and pickling vegetables thanks to Trudy. So they know where they are and they will stop, but they wanted me to tell you not to expect much because, and I quote, they don't know what the fuck is going on."

Duncan bounded into the house and returned a few seconds later, notebook and phone in hand. "I don't trust them to stop," he said. He sprinted past Jesse and Bella at a good clip.

"They seemed sincere." Jesse said it for her benefit, not Duncan's.

"I think Duncan has learned that the government can claim to be forthcoming," said Trudy, "and still do a good job of hiding anything it wants to."

Duncan was halfway to the road when the two government vehicles came into view. Trudy recognized the Garfield County Sheriff's SUV. The second vehicle, a pickup, was Parks and Wildlife.

They didn't slow.

Duncan found a final gear for his sprint, arms waving. His short, sharp whistle did the trick. Brake lights popped red and the door on the first vehicle opened.

Handshakes. Gestures. Duncan folded his arms. Listened. Took a note. Shook his head. Nodded his head. The officer from the Parks and Wildlife truck pointed to the bed of his pickup and Duncan hopped up on the bumper to have a look over the tailgate.

Between the bear tooth necklace, Allison's report of the no-information-man tied to a tree and the simmering disquiet she felt from filming a pilot for a major network—*just how presumptuous was she?*—Trudy sensed that queasy feeling from uncertainty and overload.

"Where's Colin?" said Trudy.

Jesse kept close tabs on everyone. He was the behind-the-scenes glue of Allison's operation. "Yampa. A good friend's family lost that hotel that burned down a couple days ago. He headed over to help with the mess."

"Think we should send Colin after Allison?"

"She's got a big head start."

"Do you have a rough idea of the location of the mystery tree?"

"Sort of."

"You never know," said Trudy. "Colin could pick up the trail."

"Like a bloodhound," said Jesse. "You worried about Allison?"

Trudy filled him in.

"Come on," said Jesse. "His necklace? Like pulling the ring off *El Papa*."

Out on the road, Duncan stepped back from the three government men, took pictures in the dimming light.

"I know," said Trudy. "Makes me sick."

"I'm calling Colin now." Jesse, old-school polite, asked to use the landline in the house.

"Of course, of course," said Trudy. "If you're hungry—"

"No thanks." He cut her off.

"A slice of dandelion quiche on the counter, made with tahini. And the crust has buckwheat groats and sunflower seeds."

Jesse Morales gave her a blank stare. He preferred meat with every meal.

"Seeds?" Again, the dead stare. "You used seeds to make crust? Seeds that were waiting to sprout and live full lives? You ground them down before they even had a chance."

Jesse shook his head in grim fashion.

Trudy laughed. "There are more where those came from."

A two-hour drive down from Yampa would put Colin back in Sweetwater tonight. He would be on Allison's trail in the morning. Or, could be. Allison rarely minded alone time.

But she would want to know about Devo's necklace.

And if you knew what would impact Allison's world, it was never a good idea to keep her in the dark for long.

Nine

Sunday Morning
Allison

Darkness caved to the gentle nudge of dawn. A whisper of blue broke the back of night and, for about the four hundredth time, Allison imagined herself being pierced by the long lance of light connected straight back to its source, ninety-three million miles away. It never hurt to remember that the evolution of cells on this particular planet was all a random fucking miracle.

A palm-size fire begged for more fuel, but she needed only enough heat to boil water. All days that started with coffee and ended with tequila were good days. A Flip N' Drip thermos waited to perform its sole duty—make one cup of coffee and keep it hot.

Sunny Boy munched on oats from a bag with an eager, noshing rhythm. She'd already packed the tent, a newfangled nylon number dubbed the "tadpole" model, which seemed perfect. She was small and hoped like hell she was unimportant, if you could be unimportant and pissed off at the same time.

She poured the boiling water into the bottom canister, snapped on the top two sections and waited the agonizing three minutes for the water to drip down through the filter chamber, hidden away like magic. Allison ate a crackling Gala apple, fed Sunny Boy the core and sipped coffee from the detachable cup. She had stolen-borrowed the organic blend from Trudy's cache.

"By the way," she said, "the answer to your question is I have no idea how much farther."

She'd go until she satisfied her curiosity, until she found what

Mr. Tree wouldn't or couldn't tell her. Having expected him to stay put until a full rescue team arrived, she felt oddly determined to finish the story.

Sunny Boy's incisors made juicy work of another apple, this time a whole one, as she held it. Four bites. He could be a dainty eater when he wanted to be. "Water back, coming right up," said Allison. "Same pothole spot as last night, if that's to your liking."

Up on Sunny Boy, she held the reins in one hand and capped coffee cup in the other, happy about the slight tongue burn.

From the saddle, tracking had proven to be a snap. Mr. Tree and his savior, if that was his role, were unconcerned about their tracks. Stopping to glass at high spots, so far, had proved fruitless. Their pace didn't sag. Their route snaked. They had headed straight across the plateau. At midafternoon yesterday, Allison guessed they were heading to West Mountain Trail and might then head north straight across the heart of the plateau, or south, back in the general direction of Sweetwater. But they crossed the trail as if they didn't even see it and slipped down into the woods that filled the canyon that climbed to Crescent Lake.

With morning sun now lighting the undergrowth, she hoped they found whatever the hell they were looking for. If you didn't know it well, there were sections of the Flat Tops that mimicked each other. To make navigation even trickier, the whole scene could change from dawn to dusk as long shadows retreated and later clawed their way back, rendering new details and altering the relief.

They crossed the South Fork of the Derby Creek and headed east down the spine of the canyon. They paralleled the Jeep Trail, which provided a zero-calories-burned access for day-trippers and fishermen to visit the mountain lake, and she found where they had spent the night with a campfire spot and eight more cigarette butts. The gap between her and them would depend on what time they had woken and packed up.

Allison kept Sunny Boy at a walk. She let him pick his way down steep, rocky bivouacs.

She didn't have a scrap of evidence for the DA, but three times yesterday she had pulled Sunny Boy to a full stop in response to an overwhelming urge to look around to the rear.

A circling hawk might be able to take in the whole sweep of high plateau and dense stands of forest behind her and declare her prime material for the nuthouse. But she had no high spot, only the gnawing notion to *look around, look around, look around*.

Aspen leaves fluttered and clacked in the warm breeze. Cooler temperatures were still a few weeks off—cooler temperatures that would trigger the alchemical transformation of the leaves from green to gold. Underbrush crackled as Sunny Boy shifted for better footing. She waited for the *look around* sensation to manifest itself as another rider. Hell, she'd take a hungry wolverine if it meant her gut radar wasn't faulty.

Colin? She chased the thought away. He had gone to Yampa.

She'd much rather go two-on-two, of course, with whatever waited up ahead.

But she also didn't mind the alone time.

Sad, but true.

There it was.

She didn't go out of her way to dwell on how the space between her and Colin had shifted. The minor earthquake from the previous summer, when Colin hadn't come clean about all he knew about his father and brother's involvement in a vile anti-government conspiracy, still generated aftershocks. Colin played it cool for the first month after the near-blowup. He gave her space and only tiptoed back into her heart when she had decompressed enough and most likely when she had issued an invisible signal that the door had opened, if only a crack. Climbing back into their routines generated laughs and fun and more than a few feisty, horny, baby-it's-been-way-too-long romps. He had saved her life. She had to remember that. He had tried to straddle two worlds—and failed. But he had done it out of instinctive loyalty to his family, nothing else. When the emotional reconnect finally happened, the conversation about "it" involved one night, a hefty dent in a bottle of tequila, and done.

They resumed old ways.

But that didn't account for why she relished days like these.

Days like these . . .

Alone . . .

The earthquake created a fissure in the back forty but the house still stood. So what the hell? They had come through it, but it took extra effort to scold the ungrateful internal bitch that tried to dominate the interior spat over the best course of action.

Repeat after me—*Colin saved your life.*

Should she be forced to etch that fact into granite with a butter knife? Times New Roman, letters each a foot high and carved cleaner than an old-school typesetter?

Maybe she didn't deserve him.

Sunny Boy channeled his inner bloodhound.

The wanderers had tightened their search in an area around the top of Crescent Lake Canyon. They had crossed the Jeep Trail again and set a more confident heading that kept Crescent Lake to the west. Thick woods and the resulting shade left the soil slightly damp. Tracking them would be easier if they dipped their feet in a fresh bucket of paint every hundred yards, but you couldn't ask for everything. Their route climbed the north face of the canyon, but Allison knew if they were looking for a spot on the high plateau that the modest incline would soon turn into a whopper. The switchbacks on South Derby Trail, a mile to the west, chopped the ascent into manageable pitches and might be Sunny Boy's best route to the top. But the wanderers seemed so sure now and purposeful in their direction that Allison had reason to believe they were close. Or maybe they had already arrived.

The forest yielded to the rocky incline in a clean line, with zero transition between the broad, rocky escarpment and the long line of lodgepoles that ran east and west as far as her eye could see.

She stopped Sunny Boy two strides from the dazzling daylight and her eyes quickly found the only moving things in view, her heart giving a little leap out of satisfaction or worry. Or both.

She dug out binoculars. She asked Sunny Boy for five steps in reverse, to deeper cover.

Her buddy with the shorts and beard, last seen in and on the ropes, struggled for footing in the rear.

She caught a flash of a tether. His wrists were bound and connected to a leash.

The guy was his handler, five yards ahead.

Back on Sunny Boy, she waited until the second figure, her guy, disappeared from view over the top lip of the incline. She pointed Sunny Boy up a less direct route that would bring her to the top of the pitch at a more oblique angle. She wanted to end up several hundred yards further north, and she didn't want to arrive at the top exposed.

Halfway to the top, she caught her first view of Crescent Lake and smaller Mackinaw Lake. The canyon wall ahead loomed even higher. The hair-raising switchbacks on South Derby Trail offered the best exit to the top. Whatever they had been searching for was on the flat, wide bench ahead.

Sunny Boy's hooves clacked on rocks. He huffed and snorted at the work. Allison's body jerked awake, sensing an abrupt end to the slow-motion chase.

Before their collective outline breached the line of sight from anyone on top, Allison dismounted and tied Sunny Boy to a rock. "Five minutes," she said. "Count on it."

She walked the last twenty yards to the lip, keeping a careful eye on seeing and being seen. She crawled the last few paces, head low and moving with care.

The blue plane sat facing away, to the south, about a half mile off. The pilot must have had a nerve-*ectomy* because you couldn't lose your cool putting a plane down on this hummocky, rocky strip of subalpine tundra. It might be easier to land on an outdoor windowsill on the fiftieth floor of a skyscraper. The plane appeared intact.

The carcass of a wounded cousin, however, lay upended nearby. The fuselage had burrowed or skidded as it crash-landed, no doubt smashing the prop.

She lay prone with her binoculars, steadying herself like a sniper preparing a shot.

This time the urge to check behind arrived like a jolt, as if a giant hook had yanked at her cheek.

She obeyed the urge.

And was glad she did.

Emerging from the woods, in the precise spot where she had come out, stood a familiar horse and its familiar rider.

Colin.

Ten

Sunday Afternoon
Duncan

"So you asked the deputies why they didn't even try and go after the man tied up to the tree?"

Duncan said, "They claimed they weren't prepared for that kind of a manhunt—food and gear, etcetera. There's a whole lot of nothing up there. Not what county sheriff deputies do."

"The low-flying plane? Is that an angle? Isn't there a minimum elevation for aircraft?"

Coogan enjoyed hashing things through. The Sunday call wasn't all that unusual. When Coogan found a story to love, he fell hard.

"Two thousand feet. At least, that's on paper. You know, the regulations."

"The out-of-season deer?"

"You read the quotes from the wildlife guys. The usual stern admonishments."

Coogan had texted to ask for the call. Duncan called back after a hot jog down Sweetwater Road. He knew the U-turn spot that made it an even four miles.

"So back to the guy at the tree. Why wouldn't they want to go after him or the guy who set him free?"

"I can ask again, but they went up there to retrieve him—you know? They weren't prepared for a manhunt into the woods. Like I said."

"And then there's the whole Devo angle."

"What about him?"

"Is anyone going to check on him?"

"It's complicated."

"Try me."

Even on a Sunday, with Trudy off, Duncan had made his due diligence round of calls. On both Quiet Tree Man and the case of Devo's necklace, he had peppered his full list of know-it-alls in Garfield and Rio Blanco County. In exchange for his efforts, he had the vague satisfaction that came from giving a shit, but not one decent scrap to follow.

"Allison stayed up in the woods because she thought she had a lead on what direction they were heading, but Colin—"

"That's the boyfriend?"

Coogan fooled nobody. He savored snippets of Allison-related stories and didn't hide his infatuation with the former city girl turned creature of the woods. Coogan also knew Colin McKee was the lucky boyfriend of Allison Coil. He knew that Colin got to enjoy the whole package in ways that Coogan—and Duncan—could only imagine.

"Her significant other, yes. The man standing between you and her. He is delivering the message about the necklace."

"Why can't you go up there?"

"To where?"

"To Meeker, find Devo's camp."

"Tell me when you're switching topics, okay? And I'm not sure I could find it, for starters, and then the third spinning plate is that our hash oil gourmands are getting arraigned first thing tomorrow."

"Nobody else knows where Devo is?"

"I'm sure they do. They found room on private land to set up camp and do their thing, but they don't want any outside interference. Or visitors."

"The Devo story is better. It's been awhile since we heard anything about him."

"I called around up there. Nothing public yet."

Coogan understood. A two-reporter town couldn't get to every story, but it was rare that a pair came along like these two, both with so much juice.

"But someone has to go in and see if they've seen Devo."

"Yeah," said Duncan. "Someone he trusts."

"And that someone leads right back to little Miss Coil because she and Devo have had, shall we say, *encounters*."

"What I'm thinking." Duncan knew that if Allison put her back to Sweetwater in late August, she could decide to stay up in the high country for a week, or more. "She's going to have to figure out a way to be in two places at once."

Eleven

Sunday Afternoon
Allison

Colin parked Merlin near Sunny Boy, stayed low.

"Jesus," said Colin when she'd finished her rundown.

"That's it, *Jesus*? What do you want him to do?"

"He could start by coming back to remind all the billionaires that the game isn't won by who accumulates the most."

She would never grow tired of Colin's strong jaw and deep-set eyes. Or the way the brim of his brown cowboy hat drooped down in front, setting off the whole profile.

"Don't disagree, of course. But what has that got to do with this?"

"Nothing," said Colin. "You asked, that's all. But if Jesus is around he could pray for the pilot—he's going to need it. Those Alaskan bush pilots have planes that can get off the ground from here to Sunny Boy. It's all about the engine, custom wings and the angle of attack."

"Fascinating." She feigned first-date sincerity.

"But that particular plane needs a thousand feet of runway. At least." He faked the nerdy authority right back. "Standard equipment for a technical takeoff like this one is a heavy-duty adult diaper and don't go with store brand."

"I see." She gave him all the serious intensity she could muster without laughing.

"Part of it depends on the load, of course. Do you know what cargo is being transferred from the busted ship to the intact one?"

She'd seen bags in sturdy bundles. They looked roundish, like well-stuffed laundry bags. She couldn't be sure. "No," she said.

"But one adult male came in on the plane?"

"Don't know if one or two—don't know nothing. But at least one, right? I see three different folks down there."

Or more? Distinguishing one from the other wasn't easy.

"Plus the cargo?"

Colin poked the air in front of his face as if he had access to a hologram calculator.

"Yes."

"Don't recommend it—taking off, that is. With all that load."

"Maybe one or two of them hikes back out," said Allison. "But the guy I found, the treed-up guy, was already struggling with a foot injury, ankle sprain or worse. And, by the way, there's a question I've been meaning to ask."

"I'm all ears. I've been sheer brainpower, as you can no doubt tell, up to this point. But now I'm all yours and, as I said, all ears.

57

Fire away."

No smile.

"Why did you follow me?"

Colin held up an index finger, scrambled low over the twenty steps to Merlin, retrieved something from a saddlebag and climbed back up the slope, head down.

He stretched out prone next to her, keeping the secret item tucked against his body.

"I'm afraid this is going to shift the mood a bit."

He lifted his arm. A distinct necklace dangled from his grip.

Allison felt that queasy, uncomfortable flutter she hated with a passion.

"It was delivered to Duncan's office. In a box."

"Then what the hell are we doing up here?"

"Why I came."

"Did Duncan call anyone? Cops?"

"Yeah, he did. Had 'em check the necklace and they were going to check the box, too. You know, wipe it down or whatever."

"There must be a problem."

"Then you agree with everyone."

"Everyone?"

"Duncan, Trudy. And me."

"Has anyone seen Devo lately?"

At one point, before the whole thing blew up, Devo had two dozen disciples who signed on for his attempt to devolve and re-toughen the collective DNA. They had a quasi–reality television show documenting the effort, but they were all forced to restart when National Forest officials evicted them from their would-be home on the northern flanks of the Flat Tops. Those who followed his adventures knew Devo had lost half the crew. Former members of the tribe had peeled off and been featured on television and in local newspapers as survivors of the experiment-gone-awry.

"Not that I know," said Colin.

"I thought he found private land," said Allison.

"Near Meeker, in fact."

Colin would know—it was his hometown.

"We need to find their camp, homestead, whatever it is." Devo's necklace, without Devo, made her guts shudder. Had she not chased Vulture Tree Guy, she'd already be a day closer.

A mechanical cough and sputter snapped their attention back to the working airplane. The engine caught, jerked to a stop and caught again. The prop whirred.

"They're all on?" Allison raised her voice. She hadn't been watching. Colin hadn't been watching.

"Maybe," said Colin.

The cover of forest was too far, the footing too treacherous to rush a horse.

The engine's throaty whine hung at a high pitch. The blue plane crept forward an inch. The plane's engine whined to a faster rpm. The plane started to roll, bouncing over rocks and wobbling into divots.

The pilot tweaked his heading, bearing to the spot where she and Colin were flattened out over the rim of the ridge. Too bad the horses didn't know how to lie down on command. Or how to camouflage themselves as sagebrush and bunch grass.

The plane gathered speed but at such an unimpressive rate that Allison wondered for a second if they weren't taxiing in order to take off from the opposite direction. If that was the plan, she and Colin were dead meat.

Allison hoped the horses didn't panic. They had zero experience around airplanes, making her jealous of their innocence.

A gap appeared between the bulbous tires and the makeshift runway. The engine labored and the plane reached an altitude of thirty feet when it banked to the right, still climbing, and the man in the co-pilot's seat, the sun bouncing off his sleeked-back dark sunglasses, stared straight down.

The man wore thick headphones and a microphone covered his mouth. He pointed right at them, stabbed a finger against the window.

The plane lumbered north and gained altitude, in part because the slope fell away at such a steep pitch.

The plane banked hard, circled back.

"Keep your head down," she shouted to Colin. They were on their stomachs. They listened to the plane grind. She had a half a notion to flip them the bird. Allison's heart pounded into the dirt.

The whine drowned out every thought and then the screaming bug set a course back to the north, and Allison grabbed her binoculars, rolled over and repeated the tail number out loud: "N1432X."

Up on the shelf, three sets of tire tracks scarred the terrain. Two landings, one takeoff. One of the landings had come in hard—bounced. The tires had gouged the land, ended abruptly and started again thirty yards on. The tracks ran parallel at first and then merged near the end of the run. The pilots of both landings must have stood on the brakes to avoid tumbling over the edge.

Trying to imagine a story that fit with everything she had seen since her encounter with Mr. No Answers, she hadn't registered that Colin had already tied Merlin in the shade of the upended fuselage. The tapered body pointed straight to the sky like a scared whitetail.

Colin put his hands on his knees, shook his head.

"Aw fuck," he said. "What the hell."

It wasn't a question.

The body hung in an ugly, hopeless fashion against the dashboard. It roasted in the sun blasting through the cracked windshield.

A combination of shoulder harness and lap belt strapped the body in, but it had slumped forward. It dangled oddly in the tight quarters.

His eyes were gone. At least, they had been a significant source of blood—mini, double red waterfalls. The blood soaked his beard and dripped down onto the dashboard below. The freshness was wet and sickening.

ZZ Top.

Him.

Once again, he wouldn't be answering any questions for a long, long time.

Twelve

Sunday Afternoon
Trudy

"It's not secret, but gypsum makes all the difference—gives the fruit meatiness, if that makes any sense."

Five chunks of tomato lined up in Sam Shelton's sizable palm.

"Crimson Cushion?"

"I've tried Bloody Butcher. I've tried Earliana. I always come back to Crimson Cushion. I like the size, too."

Loik.

They stood in Shelton's gleaming greenhouse on his farm in the rolling country east of Meeker and north of the White River. Every pane of the greenhouse gleamed. All the raised beds finished at matching heights. With the laboratory's spiffy brightness, Trudy felt as if she had entered the world of a former rocket scientist, not a former rock star.

"Fish meal?" said Trudy.

"Cottonseed meal and bonemeal, too." Shelton tucked another wedge of tomato into his cheek, stared at her and gave a half grin as he chewed, a small drizzle of juice escaping from one corner of his mouth. He wiped the drizzle away on his wrist. "Can you believe the taste?"

"Lovely," said Trudy. "More complex than you might think. And your compost, your bedding soil?"

Shelton had suggested the visit—to hang out, get comfortable. The producers wanted to film the visit but Shelton chased them off.

"A guy outside of Rifle makes this stuff like black tea, no worries about weeds or pests." *Pastes.* "Solid gold right there. I got a full dump truck of the stuff last fall, let the soil get happy all winter."

Wint-uhrrr. Trudy tried to stop hearing it.

The greenhouse ran like a long straight tail from Shelton's old-school farmhouse. He kept five chickens, two goats, a pet duck. He introduced her to three cats inside the house, and a few others roamed round outside or basked in the sun. Entering the greenhouse required Trudy to attest to the fact that she wore clean clothes and hadn't visited her own greenhouse that day and thereby exposed herself to any mites or insects that might have hitched a ride. She wondered if he was going to have her sign a form. In blood.

"Sorry about all the miscues up there, you know, screwups."

They had drifted back inside and sat at a simple square oak table in his sparse kitchen. Plain off-white plates sat on the table with a fork and red-checkered cloth napkin. The plates were as heavy and solid as a discus. Counter, gas oven, sink and refrigerator lined up like hard-working soldiers, all pressed against one wall. Light poured in through south-facing bay windows over the sink. The rock star touches were few—a small, framed black-and-white photograph on one wall (onstage with Pete Townshend) and an ornate wine decanter. A gift, Shelton said, from Tina Turner.

"Please," said Shelton. "You got the hang of it."

"Silly, aren't they? Nerves."

"You don't have to tell me."

"You didn't look nervous."

"Up on the hill do you mean, or back in the day?"

"Back, you know, then."

"Performing?"

Trudy wasn't clear on the rules about talking about the rock star stuff.

"Yes."

"Took me a couple years to not hurl before going on. Promoters started getting cold feet—shows starting an hour later than they should because I'm pacing between the green room and the men's, you know. I'm plankin' it."

"Really?" She wasn't sure what *plankin'* was, but had a rough idea.

"Sure, yeah, but I was a kid, you know. Getting polluted and doing the whole thing and what words came out of my cakehole might have sounded cocky, but I was an utter tool, down to my gizzards. Like we used to say, fecky the ninth." *Nointh*. "Didn't know myself."

Shelton pushed himself back from the table, rummaged around in the white refrigerator no higher than his shoulders, spent a minute slicing and chopping at his counter, and returned with fat chunks of mozzarella, sliced tomato and a stack of shiny basil leaves. He plopped a full bottle of cabernet between them on the table.

"The basil is yours, of course," said Shelton. "Market fresh right here at the store in town."

"Brett's grocery store," said Trudy. "My friend Brett Merriman."

"Best around. And the mozzarella comes from a guy in Grand Junction who makes his own for a pizza joint. Fresh as can be."

Shelton dusted his tomato with sea salt, sprinkled from pinched fingers at eye level, and fresh black pepper. He layered a sandwich with the cheese and herb. "Lunch and dinner right here—how much more do you need?" He winked.

Ex-omnivores, Trudy knew, often made the most ardent, demanding and finicky vegetarians.

"So this is it, then? No amount of cajoling will get you back out there?"

He worked his way through a big bite of the improvised sandwich. He took a good sip of the wine, studied the dark red liquid and eyed her.

"It wasn't real anymore." He took a chest-deep breath. "The songs weren't songs. It was *shtick*. They wanted us to re-create moments onstage, choreographed bits from videos from three decades ago, you know, the first wave of videos. Like ZZ Top and their cowboy boots tapping the sand at the desert gas station. And now they have a live camera and a giant screen so twenty thousand fans can see a picture of the cowboy boots— and cheer? You must be fucking kidding me? That your so-called rock show comes down to choreographed bits like that? So the fans get all choked up about the early days of MTV? A few toe taps to get their hearts fluttering? You're not selling an idea or a tune, you're selling nostalgia. You could see the thick waves of the stuff floating in the arenas. Like if Pete Fucking Townshend doesn't do the old windmill, people feel like they didn't get their money's worth. Fun, sure. Cute young girls in the front row, sure. Tits out to here, sure. Ego puffed out to here, sure. Ego getting laid, so to speak, every freaking night. But hollow? Monotonous? Bus. Hotel. Arena. Interview. Bus again, booze again. On and on."

Shelton chased his speech with a glug of wine.

"Some people in that situation might not have known how to take control."

Shelton sliced his remaining veggie sandwich into thirds, stabbed one piece with a fork and let it stand there, at the ready.

"I honored every contract, signed every autograph through the last stop on tour. We were in Tampa. I knew I would have no more obligations in a few precious hours. I'd held off my agent, told him I'd decide soon about another tour. Even that genius fucker Jack White wanted me to come to Memphis and do one of those old-fogey duet albums with everyone from Dolly Parton to Katy Perry—but you know those are all technology. Duets? Dolly arrives as a file in a computer program, her track recorded in a far-off studio."

Shelton popped a bite into his mouth. His chewing produced a smacking sound—pure enjoyment.

"I wanted a small town. I wanted animals. A few, anyway. I wanted to get my hands dirty. I'd played a festival in Grand Junction one September—a corn festival south of there, anyway, in Olathe—and I remember seeing the sun setting off the hills, right from the stage, and all I wanted to do was watch the glow.

I repeated a verse from a song that night and sparked a firestorm on Twitter. *How could he forget? Is Sam Shelton losing it?* I knew right then. Took me a year to wind everything down."

"No regrets?"

Another chunk disappeared in Shelton's mouth. She listened to the wet tomato squish.

"I'm not the only one at this table who drew a line in the sand." He smiled. "Or the dirt."

Trudy felt a faint blush, the tables being turned. There were days when she knew as a scientific fact that the cooped-up marriage to George Grumley had happened to a human being other than the one that lived in her skin now. "My hand was forced."

"You took steps."

"Did what I had to do."

He smiled, proud of his trap. "But you took action."

"All three of us in Sweetwater—Duncan and Allison, too. All had to deal with a change, one way or the other." It seemed like a good time to remind herself about Duncan, who lately seemed more distracted than ever, even a bit depressed. At least, brooding. Moving to Sweetwater had cooled his pace, but now he had reverted to the mean—a bit nervous, even.

"Sorry but I've never been too keen around reporters."

"Not all reporters are the same. Be like saying all drummers are the same."

"Ah, drummers—there are some common elements. Speeding up, for one."

"Duncan is a great guy and took quite a tumble, careerwise."

If she got to know Shelton a bit, no doubt Duncan would ask her to negotiate the opportunity to come out and write a profile.

"I want my own story back."

"Meaning?"

Another chunk of tomato sandwich, more squishing.

"Out of a hundred reporters, maybe one good one. You wouldn't believe how many times I say one thing and the print version is concocted from thin air. It's something you did not even say. It drains you, messes with your head."

Trudy used his serrated knife to slice a tomato, left space for him to fill.

"The stories start fucking each other—bet you didn't know that."

"Stories?"

"It's all one big circle of poaching and fucking. You see a phrase or a line in one interview, maybe about how I stand onstage or some bullshit, and the phrase multiplies like magical bread and fishes. It becomes the truth. I'm prey, they are the snarling jackals. You lose your way, I'm telling you. One time I had a reporter call back, through my publicist, and wanted to double-check every quote. I wanted to jump on an airplane, buy her the best dinner in town and kiss her or let her fuck me or both."

"The trade-off, however, was money," said Trudy.

"Sure. And your soul crawls off to a corner and shrivels into a dry ball of dust."

"And now?"

"Out here? It's me and the fish meal, me and the gypsum. I feel like a teenager again, you know. Flying the coop. I left home at sixteen. Back then, me mum's voice rattled around in my head for the first few months, but I started to break free, find myself. Same thing here, the first few months were rough. Self-doubt, you know. But I found a new rhythm. I got my own voice back. The real one. It's freedom, baby. Feel like you're gonna live for another hundred years."

Shelton paused and cleared his plate of the last wedge of fruit. More squishing. He smiled. "I am tomato."

Thirteen

Heavy foot traffic had tamped down the ground around the downed plane. It took a minute of circling to pick up a trail that led straight to the remnants of a small campfire, stubs of three split logs sticking out of the ash, the unburnt ends clean. Colin found the outline where a rectangular tent had smooshed down the scrappy undergrowth. The tops on a cluster of blue flax were smashed, decapitated.

"Coroner and cops are going to take time getting up here," said Allison. And then the interviews. And all the re-interviews.

They were halfway back to the plane from the campsite and already Allison caught a whiff of the rank cockpit.

They walked side by side, but not close. They each scanned the ground for scrap or stray bits.

"Routt County?" said Colin. "The boundary is right around here."

"Garfield. Same old friends."

"We going to leave him?"

"I'm not touching him."

"What if the blue plane off-loads, tries to come back?"

"They might come looking for you and me. But not here, knowing we'd find the dead guy and call in the cavalry."

"Did Mr. Tree ever ask your name?"

"For sure, no."

"Did you tell him anyway?"

"Why would I?"

Allison spotted a cigarette butt, picked it up as she had hundreds of others around camps over the years, much as she tried to insist that smokers deal with their waste. Ninety-nine percent of discarded butts looked the same but, like the one she'd found the day she spotted the vultures, this one had been smoked down to the filter. She wasn't too concerned about fingerprints or DNA, since the wrecked plane should contain vast hordes of the stuff from the crash survivors, but she plucked it with care nonetheless.

"Fuckers," said Allison. "Murdering fuckers with airplanes and a dead body and I still can't for the life of me make sense of the out-of-season dead deer. And now this."

"Litter?"

"All crimes," said Allison. "Every one."

"And now?"

"Horses need food and water. Us, too. And later today, or damn soon, we have to see if we can find Devo." The Devo thing gnawed at her. It wasn't good.

A thousand questions roared, but one more thing needed checking.

She plucked a bandana from a pocket inside her jean jacket, then draped the jacket on a bush near Sunny Boy.

The sun blasted the wide, rocky bowl and the heat poured down on this spot like a reflector, cooking the lingering pool of sour air. Overhead, the dry sky sparkled with such stunning clarity that you felt sorry for the word *blue* because *gold* had already stolen all the associations with wealth and luxury.

"Need help?" said Colin.

"Since I'm not sure this will work, I don't know."

Allison tightened the bandana and pulled off her Ropers, but not her white socks. There was no point in confusing the fingerprint folks with toe activity, though she would have to come clean about adding her small impressions to the smudgy jungle of prints left by grown men. The dead man's face reminded her of ancient Roman busts with no detail in the eyes. Her toes found purchase on the knobby dashboard and she pushed off, shimmying up on the back of the empty co-pilot's seat.

A half-size jump seat sat in the middle of the space, its back flopped down. Two seatbelt straps dangled, useless.

Allison waited a few seconds for her eyes to adjust, sipped a breath. The air wasn't that bad, the body was fresh.

Emptiness greeted her from the vertical, tapered cave.

Breathing through the bandana in an aboveground coffin of sorts, she caught a whiff of something else—not as pungent but heavy, permanent.

The cargo hold had been hollowed out. Netting, hefty mesh made of thick plastic, dropped from both sides. She ran her fingers along the floppy bones of the apparatus, her fingers coming back with a gritty dust. She reached across the narrow cabin, took another swipe. Same grit.

Allison climbed down from her perch and hopped back out into the blinding sunshine. She yanked down her bandana and cupped her hand at her face.

"Smell this," she said, offering her fingertips.

Colin inhaled. "Only one thing in the whole world smells like that."

Allison gave it another long whiff. It smelled of yesterday's skunk stirred with lemon, burnt sage, a muddy farm and a closed room after vigorous sex. Colin grabbed her fingers back.

"Do you wish we had enough to roll one?"

He smiled.

"Easy as buying a six-pack," said Allison. "We can take care of your needs."

After Colorado legalized it, and even long before, weed surfaced every now and then around camp—more with city-based hunters from the Front Range and not so much with others, she found, from the Western Slope. She could predict the ones where a de rigueur joint would materialize with the late-night whiskey. As long as nobody minded, and as long as their tents remained smoke free, she didn't care. She knew the perfect dose for end-of-the-day tequila. She'd take a hit of pot to be sociable, but the strains varied so she wasn't sure what she was getting into. She'd seen more barfing, hangovers and lost days of hunting from booze than from any lingering effects of pot. Besides, pot smokers tended to laugh. Boozers treated late-night campfires, every now and then, as if they'd found a place to be surly.

"A planeload of buds?" said Colin. "Worth a small fortune."

"Buds or the whole plant—either way." More than ever, Allison felt the rising urge to get the fuck out of there.

"At least we know what we're dealing with."

"By *we*, you mean *they*, of course."

" They?"

"The cops."

"We aren't even here," said Colin. "We spotted the wreckage on top of the ridge—figured it was faster to call it in than ride clear around. I can give them the rough GPS coordinates. Isn't that enough?"

"Look at you—all Mr. Twenty-First Century."

"If you ever need your precise global positioning, just holler."

"Isn't Flat Tops Wilderness enough of an address? Do we really need to know the numbers that go with the precise bit of dirt? Did anyone think it doesn't need or want a number?"

"You trying to stop progress?"

"If you find the switch," said Allison, "let me know."

Fourteen

Public Defender Inez Cordova stood five two in her modest pumps. Her cute frame made court time fly.

Today she opted for a strategy that had failed elsewhere. Under Colorado's laws that legalized marijuana, home enthusiasts could grow the plants they needed to produce hash oil. The issue was the care they took during production, when butane must be pumped through a tube packed with raw marijuana plants to draw out the potent, golden substance known as honey oil, earwax or shatter.

"This is not a case for the courts," said Cordova. Her dark eyebrows lifted. She oozed calm. "This is a case for the state marijuana regulators. The fire could have started from a home welder working on his automobile or a distiller making a hobby batch of whiskey. It's similar to frying a turkey at Thanksgiving and not doing it carefully — fires, unfortunately, are a part of life. They are a fundamental risk of life. That is why we have fire departments and why we let homeowners keep tanks of propane or why natural gas is run through the city streets as part of the infrastructure. It's an acceptable risk."

The couple being charged appeared as odd and unlikely in person as they had in their mug shots. Duncan's sympathies ran toward the eighteen-year-old boy — clearly a boy — because at some point he must have taught himself, or convinced himself, to align his fate with this mouth-breathing female, old enough to be his mother.

Jimmy Enriquez' distended earlobes swooped low. The three strands of barbed wire fence, tattoo variety, circled his neck. Everything about the kid screamed angry teenager. He stared straight ahead, dumbfounded.

Duncan thought—isn't smoking legal weed enough? How stupid do you have to be to think that you can manage handling pure butane around fire? Budtenders across Colorado could get you as high as a kite without having to risk injury to yourself or your house. Or your neighbor's.

They were being processed one at a time. Enriquez went first. Judge Paul McCormick, a no-nonsense sort, spoke like a benevolent priest. Duncan had seen this routine a few dozen times. Step one, set an avuncular, chatty tone. Step two, sentence offenders to a century of pounding rocks. Step three, *next!* Maybe McCormick had a stake in the thriving prison system.

Inez Cordova must know she didn't stand a chance. Her plan went further south when the prosecutor noted Enriquez' previous arrest for burglary, failure to enroll in a drug and alcohol treatment program, and a ticket for bullying at school.

Marsha Sykes went next. She stood quickly. She was taller than Enriquez and even larger, in person, than Duncan imagined. Again, the prosecutor needed five minutes to run down the rap sheet.

McCormick set sky-high bonds. The only other onlookers in the court were truck driver Cleo Bilhorn and her husband and another couple that Duncan figured were the property owners on the opposite side of the blackened epicenter of the blast.

The judge made a few statements about the distinction between reckless and intentional arson and sent each case off with a relaxed charm, as if the defendants should feel good about how they were being treated.

Out in the hall, Duncan steered clear of Cleo Bilhorn and introduced himself to the neighbors who had lived on the opposite side of the freak-show couple.

"We're upside down. You think insurance will make us whole? What little insurance we had?" Tim Miller didn't raise his voice, but he spit venom. His wife, Sandy, interweaved her right arm with her husband's left. Their hands clenched—hard. "Couple of degenerates. And they aren't gonna be able to pay us back. We're screwed."

"Did you know them?" said Duncan. "Know how long they lived there?"

"Said hi here and there," said Sandy Miller. "We weren't friends or anything."

"Any idea they were into—the hash oil?"

"None." Tim worked on the drilling rigs; she worked part-time in a private day care. "You think they invite us over for parties?"

"Smell anything, see anything?" said Duncan.

"You think I wouldn't have said something?"

"Do you think it's like any another hobby, an accidental fire?"

"Frying a turkey the same as turning your house into a drug lab?" Tim Miller shook his head. "That's ridiculous."

Duncan pondered the wisdom of the next question. But he was in no hurry. Inez Cordova remained on her cell phone. She stood down the hall, over Sandy Miller's shoulder.

"Okay," said Duncan, "let me ask your opinion of the legalization of marijuana. I mean, do you think this would have happened if marijuana wasn't legal? Do you think they would have felt as, say, comfortable about cooking up that stuff?"

"Couple of lowlifes like them?" Tim would speak for them both, that was clear. Sandy shook her head. "People have been frying up, boiling up and blowing up their shit for fucking forever. But now it's weed everywhere, as common as a beer after work. Couple puffs and boom, there you go."

"You see drugs around?" He didn't mind sounding like an idiot if it meant leveraging a good quote.

"Yeah, plenty of illegal and plenty of legal, too. Liquor. Cigarettes. And now weed everywhere. You can dial it right in. Mix it up—a handful of this, a bag of that. But you shouldn't be able to turn your house into a bomb because you want to risk playing with flammable shit like butane. Give me a break."

No matter your station in life, you could always find a way to look down your nose at the neighbors. In this case, thought Duncan, the Millers were justified.

Duncan jotted down their cell phone number for future reaction as the case progressed, then took a seat on a hallway bench. Cordova gave a sign with a quick head nod that she knew he was waiting. He checked email and Twitter, glancing always for what was trending.

"Not a test case," said Cordova. "It's fact. Marijuana, legal. Butane, legal. No different than an accident with burning trash. There's an attitude that ghettoizes anything to do with marijuana."

"So you're saying that hash oil fires are a fact of life? Get used to it?"

Cordova's dark hair fell straight, neat, precise.

"That's how you're going to play it?"

"It was a question."

"The newspaper, you know, can set the tone."

"I'm trying to understand the message to the community."

Cordova held his gaze but winced like she'd bitten a sour pickle. She tugged at the shoulder strap of a briefcase heavy enough to be toting cinder block triplets.

"The law is the message to the community. Public defenders don't run around dreaming up messages. We make sure people are treated fairly within the law, so this poor couple receive the same treatment as a rich guy who burns down a few houses when the grease in his turkey fryer goes *kablooey*."

Duncan scratched a few lines down in his notebook. He had started his voice memo app with the Millers and left it on. He got better quotes since he started recording interviews, even though they took more time to transcribe.

But clouding his thoughts now was a new line of speculation. What would it be like to have a piece of the action? Maybe he should just walk away from journalism, clean as can be, and nurture his investment, watch it more closely as a budtender or grower. But reporting and writing were all he knew.

"Jesus, Duncan." Cordova relaxed. "I thought you were grilling me for real."

He had met her for one coffee, three months ago. Then, a quick lunch at the Daily Bread a couple weeks later. All aboveboard. Casual. A little gift to his fantasy life, that was all. He'd paid with his latest credit card, a minor miracle that the plastic worked. He was *developing sources*. Everyone knew about Trudy, including Inez Cordova. The big scene in Glenwood Canyon and Hanging Lake Tunnel with the anti-government terrorists took care of that. A strong fantasy life, however, seemed harmless. He had nothing but respect for Trudy and for how she handled all that she'd been through.

"The courtroom quotes gave me plenty," said Duncan.

"If you guys do an editorial, you should weigh in."

"Sounds like you know what I'm thinking."

"Think you know the double standards I'm talking about."

"Maybe the pot shops need to run classes about producing

hash oil safely at home."

"Ventilation," said Cordova. "It's all about ventilation. I've watched all the instructional videos on YouTube, believe me."

"I do."

"You have to be careful, Duncan Bloom."

"Careful?"

Her lips formed a puffy pink button with a downward droop of disdain.

"It's a small town."

"No more beers?"

He had seen her playful, girly side the day of the beers, if only a peek.

"It's not that."

"Then what?"

"Reporters don't take sides, right?"

"We have opinions, sure."

"But I mean getting involved kind of taking sides—marching with protestors or helping a politician, say, write a speech."

Every ounce of giddy-up lust drained from Duncan's being.

"Correct." He turned two syllables into five, unsure where this was going.

Cordova raised her eyebrows one millimeter. Nothing else on her face changed. "Then be careful."

"What are you saying? About me?"

"Do you see anyone else around but me and you, Duncan Bloom?"

Cordova had the upper hand.

"You have to come clean. What do you know?"

"Nothing I can prove in a court of law, but people see things in this town. People talk. You are a known quantity. You don't know all the people who know you. And are watching." She gave her cinder blocks one more heave-ho. "Very carefully."

Fifteen

Sun blasted Cinnamon Nation's cheeks. She squatted by a lazy fire like a rice farmer. Her butt fit tight against the rear of her ankles, the bare flesh of her thin thigh sealed up against the flesh of her lower leg.

"Nine days," she said.

"Where was he headed?"

"Not like it was any big deal—I mean, you know, Devo could be gone for two, three days at a time. But . . ." Cinnamon jabbed the fire with a stick, stood up. Allison felt short around most people, and she gave away at least five inches to Cinnamon, but the woman's rugged toughness added extra presence. "Nine days. We all had to go back and count, figure it out."

Three days had passed since Allison had crawled up the innards of the wrecked plane above Crescent Lake. It had been two days since she and Colin had first laid everything out for Trudy and Duncan and then walked the Garfield County Sheriff through the same story, vultures to dead pilot. Duncan, no surprise, had gone bananas, but Allison asked that he rely only on the report that she had written out for the sheriff and to keep her name out of it. Colin's, too.

Yesterday, Trudy had made a series of calls to her friends in the grocery and herbalist community in Meeker and triangulated the location of where Devo and his mates were living off the land in their indefatigable effort to rekindle toughness in the collective DNA of mankind.

And womankind—like Cinnamon.

And *baby*kind.

The beginning of the next generation of backwards time travelers sat on a makeshift outdoor bed, sound asleep. Dock, Devo and Cinnamon's tiny six-month-old son, slept on his stomach, with his legs pulled up and his chest pressed down. Dark hair covered his head like a chocolate dome.

Driving up to the spot outside Meeker had taken all morning. Finding the property owner, earning his trust and waiting for him to shuttle back and forth three miles to the campsite—two miles on ATV, one on foot, per the rules—had eaten up the afternoon.

All along, Devo's bear tooth necklace served as their ticket.

At the sight of it dangling from Allison's palm, tears jetted down Cinnamon's weathered cheeks. She had taken it from Allison and slipped it around her head, stroking the teeth like prayer beads.

"We all took turns heading off—hunting and foraging, trying to get ready for winter." Cinnamon's skin had roasted to a medium umber. "It wasn't that big a deal. Until it was."

"Any idea what his plans were—which way he was headed?" Colin had expressed semi-dubious thoughts all day about their ability to help, other than to deliver the necklace back to Devo's camp.

"Devo?" said Cinnamon. "He does what we all do. He follows signs. He's got traps he checks on a regular basis—and if they're empty he'll go higher or find a spot to watch."

"Deer?" said Colin.

Cinnamon wiped a tear with her bicep, the shape of a small lemon.

"When he got lucky," said Cinnamon. "We have a cabin for smoking meats down by the creek, and one deer means so much to us and in so many ways."

"Favorite routes?"

"He mixed it up. We all mix it up. That's the thing." Cinnamon's hair was Rasta-ready. A bracing funk wafted off her body. Did their collective noses desensitize? Was that part of the transformation?

"Anyone bothering you?" said Colin. He stood transfixed. Cinnamon's entire deerskin garb would fit in a thimble.

Cinnamon shrugged. She swiped at a fly. "Not really."

"He tangled with someone." Vast, visible hunks of boob proving to be no distraction, Colin wanted answers.

"I'm not sure."

If anything, Cinnamon seemed dopey, mystified.

"So what's 'not really' mean?" Colin cut no slack.

"It means what it means. There are a couple of things."

"Help us," said Allison.

They were no longer alone. Four others—three well-bronzed guys and one small, pixie-like woman circled around. They weren't emaciated, but body fat in the tribe was nonexistent.

"Someone separated him from the necklace," said Colin. "Hard to imagine that went down without a struggle."

One of the guys, likely the oldest, with a wide and wispy beard, leaned on a thick walking stick. Whether through semi-crazy devolution diet or from sheer hard work, the guy's long lean torso, from neck down past taut pecs to well below the hip, was an object of Allison's admiration. Colin could have the boobs. A fair trade.

"Neighbors?" said Allison. "Was anyone giving you a hard time?"

"Tell them."

The two words were from the pixie. A sullen fog had settled over Cinnamon and the three guys, but the pixie managed a hint of smile.

"Tell them what?" said Colin.

"First," said Cinnamon. She could manage one-word sentences, at least. "What are you going to do?"

"What do you mean?" said Colin. "Try to find him."

"It is what it is," said the bearded torso. Allison had already decided his hip bones would be a painful proposition.

Cinnamon introduced the two new speakers. Lyric, the pixie. Rock, the beard.

"He ran into trouble," said Rock. Maybe. "Part of the deal out here—no guarantees about anything. It's part of the deal for him and it's part of the deal for us."

"Let's put it this way," said Allison. "If you were looking for him right now, where would you start?"

Cinnamon turned to her crew for a quick moment of consultation. From what Allison could tell, the debate involved divulging the inside plan. Shrugs, sharp whispers. One short, sharp, guttural grunt, courtesy of Rock.

"This isn't like our last camp," said Cinnamon. "So we are in the process of finding a new one."

"And that's a hard search to conduct when you're off the grid, avoiding the grid and trying to prove the grid is a fucking disaster." Pixie didn't have much energy in her rant. "We have to find a new place where we're welcome without hiring a real estate agent or posting a request on Craigslist."

"Or responding to any offers," said Cinnamon.

"So Devo was going to town?"

Allison knew he'd been torn a year ago when the authorities gave his tribe the old heave-ho from the Flat Tops. That was fine with her—they did not belong up there.

The collective pause told Allison everything she needed to know. Lyric's shrug, left in the up position for a count of five, confirmed it.

"How often?" said Colin.

Lyric shook her head. "We don't know."

"It was sort of a pretend thing," said Cinnamon. "He'd say he was off hunting, but we all knew it was an issue—to figure out where to head next."

"Did he find a lead?"

"We thought he was making progress," said Rock.

"What about the rancher here?"

John Kipling. A young guy, mid-thirties, helpful, upbeat and a new age farmer intent on raising grain-fed cattle that would rival Japanese Kobe beef.

"He's okay but we need a better place—more water, better soil," said Cinnamon. "We scoped this out pretty hard, but it's dead around here and the creek dried up three weeks ago."

"Two mile round trip to an undependable spring," said Lyric.

"And five miles to decent deer country." Rock was getting into it. "Sucks."

A patch of camp had been converted to crops, but the plants looked forlorn. They needed Trudy and her touch. Cornstalks, tomato vines, squash, beans, carrots.

"Did he ever come back with—provisions?"

Glance. Shrug.

"It's not like we can turn you in to the police for not following your own strict rules of devolution," said Colin. "But for crying out loud, give us something to go on."

"Don't you think it's a threat—dropping the necklace off with a reporter?" Allison ramped up her energy, hoped it got contagious. "You're not concerned they're coming after your whole thing back here? He must have pissed off someone."

Allison felt the clench of loss. She and Devo had been through so much. She owed him more than standing around chewing the hopeless maize.

"Of course we're worried," said Rock.

"But you can't exactly contact the authorities," said Allison.

"You got it," said Lyric.

Rock shook his head. "Ain't happening."

"Even if you're not paying taxes," said Colin, "you know, cops can get pretty fired up. Not always, but . . ."

Perhaps Colin was bluffing to get them more charged up about the possibility of mounting a full-scale search, but it didn't work.

"Devo might show up," said Cinnamon. "Any minute. Maybe he was chasing something."

"Maybe he found a new camp spot." Lyric's smile brightened, a flake of pyrite in the pan.

"Longest he's been gone before this?"

"We don't keep track," said Cinnamon.

"Guess," said Colin.

Shrug. Head shake.

"Few days," said Cinnamon. "Four. Maybe."

Did devolution mean a decline in your sense of alarm? From the moment Colin held up the necklace, Allison had not been able to quell the bubbling panic. Sorrow sawed at her gut. "I need a place to start," she said.

"What are you going to do?" Rock made it sound like he would authorize the search permit, but only if he approved of the strategy.

"Ask around," said Allison. "Ask the fuck around. See if anybody knows anything. If he's got a few haunts. Meeker might as well be Manhattan without a hint or two from you all, maybe narrow it down?"

"But no cops," said Rock.

"I've got to talk to the cops," said Allison.

"They're going to come after us," said Cinnamon. "They'll want to come out here."

"And then it's all blown up." Lyric shook her head. "Contaminated."

"They will know if . . ."

If a body turns up? Allison did not want to see Lyric cry.

" . . . if there's information that might be useful."

"Protect us," said Cinnamon. "That's all. We need to find Devo. We do."

"So do I." Allison owed Devo plenty. "So do I."

Sixteen

Wednesday Afternoon
Duncan

"Who knows? Who did you tell?"

"Nobody and nobody."

"Then how does a public defender, for crying out loud, make it clear she knows? And, I mean, in so little time?"

"Public defender?" said Rudduck.

Duncan shouldn't have mentioned the source. Rudduck might know her. Might know all of them. "During an interview related to that hash oil explosion in Rifle."

"Hash oil?" said Rudduck. "If I were you, I'd make anyone cooking up hash oil look as foolish and stupid as you possibly can. They give pot a bad name, you know? They make it look so desperate, all that butane and shit. We want our product to gain

84

respectability, like snooty wine with fancy labels."

"So you got the check?"

Duncan had delivered it to Helen Barnstone during a quick meeting in the City Market parking lot. He'd signed the papers. He had also given the check some mental juju before handing it over. *Go forth and multiply. And make it fast.*

"Of course," said Rudduck.

"And who knows about that check?"

"Nobody who can't be trusted."

Duncan paced between Trudy's kitchen—*their* kitchen—and down three steps into her ever-abundant greenhouse, attached off the rear of her Sweetwater home.

Their greenhouse, *their* home . . .

The only reliable connection from Sweetwater meant using Trudy's landline and its black, twenty-foot coiled tether, attached to the wall mount. Compared to his cell, the handset felt like an anvil.

"You haven't mentioned my name to other investors?"

"Give me a break."

"Where are you now?"

The bigger question involved Trudy's location. Dusk entered last-gasp mode.

"Silt," said Rudduck. "Why?"

"You think someone saw us at the hotel?"

"In a year, you'll quadruple the value of your investment. You'll be able to do anything you want."

Not really, thought Duncan. But it would buy him a clean slate. And stop the calls from creditors.

"If this gets out," said Duncan. "If I ever want to write books or get hired as a writer anywhere, I can't leave a newspaper, not even one in Glenwood Springs, with a cloud over my head."

"If you're worried on principle, then any reporter who owns

one share in a mutual fund should be forced to sit home and suck their thumbs because there might be a conflict."

Duncan opened the front door, hoping to see a pair of familiar headlights approaching. Since he had encouraged Trudy's new venture, he might do a better job of tracking all it entailed. Who would have thought freaking Sam Shelton would de-cloak from hermit status to appear on a NatGeo show about gardening and eating weeds in the woods? Trudy's carefully managed world could become quite large, quite public.

"That's the point—a mutual fund is so diffused it doesn't make much difference. This is a substantial amount invested in one specific thing and oh, by the way, the whole country is watching."

"You went into this with your eyes wide open, Duncan. And repeat after me—*quadruple*. No time to be nervous. Your money landed in a new home a few hours ago and it's getting used to its new surroundings. This ain't Vegas."

"Who is Helen Barnstone?"

Again, a pause. This one longer than the last.

"I'm sensing uncertainty," said Rudduck. "Businesses don't like uncertainty. We like stability. No surprises."

"Who?" said Duncan. Maybe he should have thrown the money at his debts and watched it evaporate. It would have been, at least, a good faith gesture.

"She is a partner," said Rudduck. "Look, this phone call and your concerns are now costing me money—in the form of time."

Duncan went back through the meeting in the Hotel Colorado, scanned the memory banks for one semi-familiar face. Had Rudduck been followed?

"My investment means squat in terms of coverage," said Duncan.

"Meaning?"

"There is no quid pro quo. In fact, I'm going to play it hard the other way. I'm going to play up the pothead dropouts and profile a few drug addicts who started with a gummy bear edible and ended up cooking meth in their basements."

"I don't care. Wait a year, then come roll around in your roomful of cash."

Duncan filled a tumbler with Trudy's organic Colorado merlot. The front porch made a good spot to sit and count all the ways he had screwed up. Duncan searched for the same peace Trudy managed to milk from every moment. Trudy carried serenity with her, sprinkled it from an invisible aspergillum. If Allison and Trudy were both here, they would drape the scene in such weighty moments that he'd be sucked into their vortex, drink or no. Time would crawl. Allison would read clouds like tea leaves or reveal fascinating ornithological tidbits based on the flight of a passing raven. Mostly, they would sit. And laugh. Allison, after a tequila or two, would unspool a funny or dramatic story about a hunt. Of course, having no money woes made life easy. Allison had her fat nest egg from the lawsuit settlement over the plane crash. Trudy had the Midas touch with a series of businesses. Who knew whether she sat a half a million dollars or more? Money didn't drive her. She wrote checks to charities as easy as cracking an egg, while Duncan wrote checks to cover months-old parking tickets and knew each check poached from the upcoming payday or the one after that.

His phone, resting on the porch railing, chirped.

"Duncan?"

One word dialed her in.

Inez.

"*Dig a mè.*"

"You say it so honky nobody is going to even know it's Spanish."

"Blame the wine," said Duncan. "Or let me apologize over a beer."

"Maybe soon."

The connection went fuzzy. Duncan strained to hear.

"You call with more cautions?"

"Did I rattle you?"

"Hard," said Duncan. "And I think you're required to reveal your sources."

"I'm not required to do anything." She turned breathy. "I called with a tip."

"It so happens the window that takes tips is open. Twenty-four seven as a matter of fact."

"I've been removed from the case."

"Our hash oil flamethrowers?" said Duncan.

"They have employed the services of an attorney."

"They couldn't afford pest control."

"Ask me who the lawyer is."

"Pretend I did."

"Carolyn Rice."

"Means nothing."

"With Carson-Blair."

A big-time Denver firm. Specialists in lefty causes and home to a hundred lawyers or more, offices up in the sky.

"So who is putting up the bucks?"

"Don't know," she said. "Maybe somebody with a stake in the outcome."

"Or maybe to make a splash? Or to set up a good appeal."

"It's been done before."

"And then be known as the firm that fought for the right of

homeowners everywhere to blow up their own home."

"They don't want the cannabis industry singled out."

This call was to set the coverage in motion—and send it rolling a certain way.

"You're not upset?" he said.

"About losing the hash oil clients? No. And I happen to think the innocent deserve the best defense money can buy, and you know what else? I have plenty of work."

"Got Carolyn's number handy?"

"Good luck, Duncan Bloom."

"If I get stuck?"

"You won't."

"Can I pretend?"

"Take some acting classes," said Cordova. "Work on your fake Spanish. And start using a bit more discretion."

Seventeen

Thursday Morning
Trudy

"You okay?"

Trudy knew Duncan hated the question.

"Do I not—*seem* okay?"

"Um, distracted. And last night? When was the last time you couldn't sleep?"

"I was only up for an hour."

"Seemed like more than that."

"Maybe two."

His eyes were foggy. He'd skipped shaving. She'd come home close to midnight and he was already asleep. Then she heard him get up early. He had left before she had woken.

"Allison's airplane?"

"What about it?" said Duncan.

"Is that the issue?"

"One of them. That is, both airplanes—the wrecked one and the one that took off. Two planes, one issue. No leads."

They stood outside the newspaper office in downtown Glenwood Springs. Tourists milled about, looking for gift shops, the hot springs and food. Trudy stood on the sidewalk next to her company pickup. She had pulled over and called Duncan from the street to see if he could come out. It wasn't an unusual spot for a few minutes of conversation.

"They must think they don't need your help."

"They don't realize that in a day I'm going to start writing about all the things they aren't saying."

"You said Allison got a tail number?"

"Yes, but no help. The plane was stolen from an airport in Lubbock three weeks ago. The guy didn't report the theft at first because he thought it was a repo guy who snatched it. He owed on it. He owed thousands. So that's a dead end. And no ID on the dead guy from the cops, and no idea where the plane started out. The cops claim they're interested, but nothing to show for it."

"They have to say at some point, don't they?"

"I've never seen anything like this," said Duncan. "Unless we're the only ones that give a shit."

"The dead guy's relatives?"

"The cops say that they are following all department policies in notifying next of kin. After that, it's up to the kin to come forward."

Whenever Duncan got stuck, he wore the annoyance like a face tattoo.

"You need a hike or a hot springs," said Trudy. She wanted to help. She had the urge to sit him down, walk through everything. "Or some St. John's wort."

"I need a cop with a chatty side. They claim they got nothing. How can I prove them wrong?"

Trudy wanted to see Duncan in better mettle. It beat thinking about the television show, due to start shooting for real in a week. The evening with Sam Shelton made production seem within the range of doable, if she could manage to fool herself.

"Keep asking questions," said Trudy. "It's what you do. Start over. Re-interview everyone. Nobody is more thorough than you."

"I'm leaving for Denver this afternoon—it's on that hash oil fire. I'm interviewing a lawyer late this afternoon. And I think I'll stay down there, drive back in the morning. The newspaper is popping for a Super 8."

"Good," said Trudy. "Give you time to think on the drive. And maybe something will occur to you."

His absence would give her time to relax, tend to her greenhouse, maybe bake some bread or work on her dandelion recipes.

"Have you heard anything from Allison or Colin about how Meeker went?"

"Not a peep," said Trudy. "I'm worried how Allison will take it. Of course I'm worried about Devo, too. Don't get me wrong. But coming after all the crazy business up in the woods with the plane wreck and the dead guy, she'll be loaded for bear."

Trudy smiled, gave Duncan the longest full-body hug she dared. He hugged her back, offered a solid smile.

"I've always wondered," he said. "Does that mean you've got your biggest gun or you're eager for a fight?"

"I happen to know. I once asked George the same question," said Trudy. "As far as he was concerned, it always meant both."

Eighteen

They started with Trudy's longtime grocer friend in Meeker, Brett Merriman. He greeted them like favorite family. He'd been leaving food for Devo—borderline fruits and veggies with the occasional protein, too. Devo retrieved bags from a big covered Tupperware bin placed out near the dumpsters.

"Once a week. Devo leaves notes about what they might need. Requests." Merriman carried a big frame but always came across as youthful and eager.

"And last week?" said Colin.

"All the food was still there. A day worse, but still there."

"Is there a certain day?" said Allison.

"Tuesdays most weeks," said Merriman.

If word got around—all the way around—Allison could imagine an aggressive cop who wanted to investigate for potential child abuse, with Dock up there in the woods.

"They want to move," said Colin.

"I'm aware," said Merriman.

"Had he been talking to anyone in particular?"

They stood in the asphalt parking lot, which had absorbed every degree of the day's heat. Merriman crossed his arms over a green apron. He studied the gray dusk gathering over the broad plain on the opposite side of the highway. A pair of wood ducks answered an urgent call, east to west. Their stubby wings thumped hard.

"He's been coming to my house," said Merriman. "Two times, maybe three—that's all. My wife accuses me of taking in every stray dog, but there you go. I think he wants to walk away from the whole thing."

"So he wasn't hunting." Colin stirred the statement with disappointment.

"They all know where it's coming from. I mean, spinach in neat bundles with those red twist ties? What they don't know is Devo takes a hot shower on the first day he's in town and then he's got his stops, I guess, his rounds. One time he hitched a ride from a friend over to Glenwood and that went so well that, the next time, he was gone for two days to Denver. His show was a business once—I assume he's got contacts."

"You have names—you know, some of those people?" said Colin.

"Not names, no," said Merriman. "He hung around Meeker other than the few trips. Some folks told me they saw him over in the woods north of town, a lightweight Sasquatch sighting, if you know what I mean."

"Hang out?" said Colin.

"Bounce around," said Merriman. "My wife would let him sleep at our place, but she didn't like the duplicity of it all, the fakery."

"Where should we start?" said Allison.

"Ask around," said Merriman. "If I were you, I'd find his girl-friend first."

Nineteen

They seeded the whole town of Meeker. As a backup, Allison had found a photo of him on the Internet and printed it off with the help of the kind folks at the Blue Spruce. Most knew Devo or knew *of* Devo. They got a hit at the library. A young woman told them Devo would sit at a computer for an hour or two, kept to himself. He looked unkempt and different, she said, and he smelled a bit like a campfire. But he didn't bother anyone. They got a hit at the Meeker Police Department. They had seen him walking around, but he hadn't bothered a soul. The cops were surprised to hear he was "missing" and asked exactly what that might mean. They asked at every motel on the main drag, too. And then they got a hit at the Elk, an L-shaped, one-story structure that wrapped two sides of a large parking lot with a giant spruce plunked down in the middle.

"Sure, I recognized him."

"Are you the owner or—?"

"Owner, yeah, and you two aren't cops."

"Friends of his," said Allison. "Did he ever stay here?"

Vern Watson stood behind a Formica counter, brown worn edges. He towered over them. His long face drooped like an old bloodhound. His head looked heavy, a size too big.

"I'm not in the habit of talking about my guests."

"He's been missing," said Allison. "Over a week now."

Watson sized them up. "You talked to the police?"

"We can't file a missing person report," said Colin.

94

"It's not like he has a house in town," said Allison. "You know, routines."

"He's an odd one." Watson jumped at the chance to take a whack. "Don't think I didn't watch that crazy ass show of his. Devolution, please. Wasn't sorry to see him get kicked out of the Flat Tops."

"How did he pay for the room?"

Colin leapfrogged a couple of other basic questions, but Allison admired the cut-to-the-chase mentality.

"He didn't," said Watson.

"Did you recognize her, then?" If Colin could make assumptions, so could she.

"She's not from Meeker," said Watson. "I know that much. Nobody from around here would be that obvious."

"How often, would you say?" Colin's witness.

"Once a month. Something like that."

"One night?"

"Sometimes two. I don't feel all that comfortable answering these questions."

"We know," said Colin.

"You have reason to think he's *missing* missing?"

"Several," said Colin. "What does the girlfriend drive?"

Allison pictured Devo's perfect cover. With his "wife" confined to the woods, he could dip his dick in town while allegedly on a "hunt" and then roll in a dead skunk or elk shit and wipe off any city smell before returning to the tribe. On the other hand, Allison knew she was applying a straightlaced American sense of family morality to a guy who wanted to hitchhike on a time machine back to the age of Lewis and Clark.

"A little blue pickup," said Watson. "Imported. She's small like Devo. They could be the couple on the cake at a hippie wedding. If I rented closets, that's all they would need."

95

"Age?" said Colin.

"Indeterminate. To me, Devo looked like George Harrison during his India phase—but smaller and older. She walked straight out of Woodstock, feathers in her hair. Wild hair, by the way. Sandals." Watson stood up straight, shrugged. "Every hippie needs a hippie chick."

"But?" said Colin.

"But what?"

"Looked like you were going to say something?"

The look in Watson's eye had, in fact, grown wistful.

"I don't mean to sound so cynical," he said. "They were a damn cute couple and I'm telling you, she was always sweet and smiled like she was at a never-ending love-in. They'd sit outside in the sun with their door wide open and talk—for hours."

"Any idea when they were here last?" Colin kept at it.

"About a week," said Watson.

"And you saw them both leave?"

"Wouldn't remember that much detail. That's all I got, people coming and going."

"How many nights on the last visit?"

Watson took a minute to click around his computer. "I shouldn't be doing this."

"It will help," said Colin. "His people are worried."

"Two nights."

"How about a name?"

Watson gave it some thought. "You'd have to be cops."

"We think she would want to know," said Allison. "I'm sure she would want to know."

Unless Devo had a cell phone tucked away in his deerskin loincloth—a cell phone with magic batteries that never died—they must have picked dates ahead for each dalliance. How had they met? How had they made plans?

"Did they hang around here during the day?" said Colin.

Watson gave a one-breath sigh. "It's not a sightseeing town."

"Giving us a town doesn't give us a name," said Colin. The more he took the lead, the more she was glad she'd taken the initiative last night at the Blue Spruce. She purposefully tried fucking her way back to an even keel, shedding the last clinging layer of grudge or anger that had lingered. She showed enthusiasm. She got him to laugh. She laughed. She dug out the tequila after the first round, made it clear there would be a round two. He deserved it. And she deserved to get over it.

"She put Glenwood Springs on the registration," said Watson. "Always gave me a bit of a laugh."

"Why is that?"

"Because her first name sounded like Glenwood."

"Glenda." Colin didn't miss a beat. Sex—the new brain food.

"Close," said Watson.

"Glenna," said Allison.

Watson nodded.

"And her last?" Mr. Relentless.

"Wingrove. If she wasn't writing down a fake hometown, she shouldn't be too hard to find."

They ordered cheeseburgers to go from the Meeker Café and gobbled them down as they headed south. The road paralleled the Grand Hogback that ran all the way to Rifle before turning east toward New Castle. The long, fat worm of sedimentary rock served as a swampy shoreline a mere hundred million years ago.

"Now what?" said Colin.

"You mean, stop in Glenwood?"

"Or maybe give the name to Duncan, let him go to town." Colin drove right at the speed limit as the canyon tightened down coming into West Glenwood. "You think that's her name—Glenna Wingrove?"

"It's a place to start."

"You have to wonder how they first hooked up," said Colin. "And how they kept the ball rolling."

"Once he switched from doing the solo devolution thing those first two years—it was never the same."

"And why eat nothing but nuts and berries and elk jerky when you've got cheeseburgers within a half-day's hike?"

"I see you fail to comprehend their mission," said Allison.

"What I don't see is how it was supposed to work. They'd better start propagating like rabbits if they hope to get anywhere, and then let's say in forty years they've got a couple hundred folks and they are starting to put a decent-size group together? First teenager who wanders into town and discovers ice cream and television? Game over."

You can adjust your involvement with the real world, Allison knew all too well, but if you wanted even a few modern-day creature comforts—say, tequila—you had to strike a bargain with the world.

Tequila? Creature comfort? Hell, creature *necessity*.

Twenty

Thursday Afternoon
Duncan

"Five minutes."

"I didn't come all the way to Denver for five minutes."

"Ten? You're going to use one quote or two—one minute

should do. I don't mean to be rude, Mr. Bloom, but you'll recall that I urged you to set a telephone appointment. We don't have much to say around legal strategy."

Carolyn Rice's fastidious forty-second-floor office offered a view that stretched up past Longs Peak to the Wyoming border. Outside, the Front Range glimmered and baked in the August heat, but the view knocked him out. Duncan tried not to gawk.

"How did you get onto this particular case?" Duncan tried to remember when the fussy layers of an urban professional woman seemed appealing. Rice wore maroon lipstick. She left a bright smear of it on the white plastic lid of her coffee cup when she sipped.

"I don't mean to sound hostile or brusque, Mr. Bloom, but why is that relevant?"

Her dark eyebrows were precision matches. One pluck on either side would have thrown the whole thing off.

"Were you looking for a case? I mean there have been plenty of hash oil fires."

"Fewer since they toughened the law."

"True. But why this one?"

"We may have read your story."

"And then inquired if a couple living in a trailer home on the Western Slope might want to engage the services of a Denver firm with rates that, well—" Duncan paused for effect. He made a mini-show of putting his notebook down on the edge of her gleaming black desk. "You know."

"I don't," said Rice.

"Your hourly rates might put a dent in their cash flow."

"What are you saying?"

Her navy blue suit made it challenging to nail down a sense of all the shapes within. So did the fact that her eyes watched his—nonstop. A wide silver band gripped the pinky finger of her right hand, the sole adornment other than the peach polish on perfect nails.

"Obviously, your firm has represented the needs of the marijuana industry in previous cases."

"I told you this would not amount to much in terms of substance," said Rice.

"You represented that one home-grow enthusiast who was arrested for a large operation in his basement about a month before legalization."

"And?"

"And that was high profile and would place your firm in the pro-marijuana camp."

If he ever needed a lawyer to get his money back, he couldn't afford the first ten minutes of Carson-Blair. Plus, every lawyer in the state would first laugh him out of the room. He'd signed something. He had to shake off a fresh image of Rudduck's grim stare.

"You seem like a nice guy, Mr. Bloom. My next question is a simple one back to you. So what?"

"Do you think the new, tighter law that increased penalties for home production of hash oil is unfair? A matter of consumer education?"

Rice sighed. "Do you need one good quote to make your drive worthwhile?"

Duncan smiled. "Quotes are the dime-store candy of journalism. They're filler. Please believe me when I say with all sincerity that I'm after the bigger picture—the influencers behind the scenes. I think readers want to know what the marijuana business is going to look like once it has all settled down. And it occurs to me that for every new screw that gets tightened by state law, somebody else gets hurt. Say, a medical marijuana patient who likes to cook up a batch of home shatter just *so*, to his precise liking. Perhaps it's an old family recipe. But this individual can no longer do so because of the new law—not without risk of a felony prosecution. So maybe a Denver law firm with resources has the opportunity to help, but first it needs a good case to use to make the point."

While trying not to worry about the fate of his eighty-one grand during the drive down to Denver, Duncan developed ideas for possible motivations for Carson-Blair. Rice's pleasing pause led him to think he'd hit a nerve.

"There are lots of reasons why we take cases."

"I am sure."

"Any decent reporter knows how to follow the money."

"Decent as in good?" said Duncan. "It's a matter of subjectivity."

"But you've been a big-city reporter. Right here."

"And look where it got me."

"Yes, moved to Glenwood and broke several big stories. I saw the clip on YouTube—you and Gayle King. And I remember the story, too. Who wouldn't? The evil plans for those tunnels?"

"That's what I mean by big picture. And I think my scenario— that your potential complainant is a medical marijuana user with a specific home recipe—would land on a largely sympathetic audience. I think Victor Hugo said something like you can fight off armies, but not an idea whose time has come?"

Rice smiled. "An English major?"

"Any chance I could profile this client of yours, the one waiting in the wings?"

"Didn't Victor Hugo also say something about harmony?"

Duncan felt chagrined at trying to show off. "He was a gold mine of ideas, I know that."

"To put everything in balance is good, to put it in harmony is better."

"So you think the law is out of whack? Unfair?"

"And he also said suffering comes in many forms—something to that effect."

Rice straightened folders on her desk that didn't need straightening.

"The laws regarding marijuana are evolving."

"What isn't? We used to tolerate litter, smoking in the workplace. Now homosexuals can marry, but laws governing discrimination against gays will take years to catch up."

Duncan retrieved his notebook. The conversation had lowered the wall between them.

"I can help," said Duncan. "A sympathetic portrait of your client, the one you will put on the stand to show that the law is unfair. You know, I'm sure, that it will be hard to find a jury member in Garfield County who is as liberal as, say, Dick Cheney. You plan to lose there, but you need to set it up for the long-range game plan, right?"

"And you can help?"

"With public opinion, perhaps."

Rice pushed her lips together in an odd pucker like a second-grade kiss.

"I'll keep that in mind," said Rice.

"But the general idea—I'm not incorrect?"

"You would be on safe ground."

"So you share the belief—" Duncan caught himself, tried not to rush. He needed to demonstrate evaluation, deliberation. "You share the belief that it's the negative association with hash oil that is drawing the criminal prosecution?"

"What I know is marijuana is legal to possess in Colorado. It's legal to grow, within limits. It's legal to smoke. It's legal to ingest. And the other thing I know is that accidents happen. If this was a case of burnt toast, we wouldn't be here."

Twenty-One

"I got nothing."

"Nothing?" said Allison.

"I know what you're thinking."

"You mean you got nothing or you got nothing to tell *us*?" said Colin.

Allison had worked with Deputy Robert Chadwick a couple years earlier, figuring out the location of a shooter's perch in downtown Glenwood Springs.

"We all appreciate what you did." Chadwick had an open, earnest look—a regular-guy quality to him.

In the earlier deal, they had asked for her help. Now she and Colin needed his. Chadwick downplayed the uniform. Somehow, you saw the man.

"So what you're saying is you've got it from here."

"Along those lines, yeah," said Chadwick.

"Or are you saying you can't tell us much?" said Allison.

"Or anything?" She heard Colin's agitation, hoped Chadwick did not. "Anything at all?"

"Off the record?" said Chadwick.

"What does that mean?" said Colin.

"I mean, between us chickens." He wanted full cooperation.

"Go for it," said Allison. "We are not reporters."

"But you know one." The retort came like a whipcrack. He'd been waiting.

"Tell us what you know," said Colin.

They were standing outside the sleepy police department, on tree-lined Eighth Street—idyllic except for the subject matter of murder, of throats cut, of grown men roped to trees like dogs.

Chadwick knew that if he didn't give them some idea of what the hell was going on, she and Colin would get pissed off in their own pissed-off way.

"It's more complicated than it appears."

"The dead guy?" said Colin.

"We're not releasing any information at this point."

"No name?" said Allison.

"It's an active investigation," said Chadwick.

"The tag number on the second plane?" said Allison.

Allison knew he was a patient cop with a practical streak. During the long day of debriefing about the wrecked plane and the dead guy, she noted that he must have dropped a few pounds. His uniform needed to be taken in.

"How close are you to being able to offer a few details?" she said. "To the public?"

"I don't know." Chadwick made it look like he could talk all day without saying anything. "There are layers to this thing."

"Feds?" said Allison.

Drugs, airplanes, state boundaries—made sense.

"Layers plural—yes."

"You're going to have to ID the dead pilot at some point, right?" said Colin.

Chadwick nodded. "Some point."

"Are you by any chance—boxed in?" said Allison. "Hampered?"

Chadwick smiled, eyed them for a few seconds each. He towered over them. "There's a whole team of folks on this one."

"Then we've got an easy one for you," said Allison.

Without going into any of the background details, Allison

asked him to tap one of the databases at his disposal and see if the name *Glenna Wingrove* got any hits.

"What for?" said Chadwick.

Colin kept a straight face. "We can't tell you more than that."

Chadwick grimaced. "You checked online?"

Allison chose to lie. "She didn't pop up." She didn't like using the phone as a computer. She didn't much care for the computer, either. Shortcuts, however, were always welcome.

"You got an age, DOB, anything?"

Allison shook her head. "Thirtysomething would be my guess."

Chadwick left them in the downtown sunshine.

"Utter bullshit," said Colin. "A corpse in a wrecked plane in the middle of nowhere and nobody will tell the public what the hell is going on. Those guys in the airplane saw *us*."

She appreciated Colin's irritation, felt it herself. They had no way of knowing if the jerks on the plane could have seen enough to get a good fix on them. The whole flyover lasted a few seconds. The jerks on the plane had killed the one guy who knew what Allison looked like up close. Had he been able to describe her in detail?

"They have federal agencies tangled up," said Allison.

"Doesn't federal mean shared—shared power between the states? Shared information with the local cops? Chadwick knows."

"What am I supposed to do?"

"Press," said Colin.

"Do you see an angle? Do we have anything in the form of leverage?"

"Offer to tell him about Devo."

"Tell him what? And that's the next county anyway."

"Tell him why we want to talk with this Glenna Wingrove.

She's gotta be here."

"We hope."

Chadwick returned with a long face and a purple Post-it note stuck to an index finger.

"Interesting," said Chadwick.

Allison plucked the paper off his thick digit.

"How so?" said Colin.

"Your Glenna Wingrove lives here now," said Chadwick, "but only for the past six months."

"What's interesting about that?" Nothing in Colin's tone would win friends.

"Just is," said Chadwick.

"Where did she live before?"

"Denver. Where she's from—from what I can tell."

"Associated with any others?"

Chadwick unfolded a white sheet of paper. Was excess detail on an innocuous name his peace offering for not being able to talk about the title bout?

"Parents, Tamara and Jordan Timms."

"Timms?" said Allison.

She wanted to see if a light bulb clicked on over her head.

"So Glenna Wingrove is married." Or was?

"To Mariah Wingrove," said Chadwick. "Born Mariah Casey. It's the new world, you know?"

"She have a brother named Nick?" said Allison.

Chadwick studied his Post-it, cocked his head like a cheerful spring robin listening for worms. "How did you know?"

Even Colin looked confused.

"Nick Timms. Devo before he was Devo." She turned to Colin. "Glenna ain't the girlfriend."

"Got it," said Colin. "Sister."

106

Twenty-Two

"Lightly toasted? Whole wheat?"

"Please."

"Homemade peach preserves from Palisade?"

"Please, if that's not too many *p*'s."

"Scrambled eggs and grilled slab of fresh tomato with a certain basil from a certain businesswoman I know?"

"I'll try to choke it all down."

"And coffee—?"

Trudy preferred tea, rarely ingested caffeine, but gave this some thought. "Half a cup," she said.

"Cream?"

"How long are these questions going to keep up?"

She laughed.

"Until your cook is satisfied that he has prepared precisely what is preferred—if that's not too many *p*'s."

"Such service."

He plucked a bag of coffee beans from the freezer, rattled it, opened the bag, sniffed its contents, closed his eyes and stood there by the sink like he'd taken a hit of heroin. "You're not going to believe this stuff."

Why wasn't Sam Shelton hungover? What did he think of the awkwardness from last night? Or had it not registered?

"Fine Colombian?"

"Good one." Shelton measured beans into a glass measuring cup. "Funny how one line from a Steely Dan song can hang around for decades. Don't think they were talking about java, however."

"Cocaine?"

"Marijuana," said Shelton. "Back then, Peru supplied all the coke. Colombia sent the MJ. And did you ever notice nobody covers Steely Dan songs? One-of-a-kind band right there. You can't touch 'em."

"All the ways to escape," said Trudy. "Is it worth this pain?"

"Felt good at the time, eh?"

"Why, why, why?"

Trudy rubbed her head. Most evenings, she knew the stopping point.

"We're animals," said Shelton. "*That's* the point."

"Dumb animals," said Trudy.

"Smart enough to distill whiskey, make beer, refine coca leaves and figure out cannabis."

"Because we're animals."

"Because at *heart* we're animals and our systems spend all day trying to survive. Everything we do is survival. Tossing back a brandy, we can let our guard down. We drift to another space where we feel more human, more free."

Shelton took another hearty whiff of his beans. Her own hangover might require a caffeine jolt and a bit of grease. Her toast might need an extra trowel of butter.

"You're awfully articulate for a man who still knew how to use a corkscrew in adverse conditions."

They had drunk her bottle of wine first.

Then he uncorked a Petite Syrah from a Colorado vintner she adored, and she soon knew she would not be driving. A series of plates of nibbles and nosh appeared like magic, and the conversation shifted all night from light to heavy, from the past to the future. Her unannounced pop-in visit could have been interpreted as an open invitation. She didn't know what it meant. He had been a perfect gentleman-pal-friend all evening long but then, after he'd prepared a bed on the couch, wider and more substantial than many beds she'd slept on, a long hug. Followed by a longer hug. And somewhere in there a grab of her butt and somewhere in the awkward groping, so unsure of what she wanted, her hand dropped between them and brushed his stiff cock. She had turned her hand around, not thinking, purely unconscious, and had given it a hello squeeze. Like shaking hands. Drunk hands. Not-thinking hands. It was one of the oddest things she had ever done. It jolted her into sobriety, at least for a moment. She remembered now the sound of her own goofy laugh, trying to downplay the moment. She had kissed him on the cheek and whispered "good night." After a half hour of terror, of reliving the few seconds of utter awkwardness, she slept like an exhausted five-year-old, except right below the surface of her woozy dream state she knew the whole night long that she would pay the price come morning for guzzling so much wine and, perhaps, for giving him the wrong signal.

"You know why the coyote howls?" he said.

Trudy wondered how long it would take to drink a gallon of water. It was what she needed. Her cranium throbbed. "To announce its territory?"

"Sure," said Shelton. "Maybe. Sounds good. But I like to think that melancholy sound is from the fact that the coyote knows it can never drop its guard. It will always be in survival mode. *Always.* We humans have an option. And most of us take it, you know, that freedom. It opens us up. We see things, imagine things. We tap our unconscious and it feels so good. We yearn for it all day long."

Not *every day*, thought Trudy. She might not drink for a week. And what had she said last night when she was feeling so free?

What had she done? Had she made enough references to Duncan Bloom?

Long before the kiss and her hand's strange moment of independent drunken fumbling, they had waded into the murky waters of talk about commitment and relationships—and she wondered if she could even begin to imagine the number of women he had undressed or the number of women who had approached him and offered themselves up as quick, easy, rock-star refreshment. Now, in the morning, he looked so fatherly and unlikely, but at the same time she felt drawn and comforted by all he had seen, as if he knew how the world worked. His world, now, was certain. He was done with scrambling. The wine had fired up his penchant for sweeping discussions about big ideas. He had read a book about anti-terrorism that outlined how the world needed new thinking about international politics and about the treatment of animals. He came across as a learner. Trudy had made a silent vow to read more books and, even through the fog of her grating hangover, remembered the pledge now.

She managed to eat. She chased away any attempts at compare-and-contrast—Duncan's intense boyishness against Sam Shelton's wise old head. It was presumptuous of her to think it was a choice. What had Duncan done other than to do what he had always done—ask questions, write, do his job, encourage her to try new things like this television show? During the alcohol-fueled chatter about monogamy and relationships the previous night, she found herself a bit downhearted because logic told her marriage was a tough thing to pull off, though she believed in the general concept and thought it admirable. Quaint, even. After her lone marriage ended amid a flurry of violence and a host of foul deceptions, she found herself uninterested in thinking long term. Why couldn't you commit to one man for a few years, learn what you could from each other and move on—no hard feelings? The whole "kept" thing—it made her squirm.

They sipped one last cup of coffee out on the covered porch, sitting side by side but not too close on an antique wooden bench from an old train station.

"So are you ready?" he asked.

"For what?"

"A full-bore schedule of shooting?"

"Trying not to think about it."

"But it's not weighing you down."

"Or slowing me down."

"That second bottle?"

"Unnecessary," said Trudy. "Evil. But it tasted great."

"The third?"

"There was a third?"

"Only an inch left."

"Then no wonder."

She flashed on a conversation from last night. Shelton had told the whole story about his cover of "Kicks" and, when asked by a reporter on tour in Miami, how he said he didn't disagree with the get-tough anti-drug policies of then-president Ronald Reagan. The comments blew up. He'd taken the Paul Revere and the Raiders' song and slowed it down a hair, given it an updated production and topped the charts for several months. Shelton hadn't backed down. He argued against his own lifestyle and endeared himself to conservatives on both sides of the Atlantic. At least, according to his version of the events. Trudy, a junior in high school at the time of the controversy, knew about the remarks from what she'd read online in the past couple of weeks.

"Wine makes the world go round. Fresh tomatoes, mozzarella cheese and wine. Lock me up, throw away the key. Bit of salt and pepper if you don't mind."

"And coffee?"

"If I could request a fifth sustenance."

"Basil?"

"Thank god this isn't a real choice."

He shook his head, shrugged, and chugged his remaining swallow of coffee.

"You'll be there to shore me up?"

Trudy had picked out the first four locations. The plan called for shooting the outdoor elements for the foraging before the weather turned. One about wild grass. One about knotweed and its nutritious seeds. And one each about mallow, purslane and thistle.

"We're in this together," said Shelton. "I'm your partner in the show, right? We are bandmates, so to speak."

Trudy had dialed up a few old videos. She'd even come across his interview about the "Kicks" comments on *The Today Show*. Most of her "Sam Shelton + videos" searches returned all his sexy-sly clips, backup singers with the black boots and big boobs and synchronized hip shakes appearing in several. They were his thing. In one, the singers and their long legs followed him to a gas station in the desert, to a pool hall, to a bank where it rained cash.

"How close do bandmates get—exactly?"

"Please," said Shelton. "I know what you might be thinking. I'm not here to break anything up."

The assertion came with clout, conviction.

"I was cavalier about that sort of thing, but that was then. The music business is not a breeding ground, shall we say, for integrity. I stepped away from all that bullshit and chaos for a reason. Same person—same me—but two lives. It is possible." Shelton held her gaze. He nodded slowly. His eyebrows were up. "Your pal Allison? Once a city girl, right? She knows exactly what I mean."

Twenty-Three

Friday Morning
Duncan

"Devo." Coogan sat down on the empty desk next to Duncan's. "Tell me what's new."

"He's missing," said Duncan. "But it isn't unusual."

"And the plane crash?"

"They've closed ranks all the way up," said Duncan. "Lips tighter than a worm with lockjaw. If I have to hear the phrase *agency assist* one more time, I'll barf. Nobody says they're the lead dog."

"U.S. Forest Service?"

"Agency assist."

"The FAA?"

"They care why the plane went down—and not so much about who ended up dead inside or what cargo they were carrying. And we know how long it's going to take for them to reach any conclusions. Even then, it'll be a preliminary."

"Somebody's gotta squeal." Coogan prioritized dailies over long-term work. "DiMarco?"

Duncan's longtime source within the Garfield County Sheriff's Department.

"Tried him," said Duncan. "The bricks are the same size and color as the rest of the wall."

"DEA? If that plane was chock-full of weed—"

"Not known for talking about their operations until they're good and ready—and usually when the bad guys are behind bars."

"Parks and Wildlife? Sometimes it's the lesser crime that trips them up—the out-of-season deer."

Duncan let Coogan run through all the agency names he could conjure up. The "yes, good idea" camp meant peace and love. Duncan picked his moments to challenge. This wasn't one of them. Coogan needed to process. The buzz about Colorado's legalization of marijuana had died down. The state was no longer the regular butt of jokes among late-night comedians, but it was unusual to run into two stories in the same week that had their roots, so to speak, in weed.

Duncan attacked the phones. He checked again with all his usual sources and asked each and every one for additional suggestions for names to call. He chatted up "public information officers." He cajoled "directors of communication." He shot the breeze with "communication specialists." All said zilch. He played relaxed, unhurried. "Just chatting." "Called to see what's new." "Good try," said Deputy Chadwick. "I showed your pals Allison and Colin the same frozen shank of shoulder."

Nobody would go off the record. A hint of arrogance came with each rebuff. These "get lost" messages had been prepared in an underground bunker in an undisclosed location in the northern nether regions of Norway on the coldest day in January. Then, they were given a quick coating of charm school gloss and repeated to the point of nausea. Everybody was not only on the same page, they were on the same fucking note.

What Duncan wanted to do was poke around on the political side of things. Garfield County Commissioner Bill Walters would soon be re-elected. Republican candidates in Garfield County started two inches from the finish line. All they had to do was reach out and cross the line. Democrats were still in the locker room tying up their shoes. Anyone with a giant *D* next to their name stood no chance, even if he or she espoused a conservative agenda.

The sacrificial *D* this time was Jack Hallowell, who owned a happening restaurant near the train station called Fork. It attracted hordes of singles. The menu boasted quinoa, chanterelles, pork belly and eight kinds of creamy risotto. Fork made its own beer, per hipster code.

It didn't take a journalism genius to know that Hallowell's arrival at the county level might mean a new countywide philosophy about openness to marijuana-related issues. Even if he didn't stand a chance, Duncan should get to know him better. At the same time, Duncan couldn't show too much interest in marijuana issues. At least, he'd keep his chatter in check around Coogan.

He called Melanie Barlow, a reporter friend at *The Denver Post*. She was a quiet, dogged journalist who had survived a dozen waves of downsizing over the last two decades. Barlow's quiet style belied her flesh-shredding piranha mindset, especially when it came to tearing apart hypocritical politicians. She listened while Duncan laid out the hash oil case and the story of the dead pilot in the flying weed wagon.

No surprise, she was aware of both.

"Dollars to donuts the retail shop that sold them the stuff to make the hash oil is making damn sure nobody comes after them," said Barlow.

"So they're getting inoculated?"

"If I were in their shoes, I'd make sure the people who could hurt me had damn good representation," said Barlow.

"One way of minimizing potential threats. But it's a crime to use hazardous substances for the extraction, not to sell the hazardous substance itself, right?"

"Somebody with a vested interest is footing the bill," said Barlow. "Some shop up there has connections—and fat pockets. You talked to the shop?"

"I don't know where they shopped."

"How many possibilities are there?"

Duncan let that stand as a rhetorical question. There were three. It wouldn't take long to make the rounds, though he didn't predict much success. Barlow was taking this brick by brick. He would have done the same, except for the Devo necklace, the plane crash and the man tied to a tree. Maybe Inez Cordova in the public defender's office would cough up where the trailer chefs bought their raw materials. Maybe he needed to read the arrest affidavit.

Easy pickings—and he'd missed it.

Barlow switched topics. "We ran a brief about that Flat Tops plane going down and the dead guy inside. Of course, that's all we can run are briefs. Unless a tight end for the Denver Broncos comes down with a sprained metatarsal. In that case, it's a full page and a photo spread along with a sidebar interview with experts on the grueling levels of pain and the best course of treatment."

"I'm familiar with newsroom priorities," said Duncan.

"Well, I happen to have a friend in the DEA who owes me a favor or ten."

"If you could pry out one wisp of a lead, I can take it from there."

Duncan gave her everything he had—all from Allison—including the tail number on the getaway plane.

"Dope, dope, chop, chop," said Barlow. "The big weed is over. Few shops down here closing up. All the quick-buck Chucks have had their shirts and shorts removed by the deadly combination of supply and demand. Much as the fearmongers can't believe it, it turns out not everybody wanted to smoke dope all the time."

Twenty-Four

Friday Afternoon
Allison

Glenna Wingrove broke the land speed record for fastest tears—under five minutes from introductions to utter sadness.

"He's been a mess lately." They had waited a few minutes while she composed herself. Allison looked Devo's sister square in the fuzzy hair. It was so rare to be taller than someone.

"I have had this bad feeling, it woke me up one night. It was as clear a thought as you can get in the middle of the night—*my brother is in trouble*."

The Timms family resemblance wasn't all that strong. Glenna was more fair and trim but, of course, not gaunt and underfed like Devo had been the last time she'd seen him. Her round face and small, tight features were dusted with pale freckles. She wore paint-splattered blue jean shorts and a gray V-necked T-shirt past its prime. Her hair was a loose grunge of flailing wildness, darkish blonde. Feathers and a headband would fit right in. She wore, in fact, long silver earrings now—feathers. A blue metallic dragonfly dangled from a plain silver necklace.

"Devo talked about you all the time. The time in the snow. He knows he would have died if you weren't there."

"He helped me, too," said Allison.

"By the way," said Glenna, "how did you find me?"

"The Elk." Being blunt, thought Allison, beat evasive.

"The owner? That tall guy?" said Glenna. "I knew he was paying too much attention."

"I think he's worried, too." Colin gave a look like a preacher at a funeral. "And he knew we were trying to help."

"He probably thought we were, you know—doing the motel thing."

"Not sure," said Colin. "But he didn't know you were brother and sister."

Wingrove shook her head. "Oh my. I was kind of afraid of that."

She rented a mother-in-law apartment in a house on Oak Street west of the Roaring Fork, up on the ridge. They sat outside in the shade at a small table drinking a light purple hibiscus iced tea. Colin took liquids in three colors—brown (coffee and whiskey), gold (beer) and clear (water). In his hand, purple looked like poison.

"How does he let you know when to meet?"

"For a while it was every other weekend," she said. "I moved up from Denver last May when I got the job."

"How did he find out you were up here to begin with?" said Colin. "Isn't there supposed to be an invisible wall between their world and the rest of us?"

Even in the shade, the air felt hot and close. A mild chill seeped from Wingrove's air-conditioned apartment when they had knocked, but she pointed to the table and then fetched the drinks. No grand tour.

"There are ways." Wingrove smiled. "All along we've been writing notes back and forth. Even that first year when he was by himself and shooting all those YouTube videos, we got notes in and notes out through the people picking up the raw footage and leaving him the occasional supply. Now, without the crew, we had a drop point in town. You know, in case of emergency. Devo was the one to check it, you know, for all the others, too."

"So you sent in a note and told him you were in the area?" said Colin.

"And told him what weekend I would be up in Meeker and where I would be staying. He knocked on my door at the motel about a half hour after I checked in on a Friday night last May." She shrugged. "It wasn't hard."

"Just the two of you?" said Allison.

Wingrove looked as if she didn't understand the question. "Who else would there be?"

"We heard he was making rounds of various places—restaurants and the grocery store, doing a bit of gleaning to help with the food supply back in camp."

"True."

"So he must have had other support."

"He mentioned Brett, the grocery store guy. Yeah, he had other places of support."

"And trips to Glenwood Springs? Denver?" said Colin.

"Can't say I'm surprised, but didn't know he made it that far."

"What *did* he talk about?" said Colin.

"The usual," said Wingrove. "What to do, what to do and what to do. He felt so responsible for the whole mess, the fact that they wound up in a place that didn't work and then put so much effort in trying to make a go of it."

"But no new alternative?"

Wingrove shook her head. "Not around there. He needed dependable water and a rich habitat, you know, for hunting everything, squirrels to deer."

"Like the Flat Tops," said Colin.

"The Flat Tops were perfect," said Wingrove. "A dream. And then the whole thing got too big, too out of control."

"Hard to hide," said Allison. But not impossible. *She* was still hiding. "At least, a crew that size."

"Devo wished he could put it all back in the bottle. All they wanted to do was sit around and talk about what to do next. They are a strange combination of survivalist experts and wannabe hippies—it's not a formula for organized decision-making." Glenna sighed. "I'm going off what Devo told me."

"Did you meet them? Cinnamon, Rock, Lyric?" Allison didn't mention the baby.

"Never," said Wingrove. "No thanks. A motel is about as close to camping as I like to get and based on his description, it didn't seem like anything I needed to see."

"Did you hear of anyone giving him any problems?" Colin cut to the chase.

"No." Wingrove didn't mind the question. "I mean, the other guys always know best. One was sure they could make that spot work, the one where they are now, but he never went on any of the longer hunts. Another was positive they should move quickly, but the question was always where and how did you find a list of possibilities?"

"Infighting," said Allison.

"But not like insurrection or anything," said Wingrove. "You're thinking someone hurt him?"

"First things first," said Allison. "We have to find him. What did you want him to do?"

"It didn't matter," said Wingrove. "Devo needed to come up for air, so to speak. He wasn't looking for a solution. Not from me, anyway."

"When he was with you for the weekend—did he leave to do anything else? Visit anyone else?"

Colin's cop-like thoroughness made Allison think he needed a notebook and pen.

"A few times I took Saturday afternoon or Sunday morning and drove up to Craig to visit a teacher friend—we went to Metro State together. I'd bring Devo a meal so he didn't have to go out. He slept and rested. So I didn't watch him like a hawk."

"But he didn't drive?"

"No license, no car. I mean, it's been years since he's been behind the wheel."

The thought made her smile and cry at the same time, conjuring an image she might never see. Allison felt that yanking sensation toward sorrow. Grief produced its own ecosystem and specific gravity; you could get lost.

"He was always there when you got back?" Allison thought of the sightings they'd confirmed around town—the library and other places.

"It wasn't like he could wander around, you know, fit in," said Glenna.

"But was he there?" Colin asked with all the empathy he could muster.

"You sound like detectives."

"And you're sure he went straight back when you left?" said Allison.

"I didn't follow him," said Glenna.

"Nobody is going to care as much as we do," said Allison. "Nobody even cares a lick right now, other than most of his tribemates and the three of us."

"And all his fans," said Wingrove.

Devo's television days were toast. Occasionally filmmakers and writers had come around to document the latest, but overall interest had waned. The fate of Devo and his clan of survivalists had become the cultural equivalent of a quirky roadside attraction.

"So if you've got something, it's no time to protect him," said Allison.

Wingrove steeled herself, looked down, sipped her iced tea, looked at each of them.

"You left because Devo was meeting someone." Trudy, Allison realized, would have been proud of Colin's intuitive powers.

Dual jets of tears zipped down both of Glenna Wingrove's cheeks, all the confirmation they needed.

"I don't know who it was," she said. "I've been sitting here the whole time, wracking my brain for anything he told me about her. She was somebody who offered to help, that's all I know. Someone who thought she knew what to do."

"A girlfriend," said Colin.

"I don't know," said Wingrove. "I think more a kindred spirit, sort of. Devo always got tense when I left. He had to prepare himself. I sort of had the impression she was a tough cookie."

"And she came to the Elk Motel?" said Allison.

Would Vern have noticed a second woman? Would he have mentioned it if he had?

"Once. That I know. She claimed to have the answer," said Wingrove. "That's what Devo said, at least. She was quite certain she knew what to do, but Devo was torn. Completely torn."

"You never saw her?"

Wingrove's head shook, tiny vibrations. They all heard the soft *whump* of a car door closing. Wingrove leaned forward in her chair and looked at the corner of her house. The woman who materialized there stopped the second she came into view.

"Hi honey," said Wingrove.

The woman's short dark hair was cut like a businessman's, up over the ears. She looked sleek but strong, on the trim side. In shape. Her complexion said outdoor work. Running shoes and grungy shoelaces showed the miles. She wore knee-length khaki shorts and then Allison dialed in the logo on her green shirt.

They kissed—more than a quick peck, on the lips.

Glenna Wingrove handled all the introductions, but Allison already knew her name.

"How long have you worked at Down to Earth?" said Allison.

"About eight months," said Mariah, not surprised at the question. "Since we moved up here. I don't know much about gardening, but I'm learning."

"Trudy Heath is my best friend on the planet. Best woman friend, at least." Allison smiled at Colin.

"Small world," said Mariah. "Met her once. She doesn't come around much, you know, day-to-day."

Mariah retreated to the apartment. Wingrove looked down, gathered herself. Mariah returned a minute later with a bottle of cold beer, a wedge of lime crammed into the bottle's mouth. She moved a chair to be close. Mariah hooked one arm on the back of Glenna's chair and the two exchanged a half smile.

"These two make you cry?" Mariah put a hand on Wingrove's cheek.

Wingrove gave a solid run-through, made it clear she welcomed their support, if not the news being delivered.

"But isn't that the point?" said Mariah. "If you live in the woods like Devo does, you don't have to keep to a schedule?"

"Too long to be gone," said Glenna. "It makes sense up to a point and then you have to be worried."

"Especially with how much he's been in touch with you." Mariah's words were right, if delivered with a touch of chill. "You've been wearing a groove on the road to Meeker."

"I was just telling them about this woman," said Glenna.

"The mysterious one," said Mariah, giving it a touch of melodrama. "Perhaps a figment of Devo's imagination or his excuse to get the motel room to himself so he could sleep and not have to have all those crabby voices around him all the time."

Glenna held the moment, shoved a hand under each thigh. Mariah put her hand on her wife's knee. "One weekend I planned to stay overnight up in Craig with my friend. When I left, I tried waiting across the street for an hour. I wanted to see her, don't ask me why. He never came out. She never went in. I had to get to Craig, so I left. Devo made her sound like some sort of freakish and fearless off-the-charts chick—another small one, too, but tougher than tough."

"Did he say where she lived?" said Colin.

"No."

"Mention a name?"

"That's the only thing I really know about her—her name. Devo said it was a name she gave herself."

Allison let her fill in the obvious blank.

"Atalanta."

Twenty-Five

Saturday Morning
Allison

Colin's cell phone rang as the last of the blueberry pancakes were being devoured. He had said he wanted to learn to cook full meals and he'd started with breakfast. A good cook around camp up in the woods, he seemed hell-bent on adding a few Trudyesque gourmet touches around the kitchen in their A-frame. Allison was growing used to him banging around, fixing meals. Whatever idea worm had wriggled up inside Colin and urged him to try a few new things, she approved. In fact, it made her wonder about her own patterns and grooves.

Too set? Too stuck?

Colin studied the caller ID. "Hey," he said.

Allison drizzled maple syrup over one last bite crammed with fruit.

"Yeah?"

Colin's expression sagged.

She'd put a smile on his face last night, but now she could feel the weight of the bad news emanate from every pore. She knew that look. He stared at her, shook his head. Allison felt that *uh-oh* jerking lurch, that heartless rogue wave that told her to grab hold of something solid.

Colin put down the phone. "Aw, hell," he said.

He knew to grab the keys, not bother with the dishes and within a minute they were in the pickup, hurting. And hustling. She fought off tears, asked a few questions but felt the heavy reality curl its way around her heart like a surgeon's perfect graft.

She stared out the window as Colin drove. He let her wallow. She wanted a helicopter or a zip line back to Meeker, but neither materialized in the too-bright morning sun.

The drive went by in a dazed blur, Allison remembering the first time they had spotted Devo and Colin had chased him down, the time she had found him frozen in the snow and warmed him back to life. She believed in long drinks of the Flat Tops, but Devo had gulped it down. He had learned one thing even better than she had—he knew how to hide. Fickle? For sure. Magician with the public relations? Off the charts. It wasn't hard to imagine that the national news would be all over this one. They had covered the roundup and eviction from the wilderness.

They would cover his death.

"Who are the cops going to notify?"

They had topped the highest point on Highway 13 and begun the long descent, straight north, into Meeker.

He looked over at her, his first check on her in a half hour. He hadn't touched her. Smart boy. "What do you mean?"

"Next of kin thing," she said.

"They must know where the flock hangs out."

"They won't know about Cinnamon or the baby," said Allison. "At least, I assume they wouldn't."

"Then—his parents?" said Colin.

"We could tell the cops in Meeker about Glenna, where she lives."

"Word will get out on this one—faster than the cops can control it." Colin passed one of those complicated-looking, hose-heavy trucks that had been as popular as pickups when the natural gas boom roared. She appreciated his sense of haste.

"This guy who called you—say it again?"

"A friend of my mother's, a guy named Hank Sloan. Old family friend who has been a big help since . . . you know."

The *situation*, yes. The situation that did not get discussed. The situation that led to a multiple-decade prison sentence longer than the life expectancy of his father. The situation that might allow his brother parole around the time he was ready to die.

"And Hank knew all this because?"

"He's a police junkie, a bit of a connector kind of guy. He had a police radio in his kitchen, booping and beeping all the time. He's at practically every meeting, too—school board, city council, you name it."

"Nosy."

"Overly interested."

"Isn't that the same thing?"

"He knew to call me."

"And had the number."

"He's good friends with my mom, so that would have been easy."

Char McKee had sold the ranch southeast of Meeker and

moved to a modest house in town. Legal bills nearly wiped her out. Colin's support for her had been steadfast, in person and on the telephone. He hadn't attended the trials. In fact, none of the McKees—Colin, his mother and a citified older brother, Daniel, from Colorado Springs—wanted to send confusing messages that might have been interpreted as support for Colin's father Earl and Colin's younger brother Garrett.

A half block past Brett Merriman's grocery store, they followed a left off Highway 13 onto Shaman Trail Road. The road cut due north past one end of the Meeker Airport, a single undulating strip of asphalt owned by the county. The road climbed a hill and skirted a cluster of houses rounded up on the edge of an oval cul-de-sac, modern-day covered wagons all nice and cozy. A bit of modern suburbia.

Four police vehicles jammed close together and a few neighbors had gathered gaggle-like, peering out between the houses.

Colin parked and Allison felt the weight of it, seeing a group of men and uniforms down across the field. She had the urge to click her boot heels together and see if she could make this all go away. But Allison knew she owed Devo that much, to take a look at his next-to-last resting place.

"A familiar face."

Deputy Sheriff Christie stepped away from the huddle to hold them back, twenty yards from ground zero. As she remembered, he looked ready to head up an international manhunt. A sizable pistol sat in a holster that jutted from his waist like a strange growth. Gizmos and boxes fought for space on his belt. He towered over her and looked fit and eager.

"He hasn't been dead for long," said Christie, jumping ahead over everything else.

"How long?" said Allison.

"The coroner is here," said Christie, as if that answered it.

"But the body wasn't here when the property owner was out mowing."

The back "yard" contained moonscape scrub, but a mower might be good for appearances. The fenceless back lots shared a broad swath of land.

"Yesterday evening?" said Allison.

"He said he finished mowing right before dark."

The cops clustered around the body. It lay half in the yard, brown and pounded by the sun, and half in the natural scrub. Allison caught a flash of Devo's bare, dark feet and she shuddered at the stark inertness and the cold reminder that the opposite of life is a distant place far out there beyond sleep and unconsciousness. It's stone nothing.

"May we take a look?" said Colin.

Sheriff Christie stared at Colin while he gave it a thought.

Colin said what she had been thinking, although Allison wanted to wait another couple minutes or decades until the inner ocean of sadness stopped roiling.

Allison kneeled next to Devo on one side, Colin on the other. Except for a complete lack of movement and that his eyes stared off a million miles up and didn't blink, Devo could have been napping. However he had wound up in this spot, it appeared to have been a gentle landing.

In life, Devo's size hadn't been much beyond child. Death shrunk him further—or maybe it was his body against the backdrop of the broad field. Nothing looked as still as a corpse.

His bronze beard flopped to one side. His gaunt face gave a hint of calm. His summer attire involved a deerskin vest and shorts, exposing ample midriff flesh, hairy and dark and so thin that Allison wondered if her two tiny hands could encircle it. Allison wanted to sneak a touch of his hand, to say good-bye, but knew better. His left arm rested on the ground. His right was folded up over his chest. His mouth slumped open. The scent of decay rose up. Perhaps the vultures were chattering now.

Colin whispered, "The hell?"

"I know," said Allison, barely above audible. "I don't see a single bruise—nothing."

Allison drew an imaginary line between Devo's new campsite and downtown Meeker. If Devo had been heading back to Cinnamon and the others, this spot would be smack on course. But if he'd been dead less than a day, or even a few hours, how had he been separated from his bear tooth necklace?

A wedge of dried-up drool clung to a small patch of skin near Devo's mouth where there were no whiskers. Bits of tan-yellow crud flecked his beard.

"Heart attack?" said Colin. "Even healthy people—you know, a clot or something. It happens."

"The necklace," said Allison. "Something was going on."

"That was days ago. You don't need a coroner to know Devo was alive this time yesterday."

The chances of natural causes, given Devo's outdoor savvy and a body with years of adaptation to the wilderness, seemed improbable. Perhaps he'd dived one too many dumpsters, banged around like a raccoon. It wouldn't be hard to imagine a few folks in Meeker who knew life was hard enough and who thought Devo's goofy experiment was a slap in the face. And any alleged survivalist who depended on scraps from civilization for himself and his tribe could be viewed as a maddening bit of hypocrisy.

Allison touched two fingers to her lips, gave them an invisible kiss and reached down near Devo's bare shoulder. Using her back as a shield, she pressed the fingers into the cold flesh.

She steeled herself against a tear and the tightness in her throat as she stood.

129

"Any sign of bruises on his back?" said Colin.

"Not my department." Christie dug two fingers in a shirt pocket in his green uniform, plucked out a tiny notebook. "Either of you know where he's from?"

"California." Allison realized she should have called Glenna Wingrove. "He tried acting but it didn't work. He moved to Denver, worked in a coffee shop and then came up with this whole crazy idea."

"You're wondering about next of kin?" said Colin.

"Precisely," said Christie. "Don't suppose his new family, if it is that, wants us to wander into camp."

"Know where they are?" said Allison.

"Not exactly," said Christie. "They don't want us to care and we're happy to oblige."

"How are they going to find out?"

Christie shrugged. "Same way they find out about anything else that happens in town or in the city or in the world. They crawled into a hole for a reason and one was to avoid calls by people like me. Given the fact that Devo's not much more than skin and bone, maybe this is nature taking its course."

Allison drifted away from the cop gaggle, Colin at her side. "I think I know what you're thinking," he said.

They walked slowly, eyes down. Colin knew the pace.

She scanned the choppy ground, considering it a bit of a miracle that anyone had managed to meld Kentucky bluegrass with the less-than-hospitable Colorado soil. Why were some homeowners so desperate to tend to a lawn? Was it the same as needing a mailbox and indoor plumbing? Here, the owners had opted for a tall fescue. This wasn't for backyard volleyball games

130

or parties but to define turf. *We own this.*

Allison sensed Colin expanding the space between them. She expanded her field of vision and slowed each step more.

On the edge of the final home, two full house lengths down the slope from Devo's inert body, Allison stopped. Mustard chunks, the same color as the crud in Devo's beard, littered the grass in a pool the size of a large dinner plate. Kneeling, she could see the slime that came with them—at least, the dull sheen on the grass. She was no expert on stomach volume, but it seemed to Allison that this looked like a substantial hurl, wondered if there were other spots that marked his trail.

Colin squatted next to her. "Looks painful," he said.

Allison sat down all the way on the cool grass. Tears trickled down along her cheek and she let them go.

Devo had been *sick*. It didn't make sense. Who knew he was in trouble—or suffering?

Allison had a firm belief, given Devo's tenacious outdoor skills, that nature didn't take him down, unless you included humans in the broad definition of nature. Despite their alleged intelligence, humans were beasts when it came right down to it. They always found a way to bloody up their teeth and claws.

Twenty-Six

Duncan had that look, that ease, that charm.

Trudy adored his ability in social situations to chat, ask questions, tell stories and wonder out loud.

Relax.

Colin cleared the wreckage on the table from their attack on eggplant parmesan, salad, bread. And lime purslane sorbet for dessert.

Wine bottle number four had been cracked. With the dishes piled in the kitchen, it stood as the lone source of sustenance on the table. Sam Shelton had been invited, but declined. Duncan had hoped to butter him up, get him to agree to a story. But Trudy wasn't too surprised when the "regrets" came. Trudy had wanted Shelton to meet her three closest friends on earth, but Shelton said he didn't want to make the drive down from Meeker.

Maybe it was just as well—the dinner talk had been devoted to Devo and, in a way, the evening turned into a bit of an Irish-cum-Colorado wake. All the reminiscing about quirky Devo wouldn't have made much sense to Sam Shelton. Of course Devo had a thing for Allison. Devo had tried several times to coax Allison to join his funky tribe of grit. It was funny to think about Allison joining anything, including a campaign of such dubious principles. The hardest, wine-soaked laughs had come imagining Allison Coil as grubby woodswoman willing to survive on squirrel and berries—no tequila!—in support of the ear-

132

nest Devo and his overt self-promoting ways.

The laughs, however, had been followed by tears. Trudy wept. Allison more than once buried her head in her hand. Colin welled up, too.

One thing was certain. The delivery of Devo's necklace meant he was in trouble before the day his body was found. Allison had produced a calendar and they figured it out—a week.

"Did you mention the necklace in your story?" A year ago, Colin would have said fifty words all night. Now, he participated in the flow.

"Yes, but not easily," said Duncan. "When the other reporters come to town to follow up, it would have been out anyway. The cops know. It's in a report somewhere."

"You think it's national news?" said Trudy.

"He was a quasi celebrity with a national television show," said Duncan. "It's making the rounds—Twitter and everything."

"Who is going back to tell Cinnamon and the others?" said Trudy.

"We will," said Allison. When they had called with the news, they were considering another night in Meeker to poke around, keep the pressure up. Trudy talked them out of it. She wanted some Allison time, too. "The cops are trying to find the parents. They can't imagine how it would look for a couple of cops to walk into camp. It's outside their comfy place."

"Horny skunk," said Duncan. Allison had told them everything they knew. "Carrying on an affair when he should be out hunting for his people or gathering scraps from the stores in town. Either way. Bit of a cliché, isn't it?"

Duncan didn't seem concerned at all about the time she had spent with Sam Shelton. Maybe he was too busy to be jealous. He seemed distracted lately, but Trudy knew he had his hands full.

"And he's a father," said Allison. "Father of the first baby born to the tribe, so it's hard to imagine him, you know, suddenly keeling over. He was in town, after all, getting a few more calories than the others on his motel weekends."

"And burned off calories off, too." Colin smiled.

"True. But after so many years in the woods—a hot but otherwise beautiful summer day, an easy hike for him back to camp. The guy knew his body and what it needed better than any athlete." Allison stared at her wine, perhaps hoping it would magically change to Sauza. "He didn't lay down and die. Not possible."

"Atalanta," said Duncan. "Think wild."

"You've heard the name?" said Allison.

"Greek mythology," said Duncan. "She was raised by a she-bear. Her father had wanted a son and left her on a mountaintop to die. She was raised by hunters and taught to fight like a bear. She was a runner and agreed to be married only if a suitor could outrun her in a footrace. The only way to slow her down was to roll a magic apple in front of her, to distract her."

In the bedroom, after one last toast to Devo, after sending Allison and Colin back across the meadow with tearful hugs, after a well-buzzed kitchen cleanup and a last glug of wine that Trudy knew she didn't need, she undressed and stretched out on top of the bedspread. She lit a candle, scurried three cats out of the room and opened the windows to the still night air, a touch of coolness like a top note.

Midnight.

Duncan returned from a last check of the doors and windows—part of his anti-bear vigil—and stood at the end of the bed in the soft light, naked except for the boxers.

"Nice view," he said. "Feel free to start without me."

He liked to watch. She'd done it for him before, pretending to be alone.

"What's keeping you?"

He answered by lighting a match and sliding a joint into his mouth. His cupped hand and the orange-yellow dot of fire moved back and forth to his mouth two times and he swayed, ever so slightly, like a sailor in light chop. He was drunk, which made sense. So was she.

"You don't mind?"

"Of course not," she said.

They both knew, without asking, that physical action would chase the death talk away.

"One hit," he said. "A nightcap. A night puff. A puffcap. Um. Um. A jointcap. A weedcap. We need a new word, dammit. Nightcap sounds like fucking James Bond."

He inhaled, held it, exhaled. He wasn't a regular toker, as far as she knew. She disliked how the odor clung to the bedroom. On the plus side, getting stoned wiped out his boyish energy. It always helped him last.

"Want some?"

He came around to her side of the bed and she took a quick puff. The contact high might have been plenty. In fact, the wine had been plenty—and now this.

She touched his boxers as he stood there, expecting to catch him off guard—in a natural state.

But, no.

"How do you do that?" she said.

The orange dot on the tip of the joint flared again near his mouth. "Told you. Great view."

For starters, a couple hundred kisses for her small breasts. They were slow, loving. She wrapped her legs around his butt, snuck a hand down and touched herself with one finger in the right spot. He made her squirm and laugh as he kissed her breasts and sucked, at times the nub of the nipple between his lips and the darting tongue giving a preview of how it would do its business when it found its way down between her legs.

He kissed her on the mouth, hard and long, and she tasted the sour-sweet herb and its sticky essence, like no other. He ground his hard prick around on her thighs and hips but held off going inside, and again she flew back to high school and times sneaking down by the river, at night, and taking her boy in her mouth and wondering, still to this day, what it would be like to own an appendage that expressed its needs so clearly.

The pot pulled her down, a strain of indica—Northern Lights. Her mind buzzed on the wine. Duncan kissed his way down her chest to her stomach and rolled her over, pulled back on her hips and continued his purposeful, pointed trail of kisses straight on down. She buried her head in the pillow and her mind flashed on Sam Shelton and maybe she was in a hotel room, preconcert or postconcert, and she was that night's temporary toy. Her head swam. Her body unhinged. Duncan flipped her over again, buried his head in her neck. Garlic, pot, sweat, oregano, thyme, flesh and sex. He kissed her again and she tasted herself—on the sweet side, if she didn't mind saying so. He leaned up and she guided him inside and Trudy went back to the hotel room in her head and sang a song to herself, that slow version of the Paul Revere oldie. "Kicks." Her hand helped now where Duncan's slow grind didn't really reach, not in the right way or the right rhythm. She knew where she needed to go.

Twenty-Seven

Deputy Sheriff Randall DiMarco didn't like being seen with the town's best reporter. They were outside the courthouse. He sat in his squad car, an SUV with the profile swept low like a mean race car. Duncan stood in the street.

"You can't have nothing."

"Why?"

"It's been a week," said Duncan. "There's always an ID."

"Always? You sure?"

"People want to know who was in the plane."

"Our phone ain't ringing off the hook."

"Ours neither," said Duncan.

"Nobody gives a shit. So you need to stop giving a shit."

"The news cares."

"The news can't *care*. The news ain't a thing."

"The facts matter—a plane crash and a dead body, a plane packed with weed."

"Like a beer truck spilling on the highway."

"That's the cops for you right there—so pissed off it got legalized and now you throw your hands up and hope for a big goddamn mess so you can all say 'I told you so.'"

DiMarco shrugged, checked his rearview mirror. "Maybe."

"Did the guy die inside the plane?"

DiMarco's dark complexion always made Duncan think Eastern Seaboard, like he walked out of the Bronx. He was mid-fifties. He had the pulse of an elephant.

137

"No."

"Well, there you go. Now we're getting somewhere."

"But you can't use that."

"The hell I can't. Sources said. Etcetera. We have to move the needle on this story."

"We?"

"Is the wreckage still up there?"

"Not my department," said DiMarco.

"Has the dead guy's family been notified?"

"I'm not lead dog, okay?"

"Yeah, but I believe you guys talk."

"It ain't me."

"Is it a Garfield County investigation?"

"Yes and no."

"It has to involve the county."

"Why is that?"

"Did the plane take off from anywhere near here—in this county, one nearby?"

"It was stolen in Texas, you know that much."

"Or was this an interstate deal?"

"I'd advise thinking both big and small, but mostly local."

"So right here? Our weed users, right here?"

"Like you?"

"Nice try." Duncan had showered in the morning, after the extended party with Trudy. He didn't remember falling asleep, only her warmth and how his body intertwined with hers. "Like no cop has ever lit up. Or sold meth like that sheriff in Arapahoe County."

"A few bad bananas."

"Oh wait," said Duncan. "Not sold—*traded* meth for sex with young boys. Protect and serve, yep and yep."

"Not a shining moment."

"If that's the sheriff, imagine the deputies."

"Imagine."

"But how can a dead guy be found in a plane crash where there was once a ton of weed and nobody knows nothing?"

"I wouldn't say nobody knows nothing," said DiMarco.

"Then who does?"

"It's not a city case."

"But you could track it down."

"If I was motivated."

"Isn't curiosity enough?"

One idea in the back of Duncan's head involved writing a nonfiction book about the booming marijuana business, but he'd need a good angle and a hell of a pitch. Several old reporter pals had book deals, but they still drove the same old junkers. Junkers like his previous-era Camry.

"I know they are working on it. By the way, are you asking for yourself or because your pal Allison found him?"

"All me," said Duncan. "This is a newspaper story. That's where you come in."

"Follow the money."

Duncan touched two fingers to the middle of his forehead, closed his eyes for added melodrama. "Where have I heard that before? Let me think. Oh yeah, *All the President's Fucking Men*. That's all we ever do is follow the money—advertisers, public relations dingbats, big business wants their name in the fucking paper. What does that even mean?"

"Nothing," said DiMarco. "But I always wanted to say it."

"I need a name. Name of the dead guy or the guy the plane is registered to, either the wrecked plane or the second one."

Duncan had done a bit of homework on the registration number off the second plane—and wasn't feeling optimistic about its value. In 2010, the FAA had asked for re-registration of 119,000 civil aircraft, due to out-of-date records. Owners complied at an underwhelming rate, leaving the system sloppy and loose.

"So Allison doesn't care?"

"What's this Allison thing? You got a crush?"

"And you don't?"

"Jesus, can you stick to the point?"

"Sure."

"Then help me."

"If I was in your shoes?"

"Can we cut to the chase? The only thing I can think is that maybe what happened up there is part of an ongoing investigation and since it's not over, you don't want to spill any more frijoles than necessary."

DiMarco smiled.

"So you were watching those guys?" said Duncan.

"Reminder," said DiMarco. "Not us."

"So you do know something. Where should I start?"

"Probably state."

"State's a big operation."

"When it comes to this stuff?" said DiMarco. "Not really."

Twenty-Eight

Cinnamon cried.

She sat, the bewildered Dock in her embrace, and let the tears run. Her thin chest heaved.

Cinnamon's sobs threatened to yank a companion fount from Allison.

Allison already wished she hadn't helped Colin decide to stay in Sweetwater and start getting ready for a black powder hunt. She missed his company, his insights. She missed *him*.

By the time Allison relayed the basics to Cinnamon, they had been joined by nine of the others for a mill-about, hug-each-other sob.

Soon, the nine were joined by eight more. As a group, they were undernourished walk-ons waiting around for the shoot to begin on a zombie flick. They studied her with wide-eyed wonder.

"Hi," said Allison. "Hello." "How are you?" "Good afternoon."

She got mumbles back, head nods. The mourning huddle around Cinnamon presented a mosaic of bronze flesh, deerskin shorts, deerskin vests and sullen, dazed expressions. A fire snapped under a black pot of water.

Allison stood off to the side, glugging water from a purple Hydro Flask. Her presence alone represented a blemish in the real-life diorama. The plastic bottle could have been considered an assault by its presence in this organic-everything world.

Devo's death formed a hard knot in her chest. There were two choices. First, one of his own tribe followed him out to the outskirts of Meeker and mounted his or her own personal coup, perhaps on behalf of a disgruntled sector of the tribe. Second, an entanglement in Meeker went sour and nasty. Natural causes? No way. No how.

Allison studied a loose row of four log huts and the incomplete bones of a teepee. The settlers had taken the trouble of hewing the logs for the first cabin but had skipped that step for the others. Saplings and brush and evergreen limbs were interwoven for the two enclosed roofs. Handsaws flopped on the ground. The last pair of construction projects needed two more walls and a roof, but no timber waited. She gave the builders high marks for effort and F's for craftsmanship. In the last cabin, the beginnings of a stone chimney took shape along the north wall, but the attempt at mud mortar looked lame.

Each hut looked big enough for six or a snug eight. Crude wood floors looked postearthquake. She couldn't imagine the energy burned to haul and hew the logs. As structures went, they were more than temporary shelter but not quite fit enough to keep a harsh winter at bay. It wasn't hard to imagine a variety of visions among the pseudo-architects and survival "experts" about whether this was the place to invest their energy. Construction required hard labor of chopping and shaping and fitting. Over and over. Nasty stuff without a bag of iron nails. They must have given thumbs-up to global warming. The previous winter had acted no worse than a long, cold fall. But global warming also gutted the habitat's bounty. The lack of rain and snow left the woods sagging and the undergrowth desperate. The animals could stay up higher, too, out of reach.

And now the prospect of looking for a new camp would mean abandoning all the work and walking away from the investment of muscle and sweat.

Where had Devo slept? Or did the leader keep a special spot?

Allison chose the best-looking quasi cabin and stepped inside. Loose chinking and an open door, a generous definition of the term, allowed some light inside. Evergreen and deerskin blankets formed eight bedding areas. Someone championed the open-floor concept.

Until the cracks in the wall were closed, the wind would whistle and bring along its kissing cousins, rain and snow.

A crude dream catcher dangled above one bed. Soft blue-gray feathers dangled from the circle, perhaps mountain jay. A round, old-school canteen, the kind that imbued everything it carried with a sour metallic essence, lay on the ground next to one bedding area. Long straps attached to a camo-print canvas wrapper. Tucked up against one wall, the library. A dozen or so fat paperbacks. A copy of *Centennial* looked new, but *Heart of Darkness* looked as if it had journeyed upriver in Kurtz' back pocket and *Call of the Wild* like it had spent a winter and spring in the Klondike snow and mud. The cover on this edition showed a dark silhouette of Buck against a full moon, neck outstretched in a howl.

He was mastered by the sheer surging of life, the tidal wave of being
. . .

Buck, the revenant—eternal mourning, endless grief. No doubt the sheepdog mix could have taught Devo and Cinnamon a thing or two about scavenging and survival. But when did anyone read? Who had the time? She would mourn alongside Buck until Devo's killer was found. Maybe longer.

Bleak House, On the Beach, The Road . . .

"Help you?"

"No, I'm—"

Still running with Buck . . .

The interior light dimmed. He stood in the doorway for a moment and then the light flooded in again as he ducked through.

"Snooping?"

The man sported a prominent brow, Grecian nose.

"Hi," said Allison. "Just looking around."

"What's to see?"

"Admiring your construction." What a joke. "Thinking of all the work." Not a joke. "And you are?"

"T-Bone."

"Lots of work."

"Nobody signed up for easy."

"Who is the librarian?"

"Kala. She's new," said T-Bone. "Big discussion whether books would be allowed."

T-Bone would fit right in on the Klondike, circa 1890. Give him a Mackinaw coat and wool mittens and he could mush dogs. His physique and glow suggested a recent recruit.

"We all know what you meant to Devo," he said. "You are a frequent star of his stories."

Allison liked the use of present tense. "He was one of a kind."

"It's going to take time."

"For?"

"For finding a new order, I suppose."

The room felt close. Allison stepped toward the opening and T-Bone ducked back outside first. Sunlight.

"But Devo had been off and away. Long stretches."

"You don't have to be here to set the course."

"So now?" said Allison.

"A leader will emerge."

"You?"

"It's going to be a natural process, I'm sure of that."

"Lot of responsibility, I'm sure."

The effort to rebuild the collective toughness likely also required re-establishing the "natural" order of women sliding to the background. Allison wanted zero to do with the past.

"The baby makes it harder, too."

"You in favor of moving?"

"Got to."

"That's why you stopped work on the cabins or whatever you call them."

T-Bone shrugged. "We need to be close to water—bottom line. One spring went dry. There's no reason to be here."

"Except the landowner doesn't mind."

"So we waste away on land where it's okay to make our home? Doesn't make sense."

"Did Devo ever tell you where he went?"

T-Bone took his time. Deerskin shorts clung to his thighs. His dirty-blonde dreads were splashed with purple and blue beads, hardly standard-issue Lewis and Clark gear. "His trips to town were not entirely a secret."

"What if there was more to his trips than scrounging around for scraps?" said Allison.

"We only cared about the food," said T-Bone. "Like gleaning fields, you know. So much food wasted in this country. Well, in your country."

"You're going to criticize the hand that feeds you?"

She could understand how living in these conditions might make someone humorless. But smug, too? A bummer combination.

"You could feed another country on what yours throws away."

So why wouldn't you *stay* in the real one and do something about it?

Allison swallowed a hundred comebacks.

"Where's your space?"

"The teepee." T-Bone pointed at the skeleton frame. They headed back toward Cinnamon. "There's room in the others, but we need to spread out and learn what works."

"Teepees need hide."

"The animals we need are out there—just hard to hunt."

The deer that were out there—and elk—existed because the wildlife were being managed and because society had advanced beyond the old-fashioned ways of killing everything that moved whenever it wanted.

Devo's crazy trip was whacked. Denial made it certifiable. His death, however, left the same gaping hole in her heart.

Cinnamon nuzzled Dock, rocked him. The tightest circle around Cinnamon were all women. Again, roles and expectations for the old ways. *Forget about it.*

"Good a time as any for a meeting."

Rock, with the walking stick and the two-sizes-too-small shorts, cut through the murmurs and sobs.

"Not now," said Lyric.

"What better time?" Rock took a step forward into the middle of the circle. All other chatter came to a halt.

"What's to decide?" This from a bushy-haired woman who flanked Cinnamon on the opposite side from Lyric.

"Everything," said Rock. "The next leader, for one. And how we're going to find a more suitable camp."

"We have guests," said Cinnamon. "A guest."

"I was just leaving," said Allison. Could she give the Dorothy Gale method a whirl? Maybe Ropers weren't meant for clicking.

"No, please," said Cinnamon. "By the way, where is he now?"

Allison felt all the eyes staring her down. *Stranger!* "Far as I know, with the coroner."

"And then?"

"They are trying to contact his parents. Or a sister who lives in

146

Glenwood Springs."

"He's ours," said Lyric. She had fashioned a tight necklace out of leather. Eight curved bones, bleached and spiky, dangled from the choker. "He belongs to us."

Would the coroner recognize Cinnamon's status, with nothing legal about her woodsy wife role?

"No," said Rock. "It's as if he went out for a hunt and never came back."

"He doesn't belong in a city grave," said Lyric.

"If he died right here, that's one thing," said Rock.

"Let him go." Cinnamon's voice gained strength. "All that scattering ashes stuff is for the living. We'll have a ceremony with or without his body."

"Then I'll make my way," said Allison.

Lyric cocked her head to the side. "Don't we want to know what happened?"

"Does it matter?" said T-Bone.

"Well, sure," said Lyric. "Of course."

Suddenly Allison realized something so basic about Devo's death that she couldn't believe she had overlooked it. Uttering it would spark too much speculation, and she wasn't yet sure about who to list as Devo loyalists or Devo detractors. And you couldn't live in a black hole trying to start a retro society and expect to keep tabs on an investigation in the evil modern world. At least, not without tortured logic.

T-Bone inhaled for dramatic effect. Arrogance dripped. "There's nothing more for us to do."

"Except if he was killed *because* he's one of us," said Lyric. She believed in her opinions.

"I've got to go," said Allison.

"How will we reach you?" Cinnamon handed Dock to Lyric, and Lyric gave the baby a nuzzle.

"Why would you need to?"

"In case of, you know," said Cinnamon. "Anything."

Google best outfitter in the Flat Tops . . . ?

Ditch this joke project and come have a beer with me in Sweetwater . . . ?

"I don't know," said Allison. "Did Devo ever show anyone his stops in town? His route?"

Allison felt a half dozen pairs of eyes ripping through her flesh.

"I know his contacts."

She stepped forward from the outer ring of onlookers, looking more alive and alert than her tribemates. She was topless, on the small side. A skirtlike cloth wrapped her solid hips. A bow draped over her shoulder as if she was ready to nail a rabbit. She wore long dreads that weighed her down.

"I'm Kala." Her cheeks looked plump. Her teeth looked ready for a toothpaste commercial. "I know where."

"Okay." Allison hoped for a clean break. "You're the Jack London fan," said Allison.

Kala smiled. "Yes, adaptation, you know?"

"Master or be mastered," Allison parried back. "No middle ground."

"The mysterious something." Kala's eyes smiled. "It calls, right? All times, waking and sleeping? Calls for you to come."

Allison could read *The Call of the Wild* once a year. The "law of club and fang" couldn't be overlooked for humans, either.

"I don't know why you'd need me." Allison's interest level in the purity of their execution was zero, but she did not grasp their disinterest in Devo's demise. "You can always leave a message at the grocery store."

"With Brett?" said Lyric.

Allison nodded.

Her departure received all the fanfare of waiting for license plates at the DMV.

Twenty paces away, mulling their apathetic attitude about Devo, a sharp "wait!" called after her. She turned to see Kala coming her way, Dock still in her arms. Kala looped her arm around Allison's. She kept walking, their backs to the tribe.

"Find out what happened." She'd gone stone-cold serious, in control. "Devo helped you, right? I mean, he told us the stories. Two times he helped you. Right?"

"And indirectly once more."

"If he made an enemy, I don't know. But you are the one to make sure they figure it out."

Kala stopped. She handed the baby over without asking. Dock uttered a brief protest, perhaps his first whiff of clean skin. Allison couldn't remember the last time she'd held a baby but felt an automatic urge to kiss the fontanelle. Dock relaxed, looked up, stared deep. *Who is this creature with the clothes?* He felt too light. Was it fair to Dock to choose this scrawny, scrappy destiny for him? What if he didn't thrive? Devolution and degeneration weren't that far apart.

"For me." Kala stepped back to admire the view of Dock in her arms. "For Dock and for Cinnamon and Devo, too."

"Let me ask you a question." Allison handed the baby back.

"Okay," said Kala.

"Does the name *Atalanta* mean anything to you?"

"Atalanta?" Kala studied her moccasins. "Why? What?"

"Does it?"

"I think I heard Devo mention the name."

"Know where she's from?"

"Why?"

"Something somebody mentioned. In fact, Devo's sister."

It didn't seem fair to tell Kala of Devo's nights in the motel

149

bed—or anything else. Not yet.

"You want to find her?"

"If you remember anything," said Allison, "get a message to Brett—any way you can, let me know."

Allison set a general course for south. Sun blasted through the thinned-out forest. Again she rued the fact that her business had not bothered to go to the trouble of buying a portable transporter beam. With all the questions about the crashed weed wagon still lingering, she didn't need to lose the few hours it would take to hike back out, reconnect with Colin, start looking for Atalanta and see if Duncan Bloom had squeezed any information out of the cops or anyone else. Of course, a helicopter would be a cheaper and more reliable form of transportation, but she would never find herself airborne again. She was more likely to trust her flesh and bones to quantum mechanics.

Maybe she should have asked Cinnamon or Lyric or Kala or the others the question that nagged at her now. But she didn't sense that the survivors of Devo's crew wanted to spend time chewing over questions that were pertinent to a death investigation outside their bubble of zeal.

The question was simple.

If Devo was heading back to his tribe from town, even if ill, why was he empty-handed?

Part Two

Twenty-Nine

Saturday Afternoon
Clay Rudduck

"Two months."

"I know."

"I'm nervous."

"Who isn't?"

"I'm not sleeping well."

"Me neither. Melatonin, some nights. Advil PM with a bourbon chaser on the others." Uttering the sleep-inducing combo triggered a sour sting in Clay Rudduck's stomach. He winced. "Not that it always works."

"You okay?"

"Acid," said Rudduck. "My stomach doesn't like to hear the word 'bourbon.'"

"I keep thinking that any day the phone will explode, or I'll hear a knock on the door." She rapped the bench where they sat—three times, hard. "Sometimes I worry they'll nab me when I'm walking out of the grocery store. Or anywhere out and about. The milk will spoil, the frozen pizza will thaw while I'm hauled off in handcuffs."

They sat on a bench in "Cowboy Camp" at the Glenwood Caverns Adventure Park, high on Iron Mountain across the river from downtown Glenwood Springs. A covered wagon and a frozen-in-place mock campfire provided the lame props for their journey back in time 150 years. The smell of French fries and the sight of patrons sipping giant sodas compromised the vibe. The "adventure park" drew a steady throng in the summer to its mash-up of an Old West town and its slick rides, from a zip line to a cliffside roller coaster. But it was October now and traffic had thinned. Up here, it was easy to chat without being worried about being seen together.

"Have you talked to any of them yet?" She seemed agitated.

"Still not a good idea."

"I don't get that."

"It's so much bigger than us."

That wasn't true, but it didn't hurt to suggest it.

"You said you had access—good access." Barnstone tugged a tuft of hair on her temple.

"I have to pick my moments."

"Make a moment *now*," she said.

"Why?"

"I need to find out what's going on."

"Patience. Good thing."

"*Two months.*" Said like an accusation.

"Still not a good idea. If the cops are watching, we'd give them what they're waiting for."

A bedraggled family of four with matching white T-shirts trudged up the slight incline of the asphalt path in front of them. The older daughter had used a wedge of fudge as both lipstick and makeup foundation. The path led them to Cliffhanger Roller Coaster and the Giant Canyon Swing, which left riders with a good view of straight down.

"I want out."

It wasn't a request.

"Don't panic."

"The plane crash changed everything. I didn't sign up for this part of it."

Rudduck wanted to touch her knee, bare below cotton shorts. Like the rest of her legs, the knee was tanned and the skin was smooth. The best thing about the whole Helen Barnstone package was the two boys, ages 5 and 7. Willy and Chuck. He had met with Barnstone a dozen or so times in person and he had yet to see her do anything self-conscious. She fit with the local scene, PTA to church.

"You bought a nonrefundable ticket."

A few happy-girl screams floated through the pines.

"Find my money, keep ten percent as a 'thank-you' gift or handling charge, no problem. Ten percent. And return the rest."

"It's not that easy."

"It better be."

"You knew going in."

"Or I turn myself in." She had thought this through. "Better at this fucking stage than down the road."

Until this point, all Barnstone had wanted was to end up in a "big-ass" house and to show her ex, "the moron," that he'd blown it. The ex had spent most of their marriage "investing" in hunting gear and justifying weekends in Las Vegas, where he claimed to have mastered a foolproof system at the blackjack tables. To accelerate her self-improvement plan and improve the odds of stomping on her ex's throat, at least in the metaphorical sense, she had enrolled in a business course at Colorado Mountain College.

Rudduck wasn't surprised that Duncan Bloom had grown edgy, but he hadn't expected the same from Helen Barnstone. Her investment, by his calculations, represented one-tenth of the small fortune she had inherited from her father, who for twenty-five years had been the chief operations officer for Colorado's second-largest grocery store chain. He had keeled over ten months earlier at the age of 62. His wife had drowned in a riptide five years before that off Myrtle Beach. Helen was the only child. Sad, but *bo*-nanza. The check from her father's estate, after everything was sorted out, arrived after the divorce settlement. She would make a perfect public face for the application for the new retail operation in Rifle. All the drivers' license checks at the Glenwood store let him know, by zip code, that there were plenty of Rifle customers. Tracking customer data was a snap.

Being first mattered. So did arriving with a good reputation.

"We have no idea what happened up there," said Rudduck.

"Which makes no sense to me. How *don't* you know what happened? And how can you evaluate risk factors without information to work with? Intro to Business—*bang*, right there." She could flash a legitimate scowl. "Know your risks."

"Is that what they're teaching you?"

"It's about control and about remaining engaged in your business. This is too loosey-goosey for me."

"This isn't a grocery store or a wine shop," said Rudduck. "And the upside? Hell."

"I knew it was a risky move." She half whispered.

He went full-on breathy talk. "Don't let your nerves get the best of you."

"What happened to the load on the plane that went down?"

She didn't need to know everything—and never would.

"The second plane picked up where the first plane left off."

"And then?"

"They'll come back when they can. That's all."

"You don't think the dead guy is one of our guys?"

Rudduck was her sole contact. How could she mean *our guys*?

"If they thought they needed help, they might have brought somebody on."

"And then he dies. Maybe murdered."

"We don't know."

"We don't know *nothing*. My point."

The rims of her nostrils turned white. Her mouth tightened down.

"We'll know more soon."

155

"I'll give it a week."

"Two weeks."

"Ten days."

"Two weeks. And promise to keep an open mind. If nothing changes, we're probably in the clear." He tried to say it like he believed it. "The election is two weeks from next Tuesday. We'll know then."

"Remember," said Barnstone. "My ex frittered our money away in Vegas. I hate the word 'probably.' Ten days. I don't mind risking cash on the grow. But this side business is danger-ous. Ten days, or I walk straight over to the paper and tell them where to begin digging on the plane crash that nobody gives a shit about."

Helen Barnstone left to ride the tram down first, alone.

Rudduck wondered how many lies he'd told, but it didn't matter.

Yes, they needed time.

Yes, Helen Barnstone needed to keep her shit together.

But there were two problems.

First, he knew precisely what had happened at the plane wreck because he was the one who drove up the so-called Jeep Trail all three hours at four miles per hour from Burns to Cres-cent Lake and then hiked for another two hours, fishing rod for authenticity, to the spot where they were holding the fucking informant and, when he denied it for the last time, gave him a double ear blow with cupped palms, pushed in his eyes with both thumbs, kneed him in the groin and, when he fell in a heap, rolled him over and planted a boot in his larynx. One last rock to the temple cracked his skull where the dashboard might have hit him. He'd trained on dummies for KBR and done some shit-kicking in Baghdad under a government contract. The training came back in full. It was like riding a bicycle.

The blows surprised the fucking informant, but not for long. It also surprised the other two, including the pilot who claimed to know how to fly in the mountains but did not.

Vince Hedland, not a pilot. The asswipe couldn't even make it over the Flat Tops on a blue-sky day.

Rudduck left the other two with the body and the bundles of weed that had been off-loaded from the wrecked plane. He gave them instructions and trundled down the bumpy-ass Jeep road all the way back, a luckless fisherman. He'd pulled an all-nighter, but it was worth it. Thank god for the quick thinking of Skip Grayson, who took the initiative to check out his hunch, to follow his gut about the guy Hedland said was solid.

The second problem was the man and woman on horseback up on the ridge when the plane had taken off.

Grayson said there were two unexplained water bottles with the informant when he returned.

And someone had covered up the deer.

Strange but true—that same *someone* had left the informant tied up.

It had taken some work, quietly poking around until he was pretty sure he knew the names of the two riders. The descriptions matched, right down to the horses they rode.

Thirty

Sam Shelton held up a joint, rolled so tight it looked like a thin white matchstick.

"I said I'd changed, I didn't say I was a Boy Scout," he said. "This shit is powerful."

They were well into the wine. That one-last-glass was four half-glasses ago.

"I'm know *I'm* relaxed," said Trudy.

Too drunk to drive. She had blown through the caution sign. The wine, Sutcliffe 2011 Cabernet Franc from Colorado. The food, her eggplant parmesan and his tomato-corn salad. The stories, performing during a storm on the Isle of Wight, partying all night after a taping of *Saturday Night Live*, opening for The Who on their fourth "final" tour. The stories were so damn funny she felt a bit like she'd been there. The guys in the crew had known every name, every location and every band that Sam Shelton dredged up. She remembered scraps of songs from high school. His yarns were like music-only trivia night at the bar. It was a wrap party blowout, Sam Shelton in full rock star bloom intertwined with compliments from the crew on the fine job Trudy and Sam had done taping all the episodes.

The crew had departed to the house they had commandeered in downtown New Castle. That was an hour prior. Trudy wasn't sure that they should be on the road.

Shelton took a hit off the joint and passed it over. She took a tiny hit.

158

Trudy stood, thinking bathroom. She lurched a bit. She stopped in the living room and bent over at the waist to clear a light head. She poured a glass of cool water from the bathroom tap and sipped. Certainly so much laughing—she could feel the endorphins floating free—would counteract the booze. Yes?

"Everything okay?"

She hadn't heard him come in.

Two squat, fat, vanilla-scented candles shed a faint glow. She turned into his open arms, not unhappy for the support. She let herself fall into his wingspread, all worn and owl-like. Were owls funny? Did they tell jokes? Probably not. The kiss started without hesitation, and she had no trouble interpreting the language of his tongue.

"Thank you." She leaned away. "Lovely evening."

"You can't drive." She could hear the smile in his voice.

"I know."

A hand moved down her back, all purposeful. It grabbed her butt. She put her head against his chest, let her arms drop to her sides. She let her eyes close. Her heart frolicked, but it worked out of sheer self-protection, working through all that booze.

Trudy squared up, sucked in a bucket of air and broke the embrace. She headed back to the bench on the low porch outside. He followed.

Inertia's grip had her good. The cool air whispered winter. With the blanket, she felt wrapped in a cocoon of warmth and wooziness.

He relit the joint.

"I'm going to call," she said. "Make a call."

"Please," he said.

Once vertical again, she took baby steps, not sure at first for a strange second where to find the door back inside. On her side? Or through Shelton's sticky cloud of smoke?

159

"You okay?"

She reached her hands out straight like a goofy, stumbling Frankenstein.

His joint crackled. The porch wobbled. Her breath tightened. Her left arm scraped the doorjamb and she slapped the inside wall, feeling for the light switch. A lamp popped on. She took a full stride, positive illumination would improve everything. If she walked with purpose, perhaps she could shake this torrential buzz.

Willpower, kiddo.

The floor came rolling and surging.

She stood still.

Blinked.

She stumbled to the kitchen, buried her face in a dish towel soaked in cold water. She sat on the toilet lid in the bathroom. She stretched out on the cool tile floor. Peach cobbler threatened to fly back up. She hated hurling and fought back, tasting the weed in her throat.

Her face burrowed into the tiles for coolness, but they had no give. She wouldn't drink for a month.

She pulled her knees up to her chest, call to prayer.

She stood. She soaked the washcloth again and sunk her face in pool of freezing water, hairline to neckline. Water dribbled down her chest.

All she wanted was to lie down, let blackness come. Tomorrow would be a bitch.

She fought her way back to the kitchen, one breath at a time. One step at a time. She found her phone on the counter by the coffee pot.

A blinking outline of a battery on the black screen said *you're an idiot*.

Back across the living room, this time she turned *off* the light to prove that she could manage.

Shelton dug out his phone in the darkness. He punched in his passcode.

"You're missing the party," he said.

His dark shape barely moved. A pinprick orange dot at the end of the joint gave her the needed bearings.

She steeled herself to keep a true line through the living room, not let the waves capsize her purpose.

"It's fine, of course," said Duncan when she explained.

She wanted to sound strong, at least, for a minute.

"I'm glad you're not driving," he said.

"Okay," she said. The word came out too thin and meek. She wanted to climb back in their bed, way back up in Sweetwater, a universe away.

"See you when I see you," said Duncan. "I love you."

Back outside, she waved away the offer when the pinprick orange dot came her way. How could there be anything left?

" You alright?"

She stood back up. Being back around the smoke worsened the wobbly abyss.

"I need to—"

She eased herself, slow motion, to the chesterfield couch inside. She reminded herself not to hurl the cobbler on the imported fabric, one of his prizes. She lay facedown, head cocked to the side. The room spun like a hurricane. Her heart boxed her ribs, uppercuts and in rhythm. She didn't have to touch her forehead to feel the fire.

A belt buckle clinked.

A paw pushed her over.

"Sam—"

A sound like rustling.

"No!" She shouted it. How could one syllable sound slurred

161

and slow?

"Don't worry."

She wriggled away to the corner of the couch as if a rattler had slithered into her tent.

She crawled up on the armrest, same height as the backrest. This was no tent. She was up on her knees when she felt his hands on her hips and her pants and her panties being tugged down and still the room flew and tumbled and holy crap she wanted it to stop—

She clung hard to the fat, thick armrest. Was it possible to climb on a cloud? Set anchors? She must not climb solo. She knew that much. Her butt was exposed, her pants were down. The marijuana cloud hovered. The stench wasn't helping the room slow its oceangoing ways. She reached an arm to the end table, searching for a handhold to yank herself up and away. She kicked and bucked and her hand flailed and she heard a soft crash, felt his hands on her hips, as she pushed over two fat candles and she remembered their metal holders, gifts from Elton John for a cover of "Tiny Dancer." Tiny *Fucking* Dancer.

She was naked.

Candle yanked out, slug weight in her palm, she spun hard and *guessed guessed guessed* through the haze and the darkness. She let her arm wheel itself through the cloud and she heard the crack, and then her fingers vibrated in a kind of happy pain because a couple smashed fingers felt so good when she heard him slump.

He groaned in pure pain.

She gasped for air. Tears streaked down her face.

She pulled up her pants.

He didn't move. She fought through the crazy-shit room wobbles and focused on one simple idea.

Get away, get away, get away.

162

Thirty-One

The kid was maybe 25, but could pass for high school.

"Way too far," said Allison.

"You think? He's just sitting there."

"Eating. Standing."

"You know what I mean."

Antlers flashed in the fading light.

"All against you—distance, breeze and drop," said Allison. Only one in twenty hunters could make the shot and do it right. "And if you don't get a clean hit, we wouldn't get over there until after dark."

"We've seen so few."

"Correction," said Allison. "That's the first."

"Like I said."

All day, the kid had gone for laughs. His friend hadn't said much. At all.

"Where there's one, there's others." An utter lie. "We'll come back tomorrow." Or not.

"Thought it was a boulder on the hillside." The kid had baby cheeks, small and deep-set eyes. "And then it moved."

Allison had seen it, but didn't want to mention it.

"Thin eats all over," said Allison. "Good eyes, by the way."

It was the warmest October hunt in Allison's time on the Flat Tops.

"Fuck," said the kid in a whisper. He switched his binoculars for his rifle and peered through the scope. "I got him right in the

163

lungs."

"Don't," said Allison.

Even with a good shot, the dense drainage between shooter and prey would take an hour to slog through, all the way down and back up. It would be easy to lose their bearings.

The bull lifted his head and looked straight across the deep draw in their direction. He walked back under the cover of forest and its dark shield.

Allison liked happy clients, but she smiled inside this time. The day had been a bust. Less mess, less hassle. She didn't trust the kid's experience. And she couldn't figure out his stone-faced buddy. They had been last-minute add-ons who asked for a site Allison had used for drop camps, not too far from where five men from Arkansas were using Allison's best campsite and the wall tent, mess tent and eleven of her horses. Jesse Morales tended the campsite, all the cooking and cleaning, for the Arkansans. Colin guided a different hunter each day, rotating around, while the others headed off in pairs.

The new hunters were locals, from Silt. On the phone two weeks ago, the kid had said they'd gotten laid off, a drilling-related business, and had found more time to put into their cow tags. Originally, they'd been hoping to get lucky on a weekend and now had the full eight days of the second season. They'd had their eyes on the unit where Allison's outfitting business had permits and could she take them?

"Long week, lotta miles." The kid's name was Merle, a name she associated with drunk uncles and car mechanics. She put him at about 22. He had blonde, faint eyebrows.

"Like this more often than not," said Allison. They had huffed their way back up to the top of an open ridge. Allison got her bearings off the silhouette of Turret Peak. "Even in the years with more favorable temperatures, no guarantees."

"Where the hell do they all go?"

"If I knew, your tags would be full."

"Was that plane that crashed anywhere around here?"

"Which one?"

"Back in August," said Merle. "Buddy of mine said he knew somebody who knew somebody who was on that plane. Ain't that right?"

Merle turned to Dwayne, who appeared unfazed by the quarter-mile hike on a steep pitch.

"They were sure talking about it." These were Dwayne's first words since lunch. He was a good six foot four with big shoulders. His cheeks were full scruff. A fuzzy unibrow formed a row of shrubbery below an acre of forehead. He needed a week at charm school. "I've been thinking I recognized your name."

Allison felt her whole system flutter awake.

"You did?"

As far as she knew, her name wasn't out there.

"Well, these guys were talking about it and your name came up," said Merle.

The Turret Peak Trail lay dead ahead another few hundred yards. She kept her head down. It would be hard to miss, but still.

"Don't believe everything you hear."

"You're not nobody," said Merle.

"As close as it gets," said Allison. "Who were your friends?"

"Guy named Ron, lives in Silt. He owns that funky liquor store right off the highway. Ron something."

"Drummond," said Merle.

For two months, the lack of resolution left an empty ache. Dead guys didn't die without telling a story. And shit didn't happen in her hunting grounds and then get hosed down the drain without explanation.

"And his connection?" She aimed for a mode around casual chat.

"Related to that whole deal with the stoners wanting to build a place to grow weed in Silt—you know, that whole controversy."

"He's part of it?" said Allison.

"Or against it, I don't know. Probably against," said Merle. "If you sold booze, would you want to help your competition?"

"Though they do go well together," said Dwayne. "Like mustard and ketchup."

Perhaps the cover of darkness brought the mute to life. Or maybe the opportunity to display his metaphor chops.

"They knew the guy?" said Allison.

"You mean the dead guy?" said Merle.

"Yeah," said Allison. "Him."

"There were other guys too, right? You saw them, right?"

She didn't know this was a topic. A *thing*.

"I didn't see squat," said Allison.

Except a plane taking off. And one face.

"And you haven't heard nothing?"

"Has anybody?"

She had only heard that the wildlife officials remained keen on finding the shooter of the vulture-pecked doe. They could make an illegal kill sound as bad as a case of capital murder. It was.

"Like it never happened," said Merle. Allison heard a touch of genuine disappointment. "Like the world has moved on."

Enough time had passed that the conspiracy theorists must now be on their fourth iteration of how a guy could die and how his story could vanish without a trace—no sign of investigation, no friends and family in an uproar.

Duncan still poked around on the story. He'd kept her in the loop.

They were single file on the dark trail now, two miles to camp and all flat or down. Two miles to dinner. And Colin. And tequila.

She set a good pace. A few inches of snow clung to the ground in the north-facing woods but not up here on the windblown plateau.

"The guy even put the first newspaper story up," said Merle. "When it first happened. It's taped to the cash register with a sign."

"It says 'Let me know if you know anything about this,'" said Dwayne.

Allison's headlamp punched a hole in the darkness. She had an urge to leave Colin with the troops, ride out tonight and be camped on the front stoop of the liquor store by the time it opened in the morning, to question this guy.

A girl could fantasize.

"You're regulars?"

"Enough," said Merle. "Aren't a whole lot of options in Silt."

"But you don't know his connection to the crash?"

"No."

"Or the dead guy?"

"Not really," said Dwayne. "Seems kind of weird, doesn't it? Like the government not explaining those UFOs down in Area 51."

Allison liked to tell herself that odd shit in the Flat Tops was just that—odd and unusual. The last few years, now including Devo's unexplained demise, suggested otherwise. Odd shit was normal.

"I leave that to the cops," said Allison.

"But the cops haven't done anything and you were there."

"Sort of," said Allison.

Eyewitnesses couldn't see everything. Sometimes she felt that life involved a series of events where she peered down a long, dark alley and caught glimpses of the action as it flashed by in the well-lit street beyond.

"Don't you want to know?"

These guys needed acting lessons. And a better script with a few more subtleties.

"It's been a long time since I gave it much thought," said Allison.

She might have gone a whole hour—once.

Devo.

Dead guy in the flying weed wagon.

In both cases, she had pinged and ponged off every possibility. She had made more than a few inquiries, but the balls kept bouncing.

No satisfaction.

"I thought the cops would do what they do," said Allison.

"Don't you think they owe people an explanation?" said Merle.

Allison let a few strides turn time into dust. "Maybe."

"But you don't care?"

A metal clasp on Dwayne's backpack tinkled against his dangling canteen in an odd counter rhythm, as it had all day. They were up here hunting only one thing—and it sure as hell wasn't elk.

"I've learned to keep my head down," she said. "Can't really say I've got much of a stake in any of that mess."

"Strange deal," said Merle.

Allison inhaled to the count of ten, a mini-meditation. Arcturus blinked into place, low on the horizon. It marked the same spot where the sun would be if this was July.

Later, over a nightcap with Colin far off in the woods, they would come up with a plan. She couldn't peel off from camp. But she could be ready to go when the hunt ended. Her best ticket out might be filling one of the tags, but that would mean putting Colin with these two and sending them off a couple hours before dawn, leaving the Arkansas crew without the guide they'd wanted.

But Colin's success rate put the *can* in uncanny. It might work.

A kill would get her out. Even in this snowless October, Colin could conjure a plump cow. It would be standing in the clearing where he wanted it to be, no different than a chubby rabbit gnawing on a carrot at the bottom of a black top hat waiting for the magician to come along.

Thirty-Two

Monday Morning
Duncan

They sat under a picnic shelter at Two Rivers Park. On this mild day, Jack Hallowell wore cowboy boots, blue jeans and a dark blue oxford shirt with a button-down collar. His short hair was prematurely gray.

"Why not say this when you announced?" said Duncan.

"Call it trust. I want people to know why and how decisions get made. The public has a right to know how you are going about that work."

Duncan's bullshit detector pegged over in the red zone. Few ordinary Joes and Josephinas had the time or interest to track a politician's every call or email, especially at the snooze-inducing level of Garfield County Commission. Hallowell's claim that he would post every email interaction reeked of pompous. What did a restaurant owner know about managing a political office?

Duncan also felt strangely subdued, a bit uncertain. Trudy had come home midmorning Sunday, then showered and crawled into bed. A first. She said she'd been up all night. She said she would explain—at some point. He had given her a wide berth all day—and night.

"So this website."

"It will be up tomorrow." Hallowell sat with his hands folded on the table, no notes in front of him, a beaten-up leather briefcase at his side. "I think you run a campaign the way you will serve in office. We'll post all campaign contributions within twenty-four hours. That's all checks that arrive. They will go in a holding zone for further review, find out who wants what before they are cashed. I'll publish my calendar for the day, and I'll finalize on a daily basis the schedule of meetings I held once the day was done. You're not writing this down."

"Your news release covers the same ground. The incumbent you're up against—are you suggesting that he's hiding something?"

The big Republican *R* on Bill Walters' chest stood for stability in Garfield County. It maintained the existing channels for backdoor handshakes.

"He's a fine man, I'm sure," said Hallowell.

"But?"

"But I haven't yet said one negative thing about my opponent."

"But?"

"*And*—note the big difference between *but* and *and*—I want to change the culture of politics. Of representing people. It's become too confusing, too inscrutable."

A lone purple raft drifted down the Colorado River. A pair of kayaks hugged the shore further upstream. Sun sparkled off the water as it dripped from their churning paddles.

The late-season river flow, coupled with last year's poor snowpack, resulted in a fear factor the same as sitting on your living room couch. This election was no different—a smooth ride home for Bill Walters. The real election happened at the primaries on the *R* side, when Bill Walters faced no opposition.

Theoretically, Walters' ongoing reign meant good things for Clay Rudduck and, therefore, for Duncan Bloom. Duncan thought about his $81K about three hundred times a day. Sometimes it was a worry. Others, it was a prayer. Still others, it made perfectly logical sense that he should be able to pull off such an all-American thing as making a timely investment and cashing in.

"Let me ask you about other issues."

Hallowell nodded.

"Development?" said Duncan.

"We've talked plenty about that."

"A last-minute check." Duncan opened the recording app on his phone.

"I'm for the right projects. It's got to be managed."

"Health care?"

"Not a county issue."

"But a litmus test nonetheless."

"We have to move toward single payer."

"Gun control?"

"Again, it's not—"

"Same thing."

"Horses are out of the barn but, yes, tougher controls on assault weapons and amassing ammunition. And more work on mental health screenings and tightening the rules on hospital holds."

"Abortion?"

"*Roe v. Wade* is the law of the land. I'd like to see more funding for women's health programs, too, of all kinds."

Typical D . . .

"Marijuana?"

"No need to rock the boat, so to speak, at the county level. It's available, it's legal, it's here—keep it the way it is with each community deciding about retail and zoning in grow operations if they want them."

"Number one biggest issue at the county level?"

"Keeping our roads in good shape." Hallowell swiped this one from his *R* counterparts. "They're the key."

Duncan hadn't focused much on the commission campaign, given the other distractions—the ongoing question mark about Devo's demise and the big fat dead end on the plateau above Crescent Lake where the plane had crashed. He should be treating Hallowell like a contender. In theory, he was one.

But Hallowell's combination of sanctimony and naiveté, Duncan figured, would cause internal bleeding.

At his desk, he drafted the main part of a 500-word story in less than an hour. Before filing it, he did a quick online search of cities and towns where Hallowell had lived before moving to one of the condos by the river in New Castle and opening up the restaurant in downtown Glenwood Springs. Being a restaurant owner was a new thing after years in commercial real estate. Stints included Colorado Springs (three years), Kansas City (four years), Los Angeles (one year). Hallowell's skipping-stone resume made as much sense as his Pollyanna platitudes and platform. He'd gotten lucky with his eatery Fork, hoped to parlay his popularity into power.

172

Duncan needed a reaction from Walters, who treated his opponent like a pesky bug buzzing his ear.

The line to Commissioner Walters went right through, no palace guard.

"Quote me as saying that our office is an open book and has been since day one," said Walters.

"That's the verbal equivalent of Cream of Wheat," said Duncan.

"Which makes it perfect," said Walters. "I know you want a spicy jalapeno, but that's all I got."

"How about off the record?"

On his computer, a page opened up from *The Colorado Springs Gazette* that gave Duncan a juicy jolt of glee.

"Off the record," said Walters, "he sounds like an idealist who couldn't buy a clue if he had a million dollars."

"That's what I'm talking about," said Duncan.

"And if I see any part of that in print, you'll be walking back to Denver stripped of every personal possession two minutes after the paper hits the streets."

"There's the kindhearted Commissioner Walters I've grown to love and admire." Duncan pictured the diminutive man, partial to light-colored suits, Western shirts and bolo ties. Cowboy boots boosted him up a few inches, but he hadn't ridden a horse or stepped on a ranch in twenty years.

"At your service," said Walters.

Duncan knew he had started triangulating a town's power centers when a politician like Walters trusted him enough to piss all over his enemies in private, allowing the reporter to better read the political battlefield.

"What would you say if I told you that back in 2010 in Colorado Springs, one Jack Hallowell led a Christian-based campaign against the legalization of marijuana and was arrested outside a medical dispensary for disrupting its business?"

"My esteemed and scholarly opponent?"

"Him."

"Arrested?"

"Yes," said Duncan. "Crime goes up and your IQ goes down—that was the theme of his campaign. He quoted all sorts of bible, New Testament and Old."

There were nineteen arrests in all, but Hallowell served as the group's spokesperson. He was quoted as an "area businessman" affiliated with an ultraconservative Christian group known to give money to any cause that would re-center the country's values to the glory days of 1955. How had he missed this?

"Commissioner?"

Duncan thought he could hear the crack of Walter's high-backed leather chair, the one with a pump handle that put Walters on an even keel when it came to peering over his desk.

"Yes, you nosy cocksucking mole, you know the taxpayers expect as their number one priority that I wait on your journalistic needs night and day, so what do you need from me now?"

"Care to comment?"

If Hallowell had a notion to slip into office and then reveal his anti-drug sentiment, it was about to go up in, well, smoke. Duncan suddenly felt more comfortable about his investment, knowing status quo would make it easy for Rudduck to do his thing.

"No."

"Off the record?"

"Shortest campaign in the history of campaigns," said Walters. "If Mr. Hallowell hasn't come clean about his true beliefs, then I think the newspaper ought to do its public duty and make sure this righteous asshole is shown the political door. The one marked exit."

Thirty-Three

"A kiss is not a green light."

Rachel Crouse looked more teacher than lawyer.

"It feels like they're coming after *me*."

"It's a big case, big names."

Crouse wore a black turtleneck. Her likable demeanor was unpretentious and endearing, a touch Lily Tomlin. She wore a streak of gray in her long russet hair.

Trudy wanted Duncan by her side, or Allison. But then they'd know everything she'd done. She had only told Duncan that she got way higher than she'd ever been before, that she wasn't even sure what had happened inside Sam Shelton's house. She'd done her best to reassure Duncan, but she still didn't have the courage to tell him everything.

They met in Crouse's upstairs office across from the courthouse, nothing fancy.

Trudy wasn't sure what rumors were flying but it wouldn't take much to put two and two together, with the "reports of an assault" at Sam Shelton's famous tomato farm in the morning newspaper. Her months of work with Shelton were well known. Plus the crew had left the two of them there. Alone.

And there were the two deputy sheriffs who had shown up, one ten minutes after the first. And paramedics tended to Shelton and then he'd been taken to the Pioneers Medical Center. There were plenty of moments for the gossip train to leave the station.

The crack of Sam Shelton's skull had stayed with her, but not as much as the terror that led up to it and that woozy state when the room flipped and tumbled.

God, she did not want to see him ever again. Or hear one of his songs, if she could help it. And now, more than anything else, the NatGeo footage, every muffed take and every bit of the good stuff, too, must be used as tinder for a bonfire and destroyed.

"After you hit him, did he do anything further? Struggle?"

"No," said Trudy.

"And you called the police?"

"My phone was dead." She hated reliving it. "I drove into town at three miles an hour, found a convenience store and they let me use the phone."

When the first cop showed up, she'd struggled to say what had happened. No doubt he could smell the booze. And weed.

Both *legal*. Private property. Sometimes you had to remind yourself that pot was legal.

"Awful," said Crouse. "What an awful moment. Did they do a rape kit?"

"It didn't get that far."

"Did he take his pants down? Or off?"

The clink of the belt buckle—

"There was no doubt what he wanted."

"But his pants?"

"I heard the belt."

"Were his pants off?"

"I think so."

"Did he ejaculate?"

"No."

"Did he touch you?"

"It was like a tackle."

176

"You weren't feeling well?"

"Like I'd been slammed into a wall."

"You'd been drinking."

"And he smoked pot. And I inhaled." And a small drag here. And there.

"Did you pour the drinks?"

"I couldn't tell you." All memories after dinner were garbled, messy. "That's going to be a problem, isn't it?"

"Did you pour the drinks?"

Trudy shook her head. "Like I said."

"And you said it came on quickly."

"I know my limits. And I had called Duncan—"

"You used his phone then? And that was a change in plans? To not drive home?"

The implication was obvious.

"I had no plan on sleeping with him."

Had the thought of getting together with the ex-rock star crossed her mind? Had she felt the seduction of being with a man who had seen so much and yet who had taken control of his world, his environment, his time?

Yes, but . . .

"Could he have interpreted your message that you weren't heading home as something else?"

"The way he came at me wasn't like that. I'd stayed there before and he was a perfect gentleman."

Nearly perfect.

The inadvertent cock grab . . .

"Stayed there before?"

"It's a long drive from Meeker all the way home, to Sweetwater. It was another late night."

Crouse needed time to absorb that tidbit.

"Where were you right before it all happened?"

177

"Outside. On the porch."

"And did he make trips inside for wine?"

"Trips? Plural?"

"Yes."

"I'd say so, yes. Now that I'm thinking of it. Why?"

Why hadn't she given him a drunken blow job and gotten out of there? Or why hadn't she beaten his head to a pulp with the candlestick brick? Trudy had played out both scenarios a thousand times, varying the level of compliance or anger, depending on the degree of light in her daydream.

"I poked around." Crouse reached for another yellow pad that sat closer to her computer. "New York City, 1999. Charlottesville, 2004. And one after the first Bonnaroo Festival in Manchester, Tennessee. I have no idea where that is. 2002."

"And?"

A shudder rattled Trudy's chest.

"I didn't even have to dig that hard. All three said they felt drugged. The one at Bonnaroo tested positive for methaqualone."

Trudy shrugged.

"Quaaludes," said Crouse. "A friend found her unconscious in the dirt near a stranger's tent the next morning. She'd been raped. No shorts, no shoes. She last remembered walking into his motor home near the What Stage. They arrested Shelton, held him for thirty-six hours and let him go."

One word came to Trudy's mind—*fool*.

"The Bonnaroo woman heard about the Charlottesville one and she came forward, but there wasn't enough for one jurisdiction to put together a case."

"And then?"

"And then it died down."

"It was in the news?"

"Entertainment news, syndicated shows. The music press. *Drudge Report*. Came and went."

Fool, dupe. Basic stupidity . . .

"From everything we can gather, he likes them semi-unconscious."

"Quaaludes?" said Trudy. She had no question he had wanted to fuck her.

"A sedative and a hypnotic. Or Rohypnol, the date-rape drug. If it was the latter, it should have come with a bitter taste. They pack a wallop."

A drug would explain lots, but it wouldn't mean absolution.

"Do you think he could have slipped something into your drink?" said Crouse. "Would have?"

Could she assert that she hadn't encouraged him at all?

"Possible." She conjured the rolling floor like the deck of a ship. But specific detail felt elusive, like a black hole with fuzzy edges. "So where does this go?"

"It goes where we want it to go."

"I could be charged with assault."

"Possible, but Shelton's pants were down around his ankles when they found him knocked out, so I don't know about that. You hit him good."

Crouse had already estimated the time—she figured it was thirty minutes between the blow and cops heading back up to Shelton's house. How they had found him, in the living room, was included in their report.

"So I could be charged."

"I don't see Sam Shelton pressing charges. The police? Hard to tell but I can't picture it. Pretty clear case of self-defense. The question is, do you have the fortitude to go after him?"

"What about the show?"

"File a lawsuit against the producers for hiring talent with a questionable past?"

"Make sure it's never shown—anywhere."

"We could negotiate that one," said Crouse. "I think they'd listen rather than face a civil trial. It wasn't that hard to dig up his previous stunts."

"So it's the charges against him for the attempted—"

"Rape," said Crouse. "Yes."

"And you bring in the others?"

"Charlottesville, Bonarroo, everywhere. We put out the word and I bet a few more will surface—women who felt ashamed or embarrassed. Women who had no idea what happened or why they woke up naked in a strange room, you know? Strength in numbers."

"But we can't *prove* we were drugged."

"Well, it would be great if you had found a container of quaaludes while you were at his house," said Crouse. "But the fact is, that pattern will be apparent. You know, it's his method of attack. You can give the money back and walk away, or you can fight for what's right and put Sam Shelton out of business, in more ways than one. For good."

And in order to do that, she realized, she would have to discuss every single encounter that preceded the assault—the long kiss, the flirting, trips to his house, the wine and more wine, and what exactly did she expect him to think? The cock grab, too. Would he mention it? To save jail time, why wouldn't he? All she knew was that the picture of a wine-guzzling, pot-smoking Trudy Heath would not jibe well with her public image as an ultrapure vegetarian who promoted healthy lifestyles and organic gardens in each and every home.

She could let Sam Shelton off the hook and maintain her reputation, whatever that was.

Or let herself be dragged through the muck and put an asshole out of commission.

Trudy inhaled. "Whatever it takes," she said. "I'm not ready. But I'll try to get there."

Thirty-Four

Tuesday Morning
Allison

One clean shot to the lung. The elk had buckled, staggered four wobbly paces and keeled over. The bull's antlers were trophy class—long points, long beams and a wide spread.

"Nice piece of shooting right there."

Colin had worked all morning to make Merle and Dwayne feel at ease.

"Now you," said Dwayne, handing over his phone to take another photo.

"Not mine," said Merle.

"Then the both of us."

"No thanks," said Merle. "All you, bro."

Armed with a plan, Colin had promoted the 4:30 a.m. departure and the four-mile uphill hike with the enthusiasm of a summer camp counselor. They'd had to wait a day. The Arkansas crew had insisted on Colin's time. "The spot I'm thinking about is dependable," Colin had boasted. "The key is to leave it alone every other year."

Twenty minutes after sunup, the hard morning chill making it difficult to stay put, this bull walked out of the woods as if he had an appointment.

"Jesus, what a feeling," said Dwayne. "Aren't we supposed to thank him for giving us his life before we cut him to pieces?"

An elk would have a better chance of hearing the appreciation before the bullet flew, but Allison let the question go. Such statements seemed like twenty-first-century attempts to wrap yourself in a cloak of higher intelligence and pseudo-spirituality.

Plus, these guys weren't here to stock freezers.

Dwayne stood up, stepped back. He blew in his hands, then shoved them in his pockets. "How can the sun be up but it feels colder than an hour ago?"

Colin and Dwayne plucked knives out of sheaths on their belts. Merle kneeled down close, his own knife at the ready, but was left to watch as Colin and Dwayne worked like a couple of old surgeons. Allison gave the three plenty of space and found a rock for a sit, doing her best imitation of routine and normal even as she calculated the hours until she'd be able to scram. The elk had gone down on the edge of a high clearing not much bigger than the space between her A-frame and Trudy's house back in Sweetwater. The clearing fell away on a steep slope. Her perch offered a view off to the east as the sun ripped open the day. The three blaze orange vests popped out against the field of gray-green brush and sage like neon tulips.

The surgeons bagged the back strap about three minutes after they started, using Colin's gutless method of field dressing. Colin could take an elk apart in less time than it took her to make breakfast. She preferred not to watch the blow-by-blow transformation of game to food. There was no explaining her running a business that depended on random death when the mere existence of random death was the reason she had retreated to the Flat Tops.

The sharply edged horizon offered a firm reminder of the real meaning of time. She wrote poems in her head. At least, scraps. She started a few hundred a day, but had no idea about the middle or the close and no idea if words could illustrate how her heart felt about the things she sensed. She wished Whitman or Coleridge were here to whisper in her ear and tell her what she was feeling.

Thinking of Duncan snapped her back to the mission at hand and the tantalizing prospect that she was close to nailing down one firm fucking lead in the vacuum of soulless silence that had grown around the upended plane and its dead passenger, the guy she could have saved.

The wrecked plane and Devo's demise lived side by side in her head. The two puzzles took turns like tag-team wrestlers. When one grew weary, the other was ready.

They had been joined by a third problem, getting Trudy back on her feet.

Merle stood beside her, his camo-covered thigh at eye level. He cupped an unlit joint between his index finger and thumb in the classic, gotta-hide-this-stuff mini-grip.

"As long as you're in shape to help pack out," said Allison. Plenty of hunters brought a flask for a nip here or a swallow there, so what was the difference?

Merle lit the joint in quick fashion. She waved it off when he offered. He sucked hard, tipped his head back. He closed his eyes. At a point fifteen seconds beyond when Allison would have keeled over from holding her breath, he blew out the smoke. He waited ten seconds and repeated the whole process.

The stinky-sweet smell obliterated the traces of alpine. Allison thought pot smelled like a skunk perfumed-up for a date.

"Since it's early in the hunt and we still have your cow tag to fill, I can take your meat out tonight." Colin and Dwayne bagged the quarters. Allison stood to help. She'd become a master at tying pack frames. "If you want."

"Sure." Merle took another deep toke on his joint.

"You got a processor picked out?"

"We got a freezer waiting at Shames' place."

A well-known processor, Shames' service was located a quarter mile before the Sweetwater Road began at the Colorado River. Shames was known for all-nighters during the season and complete use of every scrap of meat.

"Easy," said Allison. "I know them."

"I can go with."

He took a final puff and pinched-off the remaining half with his fingers.

"Me and Sunny Boy and a packhorse or the mule," said Allison. "Probably Hercules. You guys stay and hunt."

"Coming back?"

"Sure—tomorrow or the next day," said Allison. *La-dee-dah.* "You're in good hands."

"We want the hide, too—everything," said Merle. "Dwayne has done some tanning."

Allison had no quarrels with the use-everything philosophy. "No problem," she said. It was possible the boys would need two trips.

Dwayne found a shady spot in the woods and a suitable branch to hoist up the meat they couldn't carry. They tied on their pack frames, then put their day packs on their chests. Merle tried not to show the strain from sixty pounds of dead weight. Allison got the head, a good thirty-pounder with the antlers. She'd need a wide path through the woods and a slow pace through tight spaces. No sudden moves. Colin rigged up a rope so the head wouldn't bounce. At least, that was the theory. Based on the way Merle shifted his weight and worked to get comfortable, their trek to camp would be a challenge. Thighs would burn. Ankles would ache. Allison recalibrated the day ahead, told herself to keep patience as a pal. If she was anxious, they'd know.

Inside, she churned. She'd been too willing to assume it would all come tumbling out—how a pot-filled plane could crash in the wilderness and how a guy could get murdered at the scene without anyone making a noise, registering a complaint or fucking doing anything. Wasn't there a natural order of questions-and-answers that required the information to spill?

Same with Devo. She had been too patient, assuming that law enforcement would do everything it could.

Allison insisted they all drink water. She passed out jerky and Trudy's homemade energy bars—nuts and figs and chewiness. Dwayne took an apple. He looked unconcerned about the hike and not at all tired from the hunt or the deboning work. Merle complained about the balance of his frame and Colin worked to adjust the load. They weren't yet moving and Merle already looked weary, staggering a bit under Colin's manipulations. Merle, in fact, was glassy-eyed.

"Fuckin' A." Dwayne saw it, too. "You okay, bro?"

Merle hacked and coughed. He spat.

He staggered. Colin braced him with an arm on his bicep.

Merle blew out a heavy breath, found his balance.

Merle took a tentative step but tripped on his own boot and spun around, his face to the sky.

Colin scampered out of the way as the whole live weight and dead weight came tumbling down and Merle landed on his back, and the fat backpack and his body arched with a garish thud and the short, sharp crack of busted bone.

Thirty-Five

"Why do reporters always want to go off the record?"

Duncan caught Deputy Sheriff Christie in his SUV in the parking lot behind the HQ in downtown Meeker.

"I'm trying to make a few shortcuts, that's all." Even standing, Duncan had to look up, given the height of the official rig.

"What's this connected to?"

"It's not connected to anything."

Sometimes when you chatted with businessmen or the government, it felt as if you were hollering across the Grand Canyon. When *they* needed a reporter to make a point or push an agenda, the gap was like a sidewalk crack.

"I'm not in the habit of giving reporters names of individuals we are watching for active investigations around dealing drugs," said Christie. "Do they do things differently over in Garfield County?"

He'd come on too strong. He should have angled into it, made it about the tenth question. Even then, he should have made it sound offhand.

"Anything new at all on the death of Devo?"

The radio inside the truck screeched in pain. Christie took a moment to make an adjustment.

"Is that why you drove up here?"

"One reason." He hoped this wouldn't take long, maybe head back to Glenwood Springs in a few hours. "Any official cause?"

"It's been two months—why now?"

186

"I've been calling the coroner every week, nothing new. Unusual, wouldn't you say?"

"Everything about Devo was unusual."

"Meaning?"

"Meaning from what I gather, that he was ingesting a variety of foods and substances that put his internal chemistry outside the norm."

"And you have no reason to think foul play?"

Christie shrugged. "We got no suspects, if that's what you mean, and no reason to suspect foul play. We have no wounds and no trauma, as you have reported now how many times?"

"Once or twice."

Or a dozen. Or twenty.

"We also have no major outcry, you know? Nobody seems to be too concerned except you and a few online bottom-feeders."

It occurred to Duncan to ask if the sheriff's office pursued murder investigations with zeal and pep only when there was a "major outcry," but he went for conciliatory, not smarmy.

"Was there anyone in town that Devo was seeing? You know, on his trips into Meeker for scraps?"

Duncan had asked Devo's sister, Glenna, for an interview about Devo, a kind of who-saw-him-last piece, but Glenna said she wanted to keep a low profile and declined.

"Everyone of interest could account for their whereabouts," said Christie.

"And that's that?"

"Unless the coroner coughs up a theory we can work with."

Duncan found Brett Merriman in his back office at the grocery store.

"Trudy okay?" he said.

"She's been better." Trudy was in a funk, but Duncan would not betray what little he knew.

"I saw something happened out at Sam Shelton's place," said Merriman. "Don't ask me why but I never trusted that guy—all those antics on stage seemed a bit forced to me, but what the hell do I know? We'd still welcome a visit from Trudy's smiling face—you know, tell her that would you?"

"Sure," said Duncan.

"What brings you up this way?"

"Checking on Devo," said Duncan. "Poking around on other stuff, too."

"Nothing new on Devo. What other stuff?"

Merriman's age was all wrong for the next question. So was his status as the owner of a prominent business. But Merriman always wanted to help. He was a connector, a fixer.

"I know it's a small town," said Duncan. "But there are issues, right?"

"Of course."

"Like crime."

"You've written about it."

"And drugs."

Merriman shrugged. "It's America. And, again, you've written about some cases."

"I'm doing a story about the market for other drugs and how marijuana has affected prices and availability."

A flat lie.

"So you need dealers?"

"I'm not saying you know dealers, but—"

"Try the public defender? They might know. Maybe they have something current. Or recent."

Such an obvious idea. Inez Cordova—*damn*. Right under his

nose but seventy miles back down the road. Meeker's courthouse was served by the same judicial district as Glenwood Springs.

"I had a hunch you'd have an idea."

"I knew zip-ola about that side of things until one of my employees got caught up in something."

"Who?" he said.

Following Merriman's instructions, Duncan waited near the deli. He pretended to check his phone but watched as Merriman pulled a young woman aside near the end of a far aisle. For the most part, Merriman's sizable profile blocked his view, but Duncan made out long ginger hair and pale skin on a scrawny young woman with a bit of a slouch.

Merriman negotiated terms and brought her over. She wore a full-body black apron over a purple-checked cowgirl shirt and blue jeans.

She didn't smile.

"Colleen," she said. Weak handshake, dry skin. Her eyes bounced a bit. Duncan took a minute to explain himself, weighing the pros and cons of mentioning Sam Shelton by name. The town might be protective of their rock star. "I'm not looking for names," said Duncan. "And I won't use yours."

She nodded, but barely.

"Brett said you got caught up in legal trouble?"

Colleen looked at her boss.

"He's a friend," said Merriman.

"It was a party. An end-of-school party. Last June. A bunch of them were heading off to college, trade school, the military—you know? We got the noise going, I guess. Music and stuff. And then a bonfire and somebody brought edibles and, after all that beer and tequila, you know."

Again, Colleen looked to her boss for approval. He nodded.

"Bunch of us passed out. I mean, *conk*. I guess the fire got out

189

of control and the next thing was the fire department hosing down trees."

"Where?"

"Down near the river over on the other side of town."

"And cops?"

"I woke up in the clinic. Found out later there were lots of cops."

"You were charged?"

"For the drinking, yeah, and the edibles."

"To be clear, marijuana or mushrooms?"

"Mushrooms?" She looked surprised. That answered it.

"Were there joints, too?"

Colleen kept her grim face. "Everything."

"Was there one supplier?"

"Two guys," she said. "Crashers, what else? I guess we were kind of loud."

At the courthouse, after getting details from Colleen, who testified in exchange for leniency, Duncan pulled the cases against Jimmy Ferrera, 24, and Ricardo Loya, 23. Both upstanding Meeker residents who, when arrested at the scene with two dozen recent high school graduates, all three years too young for the alcohol or the pot, had three ounces of marijuana and a wide assortment of colorful pills and edibles, including chocolates and cookies. Duncan had no question about what Jimmy and Ricardo were hoping to score if they could dial in the precise amount of relaxation that would encourage some of Meeker's recent female high school grads to lose their tops and shorts.

"You find the strangest threads."

Inez Cordova made it clear she was busy and didn't have time for the usual banter.

"You remember the case."

"Like it was yesterday."

"Think they'll know?"

Duncan stood in the park outside the courthouse. Leaves littered the lawn. A cool breeze said October was giving way to Antarctica. His gut wobbled—it warned he was chasing a wild goose. Nobody, in fact, chased the tame ones. He should ask around where to find Sam Shelton's place, jam tomatoes down his throat with a wooden spoon. Maybe fifty.

"You want me to wrangle an introduction because I defended them in court and they still got the max?"

"Maybe they know something," said Duncan. "Maybe a name came up."

"The Colorado Department of Corrections manages their routines now. Five years each—there were loaded guns in their car, too, and concentrates."

"I need one who knows the scene up here."

"You think this is Haight-Ashbury? 1968?"

"You know what I mean."

Duncan knew it took a while in any town to spot the scruffy side, the pockets where people were hanging on by their bitten-up fingernails.

"You sound so desperate I almost want to help."

"What do I have to do to get rid of the *almost*?"

"Jesus," said Cordova. "Give me three minutes."

Duncan sat on a bench near the edge of the park, checked his email, checked Facebook, checked Twitter, listened to two innocuous voice mails and thought about calling Clay Rudduck after Inez called back. But to say what?

He pulled out the mind-meld voodoo spell he cast whenever he needed a source to cough up on deadline. "Fucking call back, fucking call back, fucking call back," he muttered.

191

Her name popped on the screen.

"*Hablar conmigo*," said Duncan. That spell was a keeper.

"I'm hanging up if you attempt one more word in Spanish."

Duncan sighed. "You're no fun."

"As a matter of fact," she said, "the opposite is true."

"What did you find?"

"I called a friend in social services."

"And?"

"And it's not as if there's an address I can give you."

"How about ten? Or a dozen?"

He'd follow every lead. Then what? Ask them all if Sam Shelton was one of their customers?

"What are you looking for?"

"A person who knows easy places to score pills." He would never break Trudy's confidence.

"That's too general. What kind of drugs? It's not like there's a milk truck and a route to follow."

"Quaaludes," said Duncan. "Or anything like them."

"There's nothing quite like them."

"Speaking from experience?"

"Yes," said Cordova. "Experience in court cases. Quaaludes are long gone unless you have a way to import the street version from South Africa."

"Benzo-whatever-they-call-it, then," said Duncan.

"Benzodiazepine. You sound desperate."

"It's important."

"It's not a story?"

"Of course it's a story." Or would be. One day. A story of a certain kind.

"I had a case a couple years ago," said Cordova. "Los Koros."

Duncan remembered it—wiretaps, a few dozen people arrested, major prosecution of a network being run out of a Mexican restaurant a few blocks west from Merriman's grocery store. Cocaine, meth and wiretapped conversations from Atlanta to Oklahoma City. "The salsa case," he said.

"Class 2 felony racketeering," said Cordova.

"A big network, if I recall. Out of that little restaurant." When the wiretaps recorded frequent references to "chicken," the defense prosecutors claimed it was all innocent references to animals needed for religious sacrifice.

The jury managed to stifle a laugh. A "chicken" was a box big enough to hold a Jersey Giant—in this case, a box full of cocaine.

"Couple of those on the fringes of that operation got light sentences," said Cordova.

"Thanks to you."

"I'd like to think."

"I need names."

"That's what the court files are for."

"Except you could save me so much time."

"One kid who was helpful was a guy named Jose Osuna," said Cordova. "Probably twenty-two now, or twenty-three. I think he got a job at that big grocery store. Last I heard, anyway."

"Now what?" Merriman said it with a smile.

"Don't mean to interrupt," said Duncan. "Again."

"Anything, anytime." He had found Merriman out in the parking lot, helping load a car with groceries. "The friends-of-Trudy ticket. Name it. How was the courthouse?"

"Illuminating."

"And now?"

"You got a guy working for you named Jose Osuna?"

Merriman startled at the mention.

"Sure. He's paid his dues, though. He feels bad about the whole thing. Everybody is still wondering how a big network was being run out of a tiny town like ours, but if that's your angle you gotta leave him alone. For now."

"Is he working today?"

"Works every day, every minute I let him. He walks around like he's wounded, you know? He's rebuilding a reputation."

"I can't talk to him? With you there?"

It took ten minutes for Merriman to explain to Osuna that the information wouldn't be used against him.

Osuna was dark-skinned, medium height and scared. He wore a stained white apron. A blue-tinged net encased thick black hair. They stood out on the west side of the building at the one-slot loading dock. Duncan pled with the journalism gods for a delivery of his own.

From his back pocket, Duncan pulled a sheet of paper and unfolded a copy of a *Post-Independent* story about Sam Shelton, complete with a sharp picture of the rock star in his prime.

"Mandrax," said Duncan. "Buttons. Ludes. 714s. Soapers. Recognize him?"

"Sure." Osuna's English was perfect. "I used to make deliveries. He's a good tipper."

Thirty-Six

Merle spent the first half hour guaranteeing them it was no heart attack. He spent the next half hour moving to a sitting position, after wriggling out of his pack like an old snake shedding its last skin. The way he babied his spine and chest, Allison guessed he had at least a couple of broken ribs and damage to a vertebra or two. Every inhale generated agony. He blamed the elevation. "Head rush," he said over and over. "I get 'em."

Colin and Dwayne had gone on ahead. They would figure out a way to get help.

"Screwed this up," he said.

It wasn't the first apology.

Allison stood, sat, stood again. They were stuck in a dense pine forest. If Merle had keeled over out in the field where they'd cleaned the elk, she could be snoozing in the sunshine. Back here in the trees, a fire might make sense. Something to do. She couldn't nap, for obvious reasons.

"It happens," she said.

"I think you're blaming the pot."

"I'm not blaming." She smelled the weed on him every time she held a water bottle to his lips. Even Merle's arm movements required back muscle—a motion you took for granted until it didn't work without pain. "You get up here, you better have Plan B and Plan C right on down the line."

"I did a nice edible with breakfast, too. I'm still a little baked. What's your poison?"

The elk head sat on the ground, its cape rolled up and tucked underneath. It looked to Allison like the bull had popped his head above the ground, a funny-looking prairie dog. The giant antlers, however, were a poor choice for efficient burrowing.

"Tequila," she said.

"Pot and tequila is a damn fine combination," said Merle. "You hit the right combination and bang, you're flying."

Merle had no reason to know it, but the word *flying* failed as an enticement.

Allison dug in her pack, wending her way through the antler thicket, for another bottle of water.

"You don't get high? Legal and all?"

She did a quick inventory of the protein bars and jerky, if it came to that.

"No," she said.

"These days you can dial in your buzz and park yourself for a few hours in a peaceful and hazy spot that is to your liking—intensity and mood, everything."

She rummaged around in the dark interior of the backpack. Maybe she'd find a wormhole. Besides figuring out a way for Merle to move so they could get out of here, all his meat needed to get packed out, too. And soon.

"You got your phone on you?"

"Of course," said Merle. "What for? Useless as yours up here."

"Power it up for me. You mind?"

Merle pulled it from a shirt pocket underneath his blaze vest, his face strained in agony with every movement. He punched the power button, waited and held it out in his palm.

It was an old-school flip phone.

"No bars," said Merle. "When are they gonna put cell towers up here in the wilderness? Not a bad idea for—"

Allison closed the phone with a sharp snap and hurled it into the woods.

"What the hell?"

She could pick it up later. It hadn't flown far. The toss was for getting attention.

Allison grabbed Merle's Weatherby, leaning by a tree not too far from Merle's grasp. She put it with her stash of stuff.

"What are you—?"

"What else you got?"

Merle shrugged.

"Hand me your knife."

"What the hell?"

Allison reached in, certain he was in no shape for sudden movements, and unsnapped the clasp. She slid out a six-inch skinner knife with a black handle. It looked brand new. She gave it an underhand toss toward Mr. Elk Head. It clinked like a horseshoe against the metal frame on her pack. Mr. Elk Head remained unconcerned.

"What the hell?"

"You got another gun of any sort?"

"No—"

She was already digging into his pack. Her hand wrapped around a thick grip. She held it up.

"Forgot I'd packed that."

She hit the clip release and let it drop in her palm. A shiny silver bullet sat at the top. The witness holes showed the clip was full. So did the weight in her hand.

"Yeah," said Allison. "Believe you."

She pocketed the bullet, put the clip back in the gun and took a minute to bury the weapon deep in her pack.

"What else?"

"Nothing."

"Stand up."

"I don't get what's going on."

"Yes you do. Stand up."

"You're not going to make me stand."

"It's only pain."

"Shit," he said. "I'm empty. Knife, rifle and that gun I forgot about."

"Up," she said. "Or I hike out of here and forget where we left you. And I'm taking every bit of food and water."

The air didn't move. Way off, a woodpecker thrummed.

Merle jammed two hands against the tree trunk behind him and shimmied to a standing position, bracing himself and twisting sideways. He favored his right side. "Son of a bitch." His head tipped back. He squeezed up his whole face. Once erect, he took a few deep breaths and patted himself down.

"Nothing," he said.

"Turn around."

"What are you doing?"

"Pull your pockets inside out."

She didn't want to get too close again.

The left pocket produced a cigarette lighter, loose change and a full, fat joint. The right yielded a pack of matches, a blue thumb drive, a small, red, single-bladed pocketknife and more loose change. The knife said Greenway CC on one side. The blade was small but sharp and also looked brand new.

"Greenway?" she said.

"Hell, I don't know."

The underhand horseshoe toss. *Tink*. A ringer.

She pocketed the thumb drive, didn't try to hide it.

"Hey."

"Objection noted. What's on it?"

She stood straight in front of him, eight feet off. She still had to look up.

"Nothing," he said. "Don't even know why I had it."

"Then you won't miss it."

"Who the hell are you?"

"That'd be a better question for you."

One thing about clients—when they showed up with the right size group on the right day with the right kind of general gear and when the person who booked it said his name, there was never a point to check IDs or hunting licenses.

"Merle Fucking Bates."

"Unusual middle name."

He spat.

"Now give me something closer to the truth. Or all the way is fine if you want to save time."

"What the hell?"

"You're up here to watch me."

"You're paranoid."

"You're as obvious as a set of googly eyes."

She'd felt the stares from Merle and Dwayne. She knew for certain she'd never understand the ability of men to find a scrap of pleasure in ogling a petite, small-chested, dressed-in-layers woman up in the woods, but these two had made her feel, at times, naked.

"I don't know what the fuck you're talking about."

"And you happened to turn up in my hunt with a whole bunch of questions about the plane crash."

"The whole valley's talking about that." He palmed the right side of his rib cage and shuddered in pain. "Fuck!"

"The point is that nobody is talking about it. A plane crashes in the wilderness and nobody knows nothing. Let's see the wallet."

"Come and get it."

Merle's rifle felt good in her hands. She made a little circle with the barrel, shook her head. "Let's review," she said.

The wallet landed between them. It was overstuffed. Papers and the corner of a twenty jutted from its guts. Inside, more hundreds than she had time to count. At least fifteen, maybe more. The face on the driver's license behind a well-stained plastic sleeve looked familiar.

"So it's Merle?"

He stared at her.

"Do they call you Vic, or do you insist on Victor?"

Victor Chanute, Glenwood Springs, CO, 5'11", 225 pounds.

"Fuck you."

"And your buddy's real name?"

Chanute spat—and caught his breath in agony. "I'm going to need another prescription."

"If you dinged your spine, it won't feel much better for about another eight weeks. If it's the ribs, six weeks. Your friend?"

"Dwayne."

"Okay, well, enjoy the rest of your day."

Allison gathered the collectibles—knife, gun, wallet—and stashed them in her backpack, where Mr. Elk Head waited with unblinking patience. The phone was located after a brief search, and it joined the rest of the junk.

"Wait—"

She gave the pack a yank on the straps and perched it on her right thigh so she could tuck an arm under the strap and slip the whole thing on. If Victor Chanute had been well briefed—and there was always a chance they had kept him clueless—he should be well aware that she had no problem leaving wounded men alone in the woods. And Chanute may as well have been tied to a tree, too. His range of mobility was even less than the last guy's.

"Colin knows the way to this spot. If you stay put, we should be back tomorrow."

She pulled a bottle of water from a side pocket and tossed it in his general direction. It rolled to a stop about ten feet from his boots. A granola bar followed. "The key is to ration and stay calm. Bears can sense panic like a cat on a tuna fish."

"You can't be fuckin' serious."

A second granola bar landed as a leaner off the bottle of water. Horseshoes—that was her sport.

"Dinner," she said. "Breakfast, too. If we're running late."

"I can't move."

"Good. You'll be easier to find."

In fact, if he started answering her questions, she might be screwed. Having to help him out of here by herself would be grueling—and eat up half a week. He might need Rocky Mountain Search and Rescue. And getting the helicopter rousted would be another fat suck of time.

Allison made a show of tightening the hip belt on her backpack.

Chanute said, "Ed Steadman. That's his name."

"From?"

"Same as me—Glenwood."

Tranquility reigned. Busted ribs and a cracked vertebra were the same as a gun to the temple if you faced the prospect of a solo hike out. Or crawl. Or death march.

"Who was the dead guy on the airplane?"

"I wasn't there."

"Come on now."

"I wasn't."

"But you knew him."

"Nobody did."

"He wasn't nobody if they came back and picked him up at

the tree and took him back to the crash."

"They knew the name he was using."

"So the fake name thing, you're familiar with that?"

"I need to sit back down."

He took a deep breath, grabbed the outside of his chest with one hand and braced his back against the tree as he shimmied back down. It hurt to watch. One big wince contorted his face on the final thump to earth.

"Let's start with the name he used."

"Harlan."

"Harlan what?"

"I don't know."

"But his real name?"

"Miguel Ramirez."

"Ramirez?" He looked whiter than vanilla ice cream. "We talking about the same guy?"

"I think I know what you're thinking," said Chanute. "Doesn't look like his name, right?"

"Who figured out his real name?"

"Not sure," said Chanute. "All I know is what they found."

"*They*?"

Chanute sipped his breaths. He stared off for a moment. His head slumped down. "I'm in trouble."

"Yes, you are. What was the name of the guy *they* killed?"

"Miguel Ramirez," said Chanute. "He was working for the cops."

Thirty-Seven

Wednesday Early Morning
Clay Rudduck

The text woke him up.
Meet 911.
1:18 a.m.

Maybe they'd slept two hours, who knew? She slept on her stomach, her sweet bare ass catching moonlight from the window. "What?" she said.

"I've gotta go."

"What?"

"They're back."

"*They* they? Them?" She moaned like it hurt to think.

"Yep."

"Now?"

"Never a good time."

"But I can't leave—I'd scare the hell out of the babysitter, coming home at this hour."

"Stay here," said Rudduck. He'd figured on the next-to-nothing tits. Slim frame to begin with and then all that running. He hadn't figured on her appetite or enthusiasm. They had done it twice, though where round one ended and round two began was lost in the haze.

"Where?" She didn't stir.

"Not far. I should be back in an hour. Two. I'll bring coffee."
She had until 10 a.m.

Maybe one more round. The daylight would be better. He wanted to see every inch of her and he wanted to see what her face looked like when she was telling him to do this and telling him to do that. Church lady? Mommy? Not really. Which reminded him. At age 35, he'd just fucked his first mommy. He'd always wondered if there would be a difference. The answer, in fact, was none. At least, not with her.

In the cab of his F-150, he could smell the pot. They had gotten high by the river, kissed, and then it was off to the groping. There was plenty of room in his pickup, given her small frame, but they drove back to his place.

At the small warehouse south of downtown, Rudduck slipped in a side door, found them all sitting in the metal folding chairs around the operation's sole desk, an industrial number from World War II. Fluorescent light flickered. They had a six-pack of beer, but didn't offer him one.

Rudduck skipped right over the weather.

"You're an hour late," he said. "Wait, let me see if that's right. Oh yeah, it's not an hour. It's two months."

Skip Grayson's tired eyes stared back behind dark-rimmed glasses. He looked like every other brewpub bro in town. "What's the difference?"

"Time," said Rudduck.

Grayson popped a cigarette out of his shirt pocket, lit it. "We called you once to tell you what we saw from the plane. Given everything, we laid low."

"Instinct," said Hedland. "Being careful."

Vince Hedland had curly black hair to his shoulders. Utah had been no diet camp, that was for sure. Next to Hedland, Tommy Than could pass for a college student. He believed in regular haircuts and he had one of those ageless Vietnamese faces that would look the same for decades. To slow that process further, he was a workout fiend and health food nut.

"We even applied for jobs," said Than. "Made it look like we had just moved to town."

"Like we cared," said Hedland.

Rudduck shrugged. "I don't get it."

Hedland shook his head. "Made sense to us. With the plane crash and the dead guy, it seemed like a good idea to be extra cautious."

"Side bet," said Grayson. "Rudduck's pissed. I lose."

"Two months!" said Rudduck. His head throbbed. He burped bourbon and Philly cheesesteaks.

Grayson stood, gave his cigarette a hard pull, made a small circle as he walked, hitched his leg up so he was half sitting on the front hood of a 1967 Ford Fairlane, Springtime Yellow. Puff condition.

"Careful," said Hedland. This was his auto body shop. The back third had been partitioned off to store all the goods. A small fortune had been spent on insulation and layers to keep the smell in check.

"After a day, I make a contact," said Grayson. "We've got the plane off-loaded. We clean the inside of that sucker for another day. The last round is Q-tips, okay?"

"We ain't got all night," said Rudduck.

"Whatever," said Grayson. "The contact happens to have seen this news item about the plane crash in the mountains and mentions it and then asks if there are going to be any issues. Yeah, there's a dead guy. And there's a couple on horseback got an eyeful, what was I gonna say?"

"You could have said that was someone else's problem, that you didn't know," said Rudduck.

"He made it sound like we'd wait a day or two. Didn't seem like a big deal."

"It was like you landed at Logan-Cache." In fact, they had put down at a grass strip ten miles out, a private hunting lodge. Business was slow, with the drought and no campfires, so the owner took a small cut to look the other way.

"Third day he doesn't answer my calls. By then, Hedland here has flown the plane back to its owner and drove the eight hours back to Logan. Fourth day, the same. Fifth day, he asks where we're staying and he sends an errand boy to tell us to cool our heels, he can't make the deal. Claims the climate ain't right."

"Where's the weed?"

"We're in two separate motels—Tommy and Vince in one, me in another. We meet for coffee, beers. Tommy here wants to get in a round of golf, but I vote no. It takes too long and you can't leave in the middle."

"Where's the weed?"

"We pack in a couple of good used footlockers from Army Surplus. Re-bag, re-seal and re-bag again. At the private landing strip, there's this barn. We might as well be milking cows. Nobody cares. The biggest risk is moving it to the storage unit— four trips in the Altima."

"We leave it sitting in a dry storage locker," said Hedland. He was the curator—made sure their network of growers raised compatible strains. And Hedland was the pilot, or claimed to be. But they wouldn't be here if he knew how to fly. "So we wait. One more time the errand boy comes around—tells us week after next. When we get the cash, he gets the key to the storage unit—the codes for the security gate and all that shit."

What a mess—about the same kind of mess he'd found above Crescent Lake.

When he'd killed Ramirez at the crash site, he'd heard the whole story.

Hedland puts the plane down when he realizes they don't

have the elevation or the power to get up and over. Grayson decides to hike out with "Dwyer" while Hedland and Than stayed with the crashed plane.

A few hours into the hike, Dwyer sprains his ankle. It swells up like a pregnant grapefruit. Grayson had said.

They camp for the night, out in the open. Grayson spots a deer. He takes one shot with his "Desert Eagle Motherfucker."

In the morning, the ankle isn't any better. Grayson whacks Dwyer in the head, completely out of the blue. He leaves him in a fog, tied up, then hikes down to Sweetwater and hitches a ride to a friend's place. The friend is named LJ, or Little Johnny. Pre-legalization, LJ had been known for the quality of his flower. He had even tried to convert to a legitimate grow, but gave up in the face of all the paperwork.

Grayson jumps on LJ's computer, looking for Harlan Dwyer. No such anybody—Facebook, anything. Dwyer had claimed he was from Minturn and had worked there. Bad choice. Grayson knew a bartender in Minturn who knew everyone in town. He called him. Never heard of a Harlan Dwyer and would have remembered such a stupid name.

Google turned up nothing.

Everything turned up nothing.

So Grayson followed a big fat hunch. When he'd shot the deer, he had "Harlan Dwyer" hold the head up as if he'd killed it. Grayson had snapped a photo with his phone. They took turns. A couple of big game hunters with an itty-bitty deer. Macho. Close up.

The one place Harlan Dwyer had seemed comfortable was talking about his work in construction. Outside Oak Creek, he'd claimed. Grayson had explained the whole situation to LJ, and LJ knew someone who did construction up that way and around Routt County. Little Johnny texted him the photo and he texted right back: *Miguel Ramirez.*

Even though the guy looked like he could have walked out of a Disney movie, his name was Miguel Fucking Ramirez.

Back to Google—"Miguel Ramirez + Colorado + arrest."

He had walked out of prison one year ago, but only two years into a six-year sentence for distribution of marijuana and controlled substances.

The age matched. And so did a tiny arrest photo in the Sterling newspaper because, no doubt, the Colorado State Patrol had wanted to make it clear they were watching for drivers headed out of state with Colorado's new cash crop. The photo was small and blurry. The hair was darker, but close enough.

So Grayson hikes back up, after making all the arrangements for the backup plane, and he finds empty water bottles he didn't recognize and Ramirez still tied up.

Grayson says nothing until they're back at the crash site, apologizes for tying him up but said he wanted to make faster time and didn't want Ramirez to wander off. Ramirez was pissed. Grayson says nothing about the water bottles he didn't recognize.

Rudduck had arrived at the crash site a few hours after dawn the next day. It had taken no time to end Ramirez' informant ways. He wasn't wearing a wire. His wallet looked all fake-like, including a credit card for Harlan Dwyer and a faked-up driver's license and other garbage.

Rudduck had spent the last two months in hell. His neck was broken from looking over his shoulder.

What had Dwyer-Ramirez relayed back to authorities? Maybe he hadn't been wearing a wire for the airplane ride to Logan, but how about before that, in the months of prep leading up? If the cops snuck an informant into their circle, they had a reason.

Hedland had vouched for Dwyer-Ramirez. Was Hedland a

leak, too?

Helen Barnstone?

She didn't flinch or seem on edge. And now, she'd fucked him good. And she hadn't been wearing a wire. He'd looked everywhere.

"Where's the cash?"

Grayson stood up, hoisted a large canvas duffel from the floor to the desk.

Rudduck zipped it open. Inside, on top, sat T-shirts and jeans and sweatshirts. Rudduck reached a hand down in the guts and pulled out a black messenger bag that felt appropriately heavy and plump. He opened the flap and looked inside, pulled out a sample pack.

"All hundreds?"

"And two fat packs of twenties," said Grayson.

After the cut to their suppliers, who grew more than they could ever consume for "medicinal" purposes, there would be $350K to split.

If the cops hadn't surfaced by now—

If the boys in the woods came back with an indication that Allison Coil was showing no interest—

If Bill Walters held onto his commission seat—

If, if, if—

Then the quiet backdoor operation, the occasional roundup of extra weed being cultivated by those with medicinal licenses for home gardens, could continue to pump up the income while Helen Barnstone and a small group of thoughtful, upstanding citizens applied for the county's first grow operation.

For now, Bill Walters was Mr. Status Quo. After the election, there would be "recalibration" regarding the tax revenue lost to neighboring counties. It would be thoughtful, measured discussion. Bill Walters would weigh the decision with credible sincerity.

Somehow, the cops had slipped Harlan Dwyer-Miguel Ramirez into his inner loop.

Was it possible Ramirez had failed to gather much of use? Rudduck insisted on nicknames all the way around—no slipups. If nobody knew nobody, the potential for moles was minimized. It was possible Ramirez had made no headway or had been too chicken to contact his cop handlers.

But Hedland had let him in.

Thirty-Eight

Wednesday Morning
Duncan

"Getting inside makes no sense—a few pills in that big house? They could be anywhere. And you're not a cop. And no warrant."

The view through the Camry's windshield took in the broad, flat sweep of land between the White River and downtown Meeker. Duncan had pulled over at a scenic overlook with a historical marker about Nathan Meeker's doomed mission.

"I have this urge to look that asshole in the eye—and maybe poke one out."

"If you have a witness, that will confirm enough."

He had spent a restless night at the Blue Spruce, unsure of his next move. He wanted to tell Trudy what he had found but didn't think it was enough.

After an early breakfast, he had texted Inez Cordova to see

if she was up. She responded with a thumbs-up emoji fifteen minutes later. He had told Inez as much as he knew, that something awful had happened between Trudy and Sam Shelton and that Trudy was pretty sure she'd been drugged and she'd had to whack him over the head. The tidbits had emerged from a series of conversations, Trudy slowly letting go of her initial reluctance to discuss it.

"It would scare them—down deep—if we had the actual pills," said Duncan.

"You're not thinking straight. You're not thinking at all, Duncan Bloom. What if you get caught? Then what? And how do you even explain how they were obtained? That's why cops have warrants, right?"

"If they knew a story would break about their precious ex-rock star host gone all organic and back to nature but who drugs women with roofies so he can, well, you know—"

"Where would you look?"

"Think he ever leaves?"

"So you're going to do this? You'll be in jail before him."

"Many folks up here don't bother with locking their doors."

The signal went wonky and quiet.

"I'll call you right back," said Duncan.

"Don't do anything—"

Thirty-Nine

For the ride out, Colin would lead on Merlin. Chanute would follow on a chestnut quarter horse named Bruiser.

Allison took third place on Sunny Boy. The elk quarters and Mr. Elk Head hitched a ride on Hercules, their stalwart mule, behind her on a string. In the rear and also on the string, an easy-going packhorse named Bucky, which fit his buckskin color.

Alas for Chanute, there was no altering a horse's steady side-to-side jostle. The motion on two cracked ribs and maybe a dinged vertebra would register each step like a mini earthquake.

"You doing okay?"

Allison knew the pain of cracked ribs—a rarified anguish for true connoisseurs. The fact that the epicenter of agony lay so close to the lungs and heart made it seem as if any deep breath might poke a hole in a critical component.

"Can I borrow back my gun for one quick chore?" said Chanute.

"Think about something else."

"I'd donate a rib or two right now," said Chanute. "No anesthesia, nothing. The surgery would feel less painful than the injury."

They had left at dawn, the forest still black. Breakfast had "to go" variety—granola bars, apples, water. Saint Jesse had risen earlier to make coffee.

Victor Chanute had made it down from the spot where he'd

212

fallen, bellowing and howling on horseback the entire way. His buddy Ed, aka "Dwayne" to them, "just happened" to have oxycodone on hand. Chanute had taken two, claimed he hadn't slept.

Chanute had pled with Allison to not tell Ed of his betrayal. Chanute had been so dopey by midnight that he wouldn't have had the ability to tell "Dwayne" what had transpired between him and Allison up in the woods. Colin took turns with her, staying up to listen for any chatter.

Nothing.

They left the impression that Colin would return that night, once Chanute was delivered to medical care, but Allison planned to send Jesse Morales back up in his place. "Dwayne" wanted to head out with them, but Allison encouraged him to stay and try to fill his tag.

Colin led them up through the cool forest to a sunny, scrubby, treeless flat. He knew a spring east of Shingle Peak. Allison found her thoughts turning to a long-running puzzle—Devo's demise. The months since his body was found had turned up nothing solid. The sheriff feigned interest, but hadn't poured much into establishing a timeline of when and where Devo was last seen or what direction he was heading. His autopsy turned up liver damage, but the analysts noted Devo's odd internal chemical mix from years of feeding off the woods. Three times Allison had taken day trips to Meeker, Colin in tow, to poke around in town, see what they could find. The effort had turned up nothing, but Allison remained unwavering in her belief that Devo knew himself too well to keel over on a calm summer night.

They took a break to water the horses and Chanute needed a half hour to climb down. Or so it seemed. It was still four miles to Sweetwater, and she could already imagine Chanute's torment during a plummeting pitch down from the plateau. She could tell him to be prepared, but there was no point in piling dread on top of woe.

"So you know the undercover cop?" said Allison.

"He wasn't a *cop* cop—he was an informer," said Chanute.

"In your group, you know, who figured it out?" said Colin, showing his acting chops. They'd planned this chat.

"I've already told her what I know." Chanute chewed a peanut butter sandwich in super slo-mo. His big cheeks had grown ruddy in the sun.

"Who killed Miguel Ramirez?"

"I wasn't there."

"Steadman?" said Allison. "Ed Steadman, or whatever you said your friend's name is?"

"Neither of us," said Chanute.

"So you do know," said Colin.

"No, I only meant he wasn't there and I wasn't there, so we couldn't have killed the informer." Chanute crammed the last bite of sandwich into his mouth.

"How much weed? Where was it headed?" Colin sounded like the goddamn DEA. She didn't mind.

Chanute shrugged.

"We're taking you to the cops," said Allison.

"A doctor first. And I would be glad to tell the cops what I told you two. Nothing."

Allison gave Colin a quick look and pulled him away and off behind Sunny Boy, tied to a waist-high clump of Gambel oak. Here near the southern end of the plateau, the forest marched most of the way up the slope. On top, they were alone with an ocean of sky.

"I don't know," said Allison. "It's possible the cops will pretend to care about talking to Chanute. They already know who died and what he was doing."

Colin nodded. "You'd think the sheriff would have to pretend to care. This guy knows."

"Of course he does."

"And you're thinking—"

"We get to the top of the last pitch—I mean, Chanute will be wanting to take it real slow. I'll go on ahead. That will give me a head start to make a few calls."

"But what if the cops are all closed-ranks because they're still frying bigger fish?"

"We have to see," said Allison. It seemed a mistake, a bad one, to have left Ed Steadman out of their sights.

Over and over through her restless night of sleep, Allison had put herself in the informant's situation. You had survived a plane crash. The plane is crammed full of weed. You tried to hike out—you and one other. You leave one person to watch the stash. On the way out, you sprain an ankle.

With the injury, you can't hike out. You both decide to camp for a night. He kills a small deer out of season for food and because he's an asshole. The other guy takes off in the morning to get help but decides to make sure that his "buddy" stays put. Gets out the rope. Maybe he's suspicious. Some cowgirl shows up and offers to help. You think she can't possibly *not* help. The less you say, the better. At least, you think so.

"That Miguel Ramirez dude must have had a lot at stake." Allison snapped herself back to the moment, to Colin's *I'm waiting* look.

"Did I say that out loud?"

"Yeah, you did."

"He needed to stay. He didn't want to be yanked out of his deal with the cops."

"He had a deal?"

"And he had a helluva lot riding on it—"

"Avoiding prison."

"Or reducing a sentence."

"But they figured him out."

"The other guy," said Allison. "He goes down to make arrangements for the backup plane, has time to check a few things, too."

"He must have got a ride," said Colin.

"That's bugged me for days. Why he came toward Sweetwater Road. Crescent Lake Road is right there—closer by half a day. Do you think he knew someone?"

"Whole lot of options between Sweetwater and the river."

"All we need is the one or two who know something about weed."

Colin counted all ten fingers. A mime. Started over. "Okay, well, you've shrunk the pool of candidates by one or two."

Allison smiled. "Seriously. The guy we're looking for probably used to deal—maybe still does."

"He still needed a ride."

"Who is the first guy you'd come across?"

"Guy?" said Colin. "Us, if we had been there. Or Trudy."

"Or?"

"Jesse Morales."

Colin lit up.

"And?"

"And he's a favor machine."

"Always lending a hand."

"You think he would have mentioned to us that he gave a ride to a bedraggled hiker who stumbled out of the woods."

Allison smiled. "Gotta start somewhere."

She needed to know who ended Ramirez' life. The killer was on the blue plane, but they could have flown to Fairbanks and long since converted their cargo to cash.

The mountain of questions temporarily overshadowed concerns for what happened to Devo. But Allison knew one thing for sure.

Colin was back. They were back. Two ice cubes, same drink.

She gave him a kiss.

"What was that for?"

"Your brainpower."

"That's me." He cocked his gaze sideways. "A minute ago I was running the quadratic equation in my head for entertainment."

"Different kind of brain that I like."

She kissed him again, slipped a finger between the buttons of his shirt to tickle his warm skin. "The kind of brain that doesn't forget it's connected to the heart. And to me."

"Stupid brain for its temporary lapse in—"

"No apologies," she said. "We've been over that—"

He cut her off with another kiss—sweaty, horsey, whiskery, unshowered hay-breath kiss.

"Phew," she said. She buried her nose in his neck, hugged him hard. "Let's get out of here."

There was one problem.

Victor Chanute was missing.

Allison hopped up on the rock where Chanute had sat. It wasn't hard to guess which direction he'd headed.

Nearing the tree line, Victor Chanute stepped. And stopped again. One hand reached around to support his tender back. He'd made it all of about fifty yards.

"Fuck," said Allison. "It's going to take an hour to turn him around and coax him back up the hill."

Colin joined her on top of the rock. "There's another option," he said. "Let him go."

She shook her head.

"That's the easy way out. At that pace, he's got five days of walking—no water, no food."

"Free country."

"Mostly true," said Allison. "Not today."

Forty

Life around the garden center appeared routine, but Trudy found herself floating as if she moved inside a padded cell, drugged up and numb.

She talked to men and wondered, *how desperate do you get?*

She talked to women and thought, *if I could tell you one thing it's never put yourself in an unclear situation. If you're alone he might just—*

Customers trickled through—indoor pots, indoor herbs, indoor issues, thinking ahead to spring. Early Christmas shoppers. Trudy acknowledged greetings with the same old smile.

She supervised reorganization of the small front room given over to hand tools and the stuff of light industry—power tools to rent or buy, take your pick.

A team member named Joe—she would have been clueless on

the name without the personalized green golf shirts—showed her a cracked outdoor faucet, and he offered to take a whack at fixing it. A young female customer with the sugary enthusiasm of a recent convert, it didn't matter to what, cornered her for a long discussion over soil health. Most days, the topic would draw Trudy's unflagging insights and quizzing probes, but today the issue left her blah and indifferent. The woman's fussy top bun was too perfect and cherry red fingernails didn't look like they would ever touch the handle of a rake, let alone dirt. She smelled of tangerine and plastic.

And then a man about Sam Shelton's age and about Sam Shelton's height, with a frisky, wild beard reminiscent of Sam Shelton's grooming, needed to detail his thoughts for next year's approach in the garden—

—*with tomatoes.*

Trudy faked a forgotten phone call, a snap of her fingers so quick and convincing she might win an Oscar, and she pawned the clueless gentleman off to an eager underling.

In her office, the phone rang as if cued—or had it been ringing all the while?

"Finally," said Duncan.

Trudy glanced at her cell phone. *Missed call, missed call, missed call . . .*

"I'm sorry," she said. It was true.

"I found a guy who sold Sam Shelton whatever he needed—whatever he asked for."

"What? How did you—?"

With every upbeat thought of landing a deathblow against Sam Shelton's golden-boy sheen, she was faced with the grim prospect of conceding to the many ways she may have misled him, including the dope smoking, the free-flowing wine and the moment or three when she had wrapped her hand around his stiff, trousered cock.

"Got lucky," said Duncan. "Brett Merriman, in fact. He was a big help. Your connections, you know. Your relationships. People will do anything for you."

Will they? "That's great," said Trudy.

"I got name, phone number and email. He used to deliver drugs to Sam Shelton's house. Do you want it?"

"Of course." Trudy jotted it down.

"Give it to your lawyer," said Duncan. "The guy seemed credible. He remembered the things Shelton liked. The variety—whoa."

"Duncan, I—"

He waited a few seconds. "What?"

"Where are you now?"

"Why?"

"Still in Meeker?"

"Not Meeker proper—but close."

"Where?"

"At his home."

"What do you mean?"

"I'm calling from his kitchen. I'm standing here now."

"*What*?" She gasped, blurted it out.

"Doors unlocked, you know."

"You can't. What are you *thinking*?"

"Stash of pills in the bedroom. Dresser, top drawer. Prescription bottles. Pills aplenty."

Her heart jumped. "Get out of there!"

"Why, what?"

"You can't saunter in!"

"Easy," said Duncan.

"What?"

"I'm kidding. Sorry, Jesus, I'm kidding."

"For crying out loud."

"The door *is* unlocked, by the way, and I met a few cats but I didn't put one foot inside, though I am fucking tempted. Tempted to burn the place down, the asshole."

"Duncan, it's not all that simple."

"What?"

"Well, you know—"

The phone might make it easier, to spill all the beans this way. It seemed like a chicken's way out, so unfair. What had he done to deserve the way she had hung out with Sam Shelton, how she had led him on?

"Oh," said Duncan. "Here's the part where you tell me you weren't Miss Goody Two-Shoes?"

From her window, she had a view out over the high bluff above the Roaring Fork. The garden beds needed a rough spade. The shrubs and trees each needed a ring of bark mulch and shredded leaves. Perennials needed cutting back and deadheading.

"I wasn't." A volunteer tear followed the fold at her cheek and nose.

"Shocked," said Duncan. "Not. I mean, come on. I know you didn't sleep with him—you wouldn't have been able to step over that line. But he's a big-ass rock star and, by the way, who wouldn't try and make a play for *you*?"

"Duncan—"

"And I don't want to know," he said. "You got attacked. *Assaulted. Drugged.* You were about to be raped. 'Hold me closer, Tiny Dancer.' My ass. You gotta nail this asshole and you have to bring it with backbone, you know?"

She hadn't expected utter forgiveness. "You weren't there."

"Am I wrong?"

"But how can you be so sure?"

"Because it's obvious. If you were sleeping with him, he wouldn't have needed quaaludes. If you had been sleeping with him, you would not have whacked him."

She felt dirty, like she needed to crawl back. And Duncan was letting her walk.

"It's all true—the way I told you."

"I know it is."

"Now what?" she said.

"Now you tell your lawyer you're ready to go forward—and you can get her the guy who supplied Sam Shelton with the stuff."

"You sure?"

"He's not going anywhere."

"You sure we're okay?"

Tears bubbled from an unknown well.

"I'm heading back. Glass of wine tonight, onward, you know? Lessons learned and all of that."

Having Duncan on her side provided an enormous lift. But the next step of going public, of taking on Sam Shelton and re-visiting that night—wine, joints, cock-grabbing awful—would be rough. It could drag her down. The garden center, too. Who would be able to see her label in a store and not think of Trudy Heath half-blitzed and trying to get in the pants of the former rock star?

Trudy said good-bye to Duncan with effusive appreciation.

She made a silent vow that would serve, in a way, as self-imposed contrition.

She wouldn't stagger about. She wouldn't wallow. She'd put her chin up and charge forward.

If the tarnish on her reputation was the price of bringing down Sam Shelton and if her stepping up emboldened others to do the same, then it was a price worth paying. She needed to pour herself into action, help Allison if she could and keep her head up, force her spirits up, even if it seemed a tad fake. Extra vitamins, more sunshine, more chlorophyll, a big green salad, green juices with burdock root and dandelion, apple, ginger, lemon, spinach and local honey. *Dandelion*. She flashed back to that wicked first day, shooting the pilot with Sam Shelton. Hell.

Long walks.

Purposeful breathing.

She would shift into action mode—case closed.

Forty-One

Wednesday Afternoon
Duncan

Coogan greeted Duncan's late arrival with three assignments—a man who shot a mountain lion in his backyard off Cattle Creek Road, an outfitter with a complaint over the permitting process for rafts on the Colorado River and a news conference at noon, a mere twenty minutes hence, being called by Jack Hallowell.

"Why I was calling," said Coogan. "Save you the trip to the office. Don't give that wimp any more than he deserves, though."

"News conference?" said Duncan.

The journalism gods always got even. Fuck off for a few hours and they would snap you back into place.

"It's his way of saying he wants to talk to you, though his campaign manager called to say we better be there."

223

Duncan's story had recounted Hallowell's anti-pot crusade of 2010. Duncan threw in a bland quote from Bill Walters and a comment from Hallowell about how views have "evolved" on the subject of marijuana consumption and how he stopped affiliating himself with the Christian right.

"The big refutation," said Duncan.

Coogan smirked. "The location tells you everything."

Stan Greer was waiting, his rig all set and ready outside the Green Dragon, a rotunda of concrete, on Devereux Road.

"I think they were waiting on you," said Greer.

Hallowell and a small band of supporters stood in a huddle near a bright blue campaign van. A magnetic sign on the van's door boasted "Hallowell Harmony," red letters on white.

A matronly woman handed out copies of a "news" release, and Hallowell began speaking about the misleading impression left by an unnamed newspaper.

"I hope voters will examine how their attitudes have changed and adjusted over time—as have mine over the past half decade," he said. "I'm here today to pledge in a public fashion, and with a retail marijuana establishment as my backdrop and witness today, that I have no interest in changing anything about access to marijuana in Garfield County."

Hallowell made no mention of his former Bible-thumping self. When he finished, Hallowell's tribe offered soft applause, worthy of a golf course. Duncan knew he was never at a "news" conference when it involved ovations of any kind.

"What changed for you?" said Greer.

"Research," said Hallowell. "I still believe there is lots left to do regarding understanding how the teenage brain is impacted by pot, so I agree with being twenty-one years old before you can buy. And I do think we need an aggressive public awareness campaign. So I'm not saying pot is harmless, either."

What if Hallowell had heard about his investment? The risk seemed low. Hallowell remained an outsider. Duncan was pretty sure he'd stay that way.

Hallowell and his crew packed up after a few more softball questions from Greer. Duncan had refused to engage. Not asking questions at the denial news conference involved a matter of self-respect. Hallowell's message was clear—*I'm a new man today*. Bullshit. Down deep, Duncan believed, you didn't change your views on stuff like that except for political gain.

Inside the store, Duncan gathered reaction from a budtender, a customer and the owner. They all agreed that the fucking politicians should keep their fucking hands off legal access to good shit. Or words to that effect.

"Way to make the politicos sweat," said Greer. He was setting up for his stand-up outside. He framed-in his own quirky shots, often using mirrors and odd angles, and then recited his lines while the unmanned camera rolled.

"I smell a hypocrite," said Duncan.

"He's a bit too earnest."

"And smarmy." Duncan wondered about Hallowell's tax return. Did he still donate to Family First or the Christian mega-church in Colorado Springs? It was worth checking.

"Did you ever get in to see our hash oil enthusiasts?"

"Negative," said Duncan. "Big-city representation now, veils of secrecy and all that."

"They bonded out, right?"

"Long time ago. What are you hearing?"

"That a plea was in the works—I got a call from one of the burned-out neighbors." A plea meant nobody was happy. "I have to check it out—the guy who called me claimed to be one of the neighbors, but he didn't leave his name. Seemed legit."

Duncan wrote up the lame "I am not an anti-drug zealot" story on his laptop at Starbucks up the hill near Target. Anything beat the newsroom. He zapped it to Coogan with a few photos and a message—*going to check a solid tip on the hash oil story. Shouldn't take long.*

He pulled Tim and Sandy Miller up in his contacts under Hash Oil Neighbors. The other name was the feisty Cleo Bilhorn. Sandy answered on the first ring.

"The insurance companies are fighting now," she said. "Tim still wants them to rot in jail for a couple of decades, but I don't know. The mobile home belonged to King's Crown, but we lost everything."

"Where are you living now?"

"Doubled up with friends in Battlement Mesa. Tim lost his job with the energy company and I commute here to Rifle for the day care job."

"You're in Rifle now?"

"What difference does it make?"

A profile of the Millers could show the collateral damage from the explosion, so to speak. He could write it extra sad. It wouldn't hurt his credibility with the anti-pot crowd.

"Just curious. Could I come see you—?"

"Oh no," she said. "I can check with Tim tonight but—"

"You can confirm there's a plea deal in the works."

"That's what we're being told."

Duncan steeled himself for the call to Cleo Bilhorn. Maybe he had come at Sandy Miller too fast, too hard.

"I remember you," said Bilhorn.

"I'm doing a story about the fallout from the fire. Sort of an update."

"Not interested."

About the last thing he expected to hear.

"I've heard there's movement in the case. I'm checking back to see what's happened—"

"Not interested."

"We want to show the fallout from that fire." Unless he looked up at the high, tree-lined ridges to the south or west, Duncan realized, this two-block strip of concrete commerce could be Anywhere, USA. Target, Pier 1, Great Clips. It doesn't get much more red, white and blue than that. Market Street, he thought, my ass. "You know, all the damage done."

"Things change."

"Your husband?"

"What about him?"

"Would he care to comment?"

The phone clattered. He heard her yell. He waited a full minute. "No," she said.

"Tell me this." He pictured Cleo Bilhorn being interviewed by Stan Greer that first day at King's Crown, so pointed and angry. "Where are you two now?"

"Mobile home, another one."

"Where?"

She waited. "What does it matter?"

"I only want an idea of where you're living—how long it took to find a place."

"H Lazy F." South of downtown Glenwood Springs, not too far. "But we can't afford to stay."

Duncan grabbed his cup, started walking.

"Can I come to you? Ten minutes. That's all I need."

227

"What the hell for?"

If there was a plea and she already had a big dollar sign being dangled, this is exactly how she'd react. Maybe a gag order had been put in place, too, and she didn't want to risk anything.

"To show the—"

"No," she said. A bark. "Forget it. What good is it going to do?"

"Well, I mean—"

"No. You thought I was crazy the first time. I could see it in your eyes. That TV guy, too. You fucking pander, both of you. You think truck driver and you think one thing. Do you have any idea how much reading you can get done? You read *The Jungle* lately? Or how about *A Farewell to Arms*? Huh? You know we write children's books, sell them on CreateSpace? We've got an illustrator, a good one. Truck drivers have lots of waiting time—so we write, together. We don't make much money, but still. And you looked right through me and in the courthouse you avoided me—the neighbors on the other side looked much more normal, am I right? Whatever the hell normal is. So take a straight ruler, okay, and shove it."

His beat-up Camry, a constant reminder of his financial plight, provided the perfect place to sulk. Saying "no" might be one thing, but she'd cut him to the core.

Children's books? CreateSpace?

Cleo Bilhorn's pissy rant stabbed a hole in his soul.

But he *did* care. He cared what happened to her and the Millers and, in a way, Jimmy Enriquez and Marsha Sykes, too. But he'd given Bilhorn short shrift, a glancing blow of journalistic fakery. Reading Upton Sinclair and Ernest Hemingway, *what the hell*?

Inez Cordova answered quickly.

"Now what? And I mean that in the nicest way."

Duncan explained.

"It's not my case. Sykes and Enriquez, as you know, have representation."

"I'm aware."

"So why would you think I'm privy to a proposed settlement?"

"Because you hear things." Duncan tried to not sound harried.

"Check with the DA. Pretty basic, Duncan."

"They never reveal if a deal is being offered, you know that."

"Where did you hear this?"

Fellow reporter sounded weak. "Reliable tipster."

"Well, it wouldn't surprise me if there was a deal."

"And why is that?"

"You didn't hear about the complication?"

Duncan relished the word *complication*.

"Call me innocent."

"Never," said Cordova. "There were two couples that pretty much lost everything, right?"

"Correct."

"I can't remember their names."

"The Millers on one side, Cleo Bilhorn and her husband on the other."

"Bilhorn," said Cordova. "Her husband has arthritis. One of the bad kinds."

"Really?"

"Rheumatoid, yes."

"Really?"

"She's been growing marijuana at home for years. Helps with

229

the pain. Did you know marijuana was one of the primary pain relievers used prior to the discovery of aspirin? That is a fact-of-the-day for you, no extra charge."

Cleo Bilhorn? Truck-driving mama with nothing but venomous words for the hash oil scientists next door? It didn't compute. It was hard to picture. But—

"So what?" said Duncan.

"So she was supplying, shall we say, raw material to her neighbors."

"Then she's not in a position to complain."

"From what I gather the depositions have been interesting."

"And you can't sell what you grow."

"Complication number one."

"There's a two?"

Duncan's head spun. Bilhorn's reaction now made more sense. So did the discussion around a plea, especially if the Millers were squeaky clean and not also growing weed in their closet.

"You can count that high?"

"I'll try to keep up."

"The Bilhorns had been selling across the fence there, so to speak, for a long time. And then, suddenly, they stopped."

"But still growing?"

"Yep."

"Then why the shutdown?"

"As Marsha Sykes said in the deposition, it's a free fucking country."

Forty-Two

"Trudy?"

Trudy snuck a glance at the name tag—*Mariah.*

"Yes?"

"My partner is—*was*—Devo's sister."

Allison had mentioned a connection, but Trudy hadn't closed the loop. Another flaw, another vow.

"Yes?"

"When Allison and Colin were at our house a few weeks ago, Glenna mentioned this woman, Atalanta. I didn't mean to interrupt—"

Was the anguish on her face that obvious? "It's fine. Please."

Trudy stood, suggested that they head outside. Trudy felt a lick of brightness, as if she'd found a night-light a mile down the chute of a vast cave.

"Glenna wants to move on," said Mariah. She was sleek, tall and clean. "She wants to stop worrying about what happened to Devo. She says if the cops can't figure it out, then that's the way it goes—Devo chose his destiny."

"But."

A path through the garden center's outdoor space led them down to the high overlook above the Roaring Fork. The October sun offered a gentle warmth.

"I mean I know he's dead and everything, but his whole reputation."

"Is what?"

"Glenna doesn't read what's out there. He's being treated as a mystic, an utter romantic, a combination of Edward Abbey and Henry Thoreau."

The coverage oversimplified Devo's life and demise. Tests were still being run, or the medical examiner was still dreaming up new screens to try, from what Trudy could gather. Devo's body remained unburied and unclaimed. Devo's final fate remained in a ghoulish form of suspended animation, his body a science experiment and his legacy as an environmental pioneer growing more every week.

"I know your boyfriend is a reporter," said Mariah. "And maybe he'd want to set the record straight?"

"One of his favorite things to do."

"I mean, does it seem right to you?"

"Just know that the story might shift, but there is no one story in a situation like this."

Trudy heard herself—and knew it might come across like a know-it-all. The variety of things she'd read about what happened to her in the Hanging Lake Tunnel shattered plausibility. The accounts held such a tenuous relationship to the truth that contemplating the idea of requesting corrections seemed like a quaint notion, given the mountain of mistakes. There were "stories" out there about her breakup with Jerry and her split from George. Allison had grumbled, too, about the loose "facts" related to those incidents. What had Sam Shelton said about rumors? Was her "story" that led up to him dropping his pants a better story than his?

"Devo was living *two lives*."

"And why drag his memory through the mud?"

"Even Glenna told me Devo's camp or tribe or whatever they called it depended on scraps from the city, that the whole idea imploded, yet there is still this fable out there that what he was selling is doable. Plus, he was sleeping with this other woman and I guess she was a bit batshit, but he couldn't resist because she gave him all the sex he could handle—and more."

"This is from Glenna?"

Mariah nodded. "And we still don't know how he died."

The implication was obvious.

"So where would Duncan start? Or anyone?"

"Atalanta."

"You have to find her first."

"I think I know where to look."

Forty-Three

Wednesday Afternoon
Allison

A few times, Allison wondered if Victor Chanute might pass out from the pain. With Bruiser heading down Shingle Peak Trail, Chanute had to lean back and hold on during the horse's braced steps on the steep descent. Chanute grew creative with his cursing combinations.

Bruiser didn't care one way or the other.

The horses knew every stretch that deserved caution, the rustling crunch of loose rock skittering and scattering under twenty horse legs. The grinding rocks were the only sounds besides Chanute's bitching. Finally, the pitch mellowed and yanked them down a long straightaway through dense aspen groves all braced and waiting for winter, leafless.

"What the fuck now?"

Chanute failed to enjoy the beauty.

"Sweetwater is another hour. Or two." Colin lied. He knew down to the minute. "What else do you need to know?"

"You're calling the cops from there?"

"We're calling the cops when we feel like it," said Allison. The one issue she'd been mulling over was that "Clay," or whoever had sent Chanute and Steadman, would be expecting a report from his two scouts.

"And a doctor? I might need an MJ prescription for the potent shit," said Chanute. "And a rib transplant and a spinal fusion. Can you let this go?"

The question didn't deserve an answer.

Colin, from up front, turned around in his saddle. He gave Chanute a cold stare.

Colin knew.

Chanute did not. Chanute kept pressing.

"You don't need to tangle me up with the cops. You got enough for whatever you need to tell them."

Colin shook his head. His right hand grabbed the cantle to stay turned around.

Chanute didn't get the message. "I've told you everything I know. Let me make my way to a doctor, no cops and none of that bullshit, and you can ask me anything, anytime and I'll steer you in the right direction. Deal?"

Allison kicked Sunny Boy up alongside Bruiser, hopped off. She pulled Bruiser to a stop, one finger under Sunny Boy's noseband was all she needed to hold on. "Get off," she said.

"What?"

Chanute feigned innocence.

"Off," she said. "Or we'll drag you off, or I'll get all these horses up to a full gallop and listen to you howl."

234

"We're almost back down, you said—"

"Off!"

"Okay, I was making conversation. I mean, I'm sorry about the dead guy, but this is all about a harmless little plant—"

Allison yanked the reins away from Chanute's hands. She unbuckled Bruiser's throat latch and browband. Bruiser shook his head in relief and the bit fell out into Allison's hand. Allison held up the tack like a prize. "Should I give him a swat on the rump? Right about now?"

Chanute swung one leg over the back faster than he had moved in two days.

He landed back on earth with a series of squawks and barks. He grabbed his back where there was nothing to grab. Chanute bent over at the waist, an old man adjusting for all the mistreatments of life and searching for the sweet spot, a relative term, of least pressure on his mangled bones.

"The hell." Chanute stumbled on the path. "I don't fucking get it."

Colin hopped off Merlin. "Get what?"

"I'm not cutting deals." Allison had half a mind to tie Chanute to a tree, see if he would dig the symmetry.

"I got nothing else for you, so it doesn't matter," said Chanute. "I don't get your burning desire to include me in your whole investigation, if that's what you call it."

"Burning desire?"

Chanute's eyes flickered from pain or uncertainty or both. He rolled his left shoulder, cocked his head.

"No." Said without conviction.

"I left a man to die." She stepped to him and he flinched, put his hands up like he was catching a ball. "To *die*."

"You didn't kill him."

"I could have saved him."

"He could have saved himself."

"And I could have insisted."

"When Grayson asked about the water bottles, how they had turned up, he had to explain—"

"Who the fuck is Grayson?"

Colin cut him off, beat her to it.

"What?"

Chanute realized he had slashed open fresh turf. He reached up for purchase on Bruiser's saddle, inhaled a thin breath to steel himself against another stab of pain.

"Who is Grayson?"

"The hell," said Chanute. "Another guy, someone who knows a hell of a lot more."

"So he was the one who came back and took Miguel Ramirez back up to the plane wreck."

Chanute stood with his back to Bruiser. Allison held Sunny Boy by a finger and he'd come around with Hercules still on the string and Allison felt walled in by the animals, a state of being she would normally relish, but not now with Chanute eating up most of the space left over for humans. Chanute looked back and forth between his captors.

"Give me a break," he said. "I'm a nobody. I'll help with what I can, you know, once we get down."

Chanute's assertion was a feeble, crappy lie. They all knew it.

"No cops," he said. "Please."

"No need."

The voice came from outside the cave of horseflesh. Allison bumped Sunny Boy back with her shoulder and found the voice twenty yards up the trail behind a rifle. He was sighting down the barrel. The unibrow was one of a kind. And all that exposed forehead, collecting sunshine.

Ed Steadman.

"Real easy now," he said. "Real easy."

Inside, Allison shook her head. A guy spitting out lines from bad old Westerns probably didn't have a clue. But stupidity, in fact, always loomed as the most dangerous threat.

What were the odds of wriggling clear of this?

With his pissed-off finger touching the trigger, probability was its own dimension.

And probability didn't care.

Forty-Four

Wednesday Afternoon
Trudy

"I'm a lesbian," said Mariah. "Obvious, right?"

Trudy smiled, glanced over.

"My wife, Glenna, of course, doesn't put it out there. She's more reserved, right?"

"Glenna looks as straight as they come."

Trudy drove one of the garden center's hybrid pickups. They were on the last descent into Meeker.

"So you think you'd know what I would say about Sam Shelton based on my preference for partners. And by the way, it's not a *preference*. I don't *prefer* women to men. I've only been with women, except for one back-seat blow job in high school. That sealed the deal for me."

"I'm sure you disappointed many men along the way," said Trudy. "The ones who didn't know."

"Do you know what it's like to feel absolutely zero interest, sexually speaking?" It wasn't a real question. "But we're way off the point of my advice and what I'd do about Sam Shelton."

"I'm listening."

Trudy had told her everything. Mariah had filled the car with a strong confidence, playing the role of the old friend who won't let you wallow in the muck.

"You have to stand up and push back," said Mariah. "Don't be confused about what was going on. How you feel—how you *still* feel, and I can hear it in your voice—is the proof right there of the crime and the injury. You can't brush that aside."

Allison had staked out a similar position. Duncan, too. The lawyer, of course. Mariah's logic sounded right. Everybody's logic sounded right. So why, Trudy wondered, was she having such a hard time pressing through, taking him down?

They paid a courtesy visit to Brett Merriman at the grocery store, ate salads at the Meeker Café, and then Mariah pointed north on a road that took them up by the fairgrounds and the recreation center, past newer housing and subdivision-like neighborhoods on the rolling hills where the town ended. Trudy wondered exactly where they had found Devo's body. She only had a rough idea.

"It will be a small miracle if I can find it," said Mariah.

"How did you find it in the first place?"

Mariah shook her head. "I was fascinated by Glenna's stories about her brother. I mean, I watched all those, quote, unquote, 'reality' shows. But it was so interesting to watch Devo figure stuff out—food, shelter, hunting, scrounging, foraging. Makes you appreciate a couch and cold IPA. So his show might have had a reverse effect. Make sense? Anyway, there was a day last spring when I was doing a delivery up here and the truck pulled a flat on the way back to Glenwood."

238

Trudy nodded. It was an operational detail not at her level.

"Anyway, I had to wait overnight for the tire to be shipped from Grand Junction and so I walked back down to the grocery store, and there's Devo with a funky sort of backpack or satchel thing and even though it was kind of cool and kind of rainy, he's wearing next to nothing. He looked like he crawled out of a groundhog tunnel, no different than an underclothed, malnourished bum. It was sad."

Trudy chased off tears. "What was he doing?"

"I'm not sure. He wasn't alone. It was up a side street not too far from Brett's grocery store, and he was clearly being pestered by a woman and I'm sure it was the same woman, you know, the same woman that Glenna described."

The road bumped down from asphalt to dirt. Every square inch of barren vista looked parched and weary.

"I couldn't exactly stop and stare," said Mariah. "Part of me wanted to go talk to them, see if everything was okay or if there was anything I could do, but she was going at him pretty hard."

"About?"

"At the time, I knew nothing."

"What did she look like?"

Mariah sighed, shook her head. Smiled. "Oh my."

"You're *married*." Trudy knew it sounded too much like an accusation.

"And one reason we'll be married forever is that we both occasionally need and want intimacy with, well, others. We have an agreement."

"Now it's my turn to say 'oh my.'"

"It works," said Mariah. "DADT. Don't ask and, you know, don't tell. It's real—for us. We're not looking all the time, but when it happens—"

"You—?"

"She was a full head taller than Devo, short hair and a certain darkness. Strong but plenty feminine, too."

"You *felt* something?"

"Riveted," said Mariah.

"And Devo?"

Mariah took a moment to collect her thoughts. Trudy edged over to the side of the road as a speeding delivery truck left them in a russet fog of grit. Flecks of sand ticked off the windshield.

"He looked so tired. Forlorn. I knew he was small to begin with, but he looked emaciated. Beyond thin. And scared as hell."

"Of?"

"Of her. Intimidated at least."

"You followed her?"

"Hell no. I didn't even watch for all that long. Whatever was going on between the two of them, I wasn't going to make myself known. The space between them was tight, closed in."

"And then?"

The road rose up, banked along the edge of a small hill. They hit washboard. "I was at the Italian restaurant having pasta and a cold beer—"

"Ma Famiglia?"

"That's it. And here she comes. She'd cleaned up, looked like a million bucks—no inflation."

"Got her talking?"

"I wasn't going to waste my chance."

"But how do you know if—"

"If she likes women?"

"Yeah."

"You just do. You can pick them out. And they can pick you out."

"I've always wondered," said Trudy.

"It's no big whoop." Mariah gave a cute, small shrug. "It's being alert for signals. It's a punch in the gut, the good kind."

"You clicked?"

"Boy howdy."

"Followed her home?"

"I'm not *that* easy," said Mariah. "She wanted me to, so she described where she lived and drew me a map. Told me to stop by if I was back in town, but I'd be taking my chances because she spent most of her time in the woods."

Mariah had followed the map before. The road rose and fell through a series of hills that pulled them into a thick pine forest and they reached a plateau, still wooded, and after a mile of flat, the road wound down the more shaded backside. Bumps and ruts and rocks kept their pace at a crawl. They heard the gnawing scrape of rock on metal as they bottomed out more than once.

"You got her talking about Devo?"

"Didn't take much."

"But you didn't let on you'd seen her in town with him?"

"No. She was transfixed. She went back over decisions they made and how they went about shelter and food. She's convinced getting involved in the whole investigation, the murder of that environmentalist, was their downfall."

"Dante Soto." Trudy said his name out of respect. "But they weren't going to let them camp up there in the Flat Tops much longer anyway, not in the wilderness area, that's for sure."

"Doesn't matter. She was obsessed with Devo."

"And sleeping with him on his Meeker weekends? She went both ways?"

"Different strokes."

"Why didn't she, you know, join them? Join up with Devo?"

"That's the whole deal right there," said Mariah. "Devo wouldn't let her."

Forty-Five

The mobile homes at H Lazy F climbed a tree-dotted hill-side by the riverbank a few miles south of downtown. One dirt street wrapped the south and west sides of the park. Another dead-ended into the middle.

On his phone, Duncan had pulled up Stan Greer's news package from the first day of the hash oil fire in Rifle. The clip with Cleo Bilhorn was shot wide enough to see the shiny new tan Ford pickup in the background. That same pickup had been backed into a stub of a driveway by the side of a green trailer. Duncan knocked on the door, up three spiky metal steps from grade.

"Aw Jesus," she said. Bilhorn wore high-waisted mom jeans and a maroon hoodie.

Duncan was ready. At his best. He didn't give a lick about the hash oil case, or so he claimed. He was after the "big picture." Sincerity dripped. He held up a six-pack of Michelob. Not crafty, not generic. He apologized. He explained how much reporters get to see and complained about how many stories they have to write. "We get jaded, it's true. I should have talked to you more." He ripped his heart out on his mini metal stage. She peered back through the draining-drab Instagram filter that was her screen door. He wondered if they had moved their home grow and he thought he caught that telltale whiff, that wonderful funk, the Grand Funk Railroad, the smell of a new generation. No differ-ent, from Duncan's point of view, than the sticky, boozy mess of

242

a million billion bars.

"I came over to see if we could start over."

A flat lie. He knew what he was after, but needed to turn back the page.

The screen door opened with a tinny groan. She ushered him to an armless blue, but stained, settee. She took a brown comfy chair. *Little Dorrit* sat on the cushy armrest, a fresh cup of hot tea on the side table next to it.

"I was thinking we could write a story about your books. I mean, that's something—using your waiting time as a truck driver to write children's books."

She perked up. "Really?"

"Absolutely."

"Who is that?" The bark from down the hall.

"Never mind," she shouted, double the decibels needed.

"That's Dwight," she added, sotto voce, as if that was enough explanation. "I can show you the books."

Duncan figured patience was power at this point. She spent fifteen minutes showing him six published children's books, all with a truck-driving theme. The illustrations weren't bad. The writing looked plain but engaging. The books looked a bit self-published, but he gave her good marks for quality. And then he tried to shift topics, as gently as he could.

"The case is all under a gag order—and you know, it wouldn't even be good form for you to be here."

A gag order? For what possible reason? The big-city law firm wanting to control the message? The story? What details were big secrets unless the cops—

Fuck.

"A gag order?"

"As of two weeks ago."

"Who *is* that?" Dwight's shout roared down the hall.

Bilhorn shot up with a semi-harried *harrumph*. She padded down the narrow hall. A door slammed and Duncan heard admonishment in the tone, no words. A one-way conversation. She shook her head coming back. "Sorry," she said.

"So this attempt at a settlement?"

"Got complicated." Bilhorn folded her arms across her chest. "Again, gag order."

"Okay, off the record. Is that okay with you?"

Duncan made a big show of putting down his notebook, laying the pen on top.

"What's that mean?"

"It means the conversation never happened—and that I cannot use your name associated with any of the information."

Bilhorn opened her mouth wide, reached with a left hand to scratch her now-taut cheek. "Never?" she said.

"Ever," said Duncan.

"Sounds like a funny deal to me," she said. "But fire away."

Forty-Six

Wednesday Afternoon
Allison

The rifle didn't twitch.

Ed Steadman had kept his distance, which was smart.

Chanute ambled away and clear of the horse-human cluster, fighting each step like he was dragging a ball and chain. He grumbled at the pain.

Steadman handed his rifle to Chanute and helped him aim the weapon at Colin's gut from six feet down the trail.

The treetops caught a breeze. On the trail, the air didn't budge.

Steadman tied up the loose horses and mule. He made a big show out of slicing off a couple of lengths of rope from a full coil behind Merlin's saddle.

Steadman clamped a paw on Allison's bicep and squeezed down to the bone. He yanked the arm up behind her back. He grabbed her other arm by the wrist and jerked it back, too, and pushed her hard.

"Hey," said Colin. "What the hell?"

Colin shook his head, arms up and away from his body.

Steadman held both her wrists in one claw. She felt rope wrap her wrists. He was a bear. A whirl and a fist would have the clout of a mosquito. A whirl and a kick to the balls? She'd better be sure.

"Hey Victor, my boy." Steadman put his giant hands on her face from behind, pressed her cheeks together. "Come get a smooch from the golden girl."

Steadman moved his hands down, circled her neck. Her mouth turned to sawdust. His fingers pressed on her windpipe.

"Ed," said Chanute. He looked worried. "Don't make it worse."

"Worse?" said Steadman. His mouth spewed an acrid fume. "Yes, worse. That's my plan. Much worse."

Colin nodded, the motion minuscule.

Bile stewed in Allison's chest. Sunny Boy huffed.

Steadman tugged at her belt, python arms draped over her pulled-back shoulders. Her wrists burned.

Chanute lost his footing, regained it, his finger on the trigger.

Colin took an innocent step closer. Chanute failed to notice.

"Stop—" said Allison before a hand covered her mouth.

"Don't make it any harder than it has to be," said Steadman.

She twisted her body hard. She caught flashes of Chanute's rifle and Colin's worried face. She torqued her chest, bucked hard with her hips. Steadman stumbled. He tried to reposition and she came clear of his grip for a second, enough to start her right leg moving, and by the time she'd turned and was square to him, her bound-up hands making it hard to keep her balance, the boot was flying up and she reminded herself to follow through, to finish the kick about a foot beyond the point of impact.

Hit balls, think jaw.

The boot smacked him flush. He buckled. She hopped on both feet to keep vertical and not lose her balance, not wanting to land on her back where her screaming arms would take the blow.

Chanute lifted the gun up but it was aimed way too high, and Colin had his grip on the barrel and corkscrewed it out of Chanute's feeble grip long before the thunder from the shot died down.

Colin jabbed the butt of the rifle into Chanute's marshmallow gut. Chanute stumbled back, arms windmilling. A backwards boot caught a rock, and he went airborne for one quick second and smacked the earth with a scream of white-hot agony.

Colin flashed like a cowboy ninja over to Steadman, chambered another round as he floated over him and put the barrel above the whiskers on Steadman's grubby cheek.

Colin barked: "Leave your hands right where they are or you'll be down one face."

Colin unsnapped a holder on his belt. His gutting knife made quick work of her lashings.

Chanute tried to roll over, let out a combo platter of yelps and cries. Nothing doing. He was a puddle of misery.

It was two against one.

Steadman lunged for Colin's ankle, but Colin skipped away and replied with a sideways boot to Steadman's shoulder, no mercy. Colin flipped Steadman over, dropped a knee smack in the sacrum. His hands ablur like a calf roper at the rodeo going for speed, Colin yanked Steadman's arms around and tied his wrists. He looped rope around Steadman's neck, threaded it around the tied-up wrists and hog-tied his ankles.

Steadman yelled indecipherable words into the dirt.

Allison took a long drink of water. Her heart thumped. Sweat trickled from her temples. Was she allowed one free kick to his teeth?

Colin planted a boot on Steadman's ribs, pressed down. Steadman howled.

Colin's ropework wasn't complete.

"You can't just—"

One last length of rope ran from the harness around Steadman's collar to a trailside tree, for good measure. Allison, breaths still short, walked the horses and Hercules down the trail. Steadman's horse, an easygoing Paint named Cricket, made six. She put Cricket and Bruiser on a string with Sunny Boy, and she put Hercules and Bucky on a string with Merlin. The work gave her focus.

"Please." Chanute flopped facedown like a walrus with a broken neck. "I can't even fucking stand up."

"Chilly night ahead." Colin wasn't questioning her plans, only stating the facts.

Neither Steadman nor Chanute would be sitting on a horse—or sitting comfortably anywhere—for a long time. Walking them out would take all day. If Chanute could flop-fish his way over to Steadman, Colin's knots would need hours of unpacking. The only issue was leaving two pissed-off men, one roped up, smack on the trail. Another hunter might be hiking out and stumble

247

into unneeded trouble. But it was getting late. Allison dug for water and a plastic bag of jerky. She built a small stash. No Fig Newtons. She flopped a spare blanket over the food and water, tossed a box of matches after it. The dry fall would help—they had ample supply of fuel within a few feet. That is, if Chanute could move enough to help.

"I don't see much choice."

Allison climbed up on Sunny Boy.

"Where the hell are we?" said Chanute.

"It's not that far," said Colin. "I'd say a three-day crawl."

Forty-Seven

Cleo Bilhorn told him about Dwight's gradual decline. "The doctors shrugged. The bank account emptied. We tried everything."

"You were living here—Rifle or Glenwood?"

"Idaho at the time," said Bilhorn. "Pocatello."

"And what brought you to Colorado?"

"Good old medical marijuana. It's not a cure, but it may as well be, I'm telling you. You can see it in him—makes him relax like you wouldn't believe."

"So the hash oil. Not something you're—"

"Of course not. That's dangerous shit. Puffing on a joint compared to firing up butane? Are you fucking kidding me?"

"So you'll be pressing for everything you can? Against your neighbors?"

"Hell yes. Pain, suffering, etcetera and etcetera. Going to get what we deserve. If it happened in a fancy-ass neighborhood and a family loses their million-dollar house because of stupid-ass neighbors, no different—right? Milk the sons of bitches."

"I'm asking because I'm curious," said Duncan. Did she not think he had a nose? "When weed went legal, did you start growing your own?"

"It's the cheapest way."

"So you grow now?"

"Getting pretty good at it, too."

"And, okay, I'm going to ask only because it's a rumor and reporters need to check on crazy stuff, and every now and then rumors have a tiny seed of truth to them." Duncan knew about unfortunate pieces-of-shit "truth" better than anyone. "Were you, by any chance, supplying extra marijuana to Ms. Sykes and Mr. Enriquez perhaps, you know, for some period of time? For money?"

Duncan had no idea how he'd work it into a story if it was true, given this off-the-record information. Both Coogan and his own journalistic soul knew he needed to attribute every statement. But he'd figure it out.

Bilhorn pinched up her mouth so her lips disappeared. "Son of a bitch," she muttered.

"But then something changed, is that correct?"

If he was going to get tossed out on his ear, he may as well push the issue as far as possible.

"Is this how it works?" said Bilhorn. "You think you're in confidential legal negotiations, but it all ends up splattered all over the news?"

"Again, we're off the record." Duncan pointed to the inert pen and notebook.

"But you'll find a way to get it in there, make us look bad—when all I've been trying to do is take care of a husband with Crohn's disease—do you have any idea how much money we spent on medicine before we moved down from Pocatello?"

Duncan shook his head.

"We had no idea Marsha and Jimmy were playing around with such dangerous stuff," she said. "And if they didn't get it from us—I mean, I didn't cut 'em any deals—they'd get it from somewhere else. The point is they blew up their fucking house and destroyed ours, too. That has nothing to do with how much we're owed."

"And something went sour between you? I mean, neighbors and all—"

"Hell." Bilhorn stared off to the side and down, vacant. "Supply and demand."

"Another neighbor?"

"No."

He hoped Bilhorn hated silence as much as he did.

"One day we got a call." Bilhorn washed her hands in the dry air. "I mean, what am I going to do with an offer like that? Dwight can't puff down all the MJ we grow. Like an old Snoop Dogg video around here most days. Seemed like a waste not to get what it's worth."

Duncan tried to treat the new information matter-of-factly. "How long ago, you know, did you stop selling to your neighbors?"

"About a year," said Bilhorn. "Maybe less."

"And you're still growing?"

"Sure."

"And selling your extra?"

"It's illegal." She hissed it.

"I know." Duncan smiled. "Off the record."

"I've got bills."

"Who do you sell to now?"

"I'll get them in trouble."

"Do I look like a cop?"

She didn't answer.

"Do you get paid in cash?"

"Of course."

"Did you get a name of the guy?"

"It wasn't a guy."

That fact caught Duncan up short. He'd been getting pictures in his head and he needed to blow them up.

"Well, it was a guy who set it all up, but then we worked with a woman. Most ordinary, regular woman you'll ever meet."

"Start with the guy."

"I get a queasy feeling giving you names."

"This talk isn't even happening."

"His name was Ed Steadman."

Duncan burned it into his memory. "And hers? Does she come here?"

"We met downtown. There are ways to wrap it up, you know. So it looks ordinary and there's no smell. Nothing."

"Where do you meet?"

"Church parking lot. On Sunday mornings."

"What church?"

"Calvary."

Right downtown.

"And her name?"

"I'm not so sure I can do that."

"Of course you can."

"It seems so innocent."

"What you're doing? Selling your extra? Pretty tame on anyone's scale. I mean, you didn't make the rules up, did you?"

"And what am I supposed to do, burn what we can't use? Throw it in the trash?"

"Exactly."

"And her name?"

"You burn me, Duncan Bloom, and I'll find the place where you live and drive my Freightliner right through your front door." She didn't blink. "She's listed at five hundred horsepower."

"You got yourself a deal. And I'll tell you where I live, save you the trouble of tracking me down."

"Helen Barnstone," said Bilhorn. "Nicest lady you'll ever meet."

Forty-Eight

Wednesday Afternoon
Trudy

They skirted the edge of the mucky meadow, their sneakers squishing down with a slurp-suck sound. A faint path drew them away from the wet spot, no doubt fed by an underground spring, and led them to a clearing twenty paces inside the forest canopy. Denuded earth and a small fire ring served as front porch to a log cabin, half of it shoved under a long slope that climbed up and away to the east. It was hard not to think hobbit.

Six fresh rabbit skins flopped over a wooden rail, drying. "They're a hare damp," said Mariah, smiling. "Sorry."

The humor pierced Trudy's grim thoughts like a hot needle. So did Mariah's beautiful smile. Why so afraid? A gorgeous if chilly October day in the woods, aspen trees dangling shards of gold in the afternoon sun.

A stone chimney jutted up the face of the low-ceilinged cabin. The structure had been constructed on three hefty logs, held up off the ground on stone corners. The walls met in sharp corners, logs notched as if by machine. "Hello!" said Mariah out of courtesy before pulling on the door. It swung open from the top. A prop flopped down and seated itself neatly in a trio of hefty rocks.

They stood inside, only a few inches of clearance for Mariah. Wood planks underfoot offered no give. The inside air smelled rich, faintly of juniper and rosemary.

Trudy guessed the room was fifteen feet on each side. The air was dead. A food-prep area included a neat shelf of jars—some open, some with lids. Dried chickweed. Amaranth. A batch of late-season clover, nearly fresh. Thistle.

"Girl after my own heart," said Trudy. "Resourceful."

"And organized."

A deerskin top blanket sat on the log bed, a candle lantern topped a round table, two wood stumps for stools. A small shelf held a dozen paperbacks, including Allison's favorite, *The Call of the Wild*.

Back outside, Trudy admired the snug hovel and how it melded with the hillside.

"She's coming back for the rabbit skins," said Trudy.

"Days do you think?" said Mariah. "Weeks?"

"Soon," said Trudy.

Trudy followed a faint path that led to a fallow garden, the soil turned and chopped.

A knee-high gauze fence surrounded the patch. The location

was perfect, on the north side of the clearing. A scoop of cool soil in her hand told her the mix included bog-like material, perhaps from the edges of the nearby spring.

The path beyond the garden led to a cluster of towering Engelmann spruce. Trudy inhaled the fading forest bouquet, a lemony touch with the pine stirred with sticky, refreshing resin. A customer once told her the Japanese practiced *shinrin-yoku*, forest bathing, to reduce anxiety. The bathers sought out a specific Japanese fir and its essential oils. Trudy stood in the dimming forest light, absorbing the trace aromas of dried fruit, peach notes and damp leaves. She'd bottle it if she could.

A rich, woody funk shoved its way into the crowd of smells. It was trying too hard—the organic equivalent of an angry skunk.

The path wrapped around a tree and then the source of the olfactory stew explained itself—a homemade compost bin, slats set an inch apart to allow the slurry to breathe and cook. The sides were cedar, rot resistant. The waist-high structure emitted wisps of steam. Atalanta knew her outdoor and green thumb shit. Plump white buttons dotted the open slats on one side of the compost bin and Trudy felt a sick sensation flash in her guts.

Trudy plucked the screaming-white fungi—*Amanita phalloides*. The stem had stayed with the cap when she'd plucked it, and she eyed the bucket-like sac at the base and found herself running back toward the cabin.

Trudy found the set of old tins again in the open cupboard inside. Mariah followed, her eyes worried. Trudy held the fresh mushroom by her fingertips and thumb. The Death Cap quivered.

"Psychedelic?" said Mariah.

Trudy placed the fresh one on a crude but smooth cutting board. "Most people don't live long enough to find out."

Forty-Nine

Wednesday Evening
Allison

Allison stood outside Trudy's house in the quiet, cool evening. Twenty minutes on the phone with the sheriff got her nothing. They were too busy with a "big-ass" manhunt to send a deputy to Sweetwater. Maybe later. Maybe tomorrow.

She tried to imagine Chanute and Steadman and what they would do. Chanute would have to work in pain, but he could free Steadman.

And if they needed warmth, her barn was the first thing they'd find.

Back inside, she dug out Trudy's laptop. She popped in the flash drive she'd taken from Chanute. All she could see was useless system folders and gobbledygook.

On Google, "Greenway CC + Colorado" turned up nothing other than a "Greenway" company out of Basalt, a home-cleaning product of some sort, and a "Greenway Plan" in Clear Creek County.

No surprise. It was doubtful that a group of marijuana smugglers passed out corporate trinkets touting their brand.

She heard Colin's whistle and she went back outside. He walked toward her across the meadow. He shook his head. "Nothing," he said.

She fixed tequilas. Allison found sandwich fixings and chips. They ate on the chilly porch in the dark, not saying much. All lights off.

Trudy's house offered a better view of the meadow and the

road coming down.

They agreed to sleep at Trudy's. They would take turns checking on the slightest bump or bruise in the night.

Allison had no trouble staying awake.

Fifty

Thursday Before Dawn
Clay Rudduck

Rudduck drove Hedland's beat-up Dodge Ram. Funky transmission, tired seats and a split dashboard to match the cracked window. Hedland sat in his own goddamn shotgun seat. It was humiliating that way. Rudduck drove like a grandma. It would be dark for another two hours.

They headed south out of Glenwood Springs and left Highway 82 at Carbondale, picking up speed as 133 bored south toward Redstone.

"How did you meet Miguel Ramirez?"

"Are you hanging all this on me?"

"And the answer is?"

"At a church social. Fucking difference does it make? At a bar."

"In Glenwood?"

"So you're blaming me."

Rudduck slowed on the highway and turned right. He followed a dirt road that climbed from the get-go, enough to press them back in their seats. The road leveled off. It zigzagged round an old barn. No detail, only a looming hulk close to the road. It was still predawn. He'd rousted Hedland at an ugly hour.

Rudduck cracked a window. Icy air jabbed his temple.

"You said you checked his background."

"And nothing has fucking happened."

"Nothing?"

"Two months since the crash and all of that. They don't know the first thing."

"So no reason to worry?"

Rudduck tried not to think of it all going down the tubes. He was so close now. After all the businesses he had started since leaving KDR, nothing had worked as well as this. He'd done security gigs. And then a few with dispensaries. Then back to security, doing the armored car service for pot shops when the banks wouldn't touch their cash.

"Look," said Hedland. "They know it was their informant because cops pulled him out of the plane, right? Dwyer or Ramirez, either way, he's their guy. They've got the plane and they can trace it back to Lubbock, but that's all. The owner was paid to use the plane for a week, knew nothing about what for. Cops got nothing."

"But there's one problem."

"What?"

"How did they know to put Ramirez with you in the first place?"

Hedland mulled it over. "You're saying they targeted me?"

"You think that bar meet-up was a coincidence?"

"It felt so—"

"So what? So—*random*?"

"Yeah."

Then it hit Hedland. "Fuck."

"And you all saw what's-her-name from the airplane. She

was right there. You think she didn't go through the wreck? We should have lit that motherfucking plane on fire with Ramirez inside, cooked it down to a puddle of goo."

"What's she got that the cops don't?"

Rudduck let the question dangle on its own thin rope, a weak braid of arrogance and presumption.

The headlights caught the yellow hulk of a D3K Cat and, beyond it, the gray foundation of the county's first grow.

Rudduck stopped, killed the engine.

He climbed out and left the door open. The soft *ding-ding-ding* of the alarm pissed him off. He kicked the door shut with the heel of his boot.

He walked twenty steps into the scrub. He heard Hedland open his door and climb out. The cooling engine ticked and pinged. A precursor of daylight drew a faint silhouette of Mount Sopris looming to the east.

Hedland put a leg up on the bumper by the tailgate, the corner of the pickup bed between them. From this distance, the light from the pickup cab caught Hedland's hulking form.

"What the fuck?" said Hedland.

"Gotta piss."

Rudduck backed up his claim with a stream splattered on the hard ground.

"What the hell are we doing here?" said Hedland.

Rudduck shuddered at the chill, zipped up. He stepped to Hedland. "Yeah, what are *we* doing?"

Rudduck answered for him.

Blood gushed when the nose broke, the right fist fueled by so much anger he didn't even know. Hedland's arms rose up, but they were a half hour late. Rudduck grabbed Hedland's ears and jammed his thumbs into both eyes, following through.

Rudduck put both arms around Hedland's neck. Blood

gushed. He yanked Hedland forward. He turned him at the last second and smashed his face down on the step bumper. The skull-on-metal sound was louder than he would have guessed.

Hedland slumped down on the dirt.

Rudduck's hand came up wet. He stood and gulped the thin air, looked around.

Far below, a pair of headlights bounced up and down. The lights turned at the barn and caught its old gray slats of wood and a sad, sagging roof.

Rudduck slammed the tailgate down. He reached down and hooked Hedland under the arms and hoisted him up. Strength and panic and desperation heaved the motherfucker straight up so he was standing, sort of, but he was too dead or dying to put any weight on his feet. Rudduck shoved his body back. Hedland flopped on the bed of the pickup with a dull thud. Rudduck put his shoulder to the mass. He fought the hill. And gravity. He heard the low rumble of the car behind him. His boots looked for purchase in the thin hardpack. He slammed Hedland's head down one more time for good measure. It was soft now, like a rotted melon.

Rudduck banged the tailgate closed. He grabbed an old moving blanket, padded and thick and torn, from behind the seat in the cab. The blanket sort of covered Hedland's sizable frame, but only after Rudduck bent the dead knees.

Rudduck had no reason to be here—no hunting gear, no rifle, no hunting buddy, no lunch, no tag, no blaze orange vest, no explanation, no nothing.

He had stopped in the middle of the road.

Their road.

Rudduck shoved the door shut. He ran straight off, hoping that the edge of their advancing wedge of headlight didn't catch him sprinting, a blurry flicker on the fringes of their vision. By the time he turned and spun low, pressing himself into the scrub and dirt, he could already see the old-school station wagon inching to a stop behind his pickup.

The doors cracked open on both sides and two men, like matching twins, unfolded themselves and stood.

The station wagon's headlights caught the hunter on the close side. A blaze orange cap dotted his sizable head. He wore a camo vest and big old camo Carhartts with suspenders. He was a regular Paul Bunyan.

A metallic rasp like a sick crow shattered the stillness and the back door opened. One more hunter emerged.

The first two peered into the cab. The third guy in the back was Bunyan's brother, only bigger. Number three strode to the rear of the pickup and stretched to the sky with his free arm. The other was busy cradling a gallon-size convenience store cup, maybe coffee.

The trio huddled at the rear of the pickup. A flashlight emerged—*what the fuck for?*

Rudduck's heart pounded a hole in the earth. His nose, he realized, had been busy fending off a stinky attack from a pile of fresh cow poop. *Open range.*

A low grumble rolled across the scrub. He couldn't make out the words. The two men backed away from the pickup bed and the third leaned over.

Rudduck couldn't see where he'd fallen, but prickers clawed his ankle and said *you're fucked.*

Fifty-One

Allison woke to full morning.

Full sun made her think she'd misbehaved, gone rogue. Colin had taken the last shift and let her sleep.

She drove her black Chevy S-10 to the barn. It had rhino bars and overhead lights, a roll bar, too. It was total overkill for putting around. She found Colin brushing down Merlin for nicks and cuts. He worked the way a butler might check his master's tux before a state dinner.

They spent an hour brushing down all the horses, let them out to the paddock. They doled out food, cleaned stalls. They took turns keeping an eye where the trail came down out of the woods.

Colin wanted to be convinced of the plan to leave the horses behind, in harm's way.

He preferred to spend another night in the loft at the barn. If they could round up a couple of loaded howitzers, Colin wouldn't object. He wanted to paint "Free Beer/Hot Food" on a sign to lure them in.

"Your sense of vengeance is appreciated," said Allison. "And I wouldn't mind having something to show the cops, you know, *told you so*. But I don't think there's any need to add to the body count."

"I thought marijuana was harmless." Colin sighed. They were back in her pickup for the three-minute commute back to the meadow.

"You know, I don't think I've ever seen you smoke a joint."

Colin could sip one beer for an hour. Two fingers of whiskey provided an evening's ration. He didn't believe in blotto. The boy could slog through any grueling situation out there in the woods, but despised the notion of inflicting pain on himself, no matter the temporary payoff.

"They call it getting stupid for a reason," he said. "Ain't that enough?"

"All we do is survive," said Allison. "Every bit of how we're programmed, you know, deep down. Tequila, weed, wine all do the same thing—it's about freedom to relax, to let our guard down."

"But not really."

"It helps you forget." Allison thought of Devo—and Trudy's mushroom theory. "It loosens you up in ways you didn't know you needed to be loose. It is literally a little trip."

"Must be a good place to go."

"What?"

"So many people want to go there, to that place. The place pot takes you."

"And you don't?"

"I don't see you stocking up at the pot shops."

"Not my thing."

"Turns people stupid in more ways than one."

"You mean our criminal masterminds?"

"You're flying a plane crammed with pot out of state. You're flying, so to speak, off the radar," said Colin. "Isn't the number one thing to get up over the mountains? Not crash?"

"Or make sure, one hundred percent sure, that when you bring on a new recruit that he's not working with the cops?"

"What the hell?"

Allison braked for the same reason Colin blurted.

A giant SUV, gleaming black and shiny like a monument to metal, sat next to Trudy's house. It looked showroom ready, spit shined. It was unusual enough, an urban tank of ridiculous proportions, but in between the vehicle and the house stood the even more preposterous sight of a man holding a bubble of flowers so large that if it was a helium balloon he might have floated off.

He wasn't moving.

In fact, his feet remained riveted in place. He wore faded blue jeans and a maroon leather jacket, light blue baseball cap. Aviators.

Allison pulled the pickup to a stop. On the porch, a few feet higher than the flower man, Trudy was in the middle of a full-bore rant. Colin cracked the window.

At this distance, words could not be distinguished. There was no need for detail.

Trudy's tirade reached a shrill crescendo. She pointed at his monster truck, yelled like she was in a horror movie and stormed back into her house. The flower man waited a minute, stepped forward like a cat burglar and laid the flowers on the porch. He retreated to his armored personnel vehicle and slipped inside.

"Who's the dude?" said Colin, as casual as his flannel shirt.

"I can't say for sure," said Allison. "But the only candidate for that kind of treatment is Sam Shelton."

"The rock star?"

"Ex," said Allison. "And utter, clueless asswipe."

Fifty-Two

As crime scenes went, it was a beauty. To Duncan, Mount Sopris might be his favorite mountain of all time—a double-peaked, big-shouldered structure that sat at the fork in the valley and served as a daily reminder of geological wonders. It blotted out the entire eastern sky from this scrubby shelf of cow pasture south of Carbondale.

A gaggle of cops surrounded a sad old pickup. There had to be double the cops necessary, but murder did that. Duncan snapped a few pictures with a pocket-size Sony that took point-and-shoot to a whole new level. He had the urge to walk higher up on the slope so he could see back inside the pickup to the object of the cop's attention, the dead guy, but the slope wasn't steep enough. A hundred yards further up the road, a bright yellow bulldozer sat idle. The gray facing of a concrete foundation poked its head about four feet above grade. He might get a view from the top of the bulldozer but climbing up on private property with all those cops around didn't seem like a wise move.

As much as he enjoyed the view of Mount Sopris and as much as he enjoyed shivering in his thin, old jacket and standing around the cow patties, he didn't need a murder.

Not today, not now, not tomorrow, not next week. Not anytime soon. Murders made for good copy most of the time, but he didn't need this murder until after the election or after he got his money back or Trudy snapped back to her old self or whenever things returned to a steady, even keel, if it was okay to think about boat metaphors while staring at a mountain.

With the name from Bilhorn—*Helen Barnstone*—and the pending settlement in the hash oil case, he had plenty to deal with and lots to sort through. He'd gone straight from the H Lazy F to Helen Barnstone's house in the Westbank subdivision. No answer. He'd waited for a half hour outside. She hadn't come home. He waited another half hour down the block, with an eye on her door, and his phone on redial to Rudduck.

The description of the church parking lot cash sales of weed were perfect, a whole new angle, if only he hadn't bought a piece of the action that was one thousand percent fucking illegal. The best thing about the past fifteen hours or so was that Trudy was off to Meeker and Allison and Colin were up in the woods. He'd slept at the newspaper on a small couch. It wasn't the first time.

"Who is he?"

"Come on," said DiMarco. "Next of kin, you know."

"Was he killed here?"

Duncan and DiMarco had perfected the non-interview interview. They stood side by side, not too close. They didn't look at each other. Minimal gestures.

"Not certain."

"You've got an ID?"

"Yes."

"Age?"

"Thirty-six."

"Hometown?"

"Glenwood Springs."

"Who found him?"

"Three hunters trying to get up the road."

"They see anything?"

"They're being interviewed."

"Was it those guys in the station wagon?" He'd seen a trio of hunters in a pullout along 133.

"That's them."

"Any idea on time of death?"

"ME's call. He's on the way."

"You guys always have a hunch."

"Can't use it, right?"

"You say so."

"He's a fresh one."

"Shot?"

"No bullet holes. No stab wounds."

"What then?"

"Beaten to a pulp."

Duncan had what he needed, took a snap of Mount Sopris for the hell of it. It might be the last nature photograph he ever took.

Back down on the highway, Duncan stopped where the old woody station wagon was parked on the dirt pullout, two cop cars keeping it company. The three hunters, including two large bearlike men, stood in a camo-clad cluster. Two of the men wore blaze orange caps. The third man's cap was knit and also blaze. The trio of heads bobbed like three oversized candy corns against the drab scrub of the dry embankment. Duncan snapped a group photo from twenty yards away, in case they got squirrelly up close, and took another, on zoom, of the station wagon's license plate. Cops waved him away as he tried to get closer.

"It's their call," said Duncan.

"There's an active manhunt." The cop was young, forthright and mistaken. "They're key witnesses. It's not a good idea to have their names out there."

"Come on, I would never use names in situations like this," said Duncan.

Total bullshit.

It worked.

The would-be hunters wanted nothing to do with a reporter. The shortest served as spokesman. He boiled their collective message down to two words: "Not today."

Duncan turned to head back. It was a decent story with a murder scene close to Carbondale, killer on the loose, body found by hunters.

"Oh, one more thing." Much friendlier tone now, notebook tucked away. "Is the road where you found the body, is that national forest access up there?"

"After the open range, the road ends about a half mile further up, in the aspens. The national forest line is back up in there another ways." The spokesman's flat, slack-jawed demeanor suggested he hadn't heard or told a joke in ten years. One of the two tall boys lit the stub of a half-smoked cigar.

"Good hunting?"

"Most years."

"And that's all national forest?"

"Not for quite a hike back up in there."

"So private land where you would have been hunting?"

"Eleventh year in a row. And we get permission each time, if that's what you're after."

Duncan shrugged, smiled. He downplayed everything. "Not after anything. Got a friend who is always looking for good spots. How much land has this guy got?"

The spokesman shook his head. "More than we'll ever cover—lots. And it's a woman who owns it, leases it out for the grazing."

"Got her name?"

"Darla Cerise," said the spokesman.

"Looked like there might have been someone up there building something."

Two shrugs, one headshake.

267

"Okay, thanks," said Duncan. "I gotta ask because I gotta ask, was the guy you found, was he just, you know, laying there?"

"Under a blanket." The cigar smoker. "Like a moving pad. Like one you get when you rent at U-Haul."

"You could tell it was a body?"

"Feet sticking out. Boots."

"Face?"

The cigar smoker closed his eyes, popped his eyebrows up. "Not much left. And whoever killed him has a thing about eyes." He was into it now. See how easy it is to talk to a real live reporter? "Man, his eyes were gone."

Fifty-Three

Thursday Morning
Allison

"There are two kinds of *Amanita*s."

It had been weeks since Allison had seen Trudy this focused. It had taken time, however, to calm her down from the encounter with Sam Shelton. "We found them—"

"We?"

"Glenna's partner—wife—Mariah. Mariah took me to the cabin, and I found the *Amanita* around the compost pile out back. It's possible, in fact, that the compost was being used to grow the mushrooms on purpose. A tin of dried ones inside, too."

"*Amanita phalloides*?" Long ago Allison had focused on learning the essentials of mushroom identification. Death by fungi seemed a poor way to go. Avoidable, too. "You're sure?"

They sat on the porch. Allison needed to see as far as possible.

Trudy smiled. She was right, it was a dumb question.

"And where is Atalanta?"

"We didn't see her. Didn't look or wait around, either."

"Maybe the coroner or one of the reports would confirm your suspicions? Toxicity levels in the kidneys or liver?"

"Maybe."

In theory, Allison could dump everything she'd learned about the plane crash with the Garfield County Sheriff's Department. Then, she could head back up north, to Meeker, and track down this mystery woman who had been kept away from the devolution tribe by the main man himself. The sooner she headed back north, the better. If the mushroom cabin was being used on a somewhat regular basis, tracking shouldn't be hard.

Allison walked Trudy through everything about Chanute and Steadman. Colin had gone on another run up to the barn, to watch.

"The dead guy on the plane was a cop?" said Trudy.

"An informant," said Allison. "A guy working off time."

"And the two guys could come stumbling down the road any minute?"

"Stumbling at best," said Allison.

"And they'll come right down this road."

"The easiest way down and out to civilization."

"And you're waiting for another, what? Wrestling match? Shoot-out?"

"If they know the barn is ours and where we live, they might want to make a statement."

"Sounds like they're in no shape to do anything of the kind," said Trudy. "Give all this to Duncan."

"And head to Meeker?" said Allison. She wanted to be there now, at the cabin.

"Are you still thinking you owe something to the dead guy on the plane?"

"Of course," said Allison.

"Don't forget," said Trudy. "Even though he was tied up, he made his own decisions, too."

Fifty-Four

Thursday Noon
Duncan

Public records coughed up the license plate and its owner, Vince Hedland.

The dead guy in the pickup might be him. Thirty-six. Two convictions for possession of marijuana, probation in both cases, and one for assault, six months in jail and probation.

The assault had happened at Doc Holliday's Tavern, a bar one block north from the newspaper office.

He didn't need this story, but Coogan showed lots of interest over the clash of beautiful countryside and violent death. The detail about the eyes—the same thing Allison described when she came down from the plane wreck with the dead guy. What the freaking *hell*? Something was going to give.

Trudy had called with the news that she was heading down from Sweetwater with Allison and Colin. They were going to spend the night in Glenwood Springs to get out of the way of two pissed-off guys in the woods. A couple of hunters in Allison's group had—what? Purposely booked a trip with her to see what she knew about the airplane wreck? And then there had been a fight. He cared about that more than anything and had jotted down the names Trudy relayed: *Victor Chanute, Ed Steadman.*

Trudy sounded anxious, but clearheaded and energetic, too. She sounded good.

Pulling up the court records on the Vince Hedland assault case, Duncan spotted a welcome name.

"Sure I remember it."

Inez' voice was like a cool spring in a frying desert.

"And?"

"Two a.m. Last winter. Hedland got there right at last call, clearly to meet the victim. She'd been waiting."

"She?"

"Yes."

"Waiting?"

"When I say a word, does it not sound like that word?"

"Proceed."

"They went outside when the bar closed."

Duncan scoured his memory for any brief mention in the paper. Nothing came up.

"February second?"

"Early," said Cordova. "Long before the groundhogs. She was pushed. She fell backwards and hit her head. One witness. A good one."

"Who?"

"A cop. He was watching the bars close. He saw the whole thing, start to finish. Fortuitous."

"Injuries?"

"Two days in the hospital for her—concussion."

"And the fight was over what?"

"He owed her money."

"Her name?"

"I'll pretend you didn't ask."

"Did she testify?"

"No need. The cop cited him and he pled guilty."

"Who was the cop?"

"Your pal."

"I don't have any."

"You don't think the *bromance* is obvious?"

"What?"

"Duncan Bloom, you are oblivious. You think you're invisible?"

"Whatever."

"Everybody watches you."

"Bullshit."

"More than you know."

Duncan doodled in his notebook. Where was any of this going? Innocuous detail for the bottom of the story. *The truck where the victim was found was owned by a guy who was in a bar fight last winter . . .*

Big whoop.

"And Hedland got probation."

"Good lawyers doing their work," said Cordova. "He had the best."

"I thought there were minimums."

He could hear her smile. "Do you want me to repeat myself?"

"Oh, it was *you*." Mock sincerity. "Now I see."

"And he was contrite. Plus the cop, your pal, only testified to a push and then she slipped."

Duncan pictured DiMarco testifying. He might want to embellish, but wouldn't. "He's one honest cop," said Duncan. And then realized his mistake.

"And I thought you didn't know him."

"Whoever it is."

"Yes," said Cordova. "Steady."

Steady?

A time-warp flutter shook Duncan's chest. He'd been picturing Inez Cordova's pretty mouth, but the more productive part of his brain was putting two and fucking two together.

He stared at the note he'd taken from Trudy, two names.

Chanute.

Steadman.

He flipped back up a few pages in his notebook from the time with Cleo Bilhorn.

Steadman.

Fuck.

The Hedland murder case could go to hell.

"You okay?" said Cordova. "Still alive?"

"Yeah," said Duncan. "I think so."

Fifty-Five

Thursday Afternoon
Trudy

Trudy drove her hybrid pickup, alone, following Allison's black pickup and the trail of dust down Sweetwater Road. They had two rooms waiting at the Hanging Lake Inn, though Allison might head straight to Meeker with Colin.

Once Trudy reached the river, her cell phone worked.

Rachel Crouse perked right up. "Give me good news."

"I'm ready," said Trudy. "One hundred percent."

"Now that's what we call consent," said Crouse. "With enthusiasm. What changed?"

Hearing about Allison getting attacked? Seeing Sam Shelton's pathetic face and those stupid flowers? *Flowers*? As if a bunch of flowers would make her forget or entice her to forgive?

"Friends," said Trudy. It was true. After Shelton scampered off, there were three votes to nail the bastard, Colin leading the pack. He argued in a persuasive manner, with zeal. "Plus, he showed up at my place, trying to crawl back."

"He *what*?" Crouse barked it. "You've got a protective order."

"He was twenty feet from my doorstep."

"He's not supposed to even step foot on your property! Did you call the cops?"

"No," said Trudy. "But I took a picture with my phone."

"Text it to me—what an asshole."

"File the lawsuit," said Trudy. "Bring in as many women as you can find."

Yes, she'd toyed with the notion of fucking Sam Shelton. Yes, she'd grabbed his trousered, hard cock for point five seconds. Yes, she had smiled—maybe she had teased. Maybe she had encouraged. But she hadn't said *yes*.

Fifty-Six

Coogan, his glasses smeared and greasy from a long day, asked Duncan to pull up Google Maps and show him the precise location of where the body had been found.

In the story, Duncan had kept it vague: "Along the edge of the forest south of Carbondale and west of Highway 83."

Duncan spotted the wide-spot turnout where he'd chatted with the hunters down by the highway and then used his finger to trace the road climbing to the west, where it jogged around an old barn.

"I was digging a bit on the property owner," said Duncan.

"Why?" said Coogan.

Duncan flipped back through his notes.

"Darla Cerise," said Duncan.

Coogan rolled a chair over, his perma-frown intact. He sat backwards in the chair and lowered his head like a sad basset hound. "Why would she have anything to do with it?"

"Covering my bases," said Duncan. "I've got an ID on the dead pilot from the Flat Tops plane wreck, too."

"No shit." His expression remained stone. "At long last."

"He was an informer working for the cops. All I've got so far is his name."

"Which is?"

"Miguel Ramirez."

"From?"

"I'll find out. That is—if he was prosecuted in Colorado. Al-

275

ways a chance the cops brought in an out-of-stater, to minimize the risk that anyone in the ring would recognize him."

"If he was out of state, it didn't work."

"And I've got a lead on the group of guys who were in the plane."

"It will have to wait for another day. Or two."

"Why?"

"Prioritize the murder—it's fresh."

"Darla Cerise was building something. It's been open ranchland since a year or two after statehood. Same family."

"New barn?"

"Looked bigger than that. And then the name rang a bell," said Duncan. "*Darla*. So dramatic. I knew I hadn't seen it too long ago."

"And?"

"And then I remembered the campaign contributions for Hallowell and Walters, wanting to see what money was lining up for the commissioner election. And it turns out Darla Cerise is a generous supporter of Bill Walters. To the tune of thousands."

"Where did you get this tip, your buddy?"

"My *buddy*?"

"Your source."

"If source equals buddy, I'm the most popular guy in Colorado. What do you mean *buddy*?" Duncan was sick of people who thought they knew him. That was despite the fact that it was his cop source, Randall DiMarco, who had called with a "strong suggestion" to look into Darla Cerise and her plans.

"Didn't mean to offend," said Coogan.

"Which buddy did you mean?"

"Your cop friend."

Duncan shook his head. "Part of my job, to develop sources."

"I withdraw the assertion," said Coogan. "What can Walters

do for Darla Cerise?"

"That's what I'd like to know," said Duncan. "Or at least that's what I'd like to check off as innocent politics. If such a thing exists."

"I always thought Walters was an honorable guy."

"He might be."

"And he's another one of your *sources*." Coogan said the word with the verbal equivalent of tiptoes.

"He's always given me good shit. At least so far. And knowing him is part of my fucking job. Any appearance of *buddydom* is a by-product of what I do, like trash after a party."

"Easy," said Coogan.

First Cordova, now this. He didn't need it.

"I'm good," said Duncan. "Following shit where it flows."

"Tell me about Darla."

"I can tell you about the tip."

Coogan offered a smile so faint it made Mona Lisa look like Taylor Swift. His way of making up. "Okay."

"If the tip is right, she is the one who offered to build a new location for High Valley Farms."

Coogan took a minute to let that sink in. "The grow in Basalt causing all the ruckus with its stench."

"Yep."

"But Garfield County doesn't permit grows."

"Yep."

"And Walters is going to be re-elected."

"Unless the moon murders the sun," said Duncan. "And tries to do its job."

"So why would she be offering?"

"Or planning?" said Duncan. He'd already thought the same thing. "Walters claims he doesn't want the county to permit grows."

Was this a sign of *buddydom* with a commissioner? Or a good reporter's awareness of sitting commissioners and their positions on public policy?

"You sure?"

"We give each other back rubs every day at noon." Duncan turned in his chair, grabbed his phone. "I'll double-check."

Coogan wasn't a sarcasm kind of guy. But Coogan had no idea of Duncan's personal overload, each leg on a different slackline bouncing in the wind.

Duncan punched Bill Walters' number so hard his fingertip stung. There were more mature options at Duncan's disposal, such as making a simple, professional call at the request of his editor, but the mix of petulance and self-righteousness felt good. He needed to show Clay Rudduck a bit of the same mix and get his money back.

"Just heading out the door," said Walters. "You're the last thing I need right about now."

"Nobody ever needs a reporter," said Duncan. "Until it's time to toot your horn. Then you insist on our presence because the road crews filled a pothole and you think it's page one worthy."

"Love-hate," said Walters. "I plead guilty to the hate."

"You know Darla Cerise?"

"Family name goes way back."

"You heard about the murder?"

"I heard it was down her way."

"You trying to split hairs?"

"Being factual. Try it."

Walters sounded worried.

"Sounds like you're following this."

"She is a friend."

"And campaign contributor?"

"Like most good friends, yes."

278

"And she has offered to help provide a home for that grow in Basalt?"

"Different county," said Walters. "No clue."

"Not unless it moves to this one. Your county."

Duncan's phone throbbed on the desk. A text from Trudy— *we're outside.*

"As a commissioner, I don't discuss the status of individual parcels of land."

"Nice to have a categorical no-comment in your back pocket."

Duncan texted back: *two secs.*

"Then, are we done?"

Duncan grabbed a black permanent marker, jotted the name *Walters* on a sheet of paper, drew an arrow, jotted the name *Cerise*, drew an arrow, jotted the name *Hedland* and then drew an X through Hedland's name.

"Does the name *Vince Hedland* mean anything to you?"

Wrecked plane. Marijuana. Dead guy. Eyes poked out.

Abandoned pickup. Possible marijuana. Dead guy. Eyes poked out.

"What does *mean anything* mean? I've always wondered. But, alas, no."

"If your, quote, unquote, 'friend' had plans to serve as safe harbor for a stinky grow operation offending the neighbors in Basalt, wouldn't she know there's a change coming to the county's approach to authorizing grows?"

Walters sighed. "Nothing has changed."

Duncan jotted down the name *Cleo Bilhorn*. Then the words *better offer*. The Bilhorns should be fearing prosecution for selling their extra. The plea deal talks must be complicated.

"And nothing will change until you're re-elected."

"And here I thought we knew each other."

"How much has she donated to your campaign, maybe with

insider knowledge that you will have a change of heart?"

"Do you keep theories as pets? Keep them around for company when you're lonely?"

The line went dead.

Walters' disavowal was too emphatic. It fit perfectly with Duncan's axiom—the swifter and more firm the denial, the bigger the shovel required to dig through the bullshit.

"That look on your face says you're in no shape to leave."

Trudy managed a half smile. Duncan took solid hugs from Trudy and Allison, a quasi hug and shoulder slap from Colin.

"Fucking mess," said Duncan. The cool night air felt good for two seconds. "Tell me about this guy Ed Steadman."

"He's bad news all the way," said Allison. "He knows everything about the plane, everyone who was on it, the whole plan. He knows. And his buddy Victor Chanute knows."

Allison unspooled the story over a few fast minutes. Duncan listened, his head still spinning. He had come to one solid conclusion: *Walters knows too much.* Trudy put an arm around Allison's shoulder when she recounted the attack by Steadman. Allison's account made Duncan shudder beyond the chill.

"Steadman was in the thick of it," said Duncan. "He's a buyer. He gathers extra from medical growers. Could be dozens and dozens of so-called caregivers. Maybe hundreds. Pretty soon, you can pack a plane. Good, fresh Colorado shit."

The general, minutes-old plan came into focus. They had two rooms booked at the Hanging Lake Inn, spiffier than the generic exterior might suggest. In the morning, Allison and Colin were bound for Meeker to talk with the medical examiner about their mushroom theory and maybe go look for the forest waif who lived in the hobbit hole. Trudy had a meeting with her lawyer.

The motel-and-pizza rendezvous was set for 9 p.m. Or as soon as Duncan could get there. He would call if he was running much later than 10.

For Trudy, Duncan thought, the change of scenery might do her good. Maybe he could break through the shield she'd raised since that night at Sam Shelton's. All Duncan knew for sure was that he'd soon be asking Trudy for a mountain of forgiveness, especially if he squandered eighty-one fucking thousand dollars and got fired for investing in the controversial business he was covering. It wouldn't hurt to provide Trudy with as much leniency and grace as possible now that he was in a position to offer both. Duncan knew Trudy well enough to know that she had to first forgive herself for whatever had happened at Sam Shelton's. The motel and a jug of wine might help with the space between them. Anything physical, such as a lingering kiss, would start completely with her.

Allison weighed the idea of swinging by the police station to see if she could rouse more enthusiasm about keeping an eye on Sweetwater. And then Allison quizzed Duncan about the murder. He told them his guess on the victim's name. She lit up when he made the connection about the possible grow operation on Darla Cerise's farm.

"The eyes were poked out?" said Allison.

On the edge of his vision, Duncan sensed someone on the sidewalk—a presence. He was listening, loitering.

Duncan dropped his voice to a whisper. "The hunters who found him said they were two red splotches. But his skull was in bad shape, too. The forehead."

Duncan turned from their loose huddle, expecting to stare someone off and away.

Instead, Duncan shuddered, a deep and involuntary twitch,

as if a grizzly had sauntered onto Grand Avenue.

The man smiled. He held up a hand in a relaxed fashion, waving *hello*.

Waving *I got all day*.

Waving *you take your time*.

Clay Fucking Rudduck.

Fifty-Seven

Thursday Evening
Allison

They raided a liquor store—a bottle of Malbec for Trudy, two tallboys of Coors for Colin, a half-pint of Sauza for her. They grabbed an extra bottle of red wine for Duncan. They had not been invited into the newspaper. Duncan said Coogan had strapped on his nasty face and, besides, there was a guy on the sidewalk who had information, Duncan said, that he'd been waiting on. Allison had taken a long look at the dude, who pointed at Duncan and made some innocent gesture like he was sorry to interrupt.

They grabbed burgers (buffalo, elk, and veggie) at Vicco's Charcoalburger Drive-In and made a mess of Trudy and Duncan's motel room, snarfing food and huddling around Trudy's laptop. They took turns lobbing in ideas about how to dig up anything on Ed Steadman. They needed Duncan and his magic database.

Trudy tried Facebook, basic Google, Google Images and every

combination of "Ed Steadman, marijuana, Glenwood Springs, arrest, police, Rifle, Silt and New Castle." Nothing.

"Try flaming butthole," said Allison. Every time she closed her eyes, she felt his giant paws on her crotch.

They spent another fruitless few minutes on Miguel Ramirez, same result.

"You said you looked in here already?" Colin held up Chanute's flash drive between thumb and forefinger.

"It's empty," said Trudy.

"Did you look in the trash?" Colin flipped the drive to Trudy. It landed on the bed where Trudy had made camp.

"Trash?" said Trudy.

"Look at you," said Allison. "What cattle ranch raised you?"

"Always look in the trash," said Colin. "Whether the bucket off the back stoop or the trash on the desktop."

Trudy shoved the drive into the port. "It's called a recycle bin." Mock admonishment.

"Another case of political correctness run amok," said Colin. Mock pontification.

"Open it up." Allison plopped herself next to Trudy on the bed, tequila in the ubiquitous plastic bathroom cups of budget hotels and motels nationwide. Tequila deserved so much better.

"Fuck." Trudy deployed a healthy f-bomb twice a year, always muttered in wonder and amazement. She said it the way a ten-year-old might say "wow."

On the screen, Trudy found a spreadsheet file in the Recycle Bin and when she had moved it to the desktop and opened it up, the screen filled up with data.

Name. Address. Last date sold. Strain. Return date. Quality. Price.

There were 309 rows. The addresses ran from Craig to Rifle, Parachute to De Beque, Paonia to Montrose, Basalt to Glenwood Springs.

Glenwood Springs, in fact, seemed to have won the prize for participation.

Trudy scrolled up from the bottom. The file was organized by date, the most recent "customer," if that was the right term, added less than a month ago.

"Jean Delaney?" Trudy shook her head, stopped scrolling. "One of my customers. One of the best. Nothing I don't know about soil and herbs and short growing seasons that she doesn't know—but she's got awful arthritis. She calls them her happy sticks. You can smell it on her. She wears it on her like a badge of honor. She was at Woodstock, for crying out loud. Told me all the stories about running around naked, tripping to Jimi Hendrix."

"So she grows her own," said Allison. "But maybe grows more than she needs?"

"Everything she grows takes off like weeds, no pun intended. So she must have bushels of the stuff, even with the limits."

"Nice source of income," said Colin. "And maybe not so little."

Allison tried to connect the dots on Ed Steadman. "When Duncan was telling us how he ran across the name *Ed Steadman*, he mentioned it was the woman from the story about the hash oil fire, the neighbor."

Colin shook his head. Trudy shook her head.

"I didn't remember it, either," said Allison.

Trudy went to the newspaper website. She entered "hash oil fire + Rifle" in search and found the original story about the fire back in August, along with a pair of disturbing oddball mug shot photos of Marsha Sykes and Jimmy Enriquez. The story included a quote from a neighbor named Cleo Bilhorn.

"That was it," said Colin.

Back at the spreadsheet, the name *Bilhorn* sat right where it belonged, in the *B*'s.

"Cops need this," said Trudy.

"What was the name of the guy who was murdered today?"

"Vince Hedland," said Colin without missing a beat. "Why are you looking at me like that? Weren't you paying attention? You didn't think it mattered?"

A topo map of Rio Blanco County fanned out across Colin's lap. Allison had marked the site of Devo's current camp, and Trudy had marked the approximate location of Atalanta's cabin.

Allison wished she could rip herself in two.

Half of her needed to be back in Sweetwater, pronto. She had a bad feeling Steadman and Chanute would be lighting fires.

And half of her wanted to be outside Atalanta's cabin at dawn, ready to follow any trail or sign. Devo's death was not natural causes. She knew it in her toenails.

"No Vince Hedland on the spreadsheet," said Trudy.

"How about Sykes or Enriquez?" said Allison.

Trudy took a minute. "No. And no."

"What about Jean Delaney?" said Colin.

"What about her?"

"Maybe she knows Steadman, too."

Trudy looked up, understood the implication. "It's past nine."

Since they'd set up camp in the motel, Allison felt confined and anxious. Everything she needed to do was out there, dark or light, midnight or noon. She'd blink and see Steadman and Chanute straggling out of the woods. She'd blink again and see Devo's lifeless eyes.

What had Devo done to piss anyone off? Trudy's detail on the paperback books in Atalanta's cabin was beyond coincidence. Jack London. As Trudy might say, solely as a means of expressing astonishment, *fuck*.

"One call?" said Allison. "I mean, she does trust you, right?"

"She lives a block from Sayre Park," she said. "Five minutes from here. I'd rather knock on the door."

Fifty-Eight

Thursday Evening
Duncan

Duncan had been so busy answering Rudduck's questions that he hadn't paid close attention to where they were driving. They circled the streets of Glenwood and then, oddly, jumped on the highway and sped down to West Glenwood, exited and roared back into town.

Coogan probably thought he had stormed out, playing the role of the petulant, arrogant reporter.

Rudduck agreed it was an "odd time" to catch up. He said he'd had a drink at Doc's. He said it was a last-second decision to drift up the street and see if Duncan might be "burning the 9 p.m. oil."

Rudduck might have had a couple. Or three. But the giant Navigator stayed rock steady in the middle of the lane, even when Rudduck looked over to ask a question. He played a Boz Scaggs CD.

The dirty lowdown . . .

Duncan wanted to text Coogan. *Be right back.* But that might invite a question he didn't want to field. Rudduck kept asking about the huddle Duncan had left on the sidewalk.

"Was that Allison Fucking Coil? And her boyfriend was the

cowboy, am I right? And your girlfriend, Trudy—well, everyone in Glenwood Springs knows *her*." Maybe Rudduck would stop for gas or a snack and that would be his chance. "You hear about that murder story down south of Carbondale?"

"Well, yeah," said Duncan. "Working on it all day."

"Oh really? Where'd it happen?"

"About five miles south of Carbondale, east of the highway. The way my editor went nuts you'd have thought it was 1963 in Dallas." Bitching about Coogan might show Rudduck he was comfortable, letting him in on company politics. "The guy can go off the rails."

"They got anything?"

"The cops?"

"No, the candy stripers at the hospital."

"Funny."

"Well?"

"They aren't telling me if they do."

"Anybody see anything?"

"Doesn't seem like it."

"Where did they find the body?"

"Back of a pickup."

"Who the hell found him back up there?"

"A few guys heading up to hunt."

"The guy was dead?"

"It was a murder, so, yeah."

"How'd he die? Shot?"

"You're worse than my editor. Where the hell are we going here?"

"What are the cops saying?"

"As little as possible."

"It wasn't a suicide?"

"It would be a first. Bash your head on a tailgate, then crawl up on the bed of your pickup, cover yourself with an old packing blanket and wait to croak."

"And so who owned the property?"

"Jesus," said Duncan. "Any chance we could talk about my money?"

"So whose property?" said Rudduck. "Is that a factor?"

Rudduck's insistence knifed its way between a couple of Duncan's ribs.

Rudduck headed back north on Grand Avenue and Duncan spotted a familiar white hybrid pickup coming off the bridge. The driver stared straight ahead. She had that purposeful look.

Trudy.

Fifty-Nine

Thursday Evening
Trudy

"Trudy?"

Jean Delaney held her front door open like Trudy was old family. She gave an arm wave and a head bob. A red bandana served as a skullcap. A few gray hairs dangled loose.

"Get in out of the chill," she said. "What are you doing?"

She was tall, fit. A spattered blue sweatshirt hung loosely on her frame. Gold, rimless, round glasses hid her eyes behind a gray tint.

The bungalow's interior burst with life. Plants popped up from the floor, bookshelves and windowsills. Delaney showed her a full-size loom in the kitchen, a purple and blue pattern in the weft. A fluffy-looking, half-eaten pumpkin pie sat on the kitchen counter next to a bowl of whipped cream. Trudy declined a slice. The last stop was her work on a still life. An easel sat by the dining table. Fat avocados in a bright yellow bowl posed for the artist's eye.

"God yes, I'm stoned," she said. "My only entertainment, though the guys still come around. Tinder, you know, is a blast. You wouldn't believe you still want physical contact with all these wrinkles and saggy parts, but you do. Not so bad in the dark. Anyway, you want some?"

"I'm driving," said Trudy, jerking a thumb toward the street. "Otherwise."

"Suit yourself."

Delaney swirled red wine into two tumblers, didn't ask. She put them on a round wooden table in a rear kitchen nook. "This won't hurt you."

"You grow, correct?"

Delaney smiled. "I know one thing—you're not here for advice, whether it's pansies or pot."

"You have a medical marijuana license?"

"Since about two months after it was possible. Got one of the best lighting setups you can rig up—those plants have no idea how a regular calendar works." She leaned over like a spy slipping state secrets. "Do you have any idea how productive these plants can be?"

"Why they call it weed—right?"

"Holy mother of medicine—water, soil, light. Boom. Wanna see?"

Delaney started to stand, as if viewing a room of pot was like a chance to view a rare ghost orchid. Trudy didn't move.

"So you consume all that you grow? Store it? Smoke it?"

Delaney sat back down five times more slowly than she'd stood. "What's this about?"

"I'm helping a friend."

"Which one?"

Delaney removed her glasses, put them on the table. Her eyes looked as clear as a baby's.

"What do you mean?"

"Your reporter boyfriend or someone else?"

"Does it matter?"

"If my name got to you because I have a medical marijuana card, I guess that would concern me, yes."

"Do you consume all you grow?"

Delaney chuckled. "If I did, I'd be horizontal all day long. Especially with that indica. You know what they call it? *In da couch.* That's because all you need is a bag of Fritos and a cold beer. Sure, you can see the fabric of the universe, but it makes you so sleepy. I'm a sativa girl. I like to be able to interact with other humans, read a novel."

"But there's leftover."

Delaney's gaze dropped cool. "Are you here to buy?"

"No."

Delaney rubbed her cheek. "Have you ever tried living on a fixed income? That's why I stepped up my gardening—keep my grocery bill down. Sell a few sweaters on Etsy. Some of my crafts and a painting when it turns out, too. But those boys pay great, I'm telling you. And it's gotta help others?"

"Boys?"

"Everyone is a boy compared to me."

Trudy had jotted the names on a paper. She pulled the slip from a pocket. "Ed Steadman? Victor Chanute?"

"You say those names like there's something wrong."

Trudy took a moment, smiled. "I didn't mean it like that. I'm trying to help a friend."

"How?"

"She ran into those two guys and one of them roughed her up, grabbed at her." Trudy let that sink in. "It's a bit more complicated, might be part of a bigger operation."

"Who is your friend?"

"Allison Coil."

"Oh my," said Delaney. "Girl on a horse."

"She's no—"

"Wait," said Delaney. "They're all girls to me."

Trudy smiled. "Point taken, but—"

"I recognize the name *Victor*," said Delaney. "I'm glad you didn't go running to the cops. Don't need that."

"Ed Steadman?"

"Not that name."

"Another?"

"It's one guy at a time. I work with Victor, but the guy I started with was a guy named Clay. Clay Rudduck. I taught myself a memory device—red duck, Clay Rudduck. You put an image in your head and that helps you remember. Brain works better with pictures, especially when stoned."

"Do you know how to reach either one?"

"No," said Delaney. "They contact me on a schedule."

"And they show up here?"

Delaney swallowed hard. "It's a different routine every time. Church parking lot. Yoga place. The post office. They tell me when, where and how."

"And no idea where any of these guys live? Or phone numbers?"

"No. They call on a schedule, down to the minute, see what I've got."

"When is the next?"

"As a matter of fact, day after tomorrow. It's kind of like a bonus payday. You tend to keep track."

Sixty

Rudduck's high beams lit up the overhead lines for the adventure park tram. The dirt road climbed and switchbacked. The valley floor dropped away.

Why the hell were they going up a dark hillside? Could he pop the door and roll out, take the bumps and scrapes? He'd be bloody—but alive—and maybe he could run. Fuck the $80K, everything.

"So the property owner?"

"What?"

"Where they found the dead guy."

"Fuck it," said Duncan. "That whole story. There's another reporter. My editor gave it to her."

"Really?"

"Marina," said Duncan. "Marina Fuentes. Cute as a button, too, I'm telling you. By the way, what the hell is up here?"

Rudduck navigated another hairpin. He drove hard into the high-banking corner. The engine growled. The seat sucked on Duncan's back.

"I've always wondered—how do reporters get all of that information so quickly?"

"What do you mean?"

There had been no answer to the destination question.

"Find out shit so quickly?"

"What do you mean?"

"Get all that detail. I mean, you got a database?"

"There's lots of databases."

"And you've got 'em?"

Duncan imagined popping the seat belt, yanking the door handle, reminding himself to roll with the fall and not fight it. He would scramble off into the dark, bullets through his back the last thing he'd ever know.

"There's stuff everywhere. Public records."

A new stretch of road tackled an even steeper pitch. Rudduck sped.

"Gotcha," said Rudduck.

"What are we doing up here?"

He had been talking to Commissioner Bill Walters about Darla Cerise one minute and out on the sidewalk with Trudy and the others the next, and here comes Clay Rudduck.

Coincidence could go fuck itself.

"What are we doing up here?"

"What?" said Rudduck. "You worried? You still thinking about your investment? Hell, I wanted you to see this town at night. The whole valley. I want you to chill out. I want you to hang in there, you know?"

"I'm not sure what you mean."

Rudduck took a minute. "I mean—don't make a mess."

Sixty-One

Trudy spilled all the Jean Delaney details in two minutes flat.

"So who will be the buyer?" Allison pictured the old lady clutching a Ziploc bag of buds. Adoration of pot spanned the generations. She had heard it helped with PTSD. Allison couldn't fathom a military life, let alone going to war, but if pot helped combat troops mellow out over what they had seen or done, the federal government should supply it for free to all vets for life.

"She says it changes every time. Location changes, too. But she knows Chanute and she knows this guy Clay Rudduck."

Even with the motel room locked, Trudy half whispered.

"Day after tomorrow?"

"If nothing has changed," said Trudy. "And based on where you left those two, I think things have changed."

Allison had imagined one thousand scenarios of Steadman and Chanute making their way back to civilization. No matter what she pictured them doing, they were always banged up, pissed off and outfitted with a double bandolier chock-full of ammunition.

"She's going to call you when she hears?"

"She said she would, but it's not like we're going to observe the deal or anything like that." Trudy hadn't even taken off her jacket. She sat on the edge of the bed, as focused and calm as Allison had seen her in weeks. "That would put her in harm's way."

"Cops?" said Colin.

"No reason to put her in their crosshairs either. But she'll spill it all to Duncan—do an interview."

"Without her name," said Colin.

"Duncan will have a field day," said Trudy.

"Still can't reach him?" Allison had punched his number several times.

"Voice mail," said Trudy. "Comes up before it even rings."

"Worried?"

"About as worried as when you two disappear in the wilderness and come back a few days after you say you will."

"Is Jean Delaney solid?" said Colin.

"If I tell her she can trust Duncan to protect her name, she's good to go. You two should hustle up to Meeker."

"Or back to Sweetwater and then Meeker," said Allison. She didn't mind skipping a night of sleep.

Colin shrugged, reading her mind. "Meeker we know we can do something. Sweetwater we might sit all night on the porch with shotguns, waiting, but they could still be struggling to remain vertical. Or they could be long gone."

Or their barn and both their houses could be black patches of smoldering ash.

"They aren't going to make matters worse," said Trudy. "My hunch."

"And you?" said Allison.

"I'll be fine," said Trudy. "Nobody knows I'm here. Duncan will turn up. We'll line up the interview with Jean Delaney for tomorrow, and by the next day's papers the cops will have their hands full."

"So we leave now?" Allison shot the question at Colin.

He stood, drained the last of a Coors. "Beat the morning rush."

Sixty-Two

Thursday Evening
Duncan

The road came to a gate. Rudduck lowered a window and held a white card against a sensor box.

"Friends," he said by way of explanation. "Not like it's Fort Knox up here anyway."

He parked by a service building and climbed out. The pickup doors slammed behind him with authority.

Duncan walked uphill, into the darkness. Was there anything about this location or time of day that felt good?

Duncan gulped at the cool air. Rudduck's footsteps scuffed and crunched. His silhouette moved against a creamy fog of stars.

Duncan found the path. "Give your eyes time to adjust." Rudduck sounded as relaxed as an amateur stargazer.

Duncan shuddered. "Fucking cold up here."

He reached a wide swath of flat asphalt, a clearing of sorts. A large hulking structure, twice the size of a house, loomed over his left shoulder. Dangling tram cars hung black against the night sky. A cool breeze dug through his shirt. The wind tickled a rhythmic squeak from something on a hinge or hanger. "*Ur—urrr. Ur—urrr.*" Pause, count to three, repeat. "*Ur—urrr. Ur—urrr.*"

A path led away from the clearing, and Duncan followed the grade up and past three low buildings that seemed to stare back.

Muffled footsteps pulled him along. The path reached a crest. A break in the trees framed the nightscape city below, Grand

Avenue the thick vertebrae in a T-bone wedge of blinking light. Why hadn't he told Rudduck to go fuck himself? Just walked back into the newspaper?

"Down here."

Duncan stopped, felt a shiver flash.

High over his shoulder, the complicated knots of a roller coaster jutted in and out of the tree line. Below, a round structure. Rudduck's inert form stood on the edge of what could be a carnival carousel. Pairs of swinging seats dangled on chains. Duncan had seen plenty of shots in the newspaper from this piss-your-pants ride. It featured the opportunity to be flung out over the cliff edge every few seconds as the machine spun you around.

"Freezing my ass off," said Duncan. His hands, thrust in his pockets, clenched for warmth that didn't come.

"Small price for the view."

Duncan stepped down the slope to the ride, kept his distance.

"I got better things to do," said Duncan. "Unless you brought me all the way up here to give me my money back."

Rudduck tipped his head back to the stars. "Will you lay the fuck off that same old tired song?"

"So I'm here to be threatened."

"It's not a threat when I tell you what you're going to do and then you do that thing, whatever it might be, and you follow through in a way that protects your investment."

Duncan shook off a deep shiver. He tried to get his mouth to move despite feeling as if he'd walked into cold storage with ice packs strapped to his chest.

"I want you to think big picture."

A lighter flashed like the big bang itself. For a second, Duncan caught Rudduck's calm face, a joint jutting from his lips.

Seriously?

The lighter snapped closed. The tip of the joint flared again as Rudduck took another hit. The cloud of smoke snuggled Duncan's face.

"Want some?"

"Brandy if you've got it. With hot chocolate. And a bonfire."

"And one day weed will be as common as brandy—as easy to get, too."

"Up here for a lecture?"

"Look at that city," said Rudduck. "And then think of all the ways people strap on a good buzz each and every fucking day. And the government has authorized or approved each and every one, from Coors Light to Night Train to fucking Courvoisier."

Rudduck sounded relaxed. Maybe pensive.

"And now here comes marijuana because the people said so— don't you love the people? And now, Mr. Reporter Man, comes your opportunity to cash in, to leave your skimpy-pay job or at least sock away some genuine financial security. The reason I brought you up here is so you can see the big picture." Rudduck took another hit. "All the possibilities lie ahead."

"What I need is a blanket."

"You have to think long term."

"Short term is screaming at me."

"Tell it to go fuck itself."

"It's a real thing, this cold."

"Come on, Duncan Bloom. Focus on the facts. Think of this moment. Life is brutal. Nobody is getting anywhere. Nobody is moving up. Yet we all soldier on, believing it will all get better. But now we've got pot and it takes the edge off, and after eighty years of the government trying to arrest and imprison their way to eradication, it's over. Their fight failed. Miserably!"

Maybe they would hear that last word down on Grand Avenue. Duncan shuddered, said nothing.

"And pot shops will be as common as liquor stores, and your little investment could dig you back out of the slow-motion train wreck that is your bank account."

"How did you happen to appear outside my office, minutes after I get done talking to Commissioner Walters?"

"Did you hear a fucking word I said?"

"Pots of gold. Got it."

"What the fuck you want to know?"

"Why you happened to materialize moments after I get done talking to one of the three commissioners in the county and a man who might make it easy for High Valley Farms to move from Basalt to a place where they might soon be welcome right here in Garfield County."

Cold bored into Duncan's chest. Another few minutes, tops, and he would need to start jogging to churn the blood.

"I got your money." Rudduck held up an oversized envelope or some kind of pouch.

"Eighty-one K?"

Duncan felt a lift.

"Sixty-five," he said. "Handling fee and charge for wimping out."

"Hell of a fee."

"Hell of a pussy about it."

"How did you come up with your so-called fees? And more to the point, tell me about coming to the newspaper. Right then."

"You're going to miss the boat. An investment the size of a kayak is going to become a fat, loaded ocean liner. Loaded."

"I can only imagine." Duncan shuddered, his own personal earthquake.

"You have to want to get rich and you have to realize you are doing something very good."

"Same as opening a hospital for the poor."

"That's it!" He sounded like a kid. "Exactly! You're dragging civilization forward. And telling the moralists swirling their martinis to go fuck themselves. Pot is no different and it's safer. Are you listening? Are we still having a conversation here?"

"I'm all frozen ears."

Sixty-Three

Thursday Evening
Trudy

Trudy recognized Coogan, but she couldn't dredge up a first name. He was small, grim and mouselike. He opened the door like an exasperated servant. It had taken two knocks on the door and then a call to the main newsroom number to roust him.

"Duncan left." Coogan led her back to the newsroom.

"We were out there talking with him. About three hours ago. Then a guy he recognized came up."

Coogan pushed his glasses up on his sweaty nose. "Really?"

"They got to chatting. Duncan waved us off like all was good."

Coogan crossed his arms, put his butt on the desk. A gray phone handset sat near him, freed from its cradle. A red light blinked. It was 10 p.m.

"Duncan told you what Allison found?"

"Yes. Finally got names to work with. You tell Allison we would love to do an in-depth profile when all the dust settles."

"Not her thing." Why was Coogan still here? "Publicity, I

300

mean."

"People who shun the limelight usually make the best kinds of profiles."

"Did something happen right before Duncan came outside?"

"He pissed off someone he was talking to. Took me a half hour to bring him down off the ceiling. The guy worked me over and then called the publisher, and I'm in the middle of a shit-storm, okay? You tried Duncan's cell, same as me?"

"Voice mail."

"His Camry still out there?"

"Yes. All locked up."

So was her ride. Having drunk too much wine, Trudy had called Valley Taxi.

"Then he must have gone with whoever that was that showed up."

"Is the angry guy all calmed down now?"

Coogan frowned harder, if that was possible. "Relative term, calm."

"I might have an idea who to call. What was the issue?"

It felt good to be mucking around in other places than her vast, swampy quicksand of self-doubt.

"We don't—"

"He's missing!" Trudy heard a snap to her voice.

Coogan picked up the unmoored handset, slapped it in his palm like a cop showing off a billy club. "Look, I know Duncan will turn up. I've got a few more calls to make. And finish."

Trudy stepped over to Duncan's desk, made herself at home in his chair.

"Really," said Coogan. "If you don't mind, I'm—"

"I can't wait for him here?" said Trudy. "I mean, his car is—"

"I've got calls," said Coogan. "They're confidential."

"It's a bit late, isn't it?" Trudy eyed a sheet of paper with three names on it—Walters, Cerise and an X through another name she couldn't make out.

"Time is kind of irrelevant when a public official feels he's been wrongly accused."

Unwinding this guy, thought Trudy, would require a beach, a month of reggae and fat doobies in place of every meal.

She tucked the paper in her jacket.

"The bars are still open," said Coogan.

Out on the street, the door was closing behind her when Trudy jabbed her foot in the fast-closing gap.

"Wait a minute," she said. Coogan had already turned to head back to the office. "I've got one more question."

Sixty-Four

Thursday Evening
Duncan

Rudduck stood too close. "I want some goddamn enthusiasm around here—okay?"

Duncan tried not to breathe from the cloud of pot smoke that hovered around Rudduck's head. For a moment, the shudders stopped.

"I'm listening."

"I'm going to keep your fucking money and what are you going to do?"

"I'll guess I'll be finding out any second."

"You're going to not dig so hard."

"What the hell does that mean?"

"It means you're about to get lazy."

"Not possible. I can't fake that shit."

A hand came up on Duncan's neck.

"Tell me how the hell you happened to be on the fucking sidewalk."

Duncan grabbed Rudduck's wrist to try and yank it away. Rudduck doubled the pressure. An electric ripple of pain flashed down Duncan's shoulders.

"You ungrateful fuck. I can quadruple your money. Or I can make it all disappear—and who are you gonna complain to, the reporter gods in the fucking sky?"

Duncan kicked. No aim necessary.

Straight.

Up.

Hard.

Rudduck collapsed like a sack of dry bones.

He howled.

Something skittered off and Duncan followed the sound. He had his hand on the canvas pouch with the fat zipper, opened it up.

His hand wrapped around a thick wad of nothing.

Rudduck bellowed.

Duncan sent the pouch over the cliff like a malformed Frisbee. He fell on Rudduck. He straddled his chest and brought a fist around fast. Rudduck's jaw issued a satisfying crunch.

He patted jean pockets. He kept one arm and all his weight on Rudduck's chest as he scrambled through his jacket. His fingers clawed a clump of keys.

"Fucker," said Duncan.

He gave Rudduck a few accidental kicks to the ribs as he stood. Adrenaline surged and he felt warm, if not toasty. His hand was tender from the punch.

Duncan dangled the keys so Rudduck could hear the jingle. "Was it Walters?"

"What the hell?"

In the dim light Rudduck's lumpy form turtled forward, stopped. He rolled over and made an effort to get upright. Duncan took two quick steps and was about to give him a boot to the rib cage when a hand lurched and grabbed his ankle and yanked. Hard. Duncan twisted and gave way to the pressure. He landed with a thud. His shoulder took the fall with heavy whacks of pain.

Duncan flailed a leg out like a kid throwing a tantrum, and Rudduck stumbled and staggered to the edge of the giant disc, the lights of the city a twinkling backdrop to his lumpy silhouette.

"Was it Walters?"

Duncan scrambled to his feet and bent over the crab-walking form. Did Rudduck know where he was?

"Was it Walters?" Rudduck had the wherewithal to mock. Not good. "Maybe it was Walters."

"Who else knew I was asking questions about moving that grow down from Basalt? Who the fuck else?"

The answer hit no different than if Rudduck had jumped to his feet and smacked him in the face with a studded two-by-four.

Duncan gave Rudduck one more healthy shove and started running.

He clenched and unclenched his punching hand, nothing broken. He started to sort through all the things Chris Coogan had said.

And all the things he hadn't.

Sixty-Five

Thursday Evening
Trudy

For his height and attire, Commissioner Walters always stood out. The attire tried hard to compensate for his compact stature. Even on a Saturday night, long after working hours, he wore a crisp red button-down shirt and one of his trademark bolo ties. The clasp on this one was a shiny saddle and stirrups.

He wasn't wearing a coat.

He'd been here all along.

Maybe he'd been in a back room, listening.

Or curled up under a desk like a troll under a bridge.

Walters spotted her coming up the short passage by the receptionist's desk. Coogan had his back to her and Trudy thought she saw a quick flash in Walters' eyes, a signal.

As if to say, *watch out.*

"What the—" Coogan turned. "What now?"

She had mingled with Walters at the occasional chamber function. Walters' wife, a good six inches taller than him and known fondly as Big Red, was an avid herbalist and a regular at the garden center.

"Commissioner Walters, you were here all along?"

"Just using the facilities."

Walters produced a smile of the half-cocked and wry variety.

"And perhaps something else," said Trudy.

"I'm afraid my reason for being here tonight is none of your business," said Walters.

Coogan looked at his shoes, then tried to recover by standing

305

up like a GI at his first inspection. Awkward.

"I'm looking for Duncan," said Trudy. "Has he talked to you today—maybe a few hours ago?"

Walters shook his head. "So hard to remember."

"Did Duncan bring up the name *Darla Cerise*?"

There was no first name on Duncan's notes, but there was only one Cerise in the whole valley that mattered—the queen of Carbondale ranchers.

"I haven't said we talked."

"You're connected to her, somehow."

"She may have voted for me," said Walters, as calm as a morning chat over coffee. "You'd have to ask her."

"Friend?"

"I have many. I'm lucky like that."

Trudy felt like a gardener in a strange garden before one shoot sprouted. She didn't know where to step—or what direction.

"Please." Coogan said it in the all-encompassing way. *Please* go. *Please* fuck off. *Please* know your place.

Coogan deferred to Walters, that much was clear.

Walters was covering for them both. They would breathe a sigh of relief when she left and they could get back to their old-boy, all-boy ways.

"Please what?"

"We're closed," said Coogan.

Trudy sat at Duncan's desk, so tired of being pushed around, subordinated, dismissed. "Obviously not," she said. "If he's at a bar, he'll come back here, right?"

She spotted his keys on the desk. She gave them a hearty shake.

"It's late," said Coogan.

"I'm aware of that."

"And we can't leave you here."

"Then how is Duncan going to get his keys once he reappears from the bars or the woods? You can leave me here. I'm sure Duncan knows how to lock up."

A look flew between them, a fast roll of the eyes.

"Police HQ is two blocks," said Coogan.

"I happen to know that," said Trudy.

"And they can be here in a minute."

"And I'll show them this."

Trudy held up the paper, pointed with her finger and read aloud: "Walters, Cerise and some other name." She looked at the third name, crossed out, and felt a jolt. "And then the name right here is the name of the dead guy in Carbondale."

"Your boyfriend's imagination," said Walters. "He's not well."

"Actually, he's quite thorough," said Trudy. "We *all* know his reputation."

"But do you know everything about him?" said Walters.

"Of course not."

"He didn't tell you about his not-so-little investment?" Walters' stare came complete with curled-over lower lip.

"Investment?"

"You think he's a Boy Scout."

"Hardly."

"Squeaky-clean reporter ethics and all of that?"

Walters took a careful step forward. Coogan put a hand on Walters' shoulder, a tap, then yanked it back and tucked both hands into his armpits and went back to studying the floor. "Don't," said Coogan. "I wouldn't."

"Ask him." Walters' unblinking look dismissed all humanity. "Ask him about his plans to get rich."

Trudy knew that personal finance wasn't one of Duncan Bloom's chief talents, but she didn't think he had enough to scrape together to "invest" in a week's worth of groceries, let alone have a long-term plan. She said nothing.

"Not something he's shared?" said Walters. "I can imagine how it's not a deal he wants broadcast. So why don't you do your boyfriend and yourself a favor and quietly get the fuck out of here, and when you do find him, tell him to junk his crazy-ass theories and stop damaging reputations—good reputations—when he doesn't have a single fucking shred of proof."

Sixty-Six

Thursday Evening
Duncan

Had Coogan dipped a toe in? Or jumped off the high dive?

Duncan cut corners on the switchbacks. He startled three deer milling around on the asphalt. He kept his eyes peeled for head-lights coming up the other way.

Trudy didn't answer, but Allison answered on the first ring.

"Almost to Silt," she said.

Duncan packed everything he knew into four fast sentences. It was the best editing of his life.

"Fuckers," she said by way of summation. "We're turning around."

"Heard from Trudy?"

"We left her at the inn."

"I tried her cell—tried the room phone. She might have gone looking for me," said Duncan. "I had a bunch of missed calls."

"Did you go with that guy who was on the sidewalk?"

For weeks, Duncan had known that he would have to explain. Eventually. That day might be now. "Long story," said Duncan. "But yes."

"You okay?"

"Better than him."

"We're at the Silt exit now."

"Sorry you can't deal with Devo right away."

"He's not going anywhere," said Allison. "Neither is Miss Mushroom. Where are you now?"

"Two minutes from the inn," said Duncan. "If Trudy's not there, I'll head downtown and get my car at the office."

"What are you driving now?"

Rudduck's Navigator skidded on the dirt switchbacks. He hoped it took Rudduck all night to walk or stumble his way down.

"Long story," said Duncan.

Sixty-Seven

Thursday Evening
Allison

Colin gave the S-10 a couple cracks of the whip. They were pushing ninety. Cops were one thing, late-night deer another. Allison buried her fear. Part of this reboot with Colin was trust.

"Maybe Trudy fell asleep," said Colin. "Or left her phone on vibrate."

"Duncan said he tried the room phone, too."

They were already in the twisty canyon east of New Castle. The headlight beam on a freight train allowed for a sense of the black river, the tightening gap.

"Get off at West Glenwood. We'll check the inn first and then head to the newspaper."

"Office," said Colin.

"Newspaper, yes."

"You can't go to a *newspaper*, unless it's lying in the road."

Allison sighed. "It's so good to have you back."

Sixty-Eight

Thursday Evening
Clay Rudduck

His testicles wanted him to lie down on the dirt and go fetal. Instead, he stagger-walked, as bowlegged as possible.

"I know it's late."

Helen Barnstone answered the third time he called.

"You can't come back—not tonight."

"You need to get in your car and come get me."

"The boys are asleep."

"You'll be back before they know the difference."

He grunted. He had forgotten the safety walk. For one step.

"Where are you?"

"Up by the adventure park."

"On the *cliff*?"

"Only one I know."

"It's late, it's closed. I mean, *Jesus*."

"It's where I am."

"How did you get up there?"

"There's a road."

"Where's your car?"

"There isn't enough time to say. Not now."

Rudduck reached the gap in the trees at the crest of the walkway. He stood for a moment to give his testicles a ten-second reprieve.

"We got problems."

"How bad?"

"Bad."

"The reporter?"

"And he figured out his boss is up to his keister with it, too."

"Where's Duncan?"

"Probably back in town—or close."

"And Chris Coogan?"

"Come get me, we'll find him."

"Willy. And Chuck."

"You'll be back hours before they wake up."

"Willy is a light sleeper. The garage door alone."

"Going to take me all night to walk back down. By then—"

"By then what?"

"We don't want to know."

Rudduck heard her think.

"We're screwed."

"He doesn't know about you."

"Everyone else does. All your guys."

"Come get me."

"Then what? I don't want to make it worse."

"That's why there's no time to waste."

Sixty-Nine

Trudy hung in the shadow at the edge of Centennial Park where the row of office buildings ended. She was three doors down from where they would come out of the newspaper.

Her phone showed seven missed calls—four Duncan, three Allison.

She couldn't talk. She needed to watch and listen. Her cab waited on Grand Avenue, engine purring and the lights off. She had promised the driver, a youthful sort with one of those I-brew-beer beards, that she'd make it worth his time.

The tone in Walters' voice—that smug, condescending, dismissive tone—clung to her like she'd been sprayed by a skunk.

And *Coogan*.

The night air was cool. The cab's engine purred, maybe a bit too loudly.

Trudy risked three quick seconds to sprint through the streetlight and tap on the window on the cab's passenger side. The window slid down.

"Let's save the gas," she said. The engine clicked off, adding to the silence. "You have to be anywhere?"

"Not until Monday morning," he said. "And this beats the zombie crawl when the bars close."

"Okay." She gave him a smile. "Thanks."

The driver must have known what she'd been watching. He popped his head and she heard a door open behind her. She squatted low by the cab, pressing herself down by the curb. She hoped she had enough cover and hoped they didn't come this way.

No *they*.

Only Walters.

He stood for a moment. He pulled a vape pen from a pocket, clicked it on and blew a puff of white smoke.

He threw a quick glance in both directions and headed north toward the river, his short legs in no particular hurry.

Trudy recognized the weakness in her nonexistent plan. Tailing one of these two on foot had not been one of the options. Walters crossed Eighth Avenue at the light. He waited for three cars to clear and crossed Grand Avenue and kept heading west into the night, fast-evaporating white puffs trailing him like empty thought clouds in a comic.

Coogan emerged a moment later. A fat briefcase tugged at his left arm. A thick ski jacket added thirty pounds. The fur-lined hood flopped on his shoulders. He beelined across the quiet street. A light-colored SUV smack under the streetlight issued a jarring squeal. Four lights flared.

Trudy popped the front door of the cab and climbed inside. Her driver didn't need instructions.

Coogan jammed the car into gear and headed south, engine roaring, tires buzzing. Her driver pulled a U-turn and popped on his headlights.

Trudy's phone lit up.

"Duncan."

"Where are you? Your car is at the motel, but the room is empty."

"Following your boss. I'm in a taxi."

"Trudy look—*what*?"

"I'm a few blocks south of downtown."

"You're following Chris Coogan?"

Chris.

"In a cab. Walters was there—the commissioner."

"Where?"

"At your office. Two buttholes."

"Trudy, pull over, stop. This is dangerous. As in, very."

"I found your note." She knew it was dangerous. "Walters. Coogan. And the name of the dead guy, with his name crossed out."

"Jesus," said Duncan.

"You should have seen how they treated me, the looks on their faces."

"Are you in a Valley Taxi?"

"Yes."

"Pull over," said Duncan, but not as an order. As a request.

"Why?"

"I'm right behind you."

Seventy

Thursday Evening
Allison

It had long occurred to Allison that she had been granted a special relationship with death. She'd been given a sneak peek around the corner. She was one hundred percent sure it was pure nothingness, but the fact was that not a day had gone by since the airplane crash when she didn't realize her deal with death had changed. Mortality lived side by side with coffee and tequila. It was a daily contemplation and not shoved off in denial.

Accidents in nature were one thing—rockslides, earthquakes, tsunamis, tornadoes, hurricanes, floods. Man-made accidents were another—from a tractor rolling over a lonely farmer on the back forty to an icy pileup of cars and trucks on a foggy highway, from a train leaving the rails to an airplane unable to sustain flight. These were all part of nature now—death by car crash was as "natural" as a rockslide.

The precarious perch on life was jittery enough, given all the risks, without men killing men. And Duncan Bloom's speedy recap of the conspiracy and all the crap that led up to Miguel Ramirez getting left at the vulture tree and then left dead in the wrecked plane made her realize, not for the first time, that not much made less sense than taking another man's life because he stood in the way of your trivial mortal wants and desires. Besides that, she'd also learned when she needed help.

Collin pulled off the Interstate. He slowed for the turn that ducked back underneath the highway and snaked around the loop that would head them over the river. Allison scrolled to a key contact in her phone; she didn't keep many.

"It's late."

"I'm aware."

"I'm not in uniform."

"Doesn't reduce your authority—and there's no time to put it on."

One thing about Deputy Sheriff Chadwick. He cared. Some cops practiced inscrutability. Not Chadwick.

"What is it?"

"I think our friend Duncan Bloom has shaken the wrong bush, and it involves that body in Carbondale and the wrecked plane in the Flat Tops and that load of weed."

"Where are you?"

She heard him clattering around, making all the right noises.

"Following Duncan, who is following his boss. We stayed on Grand Avenue where 82 veers off. At Twenty-Third Street."

"Does his boss know he's being followed?"

"No clue," said Allison. "But if he doesn't now, he will soon. He turned on Twenty-Seventh and then right again on Sopris. And I think you know."

"Dead end."

Seventy-One

Duncan knew the stubby street. Work as a reporter long enough in a small town, you eventually know every inch of asphalt. He'd never been to Chris Coogan's house. No off-duty fraternization, no summer barbecues, no holiday gifts, no after-work beers. Coogan treated his job like a holy mission. But along came temptation. She came naked.

She smelled like weed.

Coogan drove a well-worn Jeep Cherokee. It reached the cul-de-sac where Sopris Avenue came to the abrupt end of its service to the residents of Glenwood Springs. The street was tucked like a knife in a sheath between Grand Avenue, which hugged the bluff above the Roaring Fork River, and Highway 82, which headed south out of town. The houses along Sopris Avenue were one-story, functional and modest. Circa Dwight Eisenhower.

Duncan pulled over and stopped at the curb. He snapped off the headlights on the giant Navigator.

"I still don't quite understand how you got this car," said Trudy. She turned around. "And someone is following us."

"Allison," said Duncan. "I hope. And Colin."

Duncan lowered his window a crack—or tried. One tap on the button and an electric buzz followed the window all the way down.

There was nothing quite like a dead-end street to underscore the fact that you didn't belong. TV light flickered around the gaps from a living room blind.

Car doors opened behind them. He caught a brief flash of interior light and he popped open his own door, perhaps out of instinct. Trudy did the same.

Duncan glanced at the window with the TV eye, half expecting to see the blind pulled aside and a head appear.

Nothing.

"Trudy. Duncan." It was Allison. And Colin. "Where did he go?"

"Straight ahead," said Duncan. "Dead center of the cul-de-sac."

"I've got a cop on the way—Chadwick," said Allison.

"What? Really?"

"Yes, really," said Allison. "You okay?"

"Got chilled up on the ridge, that's all."

"And you're sure about Coogan?"

The acid-churning question of the day had corroded his stomach all the way down from the adventure park.

"No question," said Duncan.

"You should have seen him," said Trudy. "Heard him. The commissioner, too. Bill Walters."

Twelve days until election, thought Duncan. Plenty of time to get the story in the paper. The only question was whether he would be the one to write it. Or would his name be featured prominently in a less flattering light?

"Are we waiting for the cop?" said Colin. They stood in a tight huddle. "What's the plan?"

"Tell the cop to park his car back up on Twenty-Seventh," said Duncan. "It's going to look like a cluster if he comes down here. And don't do anything just yet. I'll be right back."

Duncan turned and ran.

"Wait," said Trudy.

He didn't respond.

There was one way to figure out whether he was up to his ankles or his eyeballs.

And he didn't want to find out when everyone else was right there.

He needed the conversation with Chris Coogan to be off the fucking record.

Seventy-Two

Thursday Evening
Clay Rudduck

Helen Barnstone took the switchbacks like she'd taken driving lessons from James Bond. Her Chevy Malibu's bucket seat hit Rudduck in the wrong spot. He winced with each turn.

The pain was excruciating. But it wasn't as bad as the two

318

phone calls, one from Bill Walters and one from Chris Coogan. Walters sounded rattled. It was such a fucking stupid call to make. At this hour? A public official making a call so easily tracked? *Idiot*.

Rudduck had cut him off, told him to chill the fuck out. But he'd let Coogan ramble. The poor boy would need counseling. And a new career. Rudduck didn't listen. He spent the time thinking back over who knew what about either Vince Hedland or Miguel Ramirez.

So much depended on Duncan Bloom's next move. If Duncan went straight to the cops? Not good. To Walters? The commissioner wouldn't answer the door or the phone. To confront Coogan? Then they could reminisce about the highlights from their soon-to-end careers.

"I still don't understand," she said.

"About?"

"About how you're up here without your car."

"I had a disagreement, shall we say, with one of our investors."

"Who?"

Rudduck shuddered as Barnstone took a corner with zeal. "As the lawyers say, that's immaterial."

"He left you up here?"

"Believe me, it wasn't a wise move."

Barnstone didn't press for detail.

"Where am I taking you?"

"Sopris Avenue. Right there by the Walmart on the west side of 82." He managed a smile in the dark for the sole purpose of adding the tone to his voice. "It's right on your way."

Seventy-Three

Coogan's Cherokee idled on a slab of inclined concrete. The garage in front of it stood open to the night—shelves, paint, gear and junk. A door off the inside corner cast a wedge of light.

Two plywood steps led up from the garage.

Duncan listened to dull thumps of someone running down stairs, then a rattling crash like the lid on a washing machine slamming down. More scurrying. Duncan's chest shook.

"Coogan!"

The short hallway led past an open-shelved pantry to the kitchen. Snow boots stood on a straw welcome mat. An open duffel, packed with clothes and crap, sat nearby, its belly exploded.

"Coogan!"

Duncan stepped all the way inside, the duffel at his feet. He leaned around the corner.

A red cooler with white handles, its lid up, ate up half the kitchen counter. Three white plastic grocery bags huddled near it, packed and plump.

A distinct exhale . . .

"Duncan? What the fuck?"

"I came to tell you—"

Coogan held up his hand. He was ready for the North Pole. A heavy winter jacket with a thick sheepskin collar gave him doughboy heft. He'd changed into blue jeans. Heavy tan work boots propped him up an unnatural inch.

"What the hell?" said Coogan.

"Trudy told me about her visit." Duncan's aorta rocked as if jacked into one of those shuddering swimsuit driers at the hot springs pool. He tried to keep his exterior cool. "I think she made a few leaps."

"How did you find me?"

"Google of course. It sounded like a few feathers might have got ruffled and I think she's been under a bit of stress." Did Coogan know? It was impossible to tell. "I wanted to make sure you're—"

"Get the fuck out."

"Going somewhere?"

No hammer had dropped. Duncan felt strangely emboldened. Rudduck hadn't told Coogan his star reporter was a fellow investor.

"What the hell difference does it make to you?"

"It's nearly midnight."

"And you're Mr. Curfew?"

Duncan took a step forward, a friend looking to poach a cold one from the fridge.

Coogan didn't budge.

"You know the law about puffers." Duncan jerked a thumb back over his shoulder. "You want to see Trudy pissed off, show her a car pumping exhaust for no reason."

Coogan stabbed a slow-motion fist into his shoulder. "Get the fuck out."

Duncan went all-in with the dumb routine, said nothing.

One thing for sure—Coogan wouldn't be calling any cops.

At the least, it made sense to slow Coogan down for the arrival of Allison's cop.

"Last chance." Coogan's head bobbed to the door behind Duncan.

"I'm missing something—"

The shove came as a surprise. So did its power.

Coogan snarled. His arms flew up. The shove caught Duncan on his breastbone and he stumbled back. His hands reached for a perch that wasn't there, and he felt himself falling where a wall would have come in handy. He sensed the doorjamb flying by but he failed to find a grip, the useless side of his fingers scraping wood.

The garage floor smacked him. His head bounced. A stab of pain zapped his skull.

Seventy-Four

Thursday Evening
Clay Rudduck

"Nice work." Rudduck stared down. "Damn reporters."

Coogan stepped down into the garage. His face was flushed like a beet and sheened in a sweaty mist.

"I ain't never heard of you," said Coogan. "You ain't never heard of me."

"Maybe," said Rudduck. "Whatever. Have you seen my car?"

Barnstone took a step toward Duncan, perhaps to tend to him. Rudduck caught her by the bicep and yanked her back into formation. "Have you met Duncan Bloom's editor?"

Chris Coogan appeared to be extremely angry. "I don't know you, remember?"

Standing required care. A wide stance helped. "If this guy is in the way of whatever it is you have in mind, then we should maybe take him somewhere. You know?"

Far behind him, a car door closed.

Rudduck turned.

He stared up the dim street.

Barnstone wriggled loose of his grip, stepped away. "The boys," she said. "I have to get home."

A low bellow escaped from Duncan's inert form.

"I'd make sure he doesn't get up," said Rudduck. "Make my day, you know? The laws are on your side."

"What the hell went haywire?" said Coogan.

"If that's your car, why don't you finish packing and scram. Mexico? Venezuela?"

Duncan grunted.

"Now's your chance," said Rudduck. "Drag him over to the river, toss him in. But I'd still go all Clint Eastwood if I was you. It would look better."

"What the hell happened?"

"Now is all that matters, bucko. Getting shit cleaned up."

"Gotta go," said Barnstone.

Duncan began a slow-motion crawl on the cruddy garage floor.

Barnstone scraped the Malibu's bumper on the curb as she peeled off.

"Got a gun?" Duncan had to be dealt with. "Everyone has a gun. Come on. Go get it and shoot your damn intruder."

"Darla Cerise?" Coogan's sweaty nose shook.

"You sound like your reporter. I got a gun."

"You made it sound golden. Sure thing. Locked up tight. All that."

"Business," said Rudduck. "New challenge every day. There's no time to stand and chat."

Duncan stopped crawling. He tried a half-assed push-up. He spat blood.

Again, Rudduck sensed a stirring and motion behind him.

"Kill the engine, will ya?"

Coogan complied.

"You heard it, too?" whispered Rudduck.

"Yeah."

They stood shoulder to shoulder on the lip of the ramp.

The cul-de-sac sucked—only one way out.

"You think we'd see someone."

"It was like a car door bang. The fuck?"

"Like someone sneaking home, though."

"Happens," said Coogan. "Why the—"

"Shut up," said Rudduck.

A truck huffed on the highway. "Who else knows you're here?"

Rudduck's gaze settled on a knot of cars about eight houses up, west side of the street.

He stepped down to the middle of the ramp, doing his best to avoid aggravating that tender spot. The cluster of vehicles looked dense. If each house had its own stubby driveway, then the line of cars must be blocking one of them.

Or two.

Rudduck walked like a window-shopping grandma. He hugged the shadows, studied the gaps between the houses for movement.

A streetlight hummed. Rudduck did a slow 360, a dead stop at each quarter turn. He stared back at Coogan's garage, its box of cool white light the only wart of defiance to the buttoned-down norm.

A dog's strident holler jolted his core—*ark, ark, ark*. Rudduck turned to the noise as if a cougar was mid-leap. His heart pinballed off his ribs.

Ten more slow steps and now he made out the outline of his goddamn Navigator.

And he should have grabbed the keys from Duncan Bloom's fucking pocket.

The Navigator, however, was jammed in by a beat-up S-10, the front bumper of the black pickup licking the butt of his.

The hood was warm.

What the hell?

His Navigator was unlocked. The stupid car *ding-donged* at the intrusion, light everywhere.

His hand found the grip on the Desert Eagle .44. He left the holster and shoved the gun in the belt at the small of his back, a pleasing bit of metal coolness on his skin. He always enjoyed holding the Desert Eagle with the extra-wide grip.

Maybe he'd loan it to Coogan.

Seventy-Five

Thursday Evening
Allison

Allison led the group scamper across the exposed gap to the shadows by Coogan's house. They slipped around the back and then huddled near Coogan's parked car.

Allison had the best view around the corner of the garage— Coogan's round trips for the cooler and a duffel taking him a few feet from her nose.

In the distance, she heard a car door open and a figure silhouetted against a white blast of light. He disappeared for a moment, ducking down, and Allison got a bad feeling.

She held her hand back to signal Trudy and Colin to hang tight.

Duncan writhed on the floor of the garage. Blood pooled at his head.

Allison wanted to tend to him—with what?

Coogan tossed a bag on the shotgun seat and climbed inside. He flipped on his headlights, adding more wattage to the already well-lit scene. The fresh light caught the red sheen on Duncan's spilled blood.

Coogan jammed his car in reverse to the street, and Allison heard a *chunk* followed by a loud hum.

The garage door started to move—big, wide, heartless, uncaring.

"Go around back—break the door if you have to."

The door was halfway down. Coogan's car kicked forward and Allison spotted the ankle-high red dots of the safety beam and hopped over them. She ducked low and rolled into the garage as the door came shut.

She scampered to Duncan, heard the pleasing *chunk* again as the door reversed course, Trudy on the steps into the house, her fingers on the button.

Allison picked Duncan up gingerly and he did the best he could to help. She pulled him toward the door in the corner.

His legs stumbled underneath.

He mumbled something.

Seventy-Six

Rudduck ran.

At least, he tried.

His balls pled for pity. He gasped at the pain. If he bowed his legs, it didn't help. Each stride delivered a brutal bite of agony, shark teeth bared.

He had taken an extra minute to check that the gun was loaded. He had needed a minute to dig into the mini storage box between the front seats and load the magazine—seven bullets. Obviously, he was thinking clearly.

Good sign.

He felt like he was running through sticky fresh tar.

Once he got the keys, what then? He had the problem of the asshole car and no room to move it.

He might need to bash his way out.

The Cherokee roared toward him—much too fast. It skidded on street grit and sand as it turned, gears grabbing and high beams catching him flush. Rudduck held up an arm to cover his eyes, kept moving.

Coogan slowed, lowered his window.

Rudduck showed him the gun, the silver barrel glinting in the streetlight.

"When the weed business finally gets people who can run a tight fucking ship—well, you ain't it," said Coogan. "Don't go near my fucking house."

"You gotta focus on the long term," said Rudduck. "You re-

327

porter guys don't know how business struggles, you know? All the management issues that come along. And remember—the intruder surprised *you*."

Coogan floored the Cherokee.

Rudduck stared at the garage and started to run. At least, as much as his condition allowed.

Finally, the concrete mini-ramp. The pitch added to the fucked-up misery of his bowlegged gait.

He slowed.

The puddle of human on the garage floor began to stir.

Rudduck climbed the few remaining steps of garage slab and put the barrel of the Desert Eagle behind Duncan Bloom's ear.

There was one problem.

It wasn't Duncan Bloom.

Seventy-Seven

Thursday Evening
Allison

Allison grabbed his hand, pushed it back.

She pushed it back harder as she stood and grabbed the barrel of the gun.

His body contorted and curled over.

She put all her weight into the twist and pressure. The barrel shook. His hand bent back in a way it shouldn't go. The gun clattered to the concrete floor.

She caught the blow in her chest. The garage spun in a blur.

She tumbled and rolled and she came up ready to charge, but he had picked up the gun from the smear of blood.

He held the gun in his left hand, tucked his right under his left armpit. He twirled down and screamed: "Son of a bitch!"

"Looking for someone?" Allison scanned for a weapon.

Rudduck stood, shook his hand like he'd burned his fingertips.

Maybe it was the Ropers. Or maybe it was a spot-on description from those guys in the getaway weed plane. Or maybe Steadman and Chanute had found a pay phone in the wilderness, called it in—this hair color, that height, the jean jacket and the pissed-off look.

"Allison Fucking Coil."

Her heart thumped. She caught her breath.

"Partially right."

"Where's your buddy Mr. Bloom?"

"Indisposed."

Trudy and Colin had dragged Duncan away to tend to his tender skull.

"Get me my fucking keys. They're in his pocket."

Allison needed to slow things down. He was a big guy. He stood like he was barefoot on hot sand, trying to get comfortable.

"And you must be Clay Rudduck," she said. "Was that your first trip to Crescent Lake?"

The door flew open. Greased hinges or the victim of Duncan's outrage, the door shot clear around. It whacked the wall with a sharp thud.

Rudduck smiled.

Duncan stood like a wounded boxer. Colin had him by one arm, Trudy by the other. It was taking all their strength to restrain him.

Allison backed up two quiet steps.

"It's over." Duncan barked the words in a spray of bloody spittle.

"Your career?" Rudduck stood with his legs wide, like a human wicket. "Is that what you mean?"

"Fuck you." One of Duncan's eyes had closed up. His lips were swollen up like a pair of chubby caterpillars.

"Money you want back? Sure, say the fuck good-bye to that shit. Are you sad about your poor investment choices, Duncan Bloom? Where are my keys?"

Duncan shrugged. "I lost them."

Trudy made a show of patting down Duncan's pockets, perhaps to prolong the moment. Colin did the same.

Allison inched around to the far side of Rudduck, who was so fixated on Duncan he didn't pay any attention.

"I can open up a few holes in his pockets." Rudduck fanned the gun back and forth.

Behind Rudduck, Robert Chadwick slid into view. Both hands were wrapped around the grip of a sizable pistol.

Trudy startled, the tiniest hint of surprise in the eyes.

Rudduck saw it.

Or maybe he smelled cop.

No uniform, but a badge on the belt.

Rudduck turned. He kept his gun aimed on the three in the doorway.

Colin pushed and Trudy pulled and Duncan toppled into the pig pile as the gun fired, a world record thunderclap.

Allison fixated on the wrist with the gun, covered the few steps between her and Rudduck quickly, determined more than anything else that it not fire again. His gun whipped around to take on Chadwick and she caught Rudduck flush, her shoulder low, as the second shot fired. Rudduck's spine buckled.

He landed without bracing himself, knees first and then torso.

His arms flopped like a wounded bird. She crawled up on his back, pushed his head down to the bloody floor with one hand. She twisted the gun free of his weakened grip.

The world popped back into full surround sound.

"Fuckers," said Rudduck. "You got nothing."

"Actually." Allison felt the surge of adrenaline rattling her system. Her lungs heaved. Breath came one teaspoon at a time. "That's not the case."

Seventy-Eight

Friday Afternoon
Allison

Four hours of police quizzing while the whole neighborhood watched.

Two hours of dozing at the Hanging Lake Inn.

One hour for breakfast, delivered to the motel by a friend of Trudy's who worked at Sacred Grounds.

Ninety minutes for the drive to Meeker, including a stop for more coffee. And supplies, including food and tequila.

One hour talking to Sheriff Christie, who listened to their theories but seemed disinclined to do anything further.

Forty-five minutes to follow the map and the bumpy road to its dead end by the clearing, precisely as Trudy described.

Whatever brain cells Allison could claim, they had all been replaced by a fuzzy blur that tumbled out of control with hideous scenarios for how much worse the cul-de-sac showdown could have played out. What had propelled her to tackle Rudduck, to get him out of harm's way? It was a reaction she couldn't explain. But Chadwick's shot, a second after Rudduck's, missed.

"Dunno."

She'd said it a hundred times, a hundred different ways.

What Allison knew was simple—the fewer the bodies, the better.

The whole ride up to Meeker and the long road back through the woods had sailed along in a blue streak of recaps as she and Colin talked about each of the cops who had interviewed them. They had been questioned separately and then handed off for a chance to start all over with a new cop face.

Once they had been released, Duncan having refused a trip to the hospital and the X-ray machine more than once, they started sharing morsels.

Colin had overheard one cop's radio report that Chris Coogan had been pulled over in Routt County a few miles from the Wyoming border.

Another tidbit came from thick-mouthed Duncan. He had explained his theories about Darla Cerise's farm as the future home of High Valley, including Commissioner Walters' role in making that possible. A cop friend of Duncan's told him a man had come forward who had picked up a hitchhiker south of Carbondale, and they were planning to do a lineup later because his description, down to the comb-over, was a dead match for Clay Rudduck.

They had a mess of boot prints from the dirt road where Vince Hedland's body was found. They had isolated one set that couldn't be matched to the victim or to the hunters who found him.

Right away as the formal interviews began, Allison had begged again for someone to check Sweetwater Road for houses on fire. She still imagined Steadman and Chanute emerging from the woods with dark thoughts and evil ideas. A resourceful cop took a walk around the outside of Allison's barn and heard a man inside moaning in pain. He had found Victor Chanute inside trying to get comfortable atop two bales of hay. Ed Steadman had vanished, but Chanute was being all sorts of helpful with ideas about where to look.

Trudy had managed to get a glimpse of the car that had dropped off Clay Rudduck at Coogan's house—the make, an old Chevy Malibu, and the first three letters of the license plate. From everything she could gather, the cops were having no trouble putting those two pieces together.

"So who killed Miguel Ramirez?"

They stood in the woods, the winter-worn clearing dead ahead.

Allison thought it strange to be transported to this spot by internal combustion. She missed Sunny Boy. She missed the smell of horse.

"Chanute was there," said Allison. "He knows."

"I'd like to know," said Colin.

"Who wouldn't?"

Their plan reeked of simplicity—find Atalanta. They loaded day packs—Fig Newtons, jerky, water, an extra jacket each, gloves, headlamps, wool hats, four apples, tequila and matches.

They might be gone an hour. Or six.

They had no plans to be out for the night.

If they needed to come back tomorrow, they would drive out in the dark and start over in the morning.

Inside the hovel-cum-cabin, a few fat flies buzzed.

"How long since someone lived here?" said Allison. A dead spider sat in the kitchen sink. "Two weeks?"

"Hard to say," said Colin. "More than that, I'd reckon."

"*Reckon*?"

"Yeah, reckon."

"You sound like an old TV cowboy."

Allison studied a bedside shelf of paperbacks.

"You prefer *suppose*." Colin jacked his voice an octave, gave the word the accent and tone of a British dowager at tea.

"Yeah, but *rickin*? Rhymes with *hickin*. As in hick in the house."

Allison pulled *To Build a Fire and Other Stories* from the shelf. It sat next to *A Sand County Almanac* and *Desert Solitaire*.

"Thought you liked hicks," said Colin. "You know how easily your clothes come off at the mere sight of a cowboy."

"It's true," said Allison. "All cowboys. Boots and the hat is all it takes."

She opened the Jack London collection with care, its spine brittle and the paper tarnished in a dingy buttery yellow.

"So word choice is right there with the whole cowboy thing," said Colin. "You know, words we learn in cowboy school—a long whip is a *black snake*, a cemetery is a *bone orchard*. And we don't say *dead*. We say *buzzard food*."

"Please don't mention vultures or buzzards."

"You could have let the vultures be, you know? You didn't have to go up there."

"And I could have taken him with me, too."

"He might have killed you—or worse."

She cracked the book and gave the papers a riffle, kicking up a mini tornado of airborne flotsam. She stood and flipped the pages for Colin.

Colin waved away a cloud of dust. "I'm a good reader—but not that fast."

"No, the notes in the margins and the underlines—red ink, same handwriting. I'd bet the farm."

"You got a farm?"

"Okay, the barn. Sunny Boy, too. Every horse we own."

Colin took the book, gave it a quick look. "The same?"

"Like an obsessed English major," said Allison. "Jack London, too. The book up at the camp is *The Call of the Wild*."

Allison scanned the hippie chick faces in her head—Lyric, Kala. Had Atalanta wormed her way into the tribe once Devo wasn't around to object? Or was she there under a different name?

"But maybe Devo borrowed one of her books, brought it there?"

"Possible. But the book was in a similar kind of spot, you know? A little library. And up there at the camp the library was in this kind of group cabin." She was thinking out loud, kicking herself for not asking to see Devo's quarters—a place he must have shared with Cinnamon, one would think, and the baby. "He didn't sleep there."

"But he could have brought the book up, finished it, and somebody else borrowed it."

The cabin felt suddenly wrong—all off. She flashed on Kala's fresh cheeks. The new recruit.

They did a quick search outside. They split up without having to decide where or how far or how long or how detailed.

Allison found the compost, still cooking up its own microbial stew but well beaten down by the coming winter and lack of turning and tending. She followed a faint trail that led down to the clearing and around. The path appeared used, but skinny. Deer and other critters had kept the vegetation pushed back. She didn't turn up one footprint, fresh or stale.

She trudged through the knee-high grass, her footing damp and squishy from the fringe of a shallow swale, perhaps once a full-blown pond. She squatted on her haunches at a spot with a good view of the cabin, a hundred yards across. She watched as Colin picked his way down through the woods on the hill behind it.

Colin stopped and looked across. He held up his hands in the universal shrug that said *nada*.

She pointed to her pickup and they met there.

"An hour's drive back to Meeker and then a long haul back up to their camp. Assume we're going up in the dark."

Allison yearned for Sunny Boy. On his back, a ride straight to the tribe might be quicker. That is, assuming they hadn't scattered to the wind or relocated at Atalanta's urging. She wasn't positive of the best route and only had a rough idea of the terrain, but she felt confident she could find them.

A motel room? Hot dinner in town? Cold beer and a hot shower?

They decided to camp. Allison kept a tarp behind the seats. They could make a lean-to by the fire. One sleeping bag. They had a sleeve each of Fig Newtons, apples, waters. And a bottle of Sauza.

Colin had a hunch about a pond he knew. "Long shot," he said. "Finding it and fishing it."

She built the fire. She found a soft spot to sleep on the edge of the clearing. Colin returned an hour later with a plump trout dangling from a chain stringer. "Two-serving size," he said.

Quiet reigned. Stars turned the night sky cloudy. A jet's whine fell from five miles up. Allison watched it trace a line of blinking red across Pegasus.

The fire crackled, offering a misleading sense of warmth. Even with a horse blanket as ground cover and the lean-to catching heat, it would be a cold night. They would take turns tending the fire.

They talked about Trudy. They talked about what was going

on with Duncan. If Duncan had taken a step over the line, if he hadn't been forthright with Trudy, she might kick him to the river. Deceit might be Trudy's least favorite "thing." Trudy had once shot a man—her husband at the time—who hid a whole world of ugliness behind her back. The Sweetwater Quartet might be in for a change. Allison liked Duncan. His energy and boyish enthusiasm were a bit much at first, but she saw now how much he enjoyed his reporter role. The brashness, something Duncan could turn off and on like a switch, came with the job. He had learned how to relax. All Allison needed to know was that she wanted for Trudy whatever Trudy wanted for herself. And the only other thing Allison needed to know was that she'd gone weeks and weeks without a flicker of wondering about the quality of the space between her and Colin.

She slept first.

He woke her up two hours later and she enjoyed the utter, untarnished, blissful solitude. She appreciated that Colin didn't let her sleep all night, fall on his sword and all of that bullshit. She liked it fifty-fifty. She studied the stars, poked the fire, thought about Devo. She kept seeing Miguel Ramirez strung up at the tree. She tried not to picture him in the wrecked plane, neck broken and his eyes bloody sockets of nothing.

Pre-dawn cold crept in. She fed the fire, turned herself on a slow rotisserie. She poked Colin awake when it was his turn again. She curled back up inside the sleeping bag under the billion stars. She watched Colin's silhouette against the fire, gently rocking. A yawn yielded a puff of condensation. She closed her eyes. She let her mind go to a place she called the box of nothing. She kept it for these occasions, when her brain wanted to fly. She crawled inside her box of nothing, where all recurring thoughts were forbidden and she was only allowed to drift. The rule was you couldn't linger on a thought. A second was too long. She let her mind dredge through the stuff of dreams, the ground clutter of her subconscious, weird shapes and psychedelic craziness. She let her mind go where it wanted, a skipping stone. No lingering.

She had drifted to pre-sleep heaviness when she heard the sudden clatter—*ba-bang*—and she sensed Colin standing and she was on her feet before she could decide what to do.

Pure instinct.

A bear?

They both stared across the pitch-black clearing.

The sound came again—a clattering. A door cried, bounced as it slammed shut, wood on wood.

She gave Colin a tug, pulled him away from the light.

A shiver tap danced on her spine.

Seventy-Nine

Saturday Before Dawn
Trudy

Trudy sat curled up on her front porch. She'd bundled up in layers—sweater, sweatshirt, jacket, blanket. She wrapped her face in a wool scarf, the perfect amount of shocking coolness still creeping in. The chill dug hard for purchase. She didn't want to go back inside where Duncan Bloom, somehow, managed to sleep.

Apologies and explanations poured out all the way from Glenwood Springs. Bridge work in the canyon delayed them forty-five minutes—more time to talk. All the way up the river. All the way up Sweetwater Road and then off and on all day, hours-long rehashing and retellings. He had turned down medical treatment, so she tended to his wounds. He insisted over and over that he'd been trying to get his money back.

He reeked of contrition.

She swallowed her own.

He hadn't betrayed *her*.

His crime was against his profession. He knew he'd blown it, that it would all come tumbling out.

Coogan would spill it. Or Rudduck. Or the cops.

At the bitter end of the cop infestation in the cul-de-sac, a television news truck had pulled up and Duncan had done everything he could to stay out of the fray. He knew the reporter.

The cops gave the reporter what he needed and then the reporter turned his attention to neighbors. Duncan had sat on the bumper of Rudduck's Navigator, in the shadows and hunkered down. Glum.

Trudy needed to let Duncan wallow, to let all the ash fall and settle.

He'd been right about Commissioner Walters.

He'd been right about Clay Rudduck. She was sure he was right about Darla Cerise.

He'd flushed Chris Coogan, too.

He'd been tempted by the fast money in weed—*weed!*—and he had taken a flyer.

He had done eighty percent of the talking. Her main point was that she was in no position to judge and that she wished he felt he could have told her what was going on.

A crow called in the darkness. The morning chill jabbed at her core. When everything came out, if Sam Shelton decided to stand and fight and go blow by blow on the night in question and everything that led up to it, she'd be the one asking for a generous dose of forgiveness.

She hoped Duncan would sleep until noon.

All day would be fine. Something had changed, more than the obvious, and she couldn't quite put her finger on it.

Whenever he woke, and whenever he was ready, she would do whatever she could to help him get his emotional act back together. And her own. She had work to do, too.

As for work and his future as a reporter, that was a whole other deal.

Eighty

Saturday Before Dawn
Allison

Kala walked out of the dark.

She stood by the fire as if she'd built it.

The fire—too good, too strong—lit her up in orange.

She'd lost weight. Her face had darkened and her cheeks had gone gaunt. Thin black feathers dangled in her hair.

A tight parka, made of a twenty-first-century synthetic, covered a deerskin shirt. Her deerskin pants were well nicked and splotched.

"You can come out."

Allison huddled low with Colin, twenty yards from the fire. All of ten minutes had passed since they heard the banging at the cabin.

"Come on," said Kala. "This fire didn't start itself."

Allison stood. Swishing the dry knee-high grass was enough—Kala turned.

And smiled.

"What the hell?" she said.

"Might ask you the same." It felt good to be back by the fire. Damn good. "What are you doing?"

"At least I have an answer," said Kala. "This is my place."

"Is it *Kala*?" said Allison. "Or Atalanta?"

Kala blinked.

In the two months since Allison had seen her, she'd lost her shiny-apple sheen. She looked junkie thin, sallow.

"Isn't that your *other* adopted name?"

"Doesn't matter now."

"So it is you," said Allison.

"So?"

"So you changed your name so you could join up," said Allison.

"Big deal, big whoop," said Kala. "Devo tried to keep me away—tried to keep me to himself, out here. Came to visit as often as he could. But I wanted to be part of the whole effort, you know? By the time he caved and relented—the Atalanta name was trashed. He'd taken care of that—even getting a vote to keep me out. By the time he came around, things were so desperate up there, I needed a new brand, you know?"

"And you needed to come in more low key?" said Allison.

"It wasn't easy," said Kala. "Believe me."

"The tribe now?" said Colin. "Cinnamon and the others?"

"It's done," said Kala. "And gotten ugly."

"How ugly?"

"A split right down the middle. Half are scattering, like me. It's over."

341

"And the other?"

"I call 'em the hard-core nasties," said Kala. "They have, quite frankly, lost it. They have entered a zone where kindness goes to die. It's as if they want to be gnawing the bark off trees with their teeth and learning how to grunt in code. Did you ever see that movie *Quest for Fire*? Except they want to go back the other way. They're going feral as fast as possible."

"Cinnamon? The baby?"

"Oh yeah, she's in that bunch. Queen Zealot. The lack of nutrition is seriously impacting their brain cells."

As much weight as Kala had lost, she didn't seem desperate. She sat down, pulled her legs up around her arms in a tight ball. A first crack of dawn found the sky overhead. The weak stars blinked off. A soft pastel like pale carrots caught three small clouds, puffballs of innocence.

"This is where you and Devo met."

"Met?" said Kala. "It's where I tried to knock some sense into him, to get him to give that tribe a bit of backbone. He ceded too much power. And, yeah, we slept together. Pairing up wasn't supposed to be a thing in the tribe—you were supposed to be able to take those kinds of things day by day. You know, the coupling up. But when it came down to it, jealousy. Like intense jealousy, the worst. So you got our zealots and you got your jealots. Yeah, why aren't they called jealots, come to think of it?"

"But you were never pissed at Devo?" said Colin. "Or pissed off?"

"So you're out here because you think you know what happened?"

"We have a theory," said Colin.

"Involving *me*?" She sat up straight, put her hand to her chest. You couldn't fake her level of incredulity.

"Did he ever piss you off?"

"Enough to hurt him?" said Kala. "Hell no. It was all the indecision I found so frustrating. I've got more wilderness training than all of them combined. Outdoor Wilderness School, round trip on the PCT without a scratch, Annapurna, a ten-day trek on Antarctica. I completely agreed with everything Devo was trying to do—that's the thing. I thought his plan was pretty cool."

"So Kala is your real name?" said Allison.

"Kala Spears—Berkeley, California. Home schooled, earth schooled, lover of the outdoors. And someone who would have given Devo a spine if I knew how."

"Met him when?"

"At auditions. Few years ago. When Devo was building up the tribe. And I came back again last spring to see how it was coming along, tried to negotiate another spot." She spoke calmly. "I came to Colorado to do some high-altitude training in the San Juans. I came up to visit, followed Devo out of camp one day. We talked. He still didn't want me in the mix. I found this old cabin, spruced it up a bit, put in a garden. Gave him a spot to come relax, get away. Once Cinnamon got pregnant and had the baby, she was no longer interested in him. I figured he was fair game. Good lord, he needed a break."

"And you started spending time with the tribe, as Kala, when?"

"Early June."

"And how often here with Devo?" said Allison.

"Every ten days or so. It varied. Sometimes the hunts would last for days, you know?"

"Where were you when it happened? When Devo died?"

"The day you came to tell us?" said Kala.

"More importantly, the day before."

She gave it some thought. "Kind of a blur, you know?"

"Try us," said Colin.

"I didn't spend much time in camp," said Kala. "I mean, there wasn't much to do there. The point was to find meat and gather, you know, while the weather was decent."

"Or come here to sleep with Devo."

Kala shrugged. "It wasn't supposed to be monogamy land, you know? What's this theory?'

Allison looked at Colin. He nodded.

"The mushrooms," said Allison.

"The—?"

She stopped.

"Your crop in the compost," said Colin.

"The *Amanitas*?"

"Are there others?" said Allison.

"I used them to demonstrate," said Kala. "I was giving the tribe lessons. If you know your mushroom stuff, you can go a long way on their protein. Of course, you need deer or elk for the fat and all the tools you can make with the bones and all that, but those suckers popped out of my compost one day and I brought a whole basketful up there, and I mixed them with the harmless ones and we sorted them together so I could show them which is which. Did you know there are two thousand varieties of mushrooms in Colorado? I wanted us to slip back over to the Flat Tops, do something much more low key. The mushrooms over there are insane."

"So you brought the mushrooms to camp."

Kala needed time to absorb the idea. "What you're saying is . . ." Her voice trailed off. "You think *Devo* made a mistake?"

"We both know that wouldn't happen," said Allison. "What happened to the mushrooms after your little lesson?" said Allison.

"Not so little. It lasted for hours. I showed them ways to hunt for them, too. What kind of wood to look for, rotten logs and ground cover. I showed them all the ways that *Amanita*s try to fool you. All of that."

"And then?"

Kala tipped her head back, stared up at the rising dawn. Tears swelled in her eyes, pooled there. She shook her head. "Mother fuck," she muttered.

"Someone took them?" said Colin. "Who?"

Eighty-One

Trudy tried.

The leisurely breakfast—an omelet, toast, coffee. The check of his bruises. The check of his tender skull. Ice bags. Willow bark tea along with her explanation that the naturally occurring salicin it contained was the same as what goes in aspirin. Chased with coffee. More coffee. The list of the things he did right, repeated. She kept going off on Bill Walters and Chris Coogan. She despised being talked down to. Duncan had no problem picturing her standing up to them.

How could it not come out?

Who was writing the story this morning? Editing it? And based on what? He'd seen Stan Greer at the scene and had hid down between cars to stay the hell out of sight, his nose on the cold pavement, smelling the warm, greasy underbelly of Rudduck's rig. The story was out there now, but he wouldn't turn on the television, couldn't open the laptop or look at his phone.

There would be a cop car any minute, coming up the road. Or his phone would ring.

Who was putting out the story? Newbie Marina Fuentes and the publisher? Shouldn't she be calling him for comment? To verify? Even if Rudduck hadn't yet pointed his finger at Duncan Bloom, shouldn't someone be calling him to get his side of the story and what went down in the cul-de-sac?

Clay Rudduck must have kept records. The cops would get them and Rudduck would have no reason to sit on the fact that the reporter in question had wanted a piece of the action, had turned over a fat $81,000 in hopes of saving his financial bacon. There was Helen Barnstone, too. She knew.

Duncan's career was cooked. He couldn't imagine any criminal charges—could he?

He had been planning—could he say it with a straight face?—to quit the paper any day and become actively involved as a marijuana retailer. Right? He'd been assured by Clay Rudduck that all the appropriate paperwork would soon be filed, that all the background checks would soon be conducted. That he would soon be registered and vetted by the state.

Should he step up? Come clean? The town shot information around like an echo chamber that had slept with Gawker and produced quadruplet babbling babies of gossip. The cops would want to hurt him.

"One step at a time," said Trudy. "You have to let this sort itself out. You may have wanted to see your money make a quick return, but you changed your mind almost right away and then look at all the work you did from that point on? That has to be factored in."

He wanted to crawl in bed with Trudy and pull the covers over his head. He wondered whether it was too early to start drinking. He wondered if he was an hour from the end of his reporter career or whether it would last the entire day. All the action had taken place too late for his former paper, *The Denver Post*, to have the story in the morning edition. But it was already bouncing around town, or would be today. All his former report-er friends would know.

Laughingstock.

"Own up," said Trudy. "You made a mistake. Don't run and hide from it. As soon as you are ready, go down there and tell your story. Your reputation is too good. You got tempted and you changed your mind—that's good. Tell your story over and over. Do you think there's an email showing you asked for the money back? Did this Helen woman know?"

Duncan shook his head. "Why would Helen Barnstone want to help me? And, no, I didn't email Clay Rudduck."

"He's going away for murder," said Trudy. "Two murders."

"Doesn't mean he can't point a finger. And why else would I have gone up there to the adventure park with Clay Rudduck unless we had a business relationship? I'm sure there are secu-rity cameras or something they can figure out—it won't be hard to piece it all together. Two of us go up, one comes down. Barn-stone goes to pick him up—we all end up at Coogan's place."

Tapping his cheekbone generated hot shards of pain. The gal-lon of coffee, combined with so much uncertainty, jangled his stomach. He stretched out on the couch by the woodstove, let his thoughts gyrate.

There was only one thing to do.

If he tried to hang on, wriggle-talk his way along and try to establish an alternate narrative, it would be a long time until he'd regain credibility. How could he look Randall DiMarco in the eye? Or Inez Cordova? Or Stan Greer? Or Allison Coil? He'd be dragging his sad reputation all over town, no matter what else had come before. He'd be the guy with the cloud, the questions, the doubt, the tarnish, the blemish. He'd be the guy having to explain and squirm and hope they didn't press him. He'd be the guy trying to keep his story straight. CBS News, for crying out loud, had footage of his satellite interview with Gayle King and they would dig up that clip when the story went national.

If anything, he would need to disappear for six months or a year and then come back in another town, maybe another state, and slip in a side door and hope someone would understand or pretend they didn't know. Grow a beard. Get fat. Change his name.

He was cooked in Glenwood Springs but, for now, he needed Sweetwater.

He needed Trudy—and Trudy needed him.

During one of the bleary hours over breakfast, she'd spelled everything out and all he could think was what would have happened if he'd gotten high or drunk with Inez Cordova, if she had been more, in a word, inviting. Sam Shelton had gotten Trudy torched, slipped her a Mickey, the quaalude, like he'd done a hundred times before to others all over the world.

Trudy needed him. She was about to walk over hot coals. By the time she was done taking down Sam Shelton, she might as well have walked over those coals in her birthday suit. Every inch of her life would be exposed, and the lawyers would slash at her credibility and her ability to remember how much she'd led him on. How many times had she been out there, alone? Hadn't they kissed? Was she enamored? Smitten?

Whatever else happened, Duncan Bloom knew he'd be there for Trudy, whatever good his tarnished reputation was worth.

He had time, after all.

In fact, he had all the time in the world.

Eighty-Two

Rock didn't seem surprised.

Maybe he was too weak to show anything. That was a possibility. He was busy taking down all the lame huts and the half-assed teepee, knocking them down to grade so they could rot.

"Three-hour head start. Maybe four. But they're dragging. Six of them altogether." He pointed northeast. "There's a pretty clear trail out of camp for the first mile or so, then it gives way. You shouldn't have any trouble. What's up?"

Allison didn't answer. "Where are you headed?"

"Home for starters, get healthy. Then, we'll see."

Rock and the crew of leftovers could have been scrap pickers in a dump.

Allison counted two other guys and three women left behind. "And Dock?"

Allison had an idea.

"He went with Cinnamon. That wasn't a choice." Fatigue slowed his speech. Resignation, too. "We tried. She's, what would you say? Feisty."

The trail could have been a two-lane highway. Devo's crew developed ruts to the deep woods—the easy way. The deer and the elk read the whole scene, knew to steer clear.

Colin set a healthy pace. Still, Allison wished for their horses. Colin knew a couple horses in Meeker they could borrow, but Allison knew that would take time to locate and negotiate and

349

rig up and all of that.

The trail climbed the side of a ridge on a slow incline, then dipped down into a cold and well-shaded thicket of heavy fir that reminded Allison, oddly, of the time she'd rescued Devo in the deep snow many moons ago. But that happened in the Flat Tops Wilderness, and they were now hiking through unappreciated and underappreciated ordinary, dry Colorado—no special National Forest or wilderness designations. Compared to the bounty of the Flat Tops, these nameless ridges had seen better days, perhaps when the area served as the Bridge River Ocean when marine reptiles and ammonites rocked the ocean and dinosaurs ruled the land. The Cretaceous creatures probably thought they had it made, except survival was an everyday fact of life. But what had really changed? Not much other than the ability to pretend otherwise.

One thing to keep in mind, Allison thought, was the number of lives that have already walked these trails, treaded these waters. And how many would come after.

They came up on the sad group, nearly stumbled on them, as Cinnamon and the others rested in a treeless gap on top of a ridge.

Cinnamon stood, did not smile. T-Bone stood next to her. Neither would be winning awards for warmth or hospitality.

From fifty yards out, Allison smiled and waved like a happy frat girl after the football game victory on homecoming day. "I'm going to try something," said Allison. "Just follow along."

"If you think I'm concerned about taking on six human walking sticks who appear as emaciated and gloomy as this bunch, well, please disavow yourself of those notions."

"Emaciated?" She said it under her breath, lips moving as little as possible. "You know that has five syllables, right? Are you showing off?"

Colin turned to her, straight face. "Always," he said. "For you."

Dock sat on the ground in a deerskin baby suit, his dull gaze taking in the visitors. He uttered a softhearted attempt at a cry, warning or stress or both.

Around Cinnamon's chest a loose wrap flopped empty— Dock's riding pouch.

T-Bone shook his head.

"Hi," said Allison, ignoring him.

Perhaps these six were going to become index fossils of the future—archaeologists a couple of millennia from now would be puzzled by the curious discovery of a crude settlement that used crude tools and ate crude foods yet appeared to have been settled more than a century after the invention of the cotton gin or agave oven. Why had they not kept up with progress?

"You followed us why?" said Cinnamon.

"End of an era," said Allison. Thinking—Paleozoic, Mesozoic, Devozoic.

"Nothing has ended," said T-Bone. "Another phase."

"Where you headed then?"

Allison asked as innocently as a passing hiker. She squatted next to Dock, then sat on the ground next to him, cross-legged.

"We'll know it when we find it," said Cinnamon.

"The direction you're headed is Elk Springs, Dinosaur National Monument and a whole lot of barren valley crossings," said Colin. "Ain't much, you know?"

Cinnamon shook her head. "You assume we are going in the direction you followed us. You are thinking in today's terms, today's landmarks or whatever. We are following our instinct. We might be headed in a different direction by sundown, you know?"

Back frames held tools and supplies. Allison spotted four

bladders of water—repurposed intestines from animals of unknown origin. Cinnamon and T-Bone stood but the other four, two men and two women, huddled in a circle nearby, clearly exhausted and chilled. A cool wind whispered from Wyoming. Any mild breeze could turn a mild October chill to frozen February. A fresh rabbit carcass dangled from T-Bone's deerskin suit. The rabbit looked big enough to feed Dock—maybe.

Allison reached for Dock, hands under his shoulders. She stood in one swift motion, his legs dangling, and brought him tight. Cinnamon gasped, a faint intake of surprise, but Allison didn't acknowledge it. She pulled Dock close and gave him a hug. She smiled. He was even lighter than she remembered and that was not a good thing. His face lacked the certain essence of puffy baby and fat. Perhaps he sensed his chance. He cooed and stared at her lips.

"I'll take him," said Cinnamon.

Allison stepped away.

"No." Allison kept walking. She put eight patient paces between her and Cinnamon. She nuzzled Dock at her neck and turned back around.

"He's mine," said Cinnamon.

"And Devo's," said Allison.

"And Devo is not much help." Cinnamon took a step forward. "Not for a long time."

"Tell me why the tribe split up," said Allison.

"Why?" said Cinnamon.

"Did Devo have anything to do with the tribe busting apart?" Allison kept the tone calm, non-accusatory.

For now.

Cinnamon eyed Allison, boots to forehead. "What are you getting at?"

Allison shrugged. "Was the question not clear?"

"Oh, so miss wilderness woman follows us up here to ask a few questions about the social dynamics of Devo's tribe? Going to tell us how to get things done? Where to go? How to hunt? What to do? You don't know shit about the woods. You're a fucking poseur."

Allison grimaced. "This isn't about me."

"It's not?" said Cinnamon. "Devo thought you were the toughest girl in the woods this side of the Mississippi, but all I hear about is tents and tequila and horses packing in everything from down comforters to cast-iron stoves to keep your fucking wall tents warm. And coffee makers for your precious *coffee*. What the fuck kind of wilderness is that?"

The tequila thing stung, as did the horse jab. And the coffee. Allison smiled.

Cinnamon was on a roll.

"You want to know why the tribe broke in two? Because Devo got soft, that's why. Way too fucking soft. Running into town? Are you kidding me? For scraps? The whole point was to get to the point of desperation, to sharpen our skills, sharpen our senses, become more in touch with the land. The whole point was to toughen up. You can't do that when you're gleaning and eating blemished produce from the back of a grocery store in downtown fucking Meeker."

"He was too soft so, what? You *killed* him?"

Allison said it as a matter of fact.

"I did nothing of the—"

Allison didn't raise her voice but cut her off.

"The mushrooms."

Cinnamon stared. She shook her head.

And Allison knew.

Any quick refutation or harsh denial and Allison might have wondered. But she'd made Cinnamon think. She'd made her process. She'd had to wrap her head around strategy. She'd had to try and think through what was the best thing to say. She'd gone from future cavewoman to someone with a problem from that other world, that one she'd rather not think about.

And thinking cost her.

"He was going to kill us all," said Cinnamon.

"Oh, really?"

"His waffling, his indecision, his living in both worlds—trying to dance back and forth, one foot in Meeker and one toe with us. He wasn't committed to the cause—not really. He wasn't willing to sacrifice. He couldn't stand to see a little pain, a little agony. I mean, please. It was all about that. It was all about that very thing."

T-Bone turned to look at Cinnamon. His dreads framed a bony, gaunt face. His previous Olympic decathlete body had lost muscle and shape. His skin drooped.

"What the hell?" he said.

"Think of how much better things have been." She turned to focus on T-Bone. The other four stood, on alarm. Allison didn't consider herself great at reading the faces of the gaunt and withered, but she believed their collective looks could be interpreted as shock.

"You did what?" said T-Bone.

"The mushrooms," said Allison, stepping into the breach of silence. "*Amanita phalloides*. The death cap. It takes dead aim— liver and kidneys both. You have to have a decent supply, but a big handful will do."

T-Bone shook his head. "Kala's lessons."

Cinnamon tried a step in Allison's direction—and Dock's.

Colin stepped in front of Allison, but it didn't matter. T-Bone grabbed Cinnamon's bicep like a frog's tongue snatching a fly. Her twiggy arm disappeared in his fist. Allison waited for the snap, wasn't so sure she would mind the sound when it came.

T-Bone twisted Cinnamon around like they were engaged in a violent polka. She buckled to ease the pressure on her arm and looked up at T-bone with pleading eyes.

"I want my baby." Her mouth had opened like something reminiscent of Edvard Munch. She might have been trying to cry, but there were no tears. "You can't do this," she said. "He's the *future.*"

Eighty-Three

Saturday Evening
Allison

"There's one thing I don't understand."

Colin sat in the back corner of the high-backed booth that was Trudy's community gathering table. He'd been part of the flow of conversation all night. Duncan Bloom said half as much as usual and Colin had filled the gap.

"Yes?" said Allison.

"So who dropped off the bear tooth necklace to begin with?"

The question was greeted with shrugs—five in all. In addition to the Sweetwater Quartet, Glenna and Mariah Wingrove had joined them for an evening of food and wine. The mood was low key. The gathering was Trudy's idea and she had made bread, salad and a giant pot of risotto packed with butternut squash.

"Does it matter?" For most of the night, Duncan had given the thousand-mile stare. Now, he seemed focused. "I mean, whoever had it delivered knew Devo was in trouble, but nothing would have changed. In the end, Devo's body would have turned up just the same."

Allison didn't want to head down the "what if?" tunnel, the most pointless place to spend time. But Duncan was wrong. Without her first visit to Devo's camp, before his body was found, she doubted she would have been as prepared to understand the dynamics.

"Not everything needs an answer," said Trudy.

"Maybe Kala," said Allison. "Maybe Devo left it behind at the cabin."

"I thought he wore it all the time," said Trudy.

"Well, there are certain activities where a bear tooth necklace might not be so appealing," said Colin.

"Here's what I think," said Duncan. "I think Devo knew he was in trouble, that he needed interference. He took it off himself and told Kala or the grocer or someone to get it to Allison one way or the other, that she'd know what to do. It was his signal for help. Disruption."

"As good a theory as any," said Colin. "Maybe he knew at least that Allison wouldn't let the baby linger in those conditions."

"Then I blew it," said Allison. "I should have reported it, the baby and all. That's what Devo wanted, to have the authorities bust it all up. Again."

"You had other things going on."

"There were two whole months when I did next to nothing," said Allison. "Except worry and wonder."

"But everything is okay now," said Trudy.

"We have to get to a better place than okay," said Allison.

"It's a place to start," said Colin, raising a glass.

Six glasses clinked, not a smile to go with. Everyone was too tired or too stressed.

"Okay doesn't suck," said Glenna. "You have to appreciate what you did and that goes for all of you, including Duncan."

"Thanks, I guess," said Duncan. "Hard to see right now."

"List the good things," said Mariah. "That's what my father taught me. When it's dark, you add a little light with each item on the list. You can make the sun shine."

"How about filling up the jails?" said Colin. "That's one. Clay Rudduck in Glenwood Springs and they already found that other guy, Skip Grayson, and that Vietnamese kid, too. Cinnamon in Meeker."

"Her given name," said Allison. They had marched out of the wilderness. She had complained and railed the whole way, not one sympathizer among her troops. "Cinnamon Black. Originally from Gibraltar, Wisconsin."

"You're keeping the prosecutors busy," said Glenna. "That's got to be a good thing."

"And what about the commissioner stepping down?" said Mariah.

"He hasn't yet," said Duncan. "But he won't have much choice."

"And exposing a major loophole in the law—marijuana caregivers, give me a break." Allison enjoyed this version of Colin, the opinion machine. "Did they think the caregivers would put their extra down the disposal—*oh well, don't need so much*?"

"Goes for you too, boss."

Mariah and Glenna sat next to each other at the end of the table in chairs. Mariah sat next to Trudy.

"Me?" said Trudy.

"You've been quiet all night."

"I know," said Trudy.

Mariah, who had held hands with Glenna most of the night,

reached her left hand over and let it rest on Trudy's shoulder. "Well, you need to count the good things, too."

"I'm trying," said Trudy, fighting off a well of tears. "I know I'd start with all of you. All your support."

"We know it won't be easy," said Allison. "You know that, don't you?"

"There's going to be some stuff that will come out."

"They'll dig up everything they can," said Duncan. "We know that."

"But there will be others there, too," said Allison. "The other women he attacked. You won't be alone."

Trudy tipped her head back, let her chest rise and fall. Mariah gave Glenna a quick hug, seated variety, and a peck on the cheek. Under the table, Allison felt Colin's hand on her thigh and she put her hand on top of his. Whatever time they left the table tonight, and Trudy's house, Allison was already looking forward to stretching out in the upstairs bedroom of her tiny A-frame with Colin by her side, under the covers with only the stars through the window.

Trudy smiled—faint but there. Duncan sat next to her in the booth and she looped an arm around his neck, pulled him close.

"Lonely isn't an issue in Sweetwater," said Trudy. "And things around here are going to get a whole lot busier, no matter what else happens, right around May."

Trudy put a hand on her nothing stomach, tapped it. She stared at Allison and smiled, a flash of the old happiness.

Duncan had reached for his wine. The glass braked halfway to his lips.

He turned to look at Trudy and his mouth froze in the open position.

For one long moment.

She smiled.

"Holy shit," he said. "Does that mean I get to stay?"

358

Acknowledgements

As always, I have had a small army of willing helpers, editors, reviewers, and people willing to answer questions. Thanks to Amy Kolquist, Maria Kelson, Mark Eddy, Gregory Hill, Daiva Chesonis, Bobbi Smith, Karen Haverkamp, Danielle Burby, Josh Getzler, Linda Hull, Stephen Singular, Bob Hoban, Terri Bischoff, Christine Carbo, Mark Graham, John Graham, Mike Keefe, Manuel Ramos, Dan Slattery, Parry Burnap, Ted Pinkowitz, Susan Pinkowitz, Laura Snapp, Katrina Blair, and all the helpful folks at Medicine Man. Special thanks to Jody Chapel for the stellar cover and sharp interior design and to Karen Haverkamp, who taught the eagles how to use their eyes. Thanks also to all the fine independent booksellers in Colorado, to Rocky Mountain Fiction Writers, and Mystery Writers of America.

CPSIA information can be obtained
at www.ICGtesting.com
Printed in the USA
BVHW03s0758181018
530509BV00001B/20/P